THE NIGHT VISITOR . . .

Stan could feel the cold from the glass as he put his nose to the icy surface. It was a moment before he realized he was looking directly into the loveless eyes of Evil.

Bargolas looked into the eyes of the man-child and began to weave his spell . . . his brain generated the image of a girl, to weave it into Stan's mind.

Stan started to back away, but something kept him—a flicker of light, the pale scent of perfume. The black void of the eyes transformed into human orbs rimmed in pale blue. The face became feminine; pink lips pouted seductively . . . Cynthia.

She reached up with long fingernails and ripped the screen apart. Then she took a step forward and placed her talons in Stan's trembling hand. With his other hand, he brushed back the sun-bleached strands of her hair. Gently, he traced the curve of her brow, the outline of her lips. He leaned forward and covered her mouth with his, and she wrapped her arms around him. Stan pressed his body closer to her, trying to ignore the screaming in the far corner of his mind.

Mike stood crouching at his bedroom door, lungs burning from his screams; he reeled from the obscene sight of Stan locked in a passionate embrace with the monster . . .

THE
SUMMONED

STEVEN RAY FULGHAM

DIAMOND BOOKS, NEW YORK

THE SUMMONED

A Diamond Book / published by arrangement with
the author

PRINTING HISTORY
Diamond edition / June 1991

ISBN: 1-55773-526-3

Diamond Books are published by The Berkley Publishing Group,
200 Madison Avenue, New York, New York 10016.
The name ''DIAMOND'' and its logo
are trademarks belonging to Charter Communications, Inc.

10 9 8 7 6 5 4 3 2 1

I wish to dedicate this book to three people:

To Vivian Garza for her support and interest all through the process of writing this book. Vivian became my audience to shock and frighten, but she also bolstered my confidence in my skills which gave me the determination to see this project through.

To Nancy Jacobs for her support in the whole concept of this book. Also a special thanks for her stubborn insistence in choosing an editor for me.

To David Paul, my editor, for the transformations he accomplished with his skill while nurturing me as a writer. He became a wonderful teacher for me.

"The incubus can assume either a male or a female shape; sometimes he appears as a full-grown man, sometimes as a satyr . . . A young witch in Rostock, in 1698, had a new demon lover every few years; she summoned her incubus whenever she wished by calling . . ."

—From *The Encyclopedia of Witchcraft and Demonology* (Robbins, 1959)

THE
SUMMONED

1

Othello, Washington, 1970

Darkness loomed unavoidable. The door, open only a crack, oozed the weighty, odorless absence of light. Stan widened the opening and blackness pushed hard against his eyes, thrusting them back painfully into their sockets.

He could have turned on the light, but it would have been an act of cowardice. His mouth suddenly dried up under his fear, and the lack of light threatened to topple his equilibrium. Wiping his clammy hands down the sides of his blue jeans, he stepped one step down and closed the door softly behind him.

Immersed in the liquid darkness, he felt it soak through his clothes, draining into his ears, muffling the sound of his breathing. Moving slowly through the thickness, he took another step down.

The stair creaked, the way old wood does, but he started nonetheless at the unexpected sound, fearful that it would awaken his parents or brothers from their midnight dreams. He took another step, again accompanied by the creaking of wood; then another, but this one was silent.

His breathing was ragged and shallow. He stopped for a moment to calm himself. It seemed that his heart was in his ears, pounding dully. Trickles of cold sweat ran from his armpits to his elbows. He took two more steps and thought

to himself, How many is that? Five . . . six . . . halfway
there?

Stan breathed deeply again and took another blind step. His
heel caught and he pitched forward. Instinctively he bent his
knees and tried to find the next step with his other foot, but
he only slid sideways. Just as he felt he was going to roll
headfirst down the stairs, he caught hold of a two-by-four.

Pressing up against the unfinished wall, he could smell the
wood. The dust tickled his nose. There had been a *thunk*
when he lost his balance and stumbled; now he remained still,
listening for any sounds indicating that someone had gotten
out of bed to investigate. After endless minutes of waiting,
he decided to continue. A few moments later he stepped onto
the bare concrete floor of the basement.

His T-shirt was completely soaked with sweat as he felt his
way to the other side of the cool basement. When he was
certain that he was near the right spot, he began feeling around
gently on the floor. After a moment of groping, his hands
closed around a candle and a box of matches. A moment later
the darkness was split open by the sharp brightness of the
lighted candle, and the smell of sulfur burned in his nose.
After dripping a few drops of wax in the middle of the concrete floor, he stood the special white candle upright.

The teenager took a few steps backward, gazed at the light
and the eerie shadows, and stripped naked. He walked a few
steps over to a cardboard box hidden in a shadowy corner
and pulled off the top. Bending to reach inside, he removed
a stick of white chalk and a piece of paper with a design on
it. Soon he was at work, crouching over the floor around the
candle, copying the design from the paper onto the concrete.
The candle became the center from which the design evolved.

For the innermost part of the design, Stan drew two linked
triangles, about two feet across, forming a Star of David. At
each of the star's points he added a small circle a few inches
in diameter and, inside that, a pentagram. Then he stood up
again, nodding with satisfaction as he examined the drawing
on the floor, its white luminescence reaching up from the dull
gray concrete. He then returned to the cardboard box for more
materials. Crouching again over the design, he placed alternately, on top of the pentagrams, a mound of salt, a quartz

crystal, a cup of water, another small candle, a vial of blood, and a burning stick of incense.

Now he enclosed the entire design within a circle, then drew another circle a foot outside the first. Inside the ring, he carefully laid down the ancient designs copied from a book on demonology he had sent away for last month.

Stan walked over to his pile of clothes and picked up his wristwatch. 12:48. He must hurry; the timing was very important. Quickly, he walked back to the cardboard box and reached inside to remove a knife—his *Athame*. Holding the *Athame* across both of his open palms, he closed his eyes and, in a cool whisper, blessed the knife:

PROTECT ME FROM ALL HOSTILITY, DECEIT, AND ILLUSION,
IN THE NAME OF ABDIA!
DESTROY THE HOSTILITY, DECEIT, AND ILLUSION,
IN THE NAME OF BALLATHER!

Stan gazed lovingly at the knife and admired the runes he had painted in white on the shiny black leather handle. Reaching back into the box, he removed a vial of philter. The philter was composed of wormwood, vervain, lignum aloes, and several dried flakes of his own blood, all ground together under a full moon two months earlier. He pulled the cork from the vial and sprinkled the philter over the blackened blade of the knife. His heart rate quickening, he stepped forward into the circle of white chalk.

Bending down with the knife in his right hand and his left hand covering his throat, he passed the blade back and forth through the flame of the large center candle. The philter sparked and hissed as the blade heated up. Then slowly he waved the knife through the thick blue smoke of juniper incense. As the teenager peered more closely at the knife, the blade appeared to take on a reddish cast. Stan stared at the knife; he'd been certain it was supposed to turn blue. He continued, shrugging his shoulders—he would not be dissuaded.

Stan dipped his fingers into the water at a point of one of the pentagrams and dribbled the tepid liquid on the blade.

Watching intently for some further change to occur, he was momentarily disappointed. But just as he started to look away, a red glow began to etch its way around the outside of the blade. If he looked directly at the blade, he couldn't see the glow. But if he focused just off to the side of the *Athame*, the glow was obvious.

His heart racing, he began the next phase of the ceremony. Standing up, he started with the very center of the design drawn in chalk. Pointing the *Athame* down to the cement floor, he spoke the first incantation aloud:

IT IS NOT THIS HUMAN HAND OF MINE THAT DOES
   THIS DEED.
NO, IT IS THE HAND OF CERNUNNOS, THE GREAT
   HORNED ONE!
INVOCET VIRGO IMAGINEM DEI M.I.N.I.S. DEINDE
   SILENTIUM FRANGAT
SACERDOS CUN VERBIS VERSICULI SANCTI DEI
   CAVEAT; IGNEM ET
FLAMAMAN AETERNAEA CARITATIS!

Warmth crept from the *Athame* into his hand and up his arm. Suddenly, the dull red glow flowed from the tip of the blade. The boy slowly began to retrace the entire design with the glow of the *Athame*. After a minute, he finished and the knife began to cool. After setting the *Athame* back into the box, he turned back to the circle. He was awestruck, for he could actually see the dull red glow of the design he had just traced. However, just as with the knife, the glow was much easier to see if he didn't focus directly on it. His body quivering in anticipation, he continued.

It was nearly time. Stan pulled a bag of rock salt from the box and began to surround the entire design slowly with a circle of salt. He stopped just before closing the circle and returned again to the box. He removed a large black book from it and walked back into the center of the circle, set the book on the cold cement, and closed the circle of salt.

He knelt, facing the center candle, and opened the book to a marked place. The cold dark chilled him and turned the sweat dripping from his arms into icy trickles. Filled with urgency, excitement, and fear, he began the summoning in a commanding whisper:

ARATOR SUDATOR ONERATOR COMOSTOR!
EMEN KETAN! EMEN KETAN!
I AM OF THEE, AND THOU ART MINE.
SEDUCTOR ET SEMINATOR! TENTOR!
I DIRECT, CONJURE, AND CONSTRAIN YOU!
BY THE DARK ONE AND HER HORNED CONSORT,
I CONJURE YOU! APPEAR BEFORE ME NOW!
I COMMAND YOU TO ACCOMPLISH WHAT IS COM-
    MANDED!
APPEAR BEFORE THIS CIRCLE OF DEMAND!
I CONJURE YOU. BY MY POWER
THIS I DECREE, AS MY WORD,
SO MOTE IT BE.

Stan closed his eyes and tried to feel the power surge through his body. At first he could feel nothing, but then it became a wild tide ebbing ever closer to shore. The candle crackled, startling him; he opened his eyes and saw the flame flicker. He fully expected to find a demon standing before him, ready to do as commanded. He was disappointed.

Stan looked all about himself, trying to find a demon in the shifting shadows. But there were only boxes full of Christmas ornaments, shelves of canned peaches, jars of homemade pickles, sand, and stacks of lumber waiting to become walls for the family room.

With pent-up anger, Stan quietly set the book on the floor in front of the main candle. He closed his eyes and strained every muscle in his body in order to focus on his purpose. Slowly, he took ten deep breaths. He could feel the warmth spreading through his body, and he began to speak.

His words came not from a book, but from the angry desperation in his heart. They came from sixteen years of frustration, of being different and alone. They came from his deep-seated desire for revenge upon all those who had hurt him.

I COMMAND YOU, O SPIRIT. MATERIALIZE
    BEFORE ME RIGHT NOW! COME TO ME. I

DEMAND IT! YOU ARE UNDER MY COMMAND!
COME TO ME, GODDAMMIT!

Talons clicked softly against the creature's cracked, stained
teeth. The short arms held each other tightly; the wide nostrils flared. The ragged ear holes quivered. Heartless eyes
watched as the darkness around it gave way to soft candlelight.

Stan rubbed his forehead in frustration. He glanced at the
Athame, then picked it up and held the tip in the candle flame.
After allowing the flame to heat the metal, he slowly brought
the blade up to his forehead and pressed it against his skin.
His forehead sizzled, and the smell of burnt flesh filled his
nose. He bit his lip to hold back the cry of pain.

The smell of burning flesh aroused the beast . . . It pulled
him, nudged him from his self-imposed sleep. His hiberna-
tion from the winter of desolation and despair ended and
gave way to the unholy commands of . . . a child. He smiled,
and the dim light reflected from his crooked, broken teeth.
He exhaled roughly and the candles flickered.

Once again Stan looked around him and found no demon.
No servant to do his bidding, no beast to visit his revenge
upon all. He stood up and shook his head, his knees popping
from the long period on the cement. He took a step to his
right and started to walk out of the circle.
   Suddenly, the smaller candle positioned at one of the pentagrams flickered and went out. Stan turned around just in
time to see the main candle in the center of the design like-
wise flicker and go out.
   Stan stood in the darkness, not even daring to breathe. All
of a sudden, a rank smell assaulted him—sweet, rotten. It
reminded him of the time a kitten had shit all over the front
of his T-shirt. The brown liquid had immediately soaked
through to his skin. Now the smell made him want to double
over and vomit, but he stood his ground and made his way
toward the stairs.
   Total darkness again enveloped him, and he kept his hands

out in front of himself as he tried to maintain his balance. He stopped abruptly when he stepped on a paper bag apparently filled with clothing. A moment later he touched the two-by-four studs of the unfinished wall with his hand. Gripping a two-by-four tightly, he rested for a moment before continuing on.

All at once he sucked in his breath. His heart pounded so hard it threatened to break free from his chest. Something had brushed the back of his neck. He was sure . . . but no, it was probably just cobwebs or a piece of string hanging down from the ceiling.

He began to calm down. A moment later, however, the demon once again touched the back of his neck. Stan felt a sharp finger on his shoulder . . . hot breath upon his back . . .

The stench overwhelmed him . . .

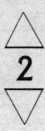

2

"Down on the floor, quick!"

"What?"

"On the floor, NOW!"

Stan reluctantly crawled onto the dark floor of the '64 Ford Ranchero as Mike slowed to a stop. Mike rolled his window down cautiously. "Hey, Zeke, how's it going?" Mike asked, just as cautiously.

"Purdy damn good, Kawaguchi. Hows 'bout you?" Not waiting for a reply, he continued, "Me and the guys were wondering if you had seen Stan Fuller around. We thought we could all have a little bit of fun. You know, maybe make him cast a spell, or conjure up a demon, or maybe even make old Peterson's dick here a mite larger than tweezer size."

Zeke grinned from ear to ear as his friends whooped it up in the backseat with their bottles of beer. Thick blue pot smoke drifted out the window, riding a wave of giggles and guffaws.

Mike looked out of the corner of his Japanese almond-shaped eye just to make sure Stan was staying put. "No, I haven't seen him around," he said, as he casually blew cigarette smoke into the chilly January air. Zeke looked suspiciously at Mike and turned to his buddies to say something Mike couldn't quite make out. They all laughed.

"Later," Zeke said and drove off in a blur of roaring white Corvette, the car kicking up a white plume of fresh, powdery snow as it slid side to side on the slick road.

Stan hoisted himself back onto the seat and looked out the passenger window. He felt indignant and angry, but also confused.

He didn't like being ordered around by Mike, but he also knew that he didn't want anything to do with Zeke and his friends. He looked out the window and became lost in the snow. The night was clear, the ground bright with the cold powder. The wheels of the Ranchero sang a soft crunching melody that seemed to keep time with Stan's breathing. In rhythm with the snow, Stan inhaled and exhaled. He could feel the snow. He could feel the weight of the truck and the grip of the tires. He could feel the breath of the boy beside him. Stan matched his breathing to Mike's.

All Stan's sensations became one breath followed by another. The breath was cold and white, and it filled his heart with fear. Gradually Stan's head lolled forward . . . His breathing became shallow and irregular.

"Cut it out!" screamed Mike at the top of his lungs. "I don't know what the fuck you're doin', but you were doing it to me, too . . . so just knock it off, goddammit, or I'll kick your ugly ass out of this car."

Stan's eyes fluttered open and he smiled slightly toward Mike. A little revenge was better than nothing, he thought. Reaching over to the radio, he turned up the volume; the music blared, tinny-sounding over the cheap speaker, washing over his discomfort and humiliation. He had made Mike afraid, and that comforted him. Music blasted from the radio. Stan laughed softly to himself.

The house was exactly eleven and a half miles due east of the desert community of Othello, in the eastern part of Washington state. It stood two stories high with a huge porch all around the first floor. It had once been painted a brilliant pure white with pale blue trim, but now what paint was left was gray. The harsh desert wind blew flakes of peeling paint along with the snow and dirt through the broken windowpanes. However, the house still stood, a testament to its suffering.

Lots of kids drove past it year after year, telling each other ghost stories. Once in a while, an especially brave bunch of teenagers ventured into the house to exert dominance over their own fears by breaking something—a window, a door. Pissing in a corner of the living room was a popular act of bravery and defiance.

In the nearly twenty years that the house had stood empty and open to the abuse of the desert, rats, termites, and high school kids, it had rarely felt the icy chill of Evil. But once in a while, if the moon was just right or if a storm vented its anger, the evil creature would emerge again and linger for a bit. It had never stayed more than a minute or two at a time, seemingly unable to remain away long from its solitary sleep, but the ensuing stress had always caused the old house to creak and moan its protest. It had wished for happier days, with warm quiet moments, the rosy cheeks of a well-fed family around a cheery fire. But those days had been long ago, before she, in all of her miserable selfish loneliness, had summoned up Evil into this world again.

"Well, I think if we're gonna go out there to do rituals and shit, we should take a good look at the place in daylight. It only makes sense to see what we're getting ourselves into before going out there in the middle of the fuckin' night. After all, everyone knows that is the house where the murders took place. Maybe we will see ghosts or somethin'."

It appeared that Mike's declaration had fallen on deaf ears. Stan just stared out the window of the A&W, his eyes fixed on the lightly falling snow. Occasionally, he blew his warm breath on the windowpane and drew symbols he had committed to memory over the last two years. Then, smiling to himself as if at some private joke, he wiped the drawings clear with the sleeve of his tattered green jacket.

Unexpectedly, Stan looked Mike square in the eye. His green eyes had an eerie cast that Mike never quite trusted.

"*WE* will not do rituals and *shit*, as you put it. *I* will perform a ceremony, *YOU* will merely observe. During this ceremony, you will do exactly as you are told. This is a very dangerous endeavor, and you and Cliff must promise me you'll cooperate completely or there will be no ceremony. Okay?"

As Stan finished speaking, Mike could feel the chill of

excitement that comes with fear. Stan Fuller was the most
interesting thing that had ever happened to Mike. Stan was
very strange—and probably crazy on top of it all. However,
his ideas and his behavior were so totally different from everyone else's that Mike couldn't help but be curious and excited at the prospects of the unknown. Yes, Stan and his
mysterious ways were becoming important to Mike . . . but
he wasn't about to let Stan know.

"Fuck you," Mike muttered, looking toward the door.

Stan got up and walked past Mike without even looking
down at him. Mike looked over his shoulder at Stan and said
as casually as he could manage, "I'll give you a call later."

Stan walked out into the fresh snow without a word. His
breath mingled with the smell of sweat and English Leather
Lime cologne. Wiping the grease of the french fries from his
mouth, he glanced at his watch. He had fifteen minutes to
walk to the old run-down motel. He was going to see Maria.
The old witch Maria. *La bruja.* She spoke only Spanish, but
Stan's Spanish was getting better. And the better his Spanish
got, the more secrets he learned about magic—both black and
white. Already he had learned more from Maria in two months
than he had in the two years he had been reading the books
he had sent away for. The only problem was that Maria moved
around quite a bit and wanted Stan to come along with her.
She was due to leave for Texas next month . . . maybe he
would go with her, after all. Who knew what his future
held?—but he knew he was too deeply into this stuff to leave
it behind him. It gave him secrets that the other kids, the kids
who never accepted him, would never have. It made him
special, worthy.

Five and a half hours later Stan walked through the front
door of the Fullers' house at 2435 Hamlet Street in Othello.
He wondered how many people in town even knew who
Shakespeare was; probably not that many.

"Stan, where have you been? You missed dinner," exclaimed his mother as she folded her apron and laid it on the
cupboard. She picked up her package of Merits, knocked out
a cigarette, and lit it. Inhaling deeply, she repeated her question. "Well, answer me. Do you think you are getting too
old to mind your mother?"

"I've been out walking."

"For three or four hours! Mike called about five. He said you left the A&W about four."

"Yeah, I was just walking . . ." His voice trailed off to nothing as he reached in the fridge to get some milk. He opened the cookie drawer and grabbed a handful of Oreos, then walked to his bedroom and shut the door silently.

In the darkness, he smelled it, an odor like wet dog fur. Stan set the milk and cookies on the dresser beside the door and started to reach for the light—but stopped. He knew just as soon as he turned on the light, the presence would be gone and all he would be left with would be embarrassment at his cowardice.

Stan's heart began to pound in his ears. He held his breath until he was sure that it was not his own breath that he heard. Someone—or something—was taking long, deep breaths. Stan tried to focus his eyes in the direction of the sound, but the more he stared, the less he saw. So he tried an old Indian trick his grandpa had taught him. He looked to the side of what he wanted to look at. And then he saw it.

For a very long time, he was frozen with terror. As though in a nightmare, he wanted to scream but couldn't find his voice. The effort left him sweating and cold. He managed to close his eyes and bring his right hand up to his left breast. From there he traced a line to the center of his forehead, down to his right breast, across to his left shoulder, then to his right shoulder, and finally back to his left breast—a star, the pentacle of protection. Then with a voice barely audible, he whispered, "Go . . . get out!"

Stan looked out into the dark room. He saw nothing. Nor could he hear or smell anything. He flipped on the light switch. The room was empty of all presences either natural or supernatural. Nevertheless, Stan walked over to the spot where he had seen the thing and looked down, expecting to see some trace left behind. But there wasn't anything. He bent down to feel whether the spot was damp or something. He reached out and made contact with the carpet, but immediately pulled back his hand as if he had burned it. The spot was indeed very, very warm. Something *had* been here!

Stan left his room and walked into the bright smokey living room. It was loud with the sounds of *The Wild Wild West*. His brothers lay in front of the TV, spaced out. His father lay back in the old ragged armchair, eyes closed and mouth open, a snore in progress.

Stan looked all about him. Everything was so normal, so unsupernatural.

He sat in front of the TV and watched James West get himself into, and then out of, dangerous situations. Odd, thought Stan, how these situations always involved beautiful young women.

After the show, Stan returned to his room. He walked back to the spot where he had seen the creature and reached out with his finger. The spot was not cold, but neither was it as hot as he remembered or imagined. Could he have just imagined the heat? Shaking his head, he clicked on his phonograph player. Ah, The Moody Blues, "In Search of the Lost Chord . . ."

While he listened to the Moodies, he scanned his occult reference books in the hope of finding a more powerful protective talisman than the forming of the pentacle. Unsatisfied with what he found, he decided to make one up. He took parts from several and combined them into one talisman, a diagram: a circle within a circle, with a pentagram, stars, moons and all kinds of symbols about which he hadn't a clue.

Quietly, he took a stick of black chalk and drew this composite of symbols upon a virgin white piece of paper. He laid this on the floor beside his bed and poured a circle of salt around the paper. In the center, on top of the pentagram, he placed a white candle.

"That should protect me against the devil himself," he muttered as he turned off the light and crawled into bed. Within minutes, he fell asleep.

Stan's eyes were wide open, but he couldn't see a thing. He didn't remember falling asleep and he didn't know what had woken him up, but his heart now pumped the blood of fear through his body. Then he heard it.

Breathing. It hadn't been there a moment before, but it was there now. The same slow, deep breaths he had heard earlier. He wondered at the failure of his homemade talisman, realizing with some futility that the candle had gone out.

Something rustled at the foot of his bed. Then the bed covers began to move. Terrorized, Stan lay on his stomach with his head turned toward the wall. Ever so slowly, the bed covers began to roll back, exposing his nakedness.

Stan lay helplessly immobile. First his shoulders were uncovered. Then, like a long flat snake, the blankets slithered down his back, caressing the smooth whiteness of his bare trunk, and finally dropped swiftly off from his feet.

Stan sweated pure fear. The window was open to the January night, chilling him. He couldn't move.

Suddenly he felt the corner of the bed sag. It sagged so far that Stan slid toward the depression created by the incredible weight. Still he couldn't find the courage to look or even call out. The Hollywood bed frame creaked and moaned like some ghostly specter. Something very hot and smooth touched his calf. It traced a line up his inner thigh to his genitals. Moving slowly away from his genitals, it traced a path up to his buttocks, lingering for some moments before moving on. Then Stan felt a tremendous grip on his neck and both his arms. Needlelike claws pierced his skin.

Pain was what it took to shake him out of his terror-induced paralysis. He began to struggle, tried to turn his head, his body, to fight this creature. He smelled something hot and foul, and he felt liquid pooling on his back. He tried with all his strength to raise up on his knees, but he was trapped under a massive weight. Suddenly that weight wedged itself between his legs. In that instant Stan realized what was about to happen. A split second later he was crushed under the most incredible pain he had ever felt. He passed into unconsciousness.

Perhaps the house knew . . . knew that the evil being was not at home tonight, that another innocent was suffering. Perhaps it felt the night and the winter chill seep into its framework. The house was cold and the darkness was unbearable. If the house had been more than a house, it would have cried. Instead, it just settled more deeply on its foundation and moaned, the sound echoing pathetically across the desert snows of Adams County.

Soon he would return here to the bowels of the house. It would bring with it the pain, the terror, and the humiliation of the boy to feed upon until it had grown stronger with a desire to shape the boy's destiny into a mirror image of its own.

If the house did know, it was powerless to change the horror that would come.

"Stan . . . Stan. Rise and shine. You'll be late for school."

Stan's mother stood in the doorway of the bedroom, looking down at her son. She loved him so much . . . but just wished that he was a bit more like the other kids. She didn't go to dances or games or do any of the things that she had done when she had been in high school. Oh, it seemed so long ago . . . she had been so popular then—not like Stan.

No, Stan was different, very different. He had never had friends. He had kept to himself most of the time, reading or just sitting alone. She didn't mind him reading so much as she minded *what* he read. He always seemed to have some sort of nonsense in his hands. Yoga or witchcraft, ESP or other crazy junk that he would probably burn in hell for reading. She blamed herself. God, she thought to herself, I pray to God that he doesn't become queer on top of everything else.

"Stan, I know you're awake. Get up and get to school! I don't have time to mess with you." Mona Fuller turned on her heel and walked out of the room, shutting the door behind her.

Stan opened his eyes. As he started to move, he was assaulted by pain. He remembered small parts of what had happened the previous night, trying to believe it had just been a nightmare. He managed to look over the edge of his bed and check on his protection spell. The candle had been knocked from the center of the paper, and the salt that had formed a circle around the paper was now spread over the floor in patterns. He recognized some of the patterns, but one thing was for certain, he thought to himself as the pain in his stomach became worse, he did not draw those patterns.

As he achingly drew up his legs to get out of bed, he noticed that they were sticky. His heart beat in his ears as he pulled back the covers to view the horror of the lower half of his body and his sheets stained with blood.

Cliff took another drag from his cigarette as he looked around the corner of the school building for any teachers.

Cliff and Mike huddled together, smoking their cigarettes and planning for the big night at the haunted house.

"We should take some girls with us," he remarked, pausing a moment to wiggle his eyebrows up and down conspiratorially at Mike.

"If we take girls," he continued, "and they get real scared, they're gonna want someone to hold on to. Shit, if we get that far we'll be home free."

"Which girls?" questioned Mike, suspiciously.

"Well . . . I bet we could get Pam and Peggy to go with us."

"Shit, those two sluts?" groaned Mike. "You can have them!"

"Fine with me," Cliff replied defensively. "I can handle *both* of them."

"Look!" exclaimed Mike. "There's Stan. Let's go give him some shit and see what's up for the weekend."

Both boys walked toward Stan, blinking their eyes against the bright morning. Their feet crunched against the frozen snow.

Stan stopped in his tracks when he saw his two "friends" approaching. He smiled, though he felt like running. He still didn't trust them . . . but then again, he couldn't think of anyone he did trust. He wanted to tell them about last night, but he knew they wouldn't believe him. He knew they already thought he was crazy. And if he told them the whole story, he wouldn't be able to stand the shame.

"Hey, Stan," Cliff started, "Mike and me were just thinking about maybe we could bring a coupla girls along to the haunted house. What do ya think?"

"I think it's stupid. There's already three of us. That's enough. Two more will only make things more difficult."

"Come *on*, Fuller! Peggy and Pam. They like you and they promised not to tell anything about what you're doing."

Stan looked back at Cliff and then to Mike, who averted his eyes as if trying to have nothing to do with the conversation. Stan looked back into Cliff's eyes and shook his head back and forth.

"Stan, I already told them they could go," said Cliff.

"Fuck! You idiot!" Mike hissed through his teeth.

"There's no telling how many people they've already told. It will probably be all over the school by noon today."

"I told them not to tell anybody. They promised. But I'll bet if we don't let them go with us, they *will* tell everybody." Cliff looked around to see if anyone was listening, then nudged Stan in the ribs with his elbow and continued, "Besides, it could be fun if the girls get real scared."

Stan looked coldly at Cliff for a few moments and said quietly, "You will be very sorry for this."

Cliff laughed nervously as the three boys stood looking out into the morning. Thirty seconds later, the bell rang for first period and they all walked toward their classes.

Just as the three teenagers were about to go their separate ways, Mike said, "We can talk about this more during study hall." A moment later they melted into the mass of students in the hall.

Third period started at 10:30. Mike and Cliff huddled in the back as far away from Miss Tackett as they could get. They sat there and waited for Stan to show up. At 10:50, something was very wrong. At 11:00, Cliff began to have a strange tickling sensation in his penis. At 11:10, he began to bleed.

Cliff felt the warm blood trickling from his piss slit. Looking down, he saw the stain forming on his white jeans. In an embarrassed panic, he motioned for Mike to follow him. Miss Tackett never even saw them leave. Cliff ran for the boys' lavatory. He unzipped his jeans and examined himself closely. The itching had stopped, and so, apparently, had the bleeding. Both boys shook their heads. Mike was afraid to ask Cliff any questions. Whatever had caused the bleeding, he didn't really want to know.

"Can you take me home so I can change my clothes?" Cliff asked meekly.

Mike nodded, and they left the lavatory, Mike walking in front to conceal the stain on Cliff's pants. As soon as the two boys got into Mike's bright red Ranchero they lit up cigarettes. Cliff found it hard to keep his hand steady. Neither one talked as the radio blared John Lennon's lyrics.

A few minutes after Cliff and Mike left study hall, Stan walked into the room. He presented Miss Tackett with a note from his mother explaining that he had had to go home for family reasons and to please excuse him for being late. Miss

Tackett nodded after reading the note and set it aside. Stan walked over to a desk and sat down. He did not even look around the room to see if Cliff and Mike were present.

The door blew open and banged against the wall. Glass fell from the already broken panes. Slowly, arrogantly, a coyote walked into the vandalized living room. There was snow on its mangy fur and traces of blood on its muzzle. It bared its white fangs, and strings of drool landed on the floor.

The coyote walked over to the steps leading upstairs. It climbed to the second floor, its sharp claws rasping on the stairs. Slowly, almost with reverence, the animal crept through a half-open door with a broken lock into the corner room. The door had a window a few inches wide and a few inches high, just large enough that someone could see through it into the room when the door was shut. This room was different from the other four rooms.

The old coyote wandered over to the mattress lying in the corner and sniffed at it. Following its nose, it looked up at the ceiling. An access panel had been removed from the ceiling, leading into the unfinished attic with its exposed rafters.

The coyote could feel the horror and the pain. Slowly, the evil essence seeped into its paws with stabbing cold—an ache creeping into its legs, reaching around to grip its heart. Suddenly, the coyote jumped to its feet, left the room, and trotted downstairs. At the bottom of the stairs, it paused. It could feel the hatred, and it was amused. Slowly it lifted its leg and urinated on the banister. In the chill, steam rose from the urine. The coyote howled, mocking, greedy, and evil. Satisfied, it trotted to the remains of the kitchen, nosed open the basement door, and trotted down the stairs into welcoming arms.

Mike thought about it for a long while. He already knew what he would do, but he was still afraid. He knew he would call Stan. Stan couldn't have been responsible for what had happened to Cliff today, but still, it was hard to figure out any other explanation. It was all just too weird.

Then again, it was also interesting and . . . cool. What if Stan did have something to do with it? What if Stan really was a witch, like some of the guys said?

"No," Mike muttered to himself, it was best not to get carried away with all this bullshit. No need to draw attention to himself. He already got too much just by hanging out with Stan.

Every time he looked in the mirror, he was surprised. All around him, in school, in town, he saw whites. But when he looked in the mirror, he saw the slanted eyes of a Japanese. But it always bothered him to look in the mirror, because he felt white, not yellow. He was a nisei, a second-generation Japanese living in the U.S. During the war his father had been sent by the Air Force to Japan to act as a translator. It was there, in Kagoshima that he had met and married Keiko. Mike had been born in Japan but had moved to Florida shortly before he was one. As a family of five they had moved around to various bases in the U.S. and several years ago had ended up in Othello.

And now Mike found that living in Othello, where there were no other Japanese, made him stand out from other kids. He was already noticed too much, and he damned sure didn't need Stan calling any more attention to him.

The phone rang. Mike was sure it was Cliff, or maybe Bill. Fucking asshole Bill had been calling almost constantly for two weeks, wanting Mike to go out and smoke a little weed with him. But he had been too busy with Stan.

"Hello?"

"Hi, Mike." It was Stan.

Mike could feel a rush of excitement as he replied, "Hi, what's up?"

"Mike, could you please come over and pick me up? There's something I want to talk to you about."

"Well, I'm pretty busy right now. I don't know if I can." Mike believed it was important to be cool and not show too much interest.

"Okay," Stan replied quietly.

Mike nearly panicked now, thinking Stan would hang up on him. "Well, I guess I could get away for a little while. I'll pick you up in ten minutes."

"Okay," returned Stan, in the same tone as before. Mike heard the click of Stan hanging up.

Twenty minutes later, Mike drove up to the Fullers' home. Stan had apparently been watching, and he walked immediately out the door to the little truck. He got in and slammed the door. "I'm hungry," he said. "Let's go to the A&W for a hamburger."

Wordlessly, Mike put the car into gear and started for the A&W. He drove carefully—unlike most of the kids his age. He liked to drive, but mostly he liked to be in control, whether it was of a car or anything else. He rarely felt comfortable in social situations, and driving his car he felt important and strong. He liked to drive.

They pulled into the back parking lot of the A&W and got out of the car. They skated down the frozen snow to the door and went in. Music blared from the jukebox. Kenny Rogers and the First Edition sang "Somethin's Burnin'." Stan walked over to the jukebox and dropped a quarter in, choosing "Ruben James," also by Kenny Rogers and the First Edition.

Mike was watching him from an orange vinyl booth across the room. Stan joined him, and the two boys ordered the teenager's staple diet of hamburgers, french fries, and Cokes.

As soon as the waitress left them, Stan looked over to Mike and began, "I've decided it would actually be a good idea to bring Peggy and Pam along. It might help keep away some of the negative energy forces I'm gonna have to deal with, and besides, if we don't take them they'll probably tell everyone at school. Since there will be five of us, we'll take my parents' car. I need to do the ceremony on the night of the new moon. That's Sunday. So we need to go take a look at the place tomorrow."

Mike nodded his agreement, feeling a surge of excitement. However, he didn't like the idea of Stan driving one bit. Stan was an awful driver. On top of that, Mike didn't trust him. But he had no choice, since his own Ranchero would only hold three.

Looking out the window, the boys saw the white Corvette pull in.

"Fuller, you better get the fuck out of here! It's Zeke and his friends. Out the back door, quick!"

Stan slid out of the booth and ran out the back door. He was too late; Zeke had seen the whole thing. Zeke nosed his car around the side of the A&W to the back parking lot, sliding on the icy pavement. Stan ran for the alley.

He looked over his shoulder, slipping. His breath was a ragged plume in the night air as the white car followed him into the alley. In panic, he ran for a fence and jumped it, landing in the snow on the other side. Running through the backyard to the front of the house, he glanced behind him again. Someone, probably Peterson, got out of the Corvette and headed for the fence. Stan heard the car pulling away. He knew Zeke would be waiting for him in front of the house.

Zeke pulled up in front of the house and waited for Stan to show, but instead it was Peterson who came around the corner.

"Motherfucker, I lost him!" yelled Peterson, at the top of his voice.

"How the fuck could you lose him? He was right in front of you," growled Zeke as he scanned the area. Then he saw Stan cut across the street at the end of the block. "There's the bastard! Quick, get in!"

Peterson climbed into the car, and the Corvette slid sideways on the ice before he could even shut the door. Zeke turned right at the Helmans' house just in time to see Stan cutting down the alley.

"Not this time, you prick," Zeke muttered.

Zeke continued around the block to wait for Stan on the other side. When Stan ran out from between two houses, Zeke and Peterson were waiting for him.

Stan was tired, and his breath was coming in gasps as Zeke and Peterson shoved him into the narrow backseat of the Corvette. He sat there and rested, knowing it was useless to try to get away. He would have to wait until he was out of the car in open space before he could escape.

Zeke drove to the day-care center outside of town. There was a half-mile of empty road from the edge of town to the day-care center and, beyond that, only flat fields covered with snow.

Zeke parked behind the day-care center so his car would not be visible from the road. Then he got out and, with Peterson's help, pulled Stan from the backseat. They threw him roughly to the ground.

"What ya running from, warlock?" Zeke taunted as he reached down and scooped up a handful of snow. Slowly he shaped it into a snowball. Peterson took the cue and began doing the same. Zeke drew back his arm and heaved the snowball at Stan. It hit Stan with a hard thunk on his right leg, then rolled off his leg and onto the ground. The snowball was so hard that it hadn't lost its round shape. Peterson then threw his iceball, hitting Stan in the head, as Zeke reached down to scoop up more icy snow.

Stan lay on the snowy ice, curled up in a fetal position to protect his face. He lay there helpless and silent as they hit him over and over with the frozen snow.

Mike left the A&W and drove up and down the streets looking for signs of Stan or the white Corvette. He wasn't worried. Zeke might have a little fun with Stan, hassle him a bit, but he wouldn't hurt him. Mike turned up the radio, lit a cigarette, and sang, completely out of tune with the music.

Helplessly, the old house moaned to itself. Again. Again and so soon. The loathsome presence was emerging. Evil was slithering up from the bowels of the house. So soon . . . again.

One of the iceballs hit Stan in the ear. It felt like he was being hit with rocks. Zeke and Peterson laughed.

"A head shot!" Peterson exclaimed, giggling to himself.

Stan could feel warm blood trickling down the side of his neck. Anger flooded his mouth. He screamed at them to stop, his voice croaking as he watched them laugh. Looking all around himself, he felt humiliation at the sight of the several dozen iceballs that had hit him. He grabbed one and, without aiming, threw it as hard as he could. The iceball hit Peterson square in the groin. Peterson screamed.

"My nuts! Oh, shit, my nuts . . . I'm gonna be sick!" Peterson cupped his groin with his hands and slumped down against the car.

When Zeke saw his friend in misery, he was enraged. He strode the ten feet over to Stan and kicked him in the back. After a moment, Peterson, back on his feet again, joined Zeke and aimed a kick at Stan's face. Stan kept his face covered, but he was unable to protect his back and kidneys.

Suddenly Zeke stopped and grabbed his stomach. He fell

to his knees and began to puke on the snow. The sharp odor of vomit was soon combined with the rich odor of shit.

Peterson, his foot poised for another kick, looked over to Zeke. Just as he was about to ask Zeke what the fuck was going on, he felt a tremendous fire in his stomach. In a few seconds, he, too, was on his knees, defecating into his pants and vomiting onto the snow.

Stan uncovered his face to look at the sight. The smells had reached him, and he was beginning to feel a little queasy and scared. Then he felt a hand slip under his arm and lift him to his feet.

A breathy voice whispered in his ear, "Run!" as he felt himself shoved forward.

Stan turned around and saw nothing but miles of flat, snow-covered fields. Confused and frightened, he ran down the road as fast as he could, remembering the pain of the night before. Fifteen minutes later, he stepped into a telephone booth and dialed Mike's number.

Stan sat in the corner of Mike's bedroom. Mrs. Kawagu-chi, Mike's mother, had brought the two boys some hot choc-olate. Stan sipped at his cup, keeping his eyes on the floor. He had wiped the blood off his neck and ear, but the whole side of his face burned as if he had a fever.

Mrs. Kawaguchi left the room. Mike shut the door behind her and sat down on his bed. "So whether you did anything to them or not, they're gonna tell everyone at school what happened, and you'll get the blame. You think you had a rep as a weirdo and a witch before . . ."

Mike walked over to his phonograph and set the needle on a record. The music of the Grass Roots flowed out of the cheap speaker.

After many minutes of ignoring Mike, Stan finally spoke. "There's one thing I haven't told you yet, and it makes me think I might not have had anything to do with them getting sick. While both of them were on the ground, someone . . . or something . . . grabbed me under the arm and lifted me to my feet, and then . . . uh . . . whispered into my ear, 'Run!' I know it sounds pretty unreal, but I think something was watching out for me."

"Well, if you smoked weed or did other drugs I might be

able to just forget all about the whole thing. I'd just call it a pipe dream. I'm not so sure it isn't just a fuckin' fantasy, anyway.'' Mike sat back down on his bed and thought for a moment before continuing. ''Let's try something. Since you think you *might* have made those two assholes sick . . . why don't you try it on Bill Byers?''

Stan gazed up with a strange look in his eyes. The idea had some appeal to him.

Mike continued, ''Bill's been buggin' me all month, ever since I started hanging around with you, that I haven't been spending enough time with him. He's gettin' to be a royal pain in the ass.'' Mike paused a moment and then said, ''Let's go!''

Stan got to his feet, still a bit disoriented. He watched Mike walk out the door and then followed him to the Ranchero. The boys drove the half-mile to Bill's house on Larch. Mike parked down the street so the Ranchero couldn't be seen from the house.

Alone, Stan got out of the truck and crunched through the snow to Bill's house. As quietly as possible, he walked around to the side of the house and crouched under Bill's window. He felt naked there under the window in the bright winter night with the freezing air biting at his nose and fingers. He wondered to himself just how he should go about his task.

Then, almost unconsciously, he took out his pocketknife and began chopping a small pentagram in the snow. Then he carved a circle around the pentagram and began to remember the sights, sounds, and smells of Zeke and Peterson being sick. Stan visualized Bill's face, and he began to hate him. He hated the way Bill talked and the way he laughed. He hated the way Bill mocked him in school. Stan began to wish Bill dead. Without thinking, Stan stabbed at the circle he had carved in the snow. Over and over and over. He lost track of the time. He didn't know how long he had been there. He'd forgotten to watch for people who might spot him crouched beneath that window in the middle of the night.

At length, Stan got to his feet. It was hard for him to walk, for his knees were cramped. His bare hands were almost frozen. He walked back to the Ranchero. When he opened the door, the blast of warm air almost knocked him over. He sat down heavily, exhausted. A moment later he was asleep.

Mike put the Ranchero into first gear and started to drive away as the front door to the Byerses' house opened. Mrs. Byers and Pete, her oldest son, had Bill by the arms and were half-carrying him to their old Chevy. When they got him in, Mrs. Byers ran around to the driver's side. A moment later the car pulled out of the driveway and headed down Seventh Street.

Mike followed at a distance to find out where they were headed. He wasn't surprised to see them pull into the emergency entrance of Othello Hospital.

Mike looked over to Stan, still asleep, and felt a chill all over his body. Could it be that the whole thing was true? Was this social reject really capable of the things he said he was? What was going to happen the night of the new moon? Mike shook his head and tried to calm down as he drove into the driveway of the Fullers' house. It was a little past midnight.

"Fuller! Hey! Wake up! You're home."

Stan sat up with some difficulty. The iceballs and the long cold night had taken their toll on his body. But he had been awake enough to pretend to be asleep, and he had seen Bill Byers taken to the hospital. Nevertheless, he looked over at Mike and said, "I wonder if Bill will get sick. Sometimes it takes a while before something happens. And then, sometimes nothing at all happens."

"Probably nothing will happen. It's not important, anyway. I'll give you a call tomorrow and we can go out and take a look at the house."

"Okay." Stan got out of the truck and walked into his house.

Slowly Mike backed out of the driveway and made his way home. Just before he went to bed, he pulled the King James Version of the Bible off his bookshelf and set it on his nightstand. Before he drifted off into sleep, he recited The Lord's Prayer to himself.

Kansas, 1946

Seth Williamson looked all around himself. Kansas, he thought, it's so flat and wide you can almost feel the presence of the Lord. For a moment he looked across the fields of wheat and corn, the buzz of insects droning in his ears. His eyes followed the horizon as it stretched out before him, meeting the clear, bright sky in a cascade of blue. The beauty, the completeness of the scene held him breathless. Kneeling down in the hot August dirt, he bowed his head and clasped his hands together in prayer.

"Thank you, Lord, thank you, Jesus!" he sang over and over to himself until his pulse raced and his breath became shallow. He rocked back and forth on his heels, praising the Lord.

"Hhhhhhooooonnnnnn," sounded an automobile horn and a black sedan roared by, waking Seth from his reverie. He turned, full of righteous indignation toward the car speeding down Highway 96 toward Beeley, and screamed, "Sinner! You will atone in hell for your mockery of the only true God!"

Seth stood up, brushing the rich dark soil from his knees. He straightened his hat and walked back to his brand-new 1946 Chevy. His daddy had bought it for him as a present for his twenty-first birthday a month earlier. The parishioners

of his daddy's church in Russellville had paid for it because
Seth was going to go forth from Georgia to spread the word
of God. He was going to set up his own church out west in
Washington state and do the Lord's work.

Seth took a deep breath, filling his lungs with pride and
determination. His heart quickened with the vision of himself
standing before his congregation behind a beautiful wooden
pulpit, with the Bible in his left hand and his right hand pointing toward a roomful of sinners. He climbed into his car and
drove toward Beeley with his hair blowing in the hot afternoon wind.

Beeley was hot. The main street, the only one that was
paved, was sending up waves of reflected heat that distorted
the shapes of buildings and people—those few people who
lacked the common sense to stay indoors with the temperature
outside at 110 degrees.

Coming into town from the east, the first thing a visitor
saw was Roy's Service Station. Next was Uncle Ike's Diner,
the gathering place for most of the town. It was here that Seth
sought refuge from the debilitating August heat by ordering
an iced tea, no sugar, thank you very much, ma'am.

There were five other customers in Uncle Ike's, three men
who looked like farmers and two young girls, May and Dotty,
who had been stealing appreciative glances at Seth from the
time he had walked in. Every so often the girls leaned toward
each other and whispered something, then giggled loudly.

Seth watched them furtively. He knew righteousness and
purity protected him, although such virtues did not keep him
from noticing that perspiration had caused the thin material
of the girls' dresses to cling to their youthful curves. His eyes
followed the contours of their waists to their ample thighs.
The creamy flesh beneath their dresses distorted the color of
the fabrics, bleeding the pale colors into their skin. Seth allowed his eyes to wander over their bodies, entranced by their
raw sexuality as a heat began to pool in his groin. He felt
himself growing hard and immediately felt ashamed. He
wanted to get up and run, but his pride—among other things—
kept him glued to his seat.

Trapped in a strong state of arousal, Seth sat on the scarred
wooden chair and glared at the two girls. He resented their
hold over him, but he was comforted by the fact that Jesus

would give him the strength to overcome this difficulty just as He had all the others.

Soon the girls stood up to pay their tab, all the time casting glances at Seth. Finished, they walked to the door and vanished in the bright summer afternoon.

A wave of relief washed over Seth, and he sighed heavily. He thanked the Lord Jesus for removing his temptation. Whores, he thought to himself with some assurance. Perhaps someday he would do a sermon on the subject. Seth sat there for another hour, lost in his daydreams about preaching the word of God. Finally, he stood and stretched out his arms in a silent yawn. Walking to his car, he spotted the two girls sitting on the curb in the shade of an old elm tree and stole a look at them. He got in his new car and drove west out of town.

An hour later, he pulled into Scott City. His clothes were completely soaked with sweat, and he was very hungry. He stopped first at a service station to fill up with gas and check the oil and water. Next, he stopped at a market to pick up some cheese, crackers, and pickles. He left the store just as it closed. It was 6:00 P.M. and the sun was lowering, but there was still plenty of light to drive a while.

After consulting the map, Seth drove north from Scott City until he reached the bustling community of Oakley. It was in Oakley that he got onto Highway 70 and headed for Denver. At 9:35, Seth pulled into Burlington, Colorado. Stopping at the first motel with a vacancy sign, he registered and paid for one night.

"Checkout time is 11:00 A.M.," muttered the elderly woman behind the counter.

The room, dark and dirty, smelled of old sweat and alcohol. Seth drew himself a cold bath. It was a good thing that he wanted a cold bath because there didn't look to be any connections for hot water. Still wet from the bath, he threw himself down upon the smelly sheets and fell immediately into a deep sleep.

It was late morning when he awoke. After an enormous breakfast of bacon, eggs, biscuits, and gravy at the corner cafe, he drove the rest of the way into Denver. Denver was a large city with cars everywhere and people rushing about in bright summer colors. On the surface, this looked to be a nice place, but Seth knew it was like every other place, populated with sinners who yearned for the word of God.

Roger and Mex were just plain mean folk. Never mind that they were more than a little down on their luck. That didn't account for all the orneriness in them. They were the kind that would kick a dog just to hear it yelp. Take that endearing quality and marry it to their recent poverty, and you had a combination that was truly dangerous.

Roger and Mex had been buddies in France during the War. The War had been pretty good to them. They had escaped almost all of the combat but still enjoyed the benefits, especially looting and raping. With so many GIs roaming around the cities and countryside, the victims didn't know who to blame—that is, when someone actually did bother to report the crimes to the American authorities. Many of the French believed the American allies weren't any better than the Germans. The world saw the Americans as saviors, the French just saw them as another occupation force imposing its will upon France.

France, Roger thought to himself, those were the good ol' days. We could get 'bout anything we wanted and anything we needed, the army provided. Now we can't even get a job . . . now we sleep in alleys or on doorsteps or worse.

Mex took a pull off the bottle when Roger handed it to him. Ah . . . it burned so nice as it trickled down his throat to his stomach. For a moment it would just sit there, then warmth and well-being would spread outward. Mex leaned back on the old army-issue sleeping bag. Handing the bottle back to Roger, he absently picked at the crud that was caked on the olive drab.

"We gotta git us some money," muttered Roger. "Sleeping outside during the summer ain't so bad, but this next winter's gonna kill us. Maybe we should head for California where it's warm all the time."

"Yeah," answered Mex, "but we're still gonna need money to git there." He pulled the bottle out of Roger's hands and upended the remainder, then passed the empty bottle back to Roger.

"Fuck, we're outa juice!" growled Roger, scratching the

black dirty stubble on his face. He tossed the bottle on the sidewalk and belched loudly, the sound echoing into the alley. "Come on, Mex, we gotta find us some money."

Seth pulled off the main road to get away from all the traffic and found himself in a grimy, depressing section of town tucked away between large warehouses. He located a filling station and turned in to it. While the attendant refueled the Chevy, Seth surveyed the area around him. Satisfied that no one was watching, he reached under the dashboard and pulled out a brown leather wallet. He took ten bucks out and counted the remainder. Two hundred and seventy dollars. This was his nest egg. This was what he had to live on until he got his own parish established.

Daddy had paid for Seth to attend the Baptist Seminary outside Augusta, using up most of the family savings. But nonetheless, Daddy had managed to scrape together three hundred and fifty dollars to get him out West. Seth closed the wallet and replaced it beneath the dashboard, unaware that he was being closely watched by the two men across the street in the alley.

After paying the attendant, Seth drove down the block, pulled into the shade of an old brick building, and walked into a no-name cafe for lunch. However, he was careful to lock the car before going in and sitting down in the relative comfort of the cafe. It was cooler here than in Kansas, but it was still plenty hot.

After eating, Seth paid his bill and walked out the door to his car. He was just about to stick the key in the lock when he heard something. He looked out and saw a tall, scruffy-looking man kicking another man who was rolling around on the ground. The man on the ground moaned and pleaded for help while the other man continued to kick him.

"Stop it!" yelled Seth, his voice cracking a bit in fear.

The tall man glanced sideways at Seth but continued kicking the one on the ground. Seth took a few steps toward the man, who looked as if he might run away. Encouraged, Seth ran toward him.

Just as Seth had hoped, the man stopped kicking the fellow on the ground and hurriedly walked away, apparently frightened by Seth's coming to the rescue. When Seth reached down to see if the assaulted man was okay, the latter suddenly sat up, doubled his fist, and hit Seth square in the nose.

Seth tumbled over backward onto the pavement. Mex got to his feet as Roger came back around the corner. As Seth started to get up, Roger hit him across the ear and Mex kicked him in the stomach. They dragged him into the darkness of the alley, making a quick check of their surroundings to see if anyone was watching. Seeing that the coast was clear, they began kicking Seth and continued until they were sure he was unconscious. They searched his pockets and found his car keys. They walked calmly across the street, unlocked the shiny black door, got in, and started the car. As the two thieves drove down the street, Mex felt under the dash and found the brown wallet.

"Hot damn!" exclaimed Roger when he opened the wallet. "California, here we come. But first we gotta stop and git us some juice!" The men laughed as they drove away, the blood drying brown on their hands and shoes.

After wiping the grease from her hands on the dingy apron, Lydia Golder untied the strings and hung it up on a small nail on the dingy wall. She called over her shoulder, "Just tomatoes all you need, Steve?"

"Pick up a dozen or so onions, too," responded the burly cook. "And mind that you don't stop at yer lover boy's, neither. I'll know. Believe me, I can smell it. So just you watch it, girl."

Lydia laughed, pulling back some loose strands of her blond hair. Then with her hands, she smoothed the cotton shirt over her breasts provocatively, winked at Steve, and walked out of the no-name cafe.

As she walked she thought about Randy. She wasn't quite sure if she loved Randy or not, but she did know that making love with him was wonderful, better than with any of the other men she had known. She loved to see him towering over her, slipping ever deeper into her, sweat falling from his brow onto her face, his sweat adding to hers. Gripping as hard as she could, adding her strength to his power, matching his moans with her screams. Yeah, no doubt about it, sex was wonderful with him . . . but after that was over, there just wasn't much to talk about.

Randy said he wasn't ready to get married. But Lydia knew it was really her. People talked. Randy knew he wasn't the only one she had slept with, and that made her a slut. Sluts were good fucking, but not exactly someone you would take home to meet the folks.

She stopped dead in her tracks. She cocked her head sideways and listened. Yep, she heard it again. It was a groan, and it was coming from the alley. She stole to the mouth of the darkened space between a warehouse and a shoe factory. She saw a man on the ground, trying to get to his feet. He had blood on his face, and he looked familiar somehow . . . Then it dawned on her—he had just been in the cafe. He'd had a club sandwich and milk. And now here he was, another neighborhood mugging victim, the third this month! She hurried over to steady him.

4

Othello, 1970

The house felt them approaching. It wanted to warn them away, reveal to them that *it* was the unwilling home of Evil. An unexpected force surged through the foundation, driving up with a monstrous intensity, pulsating through the walls and echoing screams deep into the rafters. Two sleeping rats, huddled together for warmth in the attic, quietly convulsed and died; tiny trickles of blood dribbled from their ears.

The force oppressed the house, and the house lost its sense of time; the memories dried up, the laughter and love it yearned for became lost in the warp of anger and lust. Slime pooled on the cellar stairs leading into the kitchen as a great stench wafted into the stark, empty rooms of the house.

The house tried, it tried to remember all the love and laughter and innocence it had known. But the presence was stronger, and the house forgot. The congealing existence of hate—of pure lust—did not want to grant the final comfort of death; it wanted only to cause suffering with silence and emptiness.

Stan and Mike drove up the dirt road leading to the house. Mike's Ranchero fishtailed on the frozen snow. It was evident that nobody had been out here since the last snowfall, for the white stuff was unmarred by the tracks of other vehicles.

The house wasn't visible from the turnoff. The first section of road rose up from the highway rather steeply from the flat deserted surroundings. Then the roadway cut through an embankment, curving around suddenly, and the house was revealed.

The house, a full quarter of a mile away, seemed in perfect harmony with its environment. It stood straight up with smooth, even lines extending from the flat surface of the snow. From a distance, the house had an aura of majesty. It seemed to send out a welcome. Mike could feel something odd, but he dismissed the feeling as excitement. Stan, however, knew something was emanating from the house. He didn't know if it was a good sign or one that indicated he should be prepared for the worst.

As the two boys drew closer, the house seemed to shimmer almost as though they were looking at this cold winter scene through the hot desert air. One moment it would look beautiful and warm, the next it would be old and sick—a shell not even worth bothering about.

Mike stopped the Ranchero at the base of the steps leading up to the expansive porch. The icy wind blew through the broken window glass, creating screams. The effect was eerie. Mike felt an urge to turn back and head for the safety of his bedroom and his record collection, the TV, the familiarity of home and family.

A moment later, that familiar horrible whisper touched Stan's ear once again, immobilizing him with terror. All he could think of was the excruciating pain he had felt two nights earlier.

Mike turned around to look at Stan, who just stood with his eyes bugging out and his mouth open. As much annoyed as startled by Stan's condition, Mike demanded, in an urgent whisper designed *not* to wake the dead, "What the fuck is your problem? Yer givin' me the creeps. Knock it off!"

Stan realized that his friend probably wouldn't believe him if he told him about the voice. But if Mike did believe him, Stan could certainly count on being forced to leave before he was ready.

Stan took a deep breath, the crisp air steeling his nerves. "Nothing," he said. "I just felt weird for a second. Come on, let's go inside and check the place out."

Stan pushed the door open. Glass, wedged beneath the door, crunched, gouging deep scars into the floor as Stan forced it—the house's final attempt to keep the boys out. The two boys stepped in and surveyed the living room, taking the full destruction into view. In the corner was an old television set turned on its side, the picture tube smashed in. Window glass and broken beer bottles were strewn all over the floor; walking was hazardous. The house seemed far from being haunted. Instead, it seemed an empty shell with the warm breath of two boys hanging ragged in the cold winter air.

The stairway loomed up to their left, and both boys felt themselves drawn upward as the winter wind blew through the cracked windowpanes, touching their ears with whispers—whispers of warning. They looked at each other and then around the room. The living room stretched out in front of them and behind the stairway. The dining room and living room were separated by an arch and the boys looked through the living room into the dining room and into the kitchen at the back of the house. Each in turn brushed at his ears carelessly, as if insects were buzzing around them. The spell was beginning.

Neither knew the other suffered as they brushed away the nonexistent insects. The whispers of warning had become veined with evil and were now whispers of temptation, the temptation that is the stuff of young boys' fantasies. The spell grew in strength.

Bare warm flesh quivered before their eyes. Smooth contours slick with readiness loomed before them, their lust feeding the fire of the spell like a bellows. Warm breath with a sweet-sour odor enveloped them . . . playing upon their excitement . . . carrying them further into their own desire, trapping them with their desperate wanting.

A drop of spittle formed at the corner of Mike's mouth. Slowly it trickled down his chin. Transfixed, his eyes glazed over; he slumped against the dirty wall and slid to the floor onto a bed of red satin, which was cool and inviting against his bare skin. He moved his arms back and forth against the silkiness as a female figure approached with a seductive sway to her hips. He tried to look up into her face but was instead drawn to the swell of her breasts rubbing urgently against the sheer pink fabric that barely covered them.

She stood at the foot of the bed, the warmth of her thigh
pressing against the bottom of Mike's bare foot. Reaching
down, she gently scratched the inside of his calf with a brilliant white fingernail. Mike moaned in expectation, his eyes
closing as blood trickled down his leg, darkening the red
satin. Mike reached his hand up toward her . . .

Stan turned his head to look in the direction of the moans
coming from Mike. Lazily, his eyes followed the angle of
the wall down until he saw Mike lying slumped over, his
hand reaching upward into the air; his eyes were squeezed
tightly shut, and a thin ribbon of blood ran from his mouth.
A shadow loomed over and then drained away from the boy.

At first, the situation did not register with Stan. He just
stared, his own dream weaving in and out. Then, as he gradually came out of it, he shook his head vigorously back and
forth.

"Hey! Hey, Mike!" he called. The sound of his own voice
brought him back. He felt invaded and vulnerable, just as he
had two nights ago. He knelt down and shook Mike by the
shoulder. "Hey, Mike!" he tried again.

This time Mike's eyes focused on Stan. A moment later he
was standing on his feet, confused and frightened. "Shit, I
musta cut myself on some glass," Mike muttered as he
reached down to touch the painful spot just above his ankle.
He pulled up his stained pant leg and looked at his blood-
soaked sock. Peeling back the sock, he discovered a neat slice
about two inches long. The bleeding had stopped.

"Fuckin' glass," Mike snarled at no one in particular. He
stood up, trying to be braver than he felt. He surveyed the
room and then looked up the staircase to the second floor.
"Going up?" he said, looking at Stan.

Stan nodded and fell into step behind Mike. The chipped,
cold banister wobbled from the weight of their hands. Glass
crunched beneath their feet as they ascended the stairs one by
one.

At the landing, Mike could have sworn that the house settled. The house seemed to sway slowly, but there was no
moaning or creaking.

From the landing, they saw four doors leading to four bed-
rooms described by the gables on the outside of the house.
They peered into the first three cautiously, making sure that

no one was lying in wait for them. Then they came to the last room. The door was slightly ajar. There was something definitely wrong with this room.

Then they noticed it.

First of all, the door seemed different. It was heavy, as if made from a special kind of wood. It had a hasp and hinge— on the *outside*, curiously enough. The lock was nowhere to be seen, but it was obvious that the door had been made to be locked from the outside. Its most peculiar feature, however, was the window, centered about four and a half feet from the floor. It seemed miraculous that this little window, about three inches wide by two inches tall, remained intact when all the other windows in the house were cracked or shattered.

As Stan slowly pushed the door open, the boys were met by the glare of winter snow assaulting them from the south through the only window in the room. In one corner a mattress—filthy with stains, tears in the gray-striped cloth—lay against the wall. Strewn across the floor were multicolored rags, shirts, pants, and old dingy underwear of an indeterminate gender.

In another corner stood a beat-up chest of drawers. Two drawers were missing; the other two were full of rags and rat droppings. Mike pointed out that the dresser was directly below an access hole through the ceiling leading into the attic. From the looks of the footprints on top of the dresser, someone had climbed or tried to climb up into the rafters using the chest of drawers as a ladder.

Stan felt as if a weight was pressing down upon his back, trying to force him to the ground. He stood there silently, his heart racing. The weight was all too familiar, and the remembrance of the same weight two nights earlier caused his pupils to widen in horror. He had difficulty standing as the weight increased.

"Help me up onto the dresser," said Mike.

Stan looked at Mike and tried to fathom the request. Thinking seemed to make him feel better. All at once Mike began to scream at the top of his lungs, startling Stan back to full consciousness.

"Jesus fucking Christ! Fuck! Get it off of me . . . goddamn

. . . shit . . . help me!'' screamed Mike, totally out of control.

Stan took a step toward Mike and began to examine him closely. "Hold still . . . Where . . . ? Where? I don't see anything." Stan tried to keep the fear out of his voice.

"Here!" said Mike, gritting his teeth together in a snarl of repulsion, pointing to the side of his head.

Stan examined the spot closely. Something liquid had fallen into Mike's jet-black hair. Stan wiped it off with his finger and looked at it.

"Blood," he whispered.

"Jesus fucking Christ!" stated Mike. "Something up there is bleedin'!"

The two boys looked at each other and then back up at the dark hole in the ceiling. Their hearts raced in unison as they contemplated the possibility of a corpse being up in the attic.

"Should we take a look?" asked Stan.

"Yeah, I guess . . ."

Mike walked back over to the dresser and, with a leg up from Stan, stood on it once again. He thrust his head and shoulders up through the opening. It took his eyes a moment to become accustomed to the darkness. Lowering his head a bit, he peered into the inky shadows and saw the source of the blood. Something sliced the air near his head, and a tirade of screams echoed into the rafters.

The house resisted. It would resist until it was nothing more than ashes and dust—forgotten and unloved.

The house twitched. It twitched again, and a ripple spread throughout the house. A mouth crowded with broken teeth snarled in outrage, stooping in the rafters, claws extended: emptiness where the boy should have been.

The chest of drawers that Mike was standing on suddenly shifted. The floor seemed to weave and buckle as Stan watched the chest of drawers topple over with Mike crashing down upon it.

Stan bent down to see if Mike was okay. Mike was laughing so hard that he had tears in his eyes. When he was able to regain his breath, he said, "Shit, we are such assholes. Scared little pussies. Shit, I can't believe it."

"What are you talking about? What was bleeding?"

"Coupla rats. Killed by a hawk or something. It flew near me . . . that's when I screamed and lost my balance."

Although not much was funny, the tension was broken and the boys laughed. A moment later, they were both rolling around on the dirty floor, holding their bellies. Their laughter echoed through the house, even as Evil smiled down on them from the rafters. Suddenly someone else's laughter, far off in the distance, merged with the boys' own.

Initially the boys didn't hear it, but soon it was unmistakable. They fell silent. As they looked at each other, their expressions confirmed that they both heard the same thing.

The sound was so faint it seemed to be across the highway. There were moments, however, when it seemed to be just under them. The boys got off the floor and walked out of the strange little room. With more curiosity than alarm, they went downstairs trying to locate the ethereal laughter.

When they reached the living room, the laughter seemed to have moved to a location outside the house. They stepped out and walked completely around the porch that skirted the house. As they chased the laughter, it seemed that it had shifted back inside the house. But something else had happened. It was not only laughter they heard but also faint screams and sobs, fading in and out.

The boys stood still, hardly daring to move lest the sound disappear altogether. Without realizing it, they began to listen with more than their ears; they began to feel the tidal pull of memories, and more details began to come through. They heard coarse muttering and then an occasional angry shout. More cries, then sharp slapping sounds followed by a deep thud. Then whimpering. Several more hollow, sickening thuds . . . then silence.

"God, let's get the fuck outa here!" whispered Mike.

"No, I think we should stay and look around some more. After all, we came here to see what we could see." Mike shook his head and reluctantly followed Stan through the old house into the kitchen. The kitchen was a disaster area. The cupboard doors were peeling and covered with nicks and gouges. The linoleum had been peeled off the floor, and in most places bare wood showed through. The eerie light of winter poured through the kitchen window above a once-white sink now covered in rust and grime.

The boys found nothing of interest in the kitchen, but they stood looking around just the same. After a moment, there was a tinkling of glass in the living room. Almost aimlessly, Mike wandered off in the direction of the sound.

Stan remained in the kitchen, staring at its dilapidated appearance. His eyes became fixed upon the shards of broken window glass glistening in the winter light. He followed the shine of the glass to the shine of fresh white paint upon the cupboards. A brighter gleam drew his eyes to the floor, newly waxed, and the clean smells of a well-scrubbed kitchen wafted in the air. The copper fixtures shone brightly, suggesting the work of a housewife who loved to scrub and wash, making a perfect home for her husband.

Stan glanced back again to the brightness of the floor. A beautiful, old-fashioned design of black grape leaves sparkled through the gleaming wax. Stan's eyes followed the design to the edge of the cupboards and back up their snow-white surface. The brightness dazzled his vision as his eyes moved hypnotically across the expanse of wood and enamel. Then, at the edge of his sight, something marred the white surface. Spattered across one corner of the cupboard and down the side of the wall were rivulets of fresh blood.

Mesmerized by the sharp contrast, Stan stood his ground while a hand rose up and smeared the blood across the white paint, leaving a vermilion handprint. Stan looked in the direction the hand had come from and saw a massive pool of blood on the floor. The pool widened and drifted toward his tennis shoes. The pool became even larger, and now Stan saw a body floating peacefully on the surface of the thick red fluid. The body was clad in a white blouse, and the blood formed lovely patterns, resembling autumn leaves, upon the white material. Stan stood there looking at the patterns and felt pleased, for all seemed natural and familiar.

Bending down on one knee to touch the pattern, he watched the blood soak into his overalls. As he reached out with his free hand, he noticed it was covered with blood. He looked from his hand to the smear on the cupboard and nodded his head slowly in understanding. He looked down upon the body. The lovely blond hair was matted with blood. His other hand felt heavy as he raised it above his head. He felt a rush of hatred and self-righteousness as light reflected from the long sharp piece of steel in his hand. With one last look at the lovely blond head, he brought the steel down heavily, solidly into her body. A familiar hollow *thunk* sounded as red spattered everywhere.

"Hey, man, you okay?" Mike had walked back into the kitchen and stood looking down at Stan as he knelt staring at the floor.

Mike's own voice sounded strange to himself.

Stan didn't respond; he only continued to stare down at what was left of the floor. It seemed to him that he was looking straight through a crack into the dark basement.

Mike looked curiously at Stan as he walked past him, headed for the basement door. The door already stood ajar. The darkness below seemed to be sucking all the light from the kitchen. Mike pulled the door completely open and looked down. The darkness was so thick he could see only part of the first step, a small portion of the second, and barely a spot of the third; beyond, there was only black.

The darkness rushed up to him, buzzing around his head like an angry swarm of bees. He felt movement, felt it before he actually saw it, a dark gray shadow against the coal black. A cloying scent burned his nostrils; his blood pumped hotly through his body. Then he saw the outline of a girl's face, veiled and moving up the stairs toward him.

The girl reached behind her ear and slowly pulled the veil away. My God, Mike thought to himself, it's Paula.

The creature of lust gazed up from his nest at the outline of the boy standing against the harsh glare of the light. He could feel the boy's excitement; he could smell the lust. Drool rolled in thick shimmers over the cracked yellow and brown front teeth, down the side of his cancerous lip. He hissed loudly, the hot breath carrying a stench upward.

Mike breathed deeply, inhaling the illusion of sweet perfume. "Paula," he muttered under his breath. He had lusted after her ever since she had been transferred to his third-period algebra class. Now here she was, just for him.

The girl stood naked on the stairs, glancing shyly at Mike. She moistened one fingertip with her tongue and rubbed it sensually over a nipple, moving her hips from side to side like a teasing little girl.

Mike's eyes widened, and he felt the warmth growing in

his groin. He took one step down the stairs, hearing music, soft and mellow. He was lulled by the spell of seduction. His groin grew full and hard, pulsating with the urgency of a youth untried.

The monster began to climb the stairs with slow deliberation. He languished in the sexuality of the boy, feeling it wash over his body like the warm sunshine he himself was forbidden. Only a few more steps and the boy would be his. All of him. His sex, his blood, his breath, his youth . . . his very life. Evil would consume the boy in body and in spirit. He would feed on the vital fluids in this man-child, and he would carry the boy's soul in his hot aching groin forever.

Paula took the final step toward Mike. Dropping all artifice, she gazed directly into his eyes. She reached up from one step below Mike and gently stroked the throbbing outline in his jeans. He flexed in her hand and she tilted her head backward, rolling her eyes in their sockets; softly she moaned her approval.

The moment Paula's gaze left Mike's eyes, the spell faltered. For a split second he lost sight of her, seeing instead a shadow, gray and shapeless. But it was only for an instant. When Paula looked back at him, running her moist and warm tongue over her pearl-pink lips, he was once again entranced.

Keeping her eyes steadily fixed on his, she bent to her knees. Her head tilted backward, her soft chestnut hair spilled over her shoulders. Her hands, soft and firm, loosened the top button of his jeans and slowly unzipped his fly. His pure white underwear was blotting up the clear fluid oozing from his throbbing manhood. With her fingernail, Paula sliced the cotton material away, then pulled him into her mouth. Over the moist suckling sounds, Mike heard Paula groaning . . . but it was mixed with something else . . . screaming. Someone screaming at him . . . oh . . . feels so good . . . just leave me alone . . . still someone screaming his name . . . "WHAT DO YOU WANT?"

Thousands and thousands of eyes. All looking at him. Stan would move one direction and then the next, and the eyes would follow him in turn. They were not natural eyes. Some were misshapen, distorted with growths and tumors. Others leaked fluids of various sickening colors. The eyes stared at him from inside the cupboards. A moment ago they hadn't been there, but now . . .

Stan could feel his weakness, his lack of control. I must shut my eyes, he thought to himself. But it was hard to draw his eyes away from this horrible spectacle. The house shuddered, and the cold winter wind blew a small piece of broken glass loose. It fell to the floor with a faint clink, distracting Stan from his nightmare. He squeezed his eyes shut and crossed himself with the pentacle of protection. Slowly and with great caution, he opened his eyes.

The floor was dirty and bare. The kitchen had been transported back to its disintegrating condition. There were no more eyes peering out from the cupboards.

Stan heard a low moan. His eyes searched for the sound and found it in the dark shadow of the basement door. It was Mike.

Stan called out to his friend, more curious than alarmed. After getting no response, he took a step closer. He had a feeling he wasn't going to like what he saw. With another step, he understood what was happening. He screamed at Mike to run.

The screams were getting louder and more distracting. Mike glanced with disgust toward the source of the noise. It was just Stan. But there was something about his expression . . . Never mind, Mike thought to himself; he turned his attention back to Paula. He looked down, expecting to see the cascade of hair and smooth pale skin. Instead, he screamed so hard that it felt like his throat was on fire. He tried to step backward but tripped on the step behind and fell upward into the kitchen, still screaming insanely.

Stan reached down and grabbed Mike by his coat, pulling as hard as he could. He dragged Mike across the rough kitchen floor. Without bothering to stick his privates back into his jeans, Mike struggled to his feet and followed Stan at a desperate, clumsy run through the broken glass in the living room and to the Ranchero waiting outside. Moments later, the two boys were driving down the highway screaming hotly at each other.

A few miles down the road, Mike, who had still not bothered to cover his sex organs, pulled off the road and stopped, screaming, "Get me some tissues out of the glove compartment!"

Stan fumbled in the glove compartment for the tissues and handed the package to Mike. Mike jerked it away and tore it open, sending tissues everywhere. He gathered up some tissues and began desperately wiping at his groin. Brown and gray slime stained the soft white tissue. A horrible stench wafted up from it and grabbed Mike by the throat. Unable to bear the smell, he opened the door and retched onto the snow-packed road.

Stan sat immobile, looking straight out the windshield into the fading winter light. He barely heard Mike's soft gagging sounds as he purged himself of his nightmare. They were miles from the house, but Stan knew there was still something with them. In the back of his mind he could hear something. It wasn't getting any closer, but it was still there. Screams. Furious, vengeful screams.

The wood in the house vibrated from the intensity. Pieces of loose glass tinkled brightly as they fell from a window molding. Fine dust filled the air as the sound resonated from the wall. Slowly the front door creaked as a coyote bitch nosed it open.

She lay her ears back flat against her head to block out as much of the screaming as she could, but it wasn't enough. The shrieks penetrated her flesh like long, impossibly thin shards of glass. She stumbled forward, drawn mercilessly to the waiting evil. As she stood at the basement door, her body was wracked with spasms of fear. Warm urine pooled around the pads of her hind legs as she began her descent into the last place she would ever see.

The creature, surrounded by darkness—consumed by his own desire—continued to scream. He could still taste the boy's flesh. His broken yellow-brown teeth ached with frustration and hatred. His body was in heat, consumed by his own lust, which the lust of the boy had multiplied. His own cock was so hard that it felt as if it would burst through the peeling greenish-black skin.

Unable to contain himself he sought pain as a release and bit into the smallest of his arms just above his claws. The pain soothed him for a moment as his own blood trickled down his parched throat. It would hold him until this bitch got down the stairs. She was almost there. Her scent made him drool as he grinned at her in the darkness.

He stopped screaming, breathing heavily from the effort. The coyote bitch whimpered like a pup as she approached the incubus. Still whimpering, she turned her hindquarters toward what would soon be her death. The desperate creature, vibrating with need, grabbed her back legs with two of his arms and thrust himself deep inside her. The bitch yelped bitterly. The second time he thrust into her, she screamed her pain as he smashed through her uterus into her guts. She died gratefully when he sank his teeth into her neck, ripping muscle and veins, spattering himself with her hot blood.

For a long while the terrible creature continued thrusting into her, until she was reduced to a shapeless, bloody mound of flesh and bones. For the moment, he was spent. His yellow tongue flicked casually at the bloody mass.

Stan and Mike had not calmed down much, even as they approached the familiar sights of Othello. For a long while Mike drove aimlessly around the perimeter of the town, smoking cigarette after cigarette. The boys kept the windows open despite the dropping temperature of an already frigid winter evening. The cold seemed to wash them clean of their fear. The music blaring out of the radio helped them forget for the moment what they had just gone through. Finally Mike drove into town and parked at the A&W.

As they got out of the car, they noticed Cliff's green Fairlane in the parking lot. The heat hit them like a blast of fire as they walked into the A&W; the harsh glare of the lights made them feel exposed and foolish.

"Hey, over here, guys." Cliff motioned to them.

Cliff stood on his knees in the orange vinyl booth, smiling his best smile. Peggy Blackston sat beside him, looking uncomfortable. Her eyes were lined in black, and her lashes were long and goopy. Her lips were painted almost white. From beneath her miniskirt extended stout farm-girl legs squeezed into black nylons with one little run near the knee, but they were her best pair and she wanted to look sexy for Cliff.

"Hi." She smiled at Stan and Mike, flipping her stringy dyed black hair out of her eyes.

"How's it going?" Mike responded.

Stan sat down without a word, refusing to make eye contact with anyone.

"So did you guys go out to the house today?" asked Cliff.

"Yeah," Mike said quietly, looking down at the table.

"Did ya see any ghosts?" joked Cliff. Peggy giggled.

The silence evoked by the question became uncomfortable. After a few minutes, Cliff broke the barrier and asked, "So when are we going there to cast spells? Tonight or tomorrow night?"

After a few more moments of silence, Mike looked up at Cliff. He was partly embarrassed, but mostly pissed, to be in this situation.

"I'm not going back," Mike said, with a certain degree of finality.

"Awww . . . did the big bad ghost scare duh widdle itty bitty boys?" mocked Cliff as he threw himself back into the orange vinyl, howling with laughter. Peggy joined in as everyone in the A&W turned toward them.

Mike, scarlet from embarrassment, slid out of the booth. Without a word, he left the restaurant and walked across the parking lot to his truck. A moment later Stan was there, knocking on the Ranchero's window.

"How about a ride home?"

Mike unlocked the door and the two boys drove off, leaving Cliff and Peggy to stare after them from inside the A&W.

"Wanna go to a haunted house and look for the boogeyman?" asked Cliff.

Peggy giggled and poked him in the ribs. "Okay."

5

"Come on, Pam, it'll be fun."

"Are you sure you wouldn't rather just be alone with him? You've been tryin' to get into each other's pants a month now. I'd just get in the way . . ."

"Yeah, sure, like you wouldn't if you had the chance," chided Peggy, popping her gum loudly in the mouthpiece of the phone. She looked back from the front of the A&W at Cliff, who watched the waitress generously swinging her hips as she walked past him.

"Come on," Peggy continued, "I can't keep him waiting all night. Are you comin'?"

"Oh, I guess. Swing by here when you're ready."

"Great!" exclaimed Peggy. "Be sure you dress warm— it's freezin' out there tonight. And bring some extra clothes for me—a pair of pants and a sweater. If I stop by my house, I'll never get out again."

"Okay, see you later."

" 'Bout half an hour. See ya." Peggy hung up the pay phone. As she walked back to Cliff she swung her own hips, in competition with the waitress. Cliff didn't appear to notice. He watched the tight material that clung without so much as a wrinkle over the smooth butt of the waitress as she walked back to the kitchen. The satiny brown fabric glimmered in the harsh fluorescent lights of the A&W.

Hmmm, thought Cliff to himself, I think that's Brian Balmer's baby sister . . .

"She said she'd go."

"What?" asked Cliff absently, trying to pull himself back to Peggy. "Oh, yeah? That's great! Finish up your fries and we'll pick her up and head out to *the big bad haunted house*."

They both laughed and made eyes at each other as Peggy wolfed down her fries, following with noisy slurps of Coke.

Hot damn, Cliff thought to himself, two chicks who are probably gonna be scared shitless . . . gonna need a guy to help them get through the night . . . and I got them all to myself. They're gonna be *so* grateful they'll probably give me anything I want.

Cliff stared out into the bright night. He could see that the moon was almost full and there wasn't a cloud in the sky. He couldn't wait to get the girls alone.

"Cliff! I said I'm ready," whined Peggy, trying to draw Cliff back from his lusty daydream.

"Yeah, yeah, I heard you. Okay, let's go. We'll stop by my house first so I can pick up a couple of joints. I've got some great bud." Cliff smiled from ear to ear as they slid noisily across the orange vinyl seats.

Screams of delight echoed into the silvery night. The moon shone with winter clarity, harsh and brassy. A soft, gauzy corona rose from the snow and wrapped its misty arms around the muscular dark-veined body. The creature caressed the gossamer with his yellow tongue and sang out in an ear-piercing shriek which mutated into laughter punctuated by a wet throaty gurgle. Presently, he stood and stared silently into the moonlight.

Black glossy eyes the size of golf balls, totally devoid of whites, reflected the luminosity of the silver-white moon. He stood, emanating desires growing more and more defined, silently savoring the conscious memories of the recently dead coyote bitch. Not long ago she had stood near this spot howling up at the moon in joyful abandon. She had borne a litter of pups just two summers ago. He could feel the coyote bitch inside him just as he had been inside her. For the moment, he was sated. But even as he stood on the ice-encrusted snow, he could feel lust taking hold of him again. His recent kill and feeding had satisfied his lust, only to make him more physical. As he grew stronger, his lust also grew. He recalled the taste of the bitch on his tongue, her bloody warmth running down his body scented with the acrid odor of his own fertile seed. Lust gripped him, propelling him quietly up a small hill.

He skittered across the snow, hardly breaking the smooth surface despite his enormous weight. He ran on talons nearly two inches long that extended from his feet and left puncture holes in the hard snow. The only sound of his running was a clickety-click, like the sound a woman might make by tapping her fingernails on a hard surface.

Suddenly the beast froze in his tracks. The crust of the snow gave way under his weight, and he settled ankle-deep in white. He stared off into the distance, listening. As he listened, his naked flesh began to tingle in anticipation. He stood motionless against the sky; he was invisible—his skin white against the snow—except for his glossy eyes and stained claws.

Swooping down from the night sky was a great snowy owl. Beautiful white feathers spread out to utilize the dense air as the owl circled in graceful arcs in search of her evening meal. With two strong flapping motions, the owl swooped up a small hill and then angled off at the last moment, perhaps sensing the danger. But it was too late and a blizzard of feathers was tossed furiously in the cold air as the owl fell silently to the snow. Moments later, the loose feathers drifted through the dense cold air and settled upon the dead owl. The bird had been split from the throat through the abdomen. Warm bloody entrails spilled out from the wound onto the melting snow.

He hunkered down in front of his kill and dipped his finger into the warmth. Blood and gore ran down his finger and he licked it off with his swollen tongue. He smiled and screamed with delight. Cackling softly to himself, he looked off into the distance and quickly forgot about the bird.

He looked longingly at the lights in the distance. People—many, many people. As he looked at the lights of Othello, he remembered the boy who had called him two nights be-

fore. This boy was special. He was like Lydia, who had summoned him for her pleasure. His pleasure had become her
pleasure. She was gone and the boy would take her place: he
would protect Evil. The boy knew many of the ancient ways.
The boy was going to be his, to help him get all that he
needed, all he lusted after. And now, the boy was down there
among the lights.

Smiling to himself, he turned his smooth, shiny head back
toward the house. A pair of headlights moved slowly up the
road. As he skittered across the snow toward the moving car,
his skin grew lighter. In a few moments it was the color of
the snow, with only his moon shadow to give him away. He
ran down the road and perched atop the embankment above
the highway.

"Fred, watch out for this corner up here, it looks real
slick."

"Alberta, I've told you a million times, only one of us is
going to drive this car."

Alberta sat quietly as Fred eased them around the corner.
Suddenly the car rocked slightly and the front windshield was
showered by icy snow.

"Oh my God, what was that?" croaked Alberta, her heart
pounding rapidly.

"Ah, take it easy—it was just some loose snow. It probably
melted during the day and was ready to fall."

The '65 Rambler station wagon continued down the highway. On top of the luggage rack Evil crouched, his talons
digging into the metal roof. Drops of spittle drooled from his
mouth onto the windshield as he began to darken once again.

"Look at that," said Fred. "Looks like raindrops, but there
ain't a cloud in the sky. If that don't beat all."

The Rambler continued its slow approach to Othello. The
unholy creature perched firmly atop the car, looking like just
another bundle that Fred had tied on top. Lust was building
in intensity. All he could think about was the boy.

"Stan," he whispered to himself. "Stan . . . we will serve each
other. Stan . . ." he chanted in a whisper all the way to town.

"God, I looked like a chicken shit in there just now with
Cliff and that slut." Mike blew cigarette smoke out the car

window that he had cracked open. "Fuck, it just pisses me off. I *know* there was something going on in that house this afternoon. I know there was . . ."

"Yeah," said Stan, "but I'm not sure just what it was."

"That's right, asshole, you don't know! You probably almost got us killed—or worse. Stan the Warlock! Shit! You didn't know any more about what was goin' on than I did! You're fuckin' around with things you don't have a clue about. But you pretend you know what's going on, and that pisses me off!" Mike flicked his cigarette butt into the street and watched the glow slowly fade out. Shaking his head back and forth in frustration, he started to say something but couldn't get it out.

Stan looked out the car window at the warm lights of his house. On one hand, he felt he should just go in and go to bed. But there was something pulling at him.

"Could we drive around a while?" Stan asked in an even voice, trying to keep his anger under control. "I don't feel like going in now, with all that's happened."

Mike sighed deeply, as if resigning himself to Stan's request, but actually he felt the same. He was too strung out to go home right now. "Yeah, I guess . . . for a while, anyway."

Mike put the Ranchero into gear and pulled away from the Fullers' house.

The green Fairlane flew down the icy streets on its way out of town. Cliff, Peggy, and Pam shared a joint and giggled over some unspoken joke as they listened to the radio. Just as they pulled through the stoplight at Killer Corner, they hit a patch of black ice and fishtailed. The teenagers whooped and hollered as Cliff corrected the problem, but not before he almost sideswiped a green Rambler station wagon on its way into town.

"Did you see that?" asked Pam. "Looked like ol' Fred was carrying a dog or somethin' on top of his car."

"Well, it looks like Pam's had enough weed for tonight," laughed Cliff.

They all giggled as Cliff worked his hand up the side of Peggy's thigh. The house was only another seven miles away.

Unnoticed by the passengers of the Rambler, the creature had jumped from the roof to the snowy road. He skittered quickly across the road, wedging himself between a pale house and a tall green arborvitae. His wide nostrils flared as he caught the scent of a dog, moments before the Golden Labrador in the backyard smelled the fetid odor of this supernatural creature. Immediately, the Lab began to whimper as he crawled farther back into the doghouse that Mr. Thompson had made for him just last summer.

Ricky, Mr. Thompson's seven-year-old son, had painted the doghouse bright red with a black roof. Ricky called the dog Bark. Bark and Ricky had played together all summer, and only one bad thing had happened. Ricky brought Bark into the house one morning, and Bark was so excited that he peed on the living room carpet. Ricky hit him on the nose. Bark didn't really understand; his big brown eyes welled up with tears. He could tell that Ricky was sorry he had hit him, but Mrs. Thompson made Bark stay on the chain next to the doghouse the rest of the day. He didn't see Ricky until the next morning. That was the longest day Bark could ever remember.

Now, as the terrifying odor became stronger, Bark wished for Ricky to come out and play, to make him forget about the bad smell . . . they could run from the fearful thing together.

When he saw the clawed foot of the monster upon the bright snow, Bark howled once for Ricky. Bark turned his head away and rolled his eyes toward the foul smell.

The piercing yelp woke Ricky from his dreams. That sounds like Bark, Ricky thought to himself.

"Mom? Dad?" Ricky called out into the darkness.

Mr. Thompson had heard the animal, too. Ricky could see that his dad had flicked on the light, for its luminescence spread outward from the crack beneath his parents' bedroom door.

"Dad?" Ricky called out once again.

"Yeah, it's me, Ricky. Go back to sleep, I'll just check on Bark. I'll be right back." He was up and had thrown his bathrobe over his pajamas.

Ricky stood on his bed and pulled back the curtains to the bright winter night as his father slipped on his boots and walked out the back door. His father looked sideways and could see Ricky standing in the window.

"Bark?" whispered Mr. Thompson, trying not to alarm any of the neighbors. "Bark. Here, puppy . . . come here, Bark."

Ricky's father approached the bright doghouse and looked into the darkness. After a moment of allowing his eyes to adjust, he saw Bark lying motionless inside. He smiled to himself and thought, Silly dog must have been dreaming. Extending his arm into the darkness, Mr. Thompson patted Bark on his hindquarters affectionately—and quickly withdrew his hand.

Ricky stood watching from his window. He couldn't figure out why his dad just sat there looking at his hand and shaking his head back and forth.

Stan sat quietly in the warm truck with his arms folded across his chest. He was feeling distant from Mike, who had been pretty hard on him the past few minutes. Stan stared straight ahead as the Ranchero's heater blasted his face with a heat that was almost uncomfortable.

Stan felt himself getting tired. His eyes were drying out, and all he wanted to do was sleep. He tilted his head back a little as Mike fiddled with the radio. The music faded in and out. Finally Smokey Robinson's "Tears of a Clown" came in loud and clear.

He licked at his lips. The taste was warm and rich. It struck an elemental chord in his being. He felt like a hunter . . . the taste of the kill. He began licking at his fingers; the taste was beginning to overwhelm him, throwing him into a state of agitation. Blood. Rich, warm blood coated the insides of his fingers. Stan extended his tongue, running it along the palm of his hand and up and down his fingers. The blood told him many things. It told him of happiness, of a little boy who played with him, of fetching a red ball, of table scraps and Gravy Train, of swimming in cold water on a hot summer day . . .

Mike sat there a moment with his mouth open, watching Stan lick his hands like an animal. More angry than shocked, Mike yelled for Stan to stop. "Knock it off! What the fuck do you think you're doing?"

Stan looked down at his hand and realized what he was doing. Stopping abruptly, he looked Mike in the eye. "Something's happenin'," said Stan with a look of terror on his face. "Something's definitely wrong."

Crouching beside some sagebrush, he was white as the snow and motionless. He stared intently at the little red pickup parked at the end of the access road. Though they were over a quarter of a mile away, the creature could hear their words. Closing the distance between him and the little red truck, twin hearts of the creature beat in excitement. He was torn between his bloodlust and his long-term survival. The boy Stan could ultimately provide him with everything he lusted for . . . or he could destroy him. Still, his lust was all-consuming as he crouched beside the truck. He could smell the cigarette smoke as his skin began to darken. The hunt had begun.

"Wow, it really looks dark in there." Peggy shivered, holding Cliff's hand tightly. Pam quickly brought up the rear.
"Don't worry, I brought a flashlight." Cliff pulled the flashlight out of his pocket and switched it on. The dim beam showed up as only a small patch of light on the porch; it was pale compared to the light of the moon on this winter's night.
The three of them stood on the ground in front of the steps leading up to the porch, the moon casting black shadows over the old wooden structure. The next moment, when Cliff stepped upon the first wooden stair, the house sang out a warning with the old creaking of wood.
"Run away . . . run far away . . ." creaked the house. "There is danger here . . . run away!"

The beast crouched in the corner of the truck bed just under the back window. He was black, blending into the shadows. He dug one talon into the side of the truck bed as Mike turned the corner sharply into Othello. The two boys had calmed down considerably, and Mike was taking Stan home.
Mike pulled up in front of the Fullers' house and let Stan get out. "I'll call you tomorrow," said Mike out the open window as Stan walked across the snow-covered front yard.
"Okay," replied Stan as Mike drove off. While Mike disappeared into the night, Stan turned to watch him and noticed

something odd. It appeared that there was something in the back of the truck. It looked like a sack or something. Stan had an eerie feeling about it and decided to call Mike about it as soon as Mike got home. Shaking his head, Stan opened the front door and walked in.

The evil creature contemplated the boy driving the small truck: the boy who he had tasted, the boy who was so full of lust. He smiled and ran his swollen yellow tongue over his cracked brown teeth. He was waiting for just the right moment. As the truck turned down a dark street, he raised his head from hiding and peered inside.

Mike felt strange, all at once, anxious—sort of like he did just before he had to take a test, or when he asked a girl out on a date. As he flipped his cigarette butt out the window, he glanced into his rearview mirror.

Looking back at him was a large dark head with bulbous black eyes staring right into his. He screamed and slammed on his brakes. The creature held tightly with his claws. Mike continued to scream the white-hot screams of terror, wrenching the steering wheel back and forth.

He hit the accelerator hard, hoping to get to somewhere or someone who could help him. He glanced back in his rearview mirror and saw nothing. In the next instant, his door handle rattled. From his side mirror he saw the creature trying to open the door.

With frantic desperation Mike drove over the slick road, heading for anyone who could help him. Reaching up to lock the door, he found the lock pulled just out of his reach. Cold air rushed into the cab of the Ranchero. Sharp talons sank into his shoulder. Mike wailed his terror, a cross between a plea and a scream.

The Ranchero skidded sideways across the frozen roadway, and was suddenly hit by an oncoming black Impala, and pushed across the snow-packed street. The passenger side where the impact had taken place was dented in, and the windshield cracked.

Ken Bliss jumped out of the Impala and ran up to the Ranchero yelling, "Kawaguchi! Kawaguchi . . . are you okay? Oh my God!"

Ken reached into the Ranchero and pulled Mike out. Mike was able to move himself, though with difficulty. Ken noticed blood dripping down the side of the boy's face and guessed it was from bumping his head on the steering wheel.

"Oh, thank God, you're okay, Mike. I tried to stop, I really did, but you were going so fast I just didn't have a chance . . ."

"Yeah . . . I think I'm okay," Mike muttered to Ken, remembering why he was driving so crazily on bad roads.

"Hang on, Mike, I'll call for help."

"No!" yelled Mike quickly. "Just stay here with me. I'm sure someone else has already called the cops."

"Sure, man, no problem. You want me to find your dog?"

"What dog?"

"Whadda ya mean? Your dog was ridin' in the back of the truck. When we crashed, it ran off."

Mike looked down at his hands; they were shaking violently. Mike knew it wasn't from the crash.

"Hey, Ken, you got a cigarette?"

The evil one crouched at the corner of a nearby house. He ground his teeth together in frustration. He had missed that boy twice. A couple blocks away he could see the flashing red light of the police cars coming to the accident. Evil turned on his heels and loped across the frozen lawns, changing his skin color to a snowy white. He ran six blocks until he came to the open snow-covered fields, where he ran across the surface, pulling each new step toward him with his long claws. His feet barely touched the frozen surface. He held his short arms to his chest as he ran, allowing the longer ones to swing in alternate strokes, feeding his momentum and speed. He held his mouth open, breathing in deep lungfuls of crisp air. His yellow tongue flopped loosely about, covering the side of his face with foul brown strands of saliva that froze instantly. He ran in the direction of the house, where he had last been summoned into this world once again.

Denver, 1946

Seth had been lying in Lydia's one-bedroom walk-up for two days. His bruises had healed up fine, but he was depressed. He felt like a failure. He had been robbed and his car had been stolen. The miserable, godforsaken sinners stole more than his money and car—they had robbed him of his dream.

Lydia unlocked the front door of the dingy apartment just five blocks from where she worked. Out of breath from the sudden exertion, she dropped the bag of groceries on the kitchen counter. Sweat matted the fine loose hairs across her forehead and she brushed them away with the back of her hand.

"God, I think it's hotter today than it was yesterday," she said loudly enough for Seth to hear in the bedroom where she had put him right after rescuing him. Not having had any sort of response from him since she had picked him up off the street, she was beginning to worry about the whole situation.

He was a handsome man, she certainly had to admit that, but he wasn't showing many signs of life. He wouldn't eat any of the food that she fixed him, and she never saw him use the bathroom. All he did was sleep or stare at the wall.

Well, she thought, I can't worry about it right now. I gotta take a bath and get to work.

Her leather-soled shoes rapped sharply on the wooden floor

as she walked through the bedroom and into the bathroom. As she walked through the bedroom, she glanced at Seth. He lay naked on his side, facing the wall. The mid-morning heat caused a trickle of sweat to run from under his arm down his back. His skin was almost as white as hers, and he didn't have an ounce of fat on him. He was firm and young and very attractive.

Raising her eyebrows in surprise at her own feelings, she turned the water on to a nice cool temperature for her bath. Stripping off her clothes, she eased herself into the water. The sensation of the bathwater was wonderful. She felt that she could stay there all day and not get tired of it.

Seth lay in bed as Lydia took her bath. He had watched her undressing out of the corner of his eye. Lying there all day long, smelling her odors and seeing her femininity, had brought out suppressed desires. He no longer had any money, had no transportation, no way to fulfill his dreams of establishing a ministry of his own. Now he was helpless. Unable to realize his vision, he was succumbing to the temptations of the flesh.

He could hear Lydia splashing around in the bathtub, humming to herself softly. He thought of her smooth skin and the supple curves of her breasts. Her dark areolas were becoming a constant source of desire. Aware of his arousal, he pulled the sheet up to cover his embarrassment.

Lydia stepped out of the tub and began rubbing herself dry with a rough white towel. Wrapping the white cloth around her, she turned to the sink and picked up her toothbrush. After she had finished cleaning her teeth, she replaced the brush and walked out into the bedroom to get dressed. She had been sleeping on the couch these past two days, but right now she didn't really want to go to work and her bed did look inviting.

She gazed at Seth lying there motionlessly. Noticing that he had pulled the sheet up around his waist, she gently settled her weight on the bed. She pulled the damp towel off her body awkwardly and tossed it to the floor. Stretching herself out alongside Seth's body, she allowed her hand to drift over to his side and gently played with his chest hair. She brushed it back and forth with her fingertips, hoping to arouse him.

Making the decision, she slid her hand down the flatness

of his stomach, circling her index finger slowly around his navel. Softly she slid her hand under the sheet and caressed the firm, pulsating flesh she found there. Running her hands down the insides of his thighs a moment, she brought her hand back up to his manhood, pulling lightly on it. She could feel the oozing slickness on her fingertips, and she found herself alive with passion.

Lydia pulled away the sheet, turned Seth around to face her, and maneuvered his position until he was inside her. His breathing deepened and quickened. His thrusting movements came quite naturally as his mouth found her breast. His passion drove him deeper with increasing speed, as Lydia's moans filled the small apartment. Suddenly Seth grabbed her forearms and plunged hard into her, his pendulous scrotum slapping against her buttocks. He issued a couple guttural groans and collapsed on Lydia's quivering body.

"I've told you three times now, I have a little money saved. I got enough to get us train tickets to Yakima, Washington."

Seth looked away, trying to think of some other alternative. He had been living in shame for the past two weeks—shame from having failed God's work and shame from having given into the temptations of the flesh. In his heart he knew what he must do.

"We need to get married, Lydia," he began, unsteadily. "We cannot continue to live in sin. We must marry!"

Lydia looked at him coolly. She had known that this was coming but was still caught a bit off guard. She wanted to get married . . . but did she want to marry Seth? Randy had called her several times and she had put him off. God, she knew the problem: she wanted to marry Randy. But she also knew that there was no way Randy would ever ask her. To him, she was just an easy woman, nothing more.

Seth was a different matter. He wasn't as much fun in bed as Randy; however, as Seth had admitted, she *was* his first woman. Seth was going places. He was moving to the West Coast and setting up a church. She could get away from her reputation and settle down. Have some kids. She had always wanted to be a mother.

"Are you sure that's what you want to do, Seth? Maybe you should think about it for a while." She turned her head and looked out the window, still not sure of what she should do, yet hoping he wouldn't change his mind. She watched the dreary little neighborhood below her; she knew she wouldn't have a very attractive future if she stayed in this town.

"It is what we must do! It is God's will. We will marry this Sunday. Do you know where there is a Baptist minister?"

She shook her head, overwhelmed by how fast her life was changing.

Seth paced up and down the floor, his fingers tapping lightly on his chin. Abruptly, he stopped in front of Lydia and looked into her face.

"What are we going to do when we get to Washington?" he asked her solemnly. "How are we going to live?" He looked down at the floor and stared at a dust mote swirling in the sunlight.

Lydia continued to look out the window, trying to think. "I've heard there's a lot of people picking fruit in the Yakima Valley, and you can make some fast money."

The idea didn't appeal to Seth at all, but he realized that it was probably their only recourse until they could find something else. Perhaps the good people of the Valley would need a minister. Suddenly he bowed his head in prayer. The Lord would provide, the Lord would provide . . .

7

Yakima Valley, 1946

Lydia lay on her side facing the dirty canvas, away from Seth. The air in the tent was hot and stale. She climbed down from the wooden platform that served as her bed while she picked fruit here in Grandview, and walked out into the summer evening.

Deeply, she breathed in the sweet air. It was much cooler out here. She maneuvered between the rows of tents and into the road, picking her way over ruts and large rocks. It was beautiful country, she thought to herself; nonetheless, she was worried.

She had not been surprised when Seth became a bit distant right after they were married. She knew he had married her from a sense of obligation and not love. But she had fully expected him to pull out of it by the time they were on the train to Spokane. She had expected he would try to make it work. But he didn't. He was cold and unloving ever since they left Denver. Of course, she had to admit he was working very hard.

Seth was working eleven and twelve hours a day, six days a week. He picked an enormous amount of fruit and put the money aside. Together with the money Lydia was making, they could soon make another start. He seemed obsessed by the work, and this obsession was changing him.

For the son of a Baptist minister who had never done physical labor, Seth was impressive. There was no load too heavy, no tree too high. He never complained about the hours; instead, he set his sights on a goal and set his back to the work. His body showed the result.

His skin now glistened with a sheen of sweat, a dark tan glowing through. His muscles were more pronounced, and his back and neck had a strong, ropelike texture. Lydia found him more attractive than ever before. But this was becoming a problem for her.

Seth wanted no part of her sexually. It seemed hard enough for him just to talk to her. He was always kind and gentle, and she never had to worry about him embarrassing her in public, like some of the other women's husbands. Seth always treated her with respect, but never with passion. The dull ache in her loins was becoming torture.

Nightly, before going to bed, she would wash and groom herself as best she could—with him in the tent—hoping against hope that he would start treating her like his wife instead of his sister. But gradually, after a month of trying and reaping no reward from it, she stopped. Instead, late at night when the faint moans of the other couples could be heard through the darkness, she would fantasize about Randy. Lately she had begun to watch some of the other men in the camp. One of them, a young Mexican boy with beautiful dark eyes, had stroked her leg while she stood on a ladder picking fruit.

Several more weeks passed, and most of the fruit was in. Seth had become troubled about the fact that they would soon be out of work. Luckily, on the last day of picking, a tall, red-haired Irishman named Michael O'Brian stepped directly into Seth's path.

"I see you're a hardworkin' man. How's 'bout comin' to work for me? I'm foreman for a sheep ranch in the Potholes area. There's a town nearby . . . Othello."

Seth was surprised by the jovial accent and stared at the man for a few moments before speaking. "I . . . I think . . ." He didn't really know if he wanted to go.

"Well, if you want to go, git yer wife 'n' all yer belongings and git on that old yellow school bus. I'll be leavin' in half an hour." O'Brian turned and walked away rapidly. He had five other men he needed to find in the next thirty minutes.

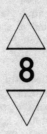

8

Othello, 1970

Cliff and the two girls walked around upstairs, peering into the rooms. Every once in a while Cliff would make some sort of noise to scare the girls, and they would huddle closer to him, even though they knew it was him trying to scare them.

"Well, so far we ain't seen any little ghosties," said Cliff. "Stan and Mike are just kids and still afraid of their own shadows."

The vile beast, however, was returning to the house. He was near and moving quickly. He *felt* the children. Impotent memories of laughter and joy drifted onto the house like winter snowflakes.

Now the color of snow, he stood on a knoll overlooking the house. He smiled as he looked down upon the car parked beside the porch. Inhaling a deep lungful of freezing air, he began leaping around joyously. Unable to contain himself, he screamed several glass-shattering cries and charged the house. As he ran, he changed his color back to a shadowy green.

"What the hell was that?" asked Cliff, trying to keep the terror he felt out of his voice.

All three walked over to the window in the bedroom and looked out into the moonlight. What they saw there at first confused them, then sent them into a frenzy of panic. Some *thing* was rushing toward them, shrieking.

He bounded up onto the roof of the Fairlane and, with a squeal, tore away at the paint. He turned his glossy black eyes toward the upstairs window and smiled.

". . . pretty, pretty children . . . can you come out and play?" he asked, in a high voice loud enough for the teenagers to hear.

Peggy began to scream. Instantly, the terror spread through the group. Pam began to scream. Cliff grabbed the two girls by the wrists and ran out of the room and down the stairs, dragging the girls behind him.

Half-expecting the creature to burst through the front door, Cliff stood in the middle of the living room trying to make the girls shut up. Their screams were making it hard for him to think. Cautiously, he walked to the door with Peggy and Pam in tow. Looking outside, he saw nothing but the night. Hissing at the girls to be quiet, he listened carefully. The frozen evening was silent.

Trembling, the panicked teenagers crept along the porch and peeked around the corner of the house. The Fairlane came into full view, but there was no monster standing on top of it. In a frantic burst of energy, they ran down the steps to the car and piled inside. Fumbling in the dark, Cliff felt for the keys in the ignition. Not finding them there, he searched through his pockets.

"Let's get the fuck outa here!" screamed Peggy.

"Shut up! We ain't going nowhere till I find the keys!"

As Peggy and Cliff felt around on the floor for the keys, Pam began to feel warm and calm inside. An image formed in her mind of the car keys; she saw them lying in the house, on the kitchen counter.

In a clear, calm voice that served to soothe Peggy and Cliff, Pam said, "The keys are still in the house. Remember when you were messing with the flashlight in the kitchen? You used your keys to scrape the dirt off the battery."

"I don't even remember being in the kitchen!" Cliff scowled, looking around himself in a panic. He was sure he'd left the keys in the ignition so they could get away fast if need be.

"Wait!" said Peggy, regaining her composure. "I remember that. We *were* in the kitchen. And you left the keys on the counter.''

Cliff, too, began to feel warm, his panic draining away. Maybe they're right, he thought, maybe I did leave the keys on the kitchen counter. In fact, in his mind he could see them now, very clearly.

''Okay,'' he said calmly, ''let's go back and get them.''

Quietly and without any panic, all three climbed out of the car and walked back up the stairs onto the porch. They pushed the front door open and walked back inside.

He stood in the rafters, listening to his young prey reenter the house. He continued weaving his spell, creating the illusions that would intensify their lust . . . feeding his power.

The house uttered a futile moan of distress. Several floorboards snapped loudly. ''Run! Run! Run away!'' they seemed to chant.

Excitement possessed the incubus; he sank his teeth into a wooden rafter. His broken teeth bit deeply into the soul of the house. Within moments, saliva dripped from the beam as a dark poison spread outward from his mouth.

The house glowed around the three teenagers. It was warm, inviting, serene. Peach-colored light flooded them. They felt as if they had walked out of the cold winter night into their own living rooms. With the light came warmth, and the three simultaneously shed their coats onto the glass-strewn floor.

''Hey, guys, you smell that?'' asked Peggy, slurring her words as she tilted her head in a dreamy state. ''It smells like Mom just made some cookies.''

Pam and Cliff, now also caught in the spell of home-baked cookies, followed Peggy's lead.

''Oatmeal-raisin,'' said Cliff.

''No, gingersnaps,'' countered Pam.

The three stood in the kitchen looking around for the cookies, their mouths watering over the anticipation of hot cookies and ice-cold milk. For a moment the spell lost its influence, and Cliff gazed down at a wrecked kitchen counter covered by rat droppings and broken glass.

The spell slipped for only an instant, however, as illusion restored itself even stronger than before. Cliff reached out and picked up an old rat turd, dry and almost frozen. Popping it

joyfully into his mouth, he chewed a moment and then swallowed.

"Nope," he said, casually smiling at the girls. "They're
chocolate chip. Careful, though, they're hot as hell . . . musta
just come outa the oven."

Peggy walked over and put her arm around Cliff's waist.
Picking up a piece of a broken beer bottle, she popped it into
her mouth. She made pleasant crunching sounds with a wide
smile across her face, as the glass sliced neatly through her
tongue several times. Shards of glass embedded themselves
deeply into her gums, and her mouth filled rapidly with blood.
A trickle of red flowed down the side of her smiling lips and
dripped off the end of her chin.

"Jesus, Peggy," said Cliff with a smile of his own, "you
don't need to make a pig of yourself. Look at you—chocolate
running down the side of your mouth!" Cliff extended his
finger and wiped her chin, then dragged his finger across his
Levi's, leaving a dark smudge.

Pam walked over and looked at the counter. "God, they
smell great! But I shouldn't eat any—I'm on a diet."

Peggy encouraged her. "Oh, go on, you can have *one*."
The whole of her chin was covered with blood; it ran in thick
rivulets down her neck and stained her blouse. As she smiled
at Pam, a great mouthful of blood gushed forward, spattering
the cupboard.

"Oh, all right," said Pam as she picked up an old piece
of tar paper and took a bite of it. She chewed for a moment
and then swallowed. "Shit, your mom really knows how to
make cookies! My mom can't cook worth a damn, even when
she's sober."

They all laughed. Peggy swallowed a mouthful of blood
and glass fragments.

His lust growing by the moment, the evil creature stood in
the shadow of the basement door, the odor of blood drifting
into his nostrils. Drooling with excitement, he clicked a talon
in a metallic rhythm against the slimy brown surface of his
teeth.

"Say, you guys, can you hear music? Sounds like it's
comin' from the basement. Let's go down and spin a few
tunes!" Cliff began walking toward the basement door, and
the two girls followed.

As Cliff opened the basement door, mellow candlelight appeared at the bottom of the stairs. They began their descent. Deep pile carpeting hushed their footfalls, and the scent of incense wafted upward. "Ina Gadda Da Vida," boomed loudly from downstairs, increasing in volume by the moment.

"Yeah! Great tune!" remarked Cliff, looking over his shoulder at Peggy as they came to the bottom of the stairs. Blood still flowed from her mouth, covering her chin, neck, and breasts.

The three teenagers looked around in the soft romantic glow of candlelight. The incense tickled their noses and pulled them deeper into the spell.

He peeked out at his prey from under the sixth stair, his eyes shiny-black and moist with his increasing arousal. Drool gathered at the corner of his mouth and dripped in sticky globs down the blue-black skin of his arm, forming a rancid puddle on the dirt floor. His short arms were clasped in front, his fingers intertwining in anticipation. The hands of his longer arms gently stroked his enormous erection, and his fingers became glossy black with the slickness of lust.

Smiling to himself, he exhaled with an odorous hiss. The dark red veins on his forehead and neck began to throb erratically with the pumping of his twin hearts. His concentration increased as he continued weaving his spell.

Filmy, ectoplasmic tendrils slowly emerged from his nostrils and ragged ear holes. Within moments, the dank air surrounding his head was swimming with ectoplasmic worms. His concentration shifted, and these ethereal extensions of himself began to drift languidly toward the three teenagers, who stood in the dim light of a single candle. A moment later, he began to rub the hands of his short arms together with childish glee.

Cliff basked in the soothing glow of the candles surrounding him—hundreds of them. Crossing the room to the beautifully ornate bed, he reached out to touch the pink satin cover. The candles made him feel warm and comfortable, and the cool sensation of satin against his hand aroused him. First he imagined how it would feel against his naked body, then he began to ponder more sensations . . . the smoothness of a girl against him, both of them swaddled in the pink fabric.

The color began to take him to greater heights of excitement. The pink was the dark pink of sexual arousal: the color of glossy lips, of moist tongues, of blood-engorged sex organs. Cliff could feel the warmth flooding into his groin as he looked over at Peggy and Pam.

The lustful, evil beast could hardly contain himself. He watched Cliff rubbing his hands gently over the infested stack of broken-down cardboard boxes that served as his resting place. He snickered like a child as he watched the gossamer wormlike structures swim around Cliff's head. Smoothly and silently one worm entered directly through Cliff's right eye. A second one slid into his ear, and a third entered through his navel.

Once inside, the worms dissolved into a channel of dreams. Instantly, the worm-dreams knew every secret desire, every explicit act that Cliff had ever wanted to indulge in. The channel of dreams knew . . . and the evil one knew as well. Other worms burrowed into Peggy and Pam, ferreting out their dreams and lusts, all consequently known by Evil.

But with unexpected strength, the teenagers' raw sexuality swept into the incubus's consciousness and shattered his concentration. He reacted to this unfamiliar power with spasms of excitement. Unable to control himself, he bit through a corner of his lower lip. His black-red blood spilled into his mouth and down his chin. The orgasmic barrage bent him double, then threw him to the ground. The murky darkness spun around him . . . and the weave of the spell began to unravel.

Terrible pain etched itself into Peggy's brain. The taste of blood tore at her stomach, and the warm glow around her began to dim. She tried to cry out, but her mangled and swollen tongue muted the attempt into a painful mutter.

Pam shook her head back and forth. It felt as if there was something inside that she needed to shake out. She turned to Peggy when she heard her groan, and tried to focus her own eyes.

"Are you bleedin'? Peg, are you okay?"

Pam looked around and saw Cliff in the corner, gazing numbly into the shadows. Then she heard something—a scraping, and something else . . . a wheezing and a whistling sound, from behind the stairs. Fear pumped through Pam's head as she tried to remember where she and her companions were and how they had got there. She stumbled over to the stairs. She grabbed hold of the splintered banister and looked into the shadows. It was a moment before her eyes focused on the writhing monster before her.

She screamed and threw herself against the stairway. She gawked at the incubus, unable to tear her eyes from it. She screamed again, louder, feeling herself thrown back into childhood nightmares. "Mama! Help me, Mama!"

The screams roused his lustful sleep. His eyes opened slowly, and a cloudy-white membrane skimmed over them. Pam saw the monster's eyes open and she screamed once again, this time stumbling backward into the dirt. As she scrambled to her feet, her mouth moved, but no more screams escaped. Absolute terror gripped her. She forgot about her friends and began to claw her way up the stairs.

A second later, talons grabbed her ankle through the stairs, ripping flesh, tendon, and muscle cleanly from the bone. Pam barely felt it as she stamped at the talons with her other foot. She slipped free from the powerful grip and pulled herself to the top of the staircase.

The full moon bathed the kitchen in a silvery light. Now aware of the searing pain in her leg, Pam glanced down and saw blood spurting from her ankle. Then she saw the exposed bone. She felt faint. The horrid face loomed in her memory, and she found the strength to stumble out of the kitchen. She gasped for air as she staggered through the living room and out the front door. Dragging her mutilated leg behind her, she made her way across the porch and started down the steps toward the car. The pain shot upward from her leg, and she fell into a heap on the snow.

The incubus licked the blood from his fingers as he heard Pam running above him. Once again, he was in control of the illusion.

Cliff was sitting on the edge of the cardboard boxes, removing his shoes. He smiled slyly at Peggy, standing a few feet away while blood continued to flow from her mouth and down her chin.

He drooled, crouched in the corner, deep in shadows, continuing to weave his illusion of blood and lust.

Cliff dropped his second shoe to the carpet. He smiled at Peggy, her lips glistening red, and patted the cool satin, motioning for her to sit beside him. She smiled back and moved toward him, swinging her hips. The crimson patterns on her blouse clung to her firm breasts. Gently he put his hands on her hips and buried his face in her moist bosom. His tongue moved in small circles against the warmth, and the taste of blood brought a hard throbbing between his legs. Slowly, he unbuttoned her jeans and slid them down her long legs. Cliff smiled to himself as he noticed that she was still wearing her black nylons even though she had changed into jeans.

Peggy released the snaps on her blouse, and it fell to the floor. She stepped out of the jeans Cliff had just pushed to her ankles. With just her nylons and bra on, she got on the bed and crawled up against the ornate headboard. She watched Cliff as he stood at the foot of the bed and removed his own jeans, T-shirt, and socks.

He studied Peggy's reaction, his erect manhood bulging in his white jocky shorts. She in turn slowly spread her legs, and her dark pubic hair showed through the sheer panty hose. Cliff reached down to the floor and fumbled around in his pants pocket. When he found his knife, he opened the small blade and moved closer to Peggy.

Peggy reached out and fondled the erection pushing out toward her from his briefs. As she squeezed tightly, Cliff extended the pocketknife to the crotch of her panty hose. Dangerously, he nicked the surface of the nylon and pulled. A tear appeared. Once again, Cliff cut the nylon until there was a gaping hole.

Peggy groaned in pleasure and excitement. She pulled at the waistband of Cliff's underwear; he ripped the crotch of hers to shreds, then cut the pink ribbon that held the cups of her bra together. The bra fell away with a snap. Cliff dropped the knife to the bed and climbed on top of Peggy. He plunged his tongue into her mouth.

Urgently, Peggy kissed Cliff and tried to tear his jockey shorts from his body. Together, they slid the shorts to his ankles as Peggy hungrily grasped his pulsing heat and guided him into her.

For a long moment, they both lay motionless, allowing the heat of their union to build. Then they began to rock, slowly, in time with the music.

After a few minutes, Cliff began to thrust deeply. He withdrew until he was almost out, then pushed back in, forcefully hitting his pubic bone against Peggy's. They moaned, and their breathing became desperate. Cliff's thrusts grew shorter and faster as his release approached.

Now the incubus crept from the shadows, inching his way to them. He basked in the brilliance of their ecstasy, power, and youth. Their powerful tide was almost enough to wash him away, but he persevered and continued to weave his spell.

Suddenly, Cliff withdrew. He rolled over onto his back and stared into the warm glow of the candlelight. Standing beside the bed was a woman of unbelievable beauty. Her blue-black skin shimmered in the golden light, crimson hair spread across her shoulders and flowed down her back. She smiled a bright, seductive smile of brilliant, white teeth and fondled her own firm breasts. Her black glossy eyes threw off no light, they were simply wells of darkness. She stepped over to Peggy and ran her long fingernails down Peggy's breast.

Cliff heard Peggy's breath catch in her throat as the sharp nails sliced open her flesh. They both stared at the open wound, running dark red as the incubus lowered his head to lap up the fresh blood with his swollen yellow tongue.

The incubus flicked at the girl's wound with his tongue and then crawled upon the pile of cardboard boxes. His enormous penis poised at the entrance of Peggy's vagina. Slowly, he entered her. The sides of her vagina tried to stretch in order to accommodate this new flesh. Her membrane tore and began to bleed.

Strangely, he restrained himself, savoring his power and the pain of his lover. He reached her limit and slowly continued his upward thrust. Tissue gave way to his strength; his tool burst into her abdomen. Peggy began the first of her wailing, tortured screams that echoed through the dark freezing basement.

Cliff's lust intensified as he watched the strangely beautiful woman thrust into Peggy. He looked into Peggy's face and listened to the screams of ecstasy pouring from her crimson mouth. The woman thrust into Peggy many times and then finally bent down to her neck and kissed her lovingly. Now Peggy was silent, her desire spent and her energy consumed by this black-skinned, red-haired woman.

Cliff reached out and squeezed the nipple that was exposed through the long strands of red hair. He stroked the beauty's head as she turned her attention to him. She knelt above Cliff, gazing down upon his body. She shook her hair back out of her way and wet her lips with her tongue.

Cliff sat up and looked deeply into her eyes, seeing nothing—not even his own reflection. Gently, he placed his hand on the back of her head and guided her down to his throbbing manhood. Her hot lips encircled him, setting him on fire. Slowly she moved her head up and down, at the same time stroking his scrotum. Cliff felt his release drawing near. He arched his back and his breath came in ragged gasps. His whole body tensed. Just as his juices shot out, a sharp pain raged through his body. He screamed, filling the space that Peggy's silence had left empty.

Cliff looked up into the horrible evil face. The incubus held Cliff's face immobile with his short arms while his longer arms pinned the boy to the bloody cardboard boxes. Cliff continued to scream, consumed by agony but unable to take his eyes off the monster above him. The creature smiled, and blood splashed from his mouth into Cliff's face. The incubus slowly opened his mouth wider, revealing, inch by inch, Cliff's severed penis, covered in spit and blood. Finally, it, too, fell onto Cliff's face with a horrible moist plop.

The blood-covered cardboard boxes shifted under the incubus's great weight. Slowly he raised Cliff's legs and, amid the torment of the boy's dying screams, impaled him, ripping through his guts. Soon the screams stopped, and he had once again found his release.

He leaned back in the heap of bodies and blood, using a stomach for a pillow. Placidly, he nibbled on a mouthful of fingers and enjoyed the moist, crunching sound. By morning, the bodies would be completely consumed. They would nourish and strengthen the evil creature, and his appetite would grow until it was unquenchable. The incubus allowed the cloudy membrane to slowly cover his eyes. Finally, his blue-black lids closed gently on his dreams.

9

Spain, 1590

Bones. White, without flesh. Bones. Black and gray, rotting. Shadows cast by the tar-oil torch flickered black, up the stone walls and across the ceiling, a shifting canopy of dread. Rustling habits whispered in time with sharp, leather-on-stone footsteps. The silence laughed at their insignificance.

Their eyes stared in horror at the heaps and piles of skeletons, many still draped in rags, moldy and foul. Bones . . . bones cast out of the Church, the bones of wretches who did not deserve the last rites, did not deserve burial in consecrated ground.

In the torchlight, their expressions of revulsion elongated into faces that betrayed their true nature, that betrayed the uncontrollable lust hidden in their hearts. Here beneath the abbey, the sins of the righteous were hidden. Here in this depository which served a purpose that was not unique, lay the cuckolded lovers of God.

Pushing the torch through the darkness, the Reverend Mother led Sister Ana through the catacombs beneath the Abbey of Almansa, deep in the Sierra de la Demanda. The air was damp with the silent screams of the Inquisition. Shielding her eyes from the constant reminders of death, Sister Ana clutched the tiny living bundle tightly to her breast and stayed close to the Reverend Mother.

Soon they arrived at a special cavern with its own special purpose. The oily flame stole the darkness from the secret, revealing hundreds of infant skeletons. The Reverend Mother crossed herself; Sister Ana sobbed silently in shame.

The Reverend Mother turned to the young nun and pointed to an empty spot on the rocks.

"Leave it there," she said coldly.

"I cannot," muttered Sister Ana through her tears.

"Leave it, I order you! Please, my dear, you must."

Sister Ana screamed, "It is a boy! A living, breathing baby boy!" The walls echoed her anguish. "How can I leave him, Reverend Mother, HOW CAN I?"

"It is part of God's plan. We cannot question it simply because we do not understand."

"I have become a whore," cried Sister Ana. As her voice echoed again from the walls, it seemed to shatter the remaining innocence of her soul.

"Sister, we do the greater will of our Lord God."

"Whores for the priests . . ." Her voice became lost in tears of guilt and shame. The newborn baby boy kicked at the cloth bag in which he was imprisoned and began to cry the high, breathless wail of a baby that wants his mother's milk. Sister Ana's breasts, swollen and flushed with the fullness of her milk, ached.

The Reverend Mother wrenched the bundle from the new mother and laid it on the cold stone. Then she led her young nun back to the abbey. In the cavern behind them, all was swallowed by the darkness.

Sister Angelica stood in the doorway of the tiny, stone-gray cell. Her heart filled with sorrow for her young friend, Sister Ana, as she watched her pray beneath the small wooden cross on the wall. Tears streamed from Sister Ana's puffy red eyes, clenched in pain and anger.

"Ana, the bell has rung for supper. We must not be late. Please, Ana."

Sister Ana rose stiffly from her knees and looked into the eyes of her friend. Nodding her head silently, she clasped her hands in front of her and walked out of the cell. Together the two young nuns walked down the silent halls to their supper.

Fat congealed on the surface of the weak mutton soup.

Gray overcooked vegetables broke the surface of the tepid liquid as Sister Ana absently soaked her hard, stale bread. Bringing the bread to her lips, she sucked away the liquid. Her pursed lips pulling in the juice reminded her that her child needed to be nursed. She imagined the tiny lips pursed just as her own were now, but finding no nourishment—only the cold darkness that would soon transform itself into death.

From the pit of her stomach, anguish swimming in bile rose up with the force of a flood. Instantly she dropped her bread. Holding her hand tightly against her mouth, she slid from the rough wooden bench and fled from the dining hall into the muddy courtyard. In the privacy of darkness, she vomited her sorrow and anguish.

She leaned against the stone wall, her lips still glistening with bile, her breath coming in short puffs of steam. She could think of nothing but feeding her baby to keep him from the darkness and death. She knew at that moment that she could never eat again unless she saved her son.

Unconcerned about helping with the cleanup following the evening meal, she retired early and crawled into her rough, flea-infested bed. She waited until she heard the bells calling the community to final prayers. Still she waited. Later she heard her sisters return, the rustle of their habits giving way eventually to the silence of sleep.

Sister Ana waited and listened for a long time, hearing no movement of any kind. The night had grown black and cold. The wind slammed sheets of rain against the wooden shutters. Sister Ana felt the chill of guilt, for she was safe and cared for while her baby lay dying in the cold darkness below the abbey.

Quietly she rose and dressed in her robes. She carried her shoes, so as not to awaken anyone with her steps, and walked on the numbingly cold stone floor with her bare feet. Within minutes she had made her way from the sleeping quarters to the church.

Slowly she retraced the steps the Reverend Mother and she had taken. She went to the arch behind the choir and opened the wooden door. Darkness pooled around her feet and threatened to drown her should she advance. Fearful and apprehensive of the darkness rising up from so much death, she pulled away and walked back into the church. She removed a single burning candle. Shielding the flame with her hand, she walked back to the cloister and through the wooden door, pulling it shut behind her.

She stopped for a moment to rub warmth into her numb feet, then pulled on her shoes. She looked about to see where the walls ended and the catacombs began. They curved downward and to the right. The uneven steps were chipped directly from the rock. Centuries-old slime covered the wall and reflected some of the dim candlelight, helping to illuminate the way.

The dampness penetrated her lungs, and a sickening sweetness, the odor of decay, assaulted her nostrils and scraped away at her courage. Fear and disgust filled her chest, pressing against her aching breasts filled with milk—milk meant for her baby. She felt, more than remembered, her purpose, and pressed on past the piles of human bones.

The silent horror of the Inquisition lay strewn about her. The enemies of the Church—enemies no more.

Suddenly, Sister Ana realized she had lost her way. The maze of catacombs had led her to a stone wall. She turned around to make her way back. The candlelight caught a flicker of movement and Ana stumbled backward in fear. A throaty gurgle sounded from a man hanging from the rocks protruding from one wall. Ana put her hand to her eyes and shook her head slowly in horror.

The man was naked. His bonds of hemp were soaked with blood from cutting into his skin. Ana could not judge how long he had been thus, but his skin was stretched taut across every bone and his eyes glistened with the last flicker of life. He gurgled again, and Sister Ana turned her head away, feeling pity for the poor soul as she hurriedly retraced her steps.

Wandering through the catacombs, she saw many of the dying and the newly dead. She would not judge them; she shared their pain and hopelessness. She hurried along her way, trying not to see the death that was all around her—death that would soon take her baby if she did not find him.

"You . . ."

Sister Ana jumped in surprise, her robes swirling around her as she turned to confront the speaker. She looked into the wizened face of an ancient man barely covered in rags. The old man sat on a shelf of stone jutting out from the wall and wove back and forth as if he were about to fall over, his hands shielding his eyes from the brightness of the candle.

"You," he began again, "have left your child to die."

"Where . . . where *is* he?" she whispered urgently.

The old man hugged himself against the bone-numbing cold and pointed down a dark tunnel.

Sister Ana turned and sped down the tunnel into the darkness, but stopped after a few steps and turned toward the old man. He was gone. In his place, on the rock shelf that served as his bench, was a pile of old rags with dark bones protruding from them.

"Ghosts!" she cried sharply. She crossed herself. I have been tricked, she thought, this must not be the way. Ghosts are evil, they only lie. Ana turned back to the path she had come down, fearful of again passing the ghostly pile of rags and bones.

Then she heard a muffled cry. She stopped and held her breath, straining hard to hear further sounds over the drum-like pounding of her heart. She heard it again, and she knew it was her baby. She hastened back down the tunnel the ghostly old man had indicated.

In the dim light of the candle the sack, sewn shut at the top, appeared to writhe with life, still lying in the shallow depression of the stone where the Reverend Mother had placed it. The cries coming from within were weak and pitiful. The child cried for its mother, cried for her breast.

Quickly she dripped wax from the candle and stood it upright on the stone. Desperately she picked up the bundle and began tearing at the stitches with her teeth. With the ferocity of a lioness protecting her cubs, she tore away the threads, her soft lips slicing into them one, two, finally three times. Blood dripped from her lips and soaked into the linen bag. At last she broke through. She pulled the naked baby boy from the sack and hugged it to her breast. She kissed the child over and over, the blood from her lips staining his back and arms.

Frantically she pulled at the robes of her habit and bared her breast. The boy child instantly began to suckle. Sister Ana began to cry silent tears of hopelessness. The infant nursed for a long time, barely making any sounds. Sister Ana lay upon the cold stone, surrounded by the sins of shame and death.

She pulled her sleeping child to her and began to doze but immediately shook herself, trying not to wake her son. She looked at how far the candle had burnt. She must return to the dormitory. She stood looking at the sleeping infant. He slept naked upon the rough linen sack meant to be his coffin. Quickly she tore at the underskirts of her habit and swaddled the baby in them. Then she replaced him in the linen sack so that he would not move about and fall from the rock.

She returned him to his makeshift cradle, surrounded by the bones of newborns that had never tasted their own mothers' milk. She shuddered as she hurried from the chamber. She retraced the route and soon found herself near the stairs leading upward into the church.

Suddenly she heard footsteps, followed by the angry voices of men. Torchlight spilled from the tunnels. Sister Ana pressed herself into a dark, cold crevice and blew out her candle. All at once the torchlight flooded the room and four soldiers entered, dragging a man by his feet. Trailing behind them, in all his finery, was the Grand Inquisitor, Bishop Juan Jalisco. Sister Ana pressed as far back into the crevice as she could. The sharp rocks dug deeply into her back, but she knew at all costs she must not be discovered. Still, curiosity impelled her to tilt her head forward to see what was happening.

Two soldiers stood guard, their swords drawn. The other two kept their weapons in their scabbards, but each held firmly to one of their prisoner's feet. The Bishop glowered down at the half-conscious wretch. The prisoner's face had been beaten bloody, but after staring at him for a few minutes, Sister Ana recognized him. It was a boy who had just recently become a monk, a boy whose razor-nicked scalp had barely healed from having been roughly shaven.

"You filthy heretic!" the Bishop screamed and kicked the boy sharply on the side of the head. "You are an enemy of the Church. You are in league with the devil."

Sister Ana looked on in horror at the poor boy and wondered what he could have done do merit such punishment. Once brought to the catacombs, the enemies of God never saw the light of day again. She pitied the boy but felt sure in her heart that if the Inquisitor, her own beloved Bishop, had found the boy guilty of some terrible crime, he was indeed deserving of punishment.

"Bind his hands and hang him from the wall with only his toes touching the floor," the Inquisitor ordered coldly.

The guards dropped the boy's feet and removed the hemp from their waistbands. Tightly they lashed the young hands together and hoisted him up on the wall, directly across from the dark hiding place of Sister Ana.

A series of emotions passed through Sister Ana. She feared for the boy; she sympathized with him. She feared for herself and wanted to run away, for the boy was even younger than she. The torchlight caught the sad image of his handsome face and reflected the pain back into her own heart. She felt powerless, realizing she was trapped and tortured just as the boy across from her was. Against her better judgment, Ana leaned out farther to watch the soldiers tie the hemp to the rocks. The Bishop and soldiers had their backs to her, but one man did not: the young monk.

As they tied him, he opened his eyes, large gentle eyes that reflected the bright flickering of the torches. Sister Ana looked into them and saw that they were also looking at her. Frozen for a moment, she felt an impulse to cry out for mercy. But she knew there would be no mercy.

"Return to your duties," the Bishop commanded the soldiers.

The soldiers left one torch for the Bishop, placing it in a crack in the stone near the young monk, and kissed the hand of the Inquisitor. Soon the soldiers' flickering torchlight disappeared down the long corridor, leaving only the Bishop, the young boy, and a concealed witness.

Bishop Jalisco waited until the light of the soldiers disappeared before speaking to the boy. The only sound in the chamber was the sputtering of the oil torch. When the Bishop spoke, his voice was soft and gentle, but it echoed within the chamber with an intimidating power.

"Carlos, my dear young Carlos. Why have you done this to me?"

The young monk again opened his eyes to look upon the Inquisitor. Drawing together all of his strength, he spoke. "I entered into the Abbey of Almansa to serve the greater will of my Lord God . . . I did not . . ." The young Carlos's voice trailed off for a moment as his strength ebbed.

"And you would have served the greater will of God by serving me. You are too young and ignorant to know the will of God. *I know* the will of God. To serve me *is* to serve God . . ."

"Serving you as the nuns serve the priests in their beds does not serve the will of God. It serves the will of the dark one . . ."

The Bishop slapped the young monk once, hard, and paused for a moment. Then he slapped him again and again, until blood ran from the boy's nose and mouth. Sister Ana looked on in horror. The young monk and she were the same. She realized that this was her lesson, too. If she refused to serve as she was ordered, she too would . . . Sister Ana heard the Bishop's laughter.

The Bishop approached the boy hanging from the rocks, his weight painfully supported by his arms and aching toes. The holy man towered over the boy by a head. Gently he bent over and kissed the boy on his bleeding lips. The young monk did not react until the Bishop pulled away. Then the doomed youth spat a glob of blood upon the Bishop.

The Inquisitor didn't even bother to wipe the indignation from his face. Instead, he stepped forward and, with closed fists, began pummeling the boy's body. Suddenly he stopped and stepped back. He loosened his brightly colored robes, then stepped forward again and tore away the drawstring of the suspended monk's pants, which fell in a heap around his ankles. The Bishop spun the boy around and fell upon him with evil hunger, crying out, "To serve *me* is to serve *God!*"

Ana could not breathe. Her chest was constricted as she forced herself not to cry out. She thought of her son. If she were to save him, she had to remain unnoticed.

Suddenly the Bishop cried out, and a moment later he stepped back. The torchlight reflected off the metal of his blade, long and thin, just before it plunged repeatedly into the back of the young monk. Ana sank back into the crevice, not daring to move or even breathe. When she opened her eyes again, she was in total darkness. The Bishop had gone. She was left to grope in the total darkness to find her way to the stairs and up into the church. It was almost daybreak when she returned to her bed.

The next day, the abbey was alive with rumors. Some said there had been a witch in the abbey posing as a young monk. Others said witches had swooped down in the dead of the night and carried off a young monk. There were other variations, all revolving around the fact that yesterday there had been a young monk named Carlos working peaceably in the abbey, and today that monk was nowhere to be found.

Sister Ana closed her ears to these rumors. First in her mind was her baby. She would do or say nothing to endanger her precious child. She spent her day carrying out her duties in silence. She did not talk to her sisters, even the ones she had grown close to.

All day, she could think of nothing but her baby. In her mind, she could hear his pitiful cries. Her heart ached more painfully than her milk-swollen breasts. It took all her will not to rush from her duties and fulfill her maternal instincts. She forced herself to concentrate upon her chores and longed for nightfall.

"Sister Ana."

Ana leapt in surprise at the voice of her friend Sister Ascencion.

"Ana, my friend, I am sorry I startled you, but the Reverend Mother has asked to see you in her quarters immediately." Sister Ascencion smiled knowingly at her friend and clasped her hands between her own. "And, Ana, if you need someone to talk to . . ."

Ana nodded her head silently, trying to remain calm, but inside, she was very frightened. Her heart raced and her breathing was irregular. She wiped the perspiration from her hands on the dark robes of her habit as she made her way to the Reverend Mother's quarters.

Along the way, she stopped for a few moments to look out the window and steady her nerves. The autumn sun was high in the great blue sky. Her eyes fell onto the beautiful Sierra de la Demanda. Every time she looked at those mountains, a sense of peace settled over her, and this time was no exception.

Taking deep lungfuls of crisp air, she focused on the gray stones of the abbey. She followed the edge of the window frame in front of her, to the wall of the women's section of the abbey. From here she could just see over the main wall

separating the nuns and the monks. As she looked into the
monks' muddy courtyard, which was much like that of the
nuns, she thought back to the murder she had seen with her
own eyes the previous night.

Aware suddenly that she had been idle too long, she turned
crisply, put on a brave face, and hurried to the doorway of
the Reverend Mother's quarters. She knocked lightly.

"Come in, my dear."

Ana entered and saw that the Reverend Mother had not
bothered to turn toward her.

"Yes, Reverend Mother," Ana spoke respectfully, with her
head slightly bowed. Her hands had begun to perspire again.

"Ana." The Reverend Mother now looked up directly at
the young nun. "One of our sisters said that you were not in
your bed for much of the night."

Sister Ana's heart pounded blood savagely against her eardrums. "Ah, Reverend Mother, I . . . I couldn't sleep, and
I had to go . . ."

"Yes, yes, Sister, I know. You have gone through a terrible ordeal. But our Heavenly Father must have willed it to
be so or it would not have happened. Sometimes, it is a . . .
thing . . . that happens to the nuns. Ah, uh, but we will not,
no, indeed we cannot . . . discuss the details of the . . . incident. The pain and the sin . . . must be put behind us. God
has forgiven everyone. Now you must be strong and continue
in your calling to do God's will."

Sister Ana relaxed a bit. The Reverend Mother did not
know where she had been last night. Her baby was safe for
the moment. But something had to be done. Ana reached up
and clasped the crucifix around her neck, lightly brushing her
milk-laden breasts. The throbbing need to release the milk
matched the need of her child.

"Sister Ana, I know it has been difficult for you. You are
barely sixteen. But you must forget. Try to be more attentive
to your duties. You are excused. Go with God."

Sister Ana bowed to her superior and quietly left the room.
All she could think about was how she was going to get to
the catacombs again without being missed.

Sister Ana carried one lighted candle and two fresh ones in
the sleeves of her habit. The glare of the flame and her ex-

haustion disoriented her as she made her way from the stairway deeper into the recesses toward the catacombs. This time she did not look at the bones, nor did she hear the silent cries of the Inquisition's victims. Even when she passed the place where she felt sure the young monk had been killed the night before, she did not look up to see his ravaged young body.

Instead, with the force of a mother's will, she sought her baby boy. In her left hand she carried a small bundle of rags to clean and diaper her baby. As she approached the place, she realized that she was almost happy. She was a mother! Then she heard the cries.

At once she knew they were not the cries of a baby who is just cold and hungry; no, there was something else in them. Sister Ana broke into a run and burst a moment later into the chamber where she had left her baby. The candlelight shone upon the child, frightening the rats into the shadows.

Ana saw blood and muffled her scream with her sleeve. She set the candle stand upon the rock and examined the bundle, tearing away the blood-soaked rags. The cloth was in shreds where the sharp fangs of the rats had chewed through it. Quickly she pulled her baby from the cloth, and his cries filled the chamber.

Tears streamed down Sister Ana's face as she looked upon her innocent newborn. One ear had been completely eaten away by the rats, and the other was only a few shreds of skin. Part of the baby's nose and his upper lip had been chewed to bloody pieces. Not knowing what else to do, Sister Ana struggled with the binding cloth of her habit and released her breasts.

She pushed the baby's face against her nipple roughly. He began to suckle, blood dripping from his mouth onto Sister Ana's creamy skin. While the baby nursed, Ana sobbed, releasing great tears of helplessness and desperation.

"Oh, God, please help me," she muttered through her tears.

She heard a voice: "Little one, you are asking the wrong one for help."

Ana sucked in her breath and uttered a half-choked gasp. She whirled around to see who had spoken the words, but she saw no one. Her eyes searched every shadow and empty

space. Still she saw nothing. "Who . . . where . . . are you?"
she ventured cautiously.

No answer.

She listened as intently as she could, but she heard nothing
save for the gentle suckling of her baby boy and her own
frightened breathing. Not knowing what else to do, she tried
to put the voice out of her mind and began the pitiful task of
cleaning up the wounds of the infant child. Silent tears rolled
down her cheeks as she cleaned the blood, hoping against
hope that there was a way to save the child. Deep in her
heart, she knew her baby could not survive another night in
the catacombs.

"I will care for him if we can strike a bargain."

Trembling, Sister Ana looked around for the source of the
voice. It seemed to come out of the darkness. She shook her
head and thought to herself that she must be going mad. Still,
she pulled the child closer to her breast and searched the
shadows. No, the voice must be in her head. She was indeed
mad. No one but a madwoman would consider trying to save
a child already doomed to this hell here beneath the abbey.

"Sister, I can ask you this only once. Do you wish my
help?"

Ana spun around. It seemed as though the voice came from
immediately behind her. But no one was there.

"Who are you?" she hissed through her teeth, trying not
to disturb her child. "Where are you? Show yourself."

All around her was silence, encased in shadows. The words
sifted into her brain, crawling over her fright like a swarm of
insects. Softly at first, then with a thundering voice echoing
in her head, she heard over and over, "Do you wish my
help?"

Finally she could stand it no longer, and she cried out,
"Yes, yes. Please help me . . . please!"

Before the echo of her voice had died down, she heard a
scraping sound across the stone floor. She turned to her side.
Slowly an old man stepped into the dim candlelight—the same
old man who had pointed the way the night before. Though
the shadowy hood of his cloak covered most of his face, she
could see that his skin was wrinkled and yellow. He stooped
with age and hobbled forward with the assistance of a cane.

"Ah, my dear," he began, his voice so soft that she could

barely hear him, "your baby will be dead by morning if I do not save him."

"Save him . . . please."

"I shall. Yes, of course, I shall. But first we must strike a bargain."

"Anything . . ." Sister Ana's voice trailed off into a dreamy whisper. She closed her eyes and let the reality of the situation weigh upon her soul.

"Do you know who I am?" he asked quietly.

"Yes," she whispered.

"Good. Then let us waste no more of your precious baby's life. We shall set the terms of the bargain."

Sister Ana stared at her shoes which barely peeked out from under her robes. The words of the Reverend Mother did not touch her. She had made a pact, a bargain. She was damned to hell forever. Nothing the Reverend Mother could say would change that; all that mattered was her son.

"Sister Ana! I asked you where you went in the middle of the night. I saw with my own eyes that you were not in your bed. Answer my question."

Sister Ana slowly came around from the distant corners of her mind. Looking into the face of the Reverend Mother, she said, "I was out walking. I couldn't sleep."

"Well, perhaps if you stayed awake during the day you would feel more like sleeping at night. Your sisters have mentioned to me that you have been found sleeping while you should be working. This slothful attitude is unacceptable. What shall we do about this?"

"I don't know, Reverend Mother."

"Shall I punish you?"

Ana looked away but did not answer.

"Oh, Sister, I know it has been hard for you, but you are not alone in this. Many of your sisters have also had to endure the same, uh, situation." The Reverend Mother paused. "I am sorry, but I must not let discipline slip. You will stay on continual latrine duty for the next month. Perhaps that environment will prove more conducive to wakefulness. You may go, Sister."

Sister Ana turned and walked back down the dark hallway.

She made her way to the cleaning room and picked up a handful of rags and some lye soap.

She stared down at the child with wonderment and love. This child was of her body. How could she not love him? Ana's whole day was dedicated to waiting for the precious few hours that she had with her child at night. To hold him, to feel his warmth, to love him, that was what she now lived for. The Church and her service to God took second place.

Lovingly, she looked into his face. His luminous eyes returned her look of affection. His nose, lip, and ears had healed. The old man had been true to his word. He had even found a small cave deep in the catacombs, where not even the rats seemed to know the way. There were no bones screaming out their horror. But there was something frighteningly different about the baby.

He was barely a month old and yet had become so heavy that she could hardly hold him in her arms. Ana remembered when her brother, Pablo, had been a baby. It was almost two years before he was this heavy.

Pablo. Her family.

It seemed like years since she had seen them. She missed them so. They were too poor to feed and clothe her any longer, and it was only practical for her to come to the abbey to serve the will of God—*and* the monks, she thought to herself bitterly. She knew she was not the only nun that had passed through the secret tunnels to the men's side of the abbey. She was not the first to lie upon the rotting straw under the bulk of a grunting, stinking monk. But she tried to put all of that out of her mind.

Looking back to her child, she noticed something she had not seen before. She laid the child upon the bed of rags and brought the candle closer. Reaching out with her finger, she touched two dark lumps on the baby's chest. Horrified, she pulled her finger back. She had felt movement inside the lump, as if it contained a creature imprisoned and struggling to get out.

Ana looked up, searching the shadows for the old man. He was never far from her child. She saw the candlelight glint from the handle of the ornate silver and ebony cane.

"Yes, Sister? You have a question that perhaps I can answer?'' The voice was light as a feather and very cold against her ear.

"What are these two lumps on my son's chest?'' she demanded, fearing the answer.

"Ana. You must remember, the bargain was that the child would belong to *us*, no longer just to you."

Ana drew a deep breath and nodded her head in agreement. "You are correct, but what are the lumps?''

"The 'lumps,' as you call them, are the beginning of my gift to our child. This gift will make him different from all other men. It will be part of his strength. He will have what every man needs—another pair of hands.''

Sister Ana could barely make out the shape of the old man in the shadows. She did not notice that her lower jaw had fallen agape in reaction to his announcement.

"This cannot be true. Another pair of hands . . . real hands?''

"Yes, my dear Sister. Hands—real flesh-and-blood hands. By this token, you will remember that he is my child, too.''

Ana looked at her baby. She could not see that he was becoming a monster. She was blinded by maternal love for her child and in her eyes, he could only be perfect.

"Sister.'' The old man tried to regain her attention. "It is now time to name the child.''

Ana looked down at the child and then to the old man, who moved into the light of the candle. Helplessly, she stood and watched as the old man raised his cane above his head and brought it down lightly, touching the child's forehead.

He whispered, "You are now Bargolas, my son. Bargolas . . . Bargolas . . .''

The name echoed in the shadows. Ana felt frightened. She suspected that her nightmare was only beginning.

10

Othello, 1970

"Cold . . . so cold . . . I wish Mom would turn up the heat
. . . I'm freezin'," Pam muttered to herself as she turned her
head over on the snow. Suddenly, the pain from her ankle
rushed into her brain, blotting out her consciousness of the
cold. She squeezed her eyes shut and clenched her teeth in
an agonized moan.

She opened her eyes again onto the snow. Her ankle
throbbed wildly, and her memory returned. The terror she
had blissfully forgotten returned.

She tried to scramble to her feet but found that the pain
and cold had weakened her. She fell headlong back into the
snow. Her breath, billowing in dense columns of steam, hung
heavily in the cold moonlight and then drifted away, only to
be replaced by another breath. She turned over on her back
and, with a great effort, sat up.

Reaching out for the cracked wooden banister, she pulled
herself to her feet. Looking down at her ankle, she saw that
her jeans were torn and the whole area, including her shoe,
was covered with dried and frozen blood. She tried to put
weight on the injured ankle, but pain seized her and her vision
momentarily darkened with the threat of fainting.

Her small measure of composure began to disintegrate, and
in its place came whimpering sobs. Using the last of her

strength, she made her way the final few feet to Cliff's Fairlane. For a moment, she clung, her hands icy-blue, to the door handle. At last, her thumb depressed the button. She managed to pull the door open and fell inside.

The keys, she thought, the keys are in the house—or lost. The memory of her friends exploded into her mind, and her breath caught in her throat. Her heart pounded wildly. The keys were in the ignition, just where Cliff said he had left them. She pulled herself upright, reached for the door handle, and slammed the door shut.

The incubus belched loudly and the foul stench washed over the walls of the basement. His small arms snaked upward, and the tiny hands began to scrub away the dried blood from his mouth and chin. His protruding belly rumbled loudly. While his short arms were busy cleaning, his longer arms were folded contentedly across that distended belly.

Every few minutes, his hand would caress the smoothness of his crotch, where his genitals, now sated, lay withdrawn inside the fleshy slit between his legs.

Suddenly, ectoplasm drifted from his ears, merging with the darkness, and a vision intruded upon his lazy stupor. He saw a red-haired woman, he remembered her—her flesh was still fresh beneath his talons. She was escaping!

Slowly he rose to his feet. A smile of anticipation crossed his face. The tip of his maleness began to protrude from his crotch in readiness. He leapt toward the stairs and bounded up them just as the car's engine started.

The evil spawn leapt out the back door and ran heavily through the snow toward the front of the house. But his progress was slow. He was too full, too sluggish.

Pam turned the key in the ignition. The car cranked over slowly, then started. As she grabbed for the gear lever, she paused and thought of her two friends in the house. She didn't really know if they were still alive. Maybe she should wait, she thought. Just for a few minutes. Maybe they had heard the car start, maybe they would come running now that they knew she had the keys. Maybe . . .

As she sat in the glare of the winter moonlight, fighting panic and pain, the monster ran around the corner of the house, stopped, and glared intently at her.

She was stunned. She and the incubus stared at each other. Then the monster smiled at her, his slime-covered teeth gleaming in the light of the moon. Pam screamed and jerked the shift lever into Drive. She slammed the gas pedal to the floor. The back tires spun briefly before gripping the surface of the road. She drove madly down the driveway, screaming as the car slipped and slithered across the frozen snow.

He trotted lazily after the speeding car. His short arms were folded across his chest and his sex organs were swelling with anticipation.

"Oh pretty . . . pretty Pam," the incubus sang out in a cracking voice as he slowed to a walk. "Pretty pretty Pam, come back and play . . . Oh, pretty pretty Pam . . . very, very soon . . . my pretty pretty Pam . . ."

Giggles like cold mountain water running over rocks echoed across the desert of snow as the incubus spun round and round, his long arms and short arms intertwining like snakes.

Pam was still screaming when Deputy Sheriff Hastings forced the Fairlane to the side of the road across from the ARCO station on Main Street. She had been screaming for the whole twenty minutes it took her to drive into town, and her voice was now little more than a husky whisper.

Hastings had to use all his strength to pull her from the car. She bit and clawed at him like a trapped alley cat. As soon as she was out of the car and he could see that she had an injured leg, he managed to free one of his hands and called on the radio for an ambulance.

By the time the ambulance arrived, Pam was silent. She clung with childlike ferocity to the neck of the deputy sheriff but refused to speak or even tell him her name, although he already knew it.

"Christ!" cursed Max Reninger as he stepped out of the ambulance. "What in the fuck is wrong with Pam?"

"I've got no idea." Hastings helped Max get Pam into the back of the ambulance. "Probably drugs. Probably got hold of some bad acid and fell down somewhere, ripping the shit out of her ankle. Fuckin' crazy kids . . ."

Max nodded his head as he shut the back doors. He walked around to the front of the white van and climbed in.

Hastings looked back at the green Fairlane. The flashing

red ambulance lights reflected off the car's rear bumper. He waved at Max as the ambulance took off for the hospital, then paused and scratched his head. There was something very wrong here. This car belonged to the Agusta family, and the kid, Cliff, was usually the one speeding around town in it. So why in hell was Pam driving it screaming hysterically with her ankle all ripped to shit? Nope, it didn't take no genius to tell something was a mite out of whack.

Hastings got back into his patrol car and followed the ambulance to the hospital. He had to make two phone calls. One to Pam's mother and the other to Bill Agusta.

"Mike! Mike, wake up!" Mrs. Kawaguchi called in her thick Japanese accent.

"Whaa . . . what's up? What time is it?" Mike growled as he shielded his eyes from the bright ceiling light that his mother had turned on.

"It's four A.M., Mike. The police are here and they want to talk to you. Hurry and get dressed. They're waiting in the kitchen. I will make them coffee, but hurry."

Five minutes later, Mike walked into the glare of the kitchen, where Sheriff Johnston and Deputy Hastings sat at the counter with their hats on the bar. His mother was busy making coffee; his father leaned against the fridge chewing on an unlit stogie. All fell silent and focused their attention on Mike.

"Kinda early, isn't it, Mike? Sorry to get you out of bed, but we've got a problem that we hope you can help us with. 'Bout an hour ago, Deputy Hastings here found one of your schoolmates injured and hysterical."

Mike immediately thought of Stan. He had really gone and done something stupid this time and probably scared himself half insane. He looked down at the floor and scuffed his house slippers against the glossy linoleum, waiting for the sheriff to continue.

"Pam Getner."

Mike shrugged his shoulders, not understanding the connection.

"Your parents say you don't know her very well, but here's the rub. We picked her up in a green Ford Fairlane, your friend Cliff Agusta's. We called his dad, and he said Cliff had plans to meet you tonight, er . . . last night. Anyway, then we talked to Mrs. Getner, and she said Cliff and Peggy Blackston picked Pam up around 10:30 or 11:00.''

Mike could feel blood rush into his face. Angry at himself because he knew the policemen could see him blush, he lashed out at the two men.

"So what? What's all that got to do with me?"

Sheriff Johnston narrowed his eyes. "Well," he continued, "it doesn't really have much to do with you at all. We were just hoping you might know where they went. Something is very wrong here. Cliff is without his car, and we can't locate either him or Peggy.''

"Why don't you ask Pam?" Mike inquired cautiously.

"She won't talk to us. Partly because she's in pain and partly because she's so scared out of her wits that she lost most of her voice from screaming herself silly. However, I doubt she'd have much to say even if she had her voice. She's in a pretty bad way emotionally, if you know what I mean.''

"How bad was she hurt?" asked Mr. Kawaguchi.

"Well, that's one of the things we're worried about. Her ankle was pretty badly mangled. The flesh and muscle were torn right from the bone, just sort of hanging there in loose flaps. The doctors think it was some sort of an animal with long claws. Like a bear—'cept we got no bears around here.''

Mike felt a sharp pain in his leg and remembered how he had gotten his wound. He began to sweat. He had to get rid of the police and talk to Stan, and he couldn't let his parents, or anyone else for that matter, know he was involved in any of this voodoo bullshit.

"Well, I don't know anything, either," Mike said quietly, "but I'll ask around tomorrow and see if anyone else saw them last night.''

Sheriff Johnston picked up his hat and placed it snugly on his head. The deputy followed suit, and the two men walked toward the door. "Well, let us know if you hear anything," said the sheriff. "I've got a real bad feeling about this one. Thanks for the coffee, Mrs. Kawaguchi. Good night.''

Mike walked back to his bedroom without a word to his parents and closed the door behind him. He lay down on his bed. The spot was still a little warm. He didn't bother removing his clothes. He wasn't going to be sleeping, anyway.

He had to wait for the morning, and then he was going to
have a little talk with Stan.

On Sunday morning at eight A.M., Mike drove up to the
Fullers', and half a minute later Stan emerged from the front
door, zipping up his jacket.

"We got trouble, asshole," Mike said as Stan slid onto the
seat next to him.

"Good morning to you, too," Stan sneered. "Why did you
get me out of bed?"

"*We* got problems," Mike said, shifting into first and
checking for traffic. It was a bright Sunday morning, and
there were no cars on the street. "All hell's breaking loose,
and I'm sure it's because of you. First we see some sort of
ghosts at that fuckin' house. Then later, some goddamn monster comes at me in the truck. If Ken Bliss hadn't caused me
to come to a screeching halt, God only knows where I'd be
now. Notice the fuckin' dent and crack in the windshield, or
are you blind as well as stupid? And while you are at it, you
should take a look at my shoulder. I still have the holes in it
to prove *something* was trying to get me."

Mike rubbed his forehead, pushing his coarse black hair
out of his face.

"And now, on top of everything, the cops come to my
house and wake me up at four in the morning. They asked if
I know where Cliff and the two sluts went last night. Where
do *you* think they went?"

Stan recognized the anger and fear in Mike's voice. The
truth of the situation was revealing itself rapidly. "Well, if
Cliff was stupid, he probably went to the haunted house."

"That's right, Stan the Warlock. He was *just that* stupid.
He wanted to impress Peggy and Pam. He wanted to scare
them bad enough that they'd fuck him in gratitude for saving
them from the monster in the haunted house—the same monster that had scared the shit out of Mike and Stan!"

Mike slowed the truck down and fumbled in his coat pocket
for his cigarettes. He took one out and lit it, then opened the
window a crack and blew smoke outside.

"Do you think he really went there?"

"Fuckin' A—he went there! And he took both girls! The
cops found Pam in Cliff's car at three o'clock this morning.

She was hysterical and couldn't tell them a thing. And on top of that, they think some kind of animal ripped up her ankle! She's in the fuckin' hospital, for Christ's sake! And where the fuck are Peggy and Cliff?''

Stan stared out the window, watching the snow-covered town pass by. He shook his head as the seriousness of the problem registered. After a minute or so, he looked Mike straight in the eye. ''Mike, you know as well as I do, we gotta go back to the house and see if they're there—''

''Fuck you, asshole! Christ! What have you gotten me into?'' Mike hammered on the steering wheel in anger. After a minute, he rounded a corner and drove toward his house.

''You're goin' the wrong way,'' Stan said sheepishly, not wanting to upset Mike more than he already was.

''I'm gonna stop at home first,'' growled Mike. ''I want to pick up my Bible, a crucifix, and my hunting rifle.''

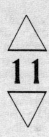

Othello, 1951

The truck turned into the drive. Lydia watched from the porch as a plume of dust rose from behind the vehicle. What a grand house, she thought to herself.

Ever since she had married Seth, she had hoped they would get a nice house. Seth's new work at the church wasn't exactly keeping them in the lap of luxury, but it had provided them with a roof over their heads and food on the table. In fact, as Lydia looked down at her body, she could see that she was putting on a bit of weight.

Even though things were going well for them with the church, they would never have been able to afford the house if the owners, who were parishioners, hadn't sold it to them for such a good price. Mr. Bainman had been transferred back East with the railroad, and Mrs. Bainman had gone along, happy to be near her aging mother again.

Yes, indeed, everything was working out for the better. Except for one thing. Seth performed all his husbandly duties save the most important one.

If only I had married a normal man for a husband instead of this *servant of God*, Lydia thought to herself for the hundredth time within a month.

But at least she had a house—that definitely made her happier. Now if only she could convince Seth to give her a child.

She was sure that a child would bring them closer together. And you can't get a baby by rubbin' noses, she thought, smiling to herself.

Seth walked in to be greeted by the aromas of a Sunday dinner. He heard Lydia bustling about in the kitchen— probably making gravy from the chicken drippings. It all reminded him of his home in Georgia and his own mother hurrying around to get Sunday dinner all ready before Daddy came home.

He shut the screen door behind him, leaving the main door open. Autumn nights in the Columbia Basin were cool, but the days were warm—thankfully, though, not as humid as Georgia. He certainly did not miss that.

He loosened his tie and pulled his shirttail from his trousers as he walked into the dining room. He sat down at the head of the table. A wisp of steam curled up from the mashed potatoes and string beans in bowls before him. The fried chicken sat in the center of the table, its grainy brown texture spiced heavily with black pepper—just the way Mama had made it for him in Georgia.

Small steps sounded around the corner of the kitchen, signaling Lydia's arrival with the gravy. She carried the gravy boat in both hands. A trickle of sweat ran down the side of her cheek as she sat down.

"I got a fresh apple pie coolin' on the cupboard. I think there's even some ice cream left in the freezer."

Making no reply to his wife, Seth bowed his head in prayer. "Dear Father in heaven, we thank you for your blessings and for the food upon this table. We thank you for bringing this family together and for the good life we have here. We give Thee praise. Amen."

He looked up and saw Lydia staring at him. It piqued his anger to know she had not bowed her head in respectful thanks to God. He reached out for the bottle of milk and poured himself a glass. Still in silence, he buttered the homemade bread and glanced back at Lydia. She was still staring at him.

"Why aren't you eating?" he said in a flat tone.

"I was just thinkin' about what you said during grace. You said thank you for bringin' this family together. We've been married for nearly five years and we still don't have any babies. Some of the women in the parish think that I'm barren. I know they do! I'm half tempted to tell them the truth!''

She glared at her husband. Her anger showed clearly, and it was obvious that this time she was not going to back down.

"Do we have to go into all that again?" Seth replied, trying to keep his voice calm—even though he was getting angry, too.

"Why don't you love me?"

"I do love you. I provide for you, and now you even have this lovely house. Remember how you said you—"

"I don't care what I said. You don't love me. You married me because you felt guilty for having sinned against your precious God!"

Lydia pushed herself away from the table and strode out of the room. Just before climbing the stairs, she turned her head and called out, "You mark my words. The next time the women ask me about children, I'm gonna tell them we don't have any because my husband hasn't touched me in over three years."

As Seth listened to the sound of her climbing the stairs, he reached to the center of the table and picked up a piece of fried chicken. He took a big bite, and juice ran down his chin. "Ummm," he said to himself, "just like Mama used to make it back in Georgia . . ."

The old woman laughed and laughed. ". . . and it was this big," she finished, holding up her hands to indicate the size.

"Oh my God, they don't come that big . . . do they?" asked Mary, nudging Lydia in the ribs with a silly smile on her face. "At least not on normal men."

All four women howled with laughter. Across the park, the men looked away from their game of horseshoes toward their laughing wives.

"Women," said Patrick. "They're always gossipin' 'bout somethin'."

Suddenly the old woman got serious. "What do you mean, man? I didn't say he was a mortal man . . ."

"Well, no wonder!" chided Mary. "What was he, a bull or a goat?"

"He was both—and he was neither."

The group of women grew suddenly silent on this autumn

afternoon. Engrossed by this strange old crone's story, they forgot about the picnic or the cooling weather.

"He was a devil," the old woman explained, cautiously, "a devil called an *incubus*. He was summoned from the place between earth and hell. And he comes solely to give women pleasure."

"Oh, gawd! I've never heard such nonsense in all my life," exclaimed Edith. "You know, they used to burn people at the stake just for talking about such things. But nowadays we know better, it's just nonsense!"

"No, it isn't. And if you want to know, all you have to do is come over to my house and I can let you see an old book that shows you how to conjure up a demon. It was written in Latin by some Catholic nun in Europe somewhere. It used to belong to the library in Baltimore, but a friend of mine stole it. And then after she was through with it, she gave it to me. She told me the whole story of how she called up this demon and he became her lover. I suspect she was crazy as a loon! But I kept the book all these years, anyway." The old woman cackled gleefully and glared at Edith.

"Hmmph," said Edith, standing up. "I am not going to sit here and listen to this blasphemy. I'm leaving! And if the rest of you had any sense you would leave, too—especially you, Lydia, the wife of a Baptist preacher! My Lord!" Edith stood up and walked away, brushing the brown grass from her pale blue dress.

Lydia stared at the old woman. The old woman looked back, searching her eyes for meaning. And when she found that meaning, she smiled. Mary saw this and jumped up to join Edith, leaving the old woman and Lydia alone.

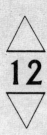

12

Spain, 1591

"Sister, I will not tell you again. You shall wait in the court-yard tonight by the north wall."

Sister Ana stared in hot anger at the Reverend Mother. Ana knew full well what waiting by the north wall meant. It was time to whore again for the monks. The north wall had an old storage area for firewood used by both halves of the ab-bey. Inside, there was a flea-ridden pallet where many of the younger and prettier sisters were required to "serve God."

"No! I will not . . . not again! I will not!"

"Sister, you seem to have forgotten who you are. You are a servant of God. You wear a wedding ring: you are married to the Church. You are wedded to our Lord, and you will serve Him as you are instructed. Now do not—"

"I will no longer whore for priests and monks who say they serve God but only serve their earthly lust!"

The Reverend Mother's face changed to the color of ash. She was shocked that one of her nuns would have the courage to address her in such a tone of voice. She stood from her chair, rushed around the table, and slapped the insolent nun across the face—not once but several times.

Sister Ana, shocked by the outburst of violence, drew back from the force of the blows and brought her own hand to her face.

"You shall do as you are told! You took vows to serve the Lord. Obedience—"

"I took vows to serve God, and if you think that lying with priests is God's work, then you don't deserve to be the Reverend Mother of this abbey!" shrieked Ana, shocked by her own rebellious behavior.

For a long while the Reverend Mother stared at Sister Ana. The truth burned with a fire in the young nun's eyes.

"You shall do as you are told or suffer the consequences. Now get out."

"I will not! I will tell . . . everything . . ." Sister Ana could not finish her sentence; her words were choked off by the pain in her throat. Tears dripped from her eyes. She turned and ran from the room.

Later that night, at the time when she was supposed to be waiting beside the north wall, Sister Ana started her familiar descent down the steps into the catacombs. As always, she carried extra candles so she could spend more time with her growing son. During the past ten months, she had learned to ignore the bones and death. But lately there had been additional horrors that she had been unable to ignore.

The tortured bodies of the Inquisition were, of course, nothing new to her. But there was something different about the newest bodies. The victims had not only been tortured, they were ripped to pieces. Of some bodies, little more was left than a heap of bloody flesh. The first time Ana had seen one such body, she had vomited. She had had to rest for many minutes before she felt strong enough to go on. Over time, she hardened herself to the horrors here. She had to for the sake of her son.

Now Sister Ana heard something. She cocked her head sideways; it hadn't sounded like a rat—she knew their noises well enough. Guards, she thought. She prepared to find herself a hiding place as she had done those many times before when her visits had been interrupted by the soldiers.

But it was not the soldiers bringing in some wretched soul. No, it was something else. Wait . . . there it was again. A *click-click-clicking*. Then silence again.

She hurried through the foreboding shadows. Suddenly, one of those shadows shifted and then rushed toward her. The shadow loomed in the candlelight. Long, dark arms tipped with claws raised above a head, while smaller arms protruding from a chest reached for her throat.

"Ahhhgrrr . . . !" screamed the creature.

Ana stepped back and gasped in horror. Then, quickly recovering from the fright, she reached out her hand and slapped the creature's face.

"Shame on you, little one. Only bad children scare their mothers in the dark." She grasped the now-docile creature by the hand. "My goodness, just look at you. You are almost as tall as I am. You are growing so fast."

Bargolas held tightly to his mother's hand as they walked together into the small chamber that served as his home. "Mama," he muttered in a high voice.

Ana set a bag down upon the stone that served as her unusual son's bed and opened it. She placed bread and some half-eaten vegetables on the bag and motioned for him to eat. He just scowled at them, however. Sister Ana looked into the corner and saw the pile of maggot-infested food she had brought to him over the past month.

"What is wrong? Why are you not eating? Is the old man bringing you food? You are growing to be such a little man already. Yes, he must be bringing you special food to make you grow faster than other boys."

She looked into her son's eyes. They had become very large and black. But she could not bring herself to look upon the small pair of arms that grew from his chest and writhed aimlessly like snakes. Her mother's love was selective. She looked at what she wished to see and ignored what frightened her. This was her child, and she would always love him—for better or worse.

"Sister Ana. You are here, as always." The old man stepped from the shadows, the ever-present cane in one hand supporting him.

"Yes," she said, not looking up at him.

"Sister Ana, you are approaching a time of grief and danger . . . great danger."

Ana nodded her head in acknowledgment.

"When . . ." the old man began cautiously, "you are gone, your son—our son—will be very sad. It will be difficult to control him."

"What do you want?" asked Sister Ana sharply, still on edge from the encounter with the Reverend Mother.

"I want your permission to take him with me when you . . . when you die. I shall take him to a place where he will be safe."

Sister Ana looked into the dark shadows for the old man but did not see him. It didn't matter, she knew who he was. But it startled her that he had mentioned her death. She knew it was a premonition. She knew, as soon as he said the words, it was too late for her. Death crept closer, and she could feel it.

"When I am dead, take him where he will be safe. He will then be your son . . . but I will always love him. I will always love him, even more than I loved God, who turned His back on me." The full impact of what she had just said struck her hard across her soul.

"Yes, indeed, Sister, you do love him more than God. And that is why your death is upon you, that is why your son has become my son." His muffled laughter danced in the shadows.

Sister Ana leaned across the stone and kissed her son on the cheek. Gently, all four of his arms encircled her and held her with the tenderness of a loving son. Tears ran from his cheeks and mingled with her tears. She pulled herself away and rushed from the chamber.

"Goodbye, my son." Her words were carried away with the dim candlelight.

The boy sat on the rock ledge, watching the candlelight drain away into the blackness. After the darkness enveloped him totally, he still heard her footsteps growing faint in the distance. For a long moment he sat there in the gloom and silence, missing his mother's touch. Then he heard the telltale shuffle behind him, and the chamber grew bright from the silver glow of the old man's cane.

The old man held his cane out in front of himself. Bargola looked up at him as he started to speak. "Come, my son. Let's find your supper."

The two of them walked from the chamber hand in hand. Soon they came upon a recent victim of the Inquisition. The confession that had been drawn from her by torture had not saved her life. The old man stood for a long while looking a the lifeless body of the young girl, whose age had been about the same as Sister Ana's. At length he turned to Bargolas and spoke.

"She was accused of witchcraft. They brought her here all the way from San Sebastián. It is said she cast the evil eye upon one of the merchants. Actually, what she did was to spurn his lustful advances. The merchant just happened to be a special friend of the Grand Inquisitor."

A smile crossed the face of the old man as he pointed to the mutilated body of the young girl.

"Here is your supper, my son."

Sister Ana refused to cry out as the tree branch crashed down upon her back once again. Was that twenty? Thirty? She had lost count. The Reverend Mother struck her again. Ana looked down at her hand and saw a thin trickle of blood running from where the blows had broken the skin. She braced herself for the next impact, but it didn't come.

Cautiously, she turned her head toward the Reverend Mother. Sweat glistened from her forehead, and her eyes were glazed from the punishing frenzy.

"I have finished. Get dressed and return to your duties in the latrine."

Sister Ana stood slowly and walked naked to her habit, which lay in a heap on the cold stone floor. Not even her mother had ever beaten her, she recalled. She couldn't imagine her parents striking her. They loved her.

She dressed, painfully slipping the habit over her wounds, and walked from the room. She did not return to the latrine. Instead, she walked out the front gate and crossed over to the monk's compound.

She knocked on the great wooden doors and was allowed to enter. She asked to see a priest and was escorted to the office of Father Antonio.

Upon entering the spacious office with its gold and leather, she was awed by the surroundings and by the presence of the priest. His eyes appeared kind and understanding; she felt safe here. She knew she could tell her story, and justice would be served.

"Sister Ana. Please sit down and make yourself comfortable."

"Thank you, Father."

"Now, my child, what can I help you with that you cannot take to the Reverend Mother?"

"The Reverend Mother is forcing me to lie down with a man—a monk from this abbey. It is sinful, and I refuse to do it."

Father Antonio nodded his head thoughtfully. Ana felt as though she were talking to her own father. She knew the priest would put a stop to all of this.

"This is a very serious accusation, Sister. I cannot believe that the Reverend Mother would ask one of her nuns to do such a thing. We are here to serve the will of God, not each other's flesh."

"Oh, Father, please believe me! It is true! In fact, it has happened before. Last year I was forced to lie with a monk and . . . and I became . . . with child." Tears fell from Sister Ana's eyes as she forced control upon herself.

The priest looked upon the nun. Her shame and weakness filled him with disgust. He picked up the quill from his desk, dabbed the nib into the black ink, and began a note to Bishop Juan Jalisco. He stopped for a moment to look back at the nun seated before him. She was staring at him. He could feel her expectation; it angered him, although he made an effort to conceal it.

"My dear Sister, the charges you have made are very serious." He leveled his gaze at the nun. "I find them most incredible. I will look into the matter, I promise you. Now if you will please return to your duties, I will take immediate action concerning this matter."

"Thank you, Father, thank you," Ana muttered, awkwardly standing up. Bowing to the priest, she took a couple steps backward and bumped into a small table. Quickly she turned and left the priest's office.

Later, as she cleaned the foul muck from the latrines, she felt as though the burden had been lifted from her. She had truly righted a wrong—not only against herself but against so many of her sisters. For the first time since she had come to the Abbey of Almansa, she felt that she had done God's work.

But suddenly she looked down at her hands covered with the recking filth and she felt the darkness of hypocrisy fill her heart. What had she done to her son? Her mother's love blinded her in many ways, but she still knew she had done evil when she struck that bargain with the old man. She had damned her soul to hell for eternity—and her son's, as well.

She plunged her hands into water to rinse the strong lye soap from them. She didn't notice the tears running down her cheeks as the two guards marched into the courtyard, accompanied by the Reverend Mother. Sister Ana turned to face them as the Reverend Mother stepped forward and spoke to her quietly.

"Sister Ana, you have made a very grave mistake. You have tried to undermine my authority and disgrace this community of God. And for that you shall be punished. Go with the guards, and may God have mercy on you."

Ana could not respond. It had not been more than two hours since she spoke with Father Antonio—and now this? Weakly she stepped up to the guards; they each placed a hand upon her wrist and led her roughly from the abbey.

Quietly and without a struggle, she allowed herself to be led around the perimeter of the north wall to the soldiers' encampment. She was taken to a small wooden structure with no windows and a sturdy door. A man with a brutal countenance stood before the cell, holding a gray bundle in his hands. He spoke after she was placed before him.

"Remove your clothes and put these on." He spat, tossing the rags beside the shocked young woman.

"But . . . but why am I here? What have I done?" More tears caressed the contours of her face.

"REMOVE YOUR CLOTHES!" demanded the vulgar Captain of the Guards as soldiers gathered around to see what was going on.

"Please, I beg of you . . . I am a nun. I can't—"

"You are no longer a holy sister in the Abbey of Almansa," raged the captain, drawing his sword. "Now remove your clothes or I will cut them from your evil flesh."

In a daze, Sister Ana started with her wimple and skullcap, allowing them to fall upon the muddy ground as her long black hair cascaded across her shoulders. Untying the crucifix that belted her black outer dress, she winced in shame as she saw a soldier biting his lip in anticipation. His comrade poked him in the ribs with his elbow and, with an ugly grin on his face, whispered something.

Shock had dried Ana's tears. They no longer flowed down her cheeks—cheeks that were now pale and cold. She had been betrayed. She had no recourse but to follow the orders of the soldiers or die.

The small group of unwashed men had grown into a crowd of jeering, slobbering animals. They drew closer as the sister pulled the black habit over her head, exposing her skin and woolen underclothes. She hugged herself across the chest, wishing to die, for she no longer had the dignity to live. Looking down at the pile of rags, she started to reach for them to cover herself.

"No! Take them all off!" the captain demanded.

Anger flooded her face hotly. In a pitiful gesture of defiance, she shook her head and stared directly at the captain. For a moment, her eyes and his were locked in a battle of will. The captain stepped forward with his hands outstretched.

Sister Ana gasped sharply as the captain's rough hands grabbed the sleeve of her blouse and yanked down, pulling Ana to her knees. Mud covered her legs and soiled her woolens. Her sleeve, from the shoulder down, had been torn away. She was determined not to give this slovenly mob the pleasure of her shame. Still in defiance, she rose to her feet and did not flinch as the captain stepped forward again, this time to the excited mutterings of his men.

Once more Sister Ana found herself lying in the mud, following the captain's onslaught. Once more she stood up, her blouse now in shreds, her breasts bare. She began to weep. Her body trembled violently, and her hands clutched at her neck as the captain stepped forward yet again and ripped the final undergarment from her body.

Some of the soldiers rubbed at their crotches. One of them stepped forward but was stopped by the captain's outstretched arm.

"There will be time for that after the Inquisition," said the captain, smiling through yellowed teeth. He then grasped Ana by the arm, led her to the door of the windowless shack, and pushed her inside. She fell in a heap onto the mud floor. A moment later, the gray rags were flung upon her and the door closed, shutting out the light of day.

* * *

Bargolas waited in the darkness. He was not hungry; in fact, he did not want for anything except the company of his mother. She hadn't come last night, and she still hadn't come this night. She had been there every previous night since he could remember, but now . . . He sensed that something wasn't right. He had visions. He saw strange scenes. Light would flood over him from all directions, and he could see his mother. She was crying. It made him want to cry, too. He didn't know what to do.

"Father," he muttered awkwardly.

There was no answer. He had never called the old man before. The old man had just been there every time he had needed him. The old man had told him over and over that he was his father. But he knew this was not true, just as he knew that his mother was his mother.

Now, without seeing him, Bargolas sensed the old man's presence. From out of the oily darkness came his voice, soft as a feather.

"She will not come again, my son. She will soon be dead."

The wooden door was thrown aside roughly, and two soldiers entered the cell to drag the woman, still stunned, into the murky autumn light. She had dressed herself in the rags two days earlier, because they afforded her the only warmth she could find. Still, she had come to believe that she would surely freeze to death.

Presently she found herself in a large room flanked by soldiers. The Grand Inquisitor, Bishop Juan Jalisco, sat in the center of the room with Father Antonio at his side. There were no other monks or nuns present. She was positioned in front of the Bishop.

She stood there in rags and with shame. She knew deep in her heart that there was no hope for her. But even though she was doomed, she could not allow the injustice of her final sentence to go without protest.

"SISTER ANA MEDINA OF THE ABBEY OF AL-MANSA, YOU HAVE SINNED AGAINST THE HOLY CATHOLIC CHURCH AND AGAINST THE SOVEREIGNTY OF SPAIN. YOU ARE ACCUSED OF THE CRIME OF WITCHCRAFT."

Ana could not believe her ears. She had known that they

would not treat her justly, but still she was shocked by the pronouncement of her crime.

"Sister, do you confess your crime freely?"

"I . . . I . . . do not confess to witchcraft. I am a woman of God," she stammered as she straightened her tired body.

"Sister, did you not admit to Father Antonio to having lain with an incubus?" questioned the Bishop keenly.

"I did not!" Ana was caught totally off guard by the question. "I told him I had been forced to lie with a monk."

"Hmmm . . . would it not be a sin for both you and the monk to commit such an act?" he asked thoughtfully.

"Yes . . ." answered Sister Ana meekly, her voice trailing off into silence.

For a long while, Father Antonio and Bishop Jalisco said nothing. They glared down at the suffering nun. Soon the woman before them began to sob quietly, the sound washing upon the Inquisitor like a pleasant morning breeze.

At length the Bishop broke the silence. "Your confession is just." He spoke calmly. "Anyone in the service of God would have felt compelled to confess such a sin, do you not agree?"

Sister Ana nodded her head in agreement, unable to find the words she needed.

"Then, my dear Sister, why has this monk with whom you had intercourse not come forward? By your own admission, anyone in the service of the one true God would feel compelled to confess such a crime. So where is this monk?"

Again, all Ana could do was to shake her head, still unable to bring forth the words. In her heart she knew what they were doing to her. She knew that all hope was gone. She could only play out this final part of her life with as much dignity as she could muster. Standing erect, she looked into the eyes of the men who were judging her and held back her tears.

"Well, Sister, since you cannot find your tongue, perhaps I can help you with the answer. Because no monk has come forward to confess such a sin, I can only assume that no such monk exists. Yet you have confessed that you had intercourse and gave birth to a child. I can only conclude—" The Bishop's voice had now risen to the intensity of a scream.

"—that you had intercourse with the devil or one of his un-holy legion!"

"No, that's not true!"

"It is true! You are a witch! Confess it!"

"No, no, no, no . . ." screamed Ana, burying her head in her hands.

"Confess your sins! Confess!"

"And what about your sins, Bishop?" Ana suddenly found the strength to respond in deafening shouts. "What about the poor young monk that you raped and stabbed deep below in the catacombs of the abbey? Isn't that also a sin?"

The Grand Inquisitor Juan Jalisco paled, and his mouth dropped open. His eyes bulged unbelievingly before the frail young woman before him.

"How could she know that?" he whispered, intending the words only for himself. Father Antonio heard him, however, and gazed at the Bishop in horror.

"What, Your Holiness . . . ?"

Realizing he had betrayed himself to the priest, Juan Jalisco became enraged. In a matter of seconds his face turned from white to the deep red of anger. The veins of his neck stood out, and his lips trembled.

"Father Antonio," began Juan Jalisco, exerting every effort to keep his voice calm and pleasant, "thank you for your help in this matter. You are excused. I will inform you of the outcome of this matter personally as soon as it has been determined."

Father Antonio now knew that the former nun was telling the truth about the Bishop. It did not come as a surprise to him. Nor was the charge of sex between the nuns and monks news. Sex was a necessary evil to keep the abbey calm and peaceful. So it had always been, and so it would always be. Father Antonio remembered fondly back to the regular encounters he had had with the Mother Superior, back when she was still a lowly nun—when they were both young. Now, obliged to respect the command of his bishop, Father Antonio left the chamber.

Ana stood rooted to the floor. Hatred for the man who sat in judgment on her caused her to shake uncontrollably.

"Confess, witch!" he commanded.

"If I am a witch, then so are you!" Ana hissed.

The Bishop looked down upon the girl coldly and then called the Captain of the Guards to his side. "Captain," said the Bishop, "give her to the soldiers for their evening pleasure, and burn her in the morning."

The captain bowed and kissed the Bishop's ring. He motioned for his men to take Ana away.

The Grand Inquisitor Juan Jalisco sat there for a long time after the chamber had emptied. He wondered how the girl could have known about the attractive young monk. He wondered if Sister Ana were indeed a witch.

Ana walked back through the abbey and out the gate, accompanied by six soldiers and their captain. They led her once again around the side of the abbey wall to the horrible little windowless shack and shoved her roughly back inside without closing the door. She lay there with the light seeping in from the open door and listened to the words of the captain as he spoke to his men.

"Do what you want with the girl. Just make sure she is alive and able to walk in the morning." He left the girl then to his men.

Ana's heart pounded savagely within her chest as soldiers crowded into the small shack, jostling each other. They grumbled and laughed. The largest and ugliest among them pushed his way to the front of the group and began to loosen his breeches. Pushing the cloth to his knees, he stooped over Ana and, with one hand, ripped the filthy rags from her body, leaving her naked and screaming. The next moment the soldier was upon her, and soon his grunting and panting were lost in her screams and the raucous encouragement of his comrades.

After a while, Ana stopped screaming. The death that she hoped would take her before the next soldier forced himself into her did not come.

Piercing screams echoed from the dark walls of the catacombs. Bargolas could feel his mother. Her pain wracked his body; her anguish burned as a fire in his heart. Helplessly, he threw himself against the slimy walls in the dark. Clawing the walls, his newly emerging talons split and cracked. His hands grew slick with his own blood.

The soft silver glow of the old man's cane emerged from the darkness. The silver light burned brighter, and the frustrated creature became still. He looked into the face of the old man and pleaded, "Help. Help . . . Mama . . ." His voice trailed off into the darkness before the old man spoke.

"I cannot. It is morning, and she will be dead very soon." The old man said this quietly, without a trace of compassion.

The child-creature lunged forward in fury and brought his powerful arm down across the neck of the old man. But no longer was the old man there—only the empty darkness. In less time than it took to draw a breath, the old man had vanished, taking the light with him.

Anger consumed Bargolas. Again, he threw himself against the wall of his dark home. Then, with the speed of a youth burning for revenge, he raced through the catacombs, scattering the bones of death in his path.

"Mama . . . I will help," he muttered to himself as he dashed toward the stairs leading up into the church.

Most of the abbey's residents had lined the north wall or crowded around the front gate to see the witch burn. It had been an hour since daybreak, and the early, soft autumn rays of sunlight found themselves swallowed up by the menacing dark clouds that threatened to rage with another storm. Between the blue and black rumbling masses, tinges of orange and violet could be seen.

· The congregation of the abbey watched as two soldiers led the former nun out into the open. Blood and slime covered her legs and trickled down to her bare feet in the cold mud. As she walked, a sharp rock punctured her foot, causing her to stumble and call out in pain. The soldiers tightened their grip on her arms and dragged her. Struggling with her dignity, she pedaled her feet until she got them under her once again and attempted to wrench herself free of the soldiers.

She looked into the foreboding sky and could find no trace of God. She doubted if God had ever been present in this horrible little place in the Sierra de la Demanda called the Abbey of Almansa. She looked ahead of her and saw a small, two-wheeled cart on a knoll. The soldiers were loading it with bundles of dry kindling. The branches and twigs were wrapped tightly together with thorny vines. The soldiers placed bundles in the cart, until the sticks stuck out the top.

Then they dragged Ana to the cart and pushed her firmly
down on the bed of wood. The sharp ends of the sticks dug
deeply into her back and legs, but she made no sound. She
was determined to give them no more pleasure.

With long pieces of hemp they tied her hands to the axles
of the wheels, the right hand to one wheel and the left to the
other. As she lay spread-eagled, looking up into the sky, the
soldiers began tying her feet to the handles of the cart. They
packed numerous bundles of kindling densely under the cart
and then all around it. The captain, carrying a blazing torch,
approached Ana.

Slamming the door aside, Bargolas emerged from the catacombs into the church. The noise startled a nun who had
chosen to scrub the floor of the church rather than watch some
poor girl being burnt to death for witchcraft. She looked up
and saw the monster running toward her. She didn't even
have time to utter a cry before sharp talons neatly removed
her head. It rolled, coming to rest against a pillar a few feet
away with a moist *thunk*.

Bargolas had gone up to get this far, so he would continue
to go up. Seeing no stairs to climb, he turned to the rough
wall and began to climb the face of the church. Within a few
minutes he had reached the top. Butting his weight against
the roof tiles until they gave way, he pushed he head up
through the roof. For a moment he was dazzled by the expanse of the world, the brightness, the color. But then his
mother's thoughts made their way to him.

*His mother, even at the end of her life, after all her pain,
worried about him. She loved him . . . She was near, but
where?*

Pulling himself higher on the roof, he looked over the peak
and down the other side. Then he saw her. She was lying in
the open—trapped, as a man approached her with fire.

In horror, he watched the man toss the flaming torch under
the wooden cart. Bargolas dug his talons into the wooden
peak of the roof, grunting in agony and frustration.

Down below, Ana looked up into the face of the captain
holding the torch. She could see his sneer as he tossed the
torch under the cart.

"Burn, witch!"

Instantly Ana could smell the tar-oil smoke and hear the crackling of the twigs underneath her. Again she told herself that she would not cry out in pain. She looked up into the sky and saw the clouds moving angrily across the sky. She saw the silhouette of the abbey. She saw movement on top of the church.

Then she felt the heat. It was on the right side of her face. Her long dark hair hung over the side of the cart; she could smell it as it started to burn. At the same time she felt the heat rise up from under her bare legs, then flames began to lick at her flesh. Fire rose up on all sides of her and sucked away the air.

Pain drove away all thoughts. Ana tossed her head back and forth, trying to escape the flames in her hair. She pulled against her bonds of hemp, for they too were on fire. But she would be dead before her bonds burned through.

The flames burned her skin, first blackening it, then melting it like wax. Finally the fat sizzled away, exposing blood-covered bones smoking in the flames, soon to add their own fuel to the blaze.

And she had screamed, her determination notwithstanding; for as long as Ana had a face and a mouth through which to draw breath, her screams echoed within every corner of the abbey. But the screams did not stop upon her death.

The people were confused. The witch had been burned; she was dead, so where were the screams coming from? They seemed to become louder. And there was something different about them, menacing. A sense of danger filled the abbey.

The thick, black smoke from the burning cart wafted on the breeze to the abbey. Everyone could smell the odor of burnt flesh and wood. Many could not bear the smell and became sick. Still the screams echoed through the courtyard.

Finally someone saw him. A nun pointed up to the wooden peak of the church and added her screams to his. Within moments the entire abbey was in a state of panic.

"A demon!" cried some of the nuns, running out of the gates with their hands clasped tightly around their crucifixes. "It is the consort of Sister Ana," cried others.

The Reverend Mother stood upon the cold mud of the courtyard and looked up. She fought panic and searched her heart for reason. After long moments of suffering through the agonizing sound, she began to put the events of the last few months together. She remembered how it had been reported that Sister Ana had been gone from her bed almost nightly since she had given birth. Birth, she thought to herself. That was the key. She had given birth to that creature!

"Oh, my Lord in heaven. What have we done?" she muttered to herself as tears welled in her eyes.

Bargolas looked down upon the strange woman who was dressed like his mother. Suddenly, a memory—though not a memory from his mind—hung before his eyes. The smell. He could smell the two women; one of them smelled of his mother. The other smelled of anger and hatred. Blood ran before his eyes as he watched his mother's skin cut and bleeding while the other woman stood there in pleasure.

The memory fading, he locked eyes with the Reverend Mother. He knew he must kill her. His gut rumbled as he started to slide down the roof toward the old nun.

Fear rooted the Reverend Mother to the spot. She felt her whole body tremble as he slid down the roof toward her. He stopped his sliding and perched, crouching, preparing to leap upon his prey like some terrible angel from hell. Just as his muscles flexed and he steadied himself for his jump, an arrow buried itself deep into his shoulder.

The captain and several of his soldiers stood on the wall separating the compounds of the monks and the nuns. The captain's sword was at the ready as his men knocked another round of arrows. Again his sword cut through the air—the signal to let fly the arrows.

Two arrows embedded themselves in the wooden beams of the roof, but two more found their marks. The first pierced the creature's back and the second his left thigh.

"My God," said the captain, "he has three arrows in him and still he stands. He truly is a creature from the darkness."

The Reverend Mother saw blackish-red blood dribble from the creature's mouth. She saw that he was dying. Suddenly, he fell to his knees when a forth arrow found purchase in his back. A moment later he plunged forward, rolling down the slanted face of the roof, breaking the arrow shafts off at the surface of his skin. He fell in a motionless heap at the feet of the Reverend Mother.

The Reverend Mother bent down to examine the creature

as the captain and his men leapt down from the wall. They knew the creature had fallen, though they did not see where he had landed.

Repulsed but curious, the Reverend Mother touched the creature's bright white skin. While she looked upon him, she observed that the creature was growing darker in color; soon he became almost black. The Reverend Mother, in horror, now saw his eyes, which had been closed, slowly open. A milky white film, like that of a mountain lizard, skimmed across his eyes before she saw that they were absolutely black. With lightning speed, two appendages snaked upward from his chest and seized the Reverend Mother by the throat. The creature's longer arms then reached up and grabbed her by the habit. A moment later the creature stood and hoisted the screaming nun up by the throat.

Bargolas heard the soldiers coming. He tightened his grip on this woman who had caused his mother so much pain and dashed into the church. Leaping over the body of the nun he had decapitated, he ran for the stairs to the catacombs, where he would be safe. The screams of the Reverend Mother intensified and rang sharply in his ears. He released one of his smaller hands from her throat and stuck it deep into her mouth; she abruptly stopped screaming.

The pain from his wounds impeded his progress only slightly. His bloodlust for revenge fueled the fire that sent him careening through the catacombs to the only home he had ever known. Behind him, he could still hear the soldiers following.

Minutes later, he found his hiding place. The chamber was dimly lit by the old man's ornate cane. Bargolas paused and looked to the old man for guidance, but all he heard was a soft chuckle.

For the first time in his young life, Bargolas felt lust. A throbbing stiffness rose up between his legs, and he looked at the Reverend Mother in a horrible new way. Clawing at her robes amid her screams, he tore them away with bloody swipes of his talons. In a flash, she lay naked before him. Her body was covered with deep scratches from which blood oozed.

The nun's protests were insignificant beside the power of the creature, and within a moment he had plunged himself

deep into her. Her screams only excited him more. He gazed
down at the woman, her mouth distended in terror, her old
teeth yellow and foul, and he placed his mouth over hers.

Her screams echoed inside him, and his tongue sought the
back of her throat. A moment later, when his tongue lodged
firmly in her throat, the screaming stopped. Bargolas squirmed
excitedly and began to suck the breath from the nun. Within
seconds, her lungs collapsed in the vacuum, and, as he increased the suction, the lungs slid moistly into his mouth. He
chewed them slowly, savoring the warm raw flavor as he
listened to the approach of the soldiers.

The soldiers rushed in just in time to see the creature with-
draw from the prostrate Reverend Mother. The creature turned
toward them with slimy pink flesh and blood oozing from its
mouth. The captain lunged forward with his torch and the
beast shrank away.

"Back to hell, demon!" commanded the captain.

With more soldiers, the Grand Inquisitor, Bishop Juan Jalisco, entered the chamber carrying an ornate crucifix. Juan
Jalisco took one look at the creature and spewed forth Latin
like vomit. His fear, however, had crushed what little faith
he had, and he staggered backward, immobile.

The captain stared into the glossy black orbs that were the
creature's eyes and was transfixed. Instantly the creature disappeared and in its place was the captain's younger sister.
She stood there, dressed for mass in her best brown dress,
her hat, veil, and shawl, embodying all the kindness and
goodness the captain had ever known. All else was forgotten
and all he could see, all he could feel, was love for her.

Juan Jalisco glared at the captain, his face illuminated
brightly in the flickering torchlight. The captain was being
bewitched, and the Bishop knew it.

"Kill it, Captain!" screamed the Bishop in a wheezing,
tiny voice.

But the captain remained mesmerized by the image of his
sister. She smiled at him and he returned the smile. "Lupita,
Lupita . . ." he muttered in loving tones.

The Bishop reached out with his crucifix and cursed the
demon. Then, hoisting the crucifix over his head like a club,
he stepped forward to strike the evil creature dead.

The captain glanced up in shock at the Bishop. Without

thinking, he unsheathed his sword and ran it through the back
of the Grand Inquisitor, Bishop Juan Jalisco. The Bishop fell
dead. Before the captain could wipe the blood from his
weapon, he felt the sharp blade of another soldier's sword
enter his heart.

Bargolas was plunged into darkness—not the darkness of
the catacombs that he knew so well, but an empty darkness
with no walls, no limits. There was nothing on which to stand
and nothing on which to lie. Bargolas drifted, not knowing
which way was up or down. A moment before, he had tasted
lustful satisfaction; now there was nothing.

"My son . . ."

Bargolas heard the old man's voice lightly against his ear
but did not see the familiar silver glow.

"I was forced to take you away from your home, for they
would have killed you. Here no one can hurt you. Here you are
safe. Here is timeless. Here you must wait. I am not with you,
for I must end my cycle. I am sorry, my son. I know you do not
understand. I am powerless to bring you back. You are too far
away, though you are really nowhere at all. Just wait. Be patient.
Someday, someone shall summon you back into the realm of
man."

13

Baltimore, 1921

Miss Clarissa Arbor read her name on the nameplate adorning her desk. She fumbled with the wooden plate and contemplated the situation. She could feel herself perspire; her nerves were getting the best of her. She plopped her chin in her hands and looked up at the great carved wooden clock in the corner. A quarter of nine. In fifteen minutes, Mr. Kloss would walk through the door, say, "Good morning, Miss Arbor," and continue into his office, shutting the door behind him. This day, however, would be different: when he sat down at his desk, Mr. Kloss would find a letter from his secretary, reciprocating the love and desire he felt toward her.

It had taken her two weeks to compose the letter, and while doing so, she had taken note of her life. Born in 1887 in Taylor, Baltimore County, she had lived with her parents until the age of eighteen. She had no prospects for marriage, and her father had described her as, at best, plain; he believed it would be best if she enrolled in the local college for ladies.

She loved Everidge College and learned well. Soon after completing her studies, she took a job in Baltimore as secretary for the law firm of Herzog, Snyderman & Hucker. That had been over twelve years ago. She had thrown herself into her work. She loved the intrigue; it compensated for the boredom of her own life.

She had no illusions about herself. At almost thirty-four years of age, with only a cat and a one-bedroom flat to call her own, she knew the face of loneliness. And she was resigned to it. She wasn't looking for anyone to make her life better—life was fine. Fine, that is, until Martin J. Kloss joined the firm.

That had been about a year earlier. The moment she saw him, she knew he was special. He was twenty-eight and already graying around the temples in a distinguished way. He carried himself proudly, and it was clear from his manner that he was accustomed to having his way. He paid a great deal of attention to Clarissa. Several times he brought her flowers. Always he wore that engaging smile. He was always polite and never demanding of her—unlike the senior partners, who took her for granted after all the years. No, Martin J. Kloss was different.

Actually, thinking back, it seemed to her that it had all started with some dreams she had had about Martin. They were romantic, very romantic. She realized that she hadn't had those kinds of thoughts since she was a girl.

The last few months, those romantic thoughts had become obsessive. She had been able to think of little else save Martin Kloss. Then one day he brought her flowers again. It was her birthday, but she had never told anyone the date was coming up. She realized then that he must care for her as much as she did for him—but that he was just shy.

She walked on air for several weeks before she finally realized that he wasn't going to make the first move. The only thing to do was to take the risk and confess her feelings to him. After all, time was getting shorter; she was already thirty-three.

The office door opened with a sharp crack, startling her. Here was Martin, in the flesh. He smiled at her, flashing his white teeth.

"Good morning, Miss Arbor. How are you today?"

"Quite well, Mr. Kloss, thank you for asking."

Martin Kloss continued walking past Clarissa and into his office. A moment later, the door shut and Clarissa's heart began to pound within her breast.

She looked up at the clock. He had been in his office for two hours and she had not heard from him. She hardly expected him to take so long. Actually, if the truth be known, she had expected him to come out as soon as he read the letter. But he had not. Now she didn't know what to do.

Finally, he strode out of the office. Clarissa prepared herself for the rush of joy she would feel when he told her that he loved her, too. But he did not even look at Clarissa. Indeed, he seemed a bit pale as he walked across the lobby to the office of Mr. Hucker. Martin knocked and then walked in.

Martin was in conference with Mr. Hucker for exactly twenty minutes. When he emerged, Martin returned to his own office without so much as a glance at Clarissa. A moment later, Mr. Hucker stepped out of his office and stared intently at Clarissa before speaking. "Miss Arbor, would you be so kind as to step into my office?"

The four other personal secretaries glanced at her, especially Mr. Hucker's own secretary, Kathleen, who glared from over the top of her wire-rimmed spectacles as Clarissa stood from her chair.

"Of course, Mr. Hucker," she said, at once crossing the lush carpet into his office.

Mr. Hucker closed the door and offered her a seat. She sat down as the senior partner walked around his desk and took his own worn leather chair. Suddenly Clarissa felt a chill, and then the hot flush of embarrassment as she saw what was upon Mr. Hucker's desktop. It was her letter to Martin.

"Miss Arbor, you have been a loyal and valued employee of this firm for many years. We have always counted ourselves lucky to have you. But now we seem to have a problem. As you undoubtedly know, Mr. Kloss and I have just been in conference, and . . . well, we have been discussing you. It seems, by this letter you wrote to Mr. Kloss, you have misinterpreted Mr. Kloss's intentions toward you."

Tears stung Clarissa's eyes as she looked down at her polished brown shoes. She nodded her head.

"You see, Miss Arbor, Mr. Kloss doesn't think that it

would be comfortable for either of you if you were to continue to work in this firm. He feels—"

"I understand," Clarissa interrupted, her voice full of emotion. ". . . I will clear my desk away and be gone within half an hour. You may send my final check to my home address."

"I'm very sorry, Miss Arbor. Perhaps we can work out something else. Perhaps a trade between secretaries or—"

"No, it is better that I leave. Thank you for your time, Mr. Hucker. I also wish to say that I, too, have enjoyed these years I have worked here. Thank you so much for your consideration."

Clarissa walked out into the lobby. All the other secretaries could see the tears in her eyes, and she felt as though she might burst out weeping at any moment. But she remained calm, restrained as much by her pride as by her embarrassment. It took her less than ten minutes to clear her personal belongings from her desk and put them in her bag.

After taking a last look around the office that had been her second home for the past twelve years, she walked out the door.

It was almost three weeks before Clarissa ventured outside her tidy little apartment. She wouldn't have left even then except that she had eaten all of the food in the house, including the last of the peanut butter and crackers. She put her hat and coat on to protect against the chill of the spring air and made her way to the market just around the corner.

As soon as she stepped onto the street, she felt naked and embarrassed. It seemed that everyone she saw looked at her with the same pitying gaze that she had seen on Mr. Hucker's face her last day of work. She knew what was wrong—she had lost her self-respect.

True, she also felt the loss of her fantasy. Martin Kloss had never been interested in her, and she knew that now. The fantasy had filled that horrible void of loneliness. And now that the illusion was gone, the black vortex of loneliness had sucked her down into melancholia.

As she walked, she tried to take encouragement from the trees that were a hazy green—they were so laden with young buds. The air was crisp, and all around her life was

entering the cycle of renewal. Still, she felt the black dog
of melancholia nipping at her heels. Young children rode
past her, screaming at the top of their lungs, but she hardly
noticed.

She had wept, but only a couple of times. She mourned
her loss of pride, not the loss of Martin. How does one lose
something that one never had? Now she realized that her
greater loss was the career she had worked so hard for, and
the place and the time that had become her life. Now not
only did she not have her illusion of requited love, but she
had lost a large part of her life as well.

It wasn't the money. Over the years, she had managed to
save a moderate nest egg. It was not necessary to rush out
and find employment in order to pay the rent. She did feel,
however, that if she did not do something to help fill the time,
loneliness and melancholia would surely devour her.

Looking over the seasonal vegetables in the Farmer's Market cheered her a bit. She thought about how she would prepare them—and then she thought of eating alone. That cast a
bit of gloom into her mood, but she ignored it as best she
could, paid for the groceries, and turned toward home. Just
before she climbed the steps to her building, she bought the
afternoon paper from a boy not more than eight years old,
who was puffing on a cigarette.

After frying some tinned meat and potatoes, she sat down
to eat with the newspaper beside her plate. Hardly bothering
to skim the headlines, she turned to the Help Wanted section.
After reading several unsuitable solicitations, she hit upon
one that sounded quiet and moderately interesting. It didn't
appear to offer the generous remuneration she had received
from Herzog, Snyderman & Hucker, but it seemed satisfactory, and she met all the qualifications.

Pressing the paper flat with both hands, she resolved to
apply for the position of librarian at the Baltimore City Library—main branch. Once the decision was made, she felt
better. She made herself a cup of tea and settled down to
listen to music on the radio.

She slumbered deeply, her peace of mind restored. In the
middle of the night, however, something disturbed her. At
first nothing registered. The weight on the bed increased and

a sweet cologne filled the room. Gently, the covers of her bed were drawn down. Clarissa opened her eyes.

For a moment she was unable to see his eyes, the reflection of light was so strong on his glasses. He smiled to her and she answered with a smile of her own.

"Martin," she whispered softly. "You have come back for me, after these few weeks you have come back for me . . ."

Martin was silent as he leaned over and kissed her lightly upon the neck. Brushing his lips along her throat, he kissed her below her ear, then he lifted his face and looked back into her eyes. He wasn't smiling any longer, but his mouth opened as he placed it over hers.

She felt him breathe into her, the heat and love penetrating the heartache and loneliness of a lifetime. She drew his warm breath of life, of love, deep into her—through her.

Martin's strong hands found the ties to her silky covering, undid them, and pulled the cloth away from her breasts. For a moment his mouth lingered there, upon the soft fullness of her flesh. Clarissa felt herself lifted up as the coolness of the room encircled her nakedness. Then slowly she felt herself settle back into the bed as Martin stood beside the bed, removing his own clothing.

Clarissa watched him as his dark clothing fell away. He placed his knee upon the bed and lowered himself, ever so gently, until his full weight rested upon her body. The breath went out of her as she sank into the warmth of the bed, and sucked in the heat of his body.

Again Martin placed his mouth over hers and they kissed. She felt his hand gently push her legs apart and she did not resist. A firm heat, strong and yet pleasing, pushed deeply into her . . .

A horrible jangle sounded near her head. Clarissa bolted upright, flailing her arms. There was a clatter—and the noise stopped. Martin's kiss was still strong upon her lips and the memory of his movement between her legs was . . . Slowly Clarissa's eyes focused. Her alarm clock lay on the floor halfway across the room. It had been a dream, just a dream. A droplet of moisture came to her eye as she threw her legs over the side of the bed and sat for a moment.

A dull ache rose up from her loins and grew until it was almost unendurable. She doubled over with the pain that is loneliness.

After a while Clarissa stopped sobbing. She washed the redness from her eyes with icy water and resolved to make a new life for herself. She would end the loneliness and despair, no matter what the cost.

The walls of books surrounding her gave her a feeling of protection against the outside world. Gradually she began to forget some of her pain and loss. Clarissa was on the road to recovery—and a difficult road it had been.

A year had passed since the head librarian had died quite suddenly and Clarissa had found herself promoted to the position. Only three years had passed, in all, since she had joined the staff, and now she was running the whole magnificent place. She loved it.

Taking on a new career had been good for her. It had been a whole new direction and she had developed a solid friendship with Bonnie. True, she had loved her job at the law firm and would probably have stayed there had she not made such a dreadful fool of herself. All in all, things had turned out quite well. But still she thought of Martin once in a while.

Falling in love with Martin—and she now was able to acknowledge that she had fallen in love with him—had been a turning point in her life. It was as if Martin had opened the floodgates of emotion that had been dammed up since she was a girl. Before Martin, she had not really thought about men or what it would be like to be with one, even just to sleep beside one. But now that was different.

Often she had difficulty concentrating on her work because of the insistent gnawing of some foreign yearning. It was a long while before she was able to identify the emotion as loneliness. Hers, however, was not the loneliness of having no one to talk to, no one to accompany her to the cinema; no, it was a more specific feeling, one that seemed to be rooted in her abdomen. It seemed like a hunger from which she could not find relief. Sometimes she felt as though the only thing that would—

"Miss Arbor, Father O'Leary is at the front desk. He wishes to speak with you."

Startled, Clarissa left her flight of fantasy and turned to her new assistant. "Thank you, Bonnie."

Clarissa walked briskly through the walls of books and up to the front desk. Her leather shoes tapped softly on the marble floor, and several people sitting at tables noted her passage. A wisp of hair had come undone from the tight bun at the back of her head. The fine strands of stray silver-brown hair rode the breeze and caught the golden rays of the summer sun streaming in through a high window.

"Father O'Leary, I am so sorry that I have missed your previous visits. What can I do for you?"

"Oh, that is quite all right, Miss Arbor, I am sure you are very busy. I am looking for some books. They were deposited here in the public library several years ago, before I took over at St. Marcus. They are scholarly books, old printings, and should, I believe, have been placed in storage. They are marked with a crucifix and the name of St. Marcus. I'm wondering if you could be so kind as to see if they still exist."

"Of course, Father. If you can give me a couple of days, I shall try to locate them. There are rooms and rooms of stored books in the basement."

"Of course, Miss Arbor. There is no hurry. I'll come back at the end of the week if that is convenient."

"Yes, that will be fine."

"Thank you so much. See you on Friday." The priest turned and walked out the great wooden and glass double doors.

Clarissa carried a kerosene lantern down the steps to the basement. The library had never bothered to have the basement wired for electricity. It was dark and smelled moldy. It reminded her a great deal of her own parents' basement, where she and her sisters had played. There they would jump out of the shadows at each other, squealing with childish delight.

She spent the better part of the morning in the basement, shifting boxes and looking for the label of St. Marcus. It turned into quite an ordeal. The dust was thick in places, and

Clarissa was seized by fits of sneezing while she hefted box after box to check their contents.

After several hours of searching, she finally came upon a pile of boxes covered with a large tarp. Peeking under the tarp, she found the label ST. MARCUS. A cloud of dust rose into the air, casting a ghostly image in the lantern light as she pulled the tarp from the boxes. In all, there were ten cartons of books. When she tried to lift one of them onto a cart, the cardboard disintegrated in her hands.

She thought of asking for help, but she had already set everyone about on other important tasks, except for Bonnie, and Bonnie was really the only one she could depend on anyway. So she and Bonnie, the closest thing she had to a friend, giggled like children and traipsed upstairs and brought back several wooden cartons, then began transferring the books from the old boxes to the wooden ones. Unfortunately, many of the books hadn't fared better than the boxes.

Clarissa checked some of the books to see what shape they were in as Bonnie returned upstairs to resume her regular duties. She thought them fascinating. One in particular caught her eye. It was badly damaged by dampness and mold. Carefully she turned the pages.

One of the first things she saw was a crude drawing of a woman tied to a cart filled with wood. A soldier stood beside the cart with a torch, setting the wood on fire. Under the picture was a handwritten caption in a flowing Latin script. On the facing page was a scholar's translation:

The witch burned for having sexual relations with an incubus.

Reading on, Clarissa surmised that this entire book was written about one particular incident in the mountains of Spain during the Inquisition. If the book was to be believed, a young nun had grown weak in her hunger for the touch of a man. Shamelessly, she had approached monks with her demands but had been spurned. Desperate, she had turned to Satan to fulfill her needs and from her loins had sprung an incubus.

It seemed that the young nun had left a record behind that had been discovered by the abbey and sealed in the church records. The record recounted her love for an unholy creature named Bargolas. It spoke of the human sacrifice that she had performed to please the Lord of Darkness. It spoke of Carnelian and Peridot, two stones that had been used to summon the incubus. The record went on to describe how all the residents of the abbey had been forced to listen to the screams of passion issuing forth from both the young nun and the incubus.

Clarissa was absolutely fascinated by the account of witchcraft. She didn't believe it, but still she was interested. As she read, she suddenly heard a scraping sound from the corner of the room. A dim, silvery glow appeared to emanate from the wall—briefly; then it was gone.

Curious, she stepped over to the wall and set the lantern down. On the floor beside the wall was a print of an old painting she had never seen. It was very odd in its execution. It appeared to be an etching. Its subject matter and perspective were much too modern to be very old. She held the print closer to the lantern. It was a picture of someone clothed in a dark robe that covered all but the person's face. The subject's sex could not be determined, but the face appeared to be wrinkled with age. In one gnarled hand, the person held a cane with an ornate handle.

Clarissa could feel her heart beating rapidly; she couldn't understand why. She replaced the picture on the floor and walked back to the books she had been packing for Father O'Leary. Just as she prepared to place the book she had been reading on the pile, she had the sensation of being touched by a voice as soft as the shadows.

"He is waiting for you, Clarissa," it seemed to say.

She looked all about for a moment, unsure whether she had actually heard something. She stopped short of putting the book in the pile to be returned to St. Marcus. Instead, she closed the cover, intending to set it aside. The title glared at her in the harsh light of the lantern: *The Maleficuarm*.

She was alone as the darkness of the subbasement rushed up to meet her. For a moment she was acutely aware of her own loneliness—and, of course, her fear. She looked out across the barren landscape of her memory and saw only desolation. At that moment, deep in the darkness with only a small candle lighting the way, she could have looked into her future, and she knew it. But she didn't. She didn't want to know what was ahead. This was a special time, and she knew it.

She had followed all the directions in *The Maleficuarm* as if it had been a cookbook. This was the correct time of year, the correct time of month, and the correct time of the night. In the bag slung over her shoulder with its leather straps pinching her skin, she carried the required stones and candles. But more important than all this paraphernalia was what she carried in her heart. Deep within her bosom, her heart beat rapidly—thunderously—with the desire for someone to love. To fulfill that desire, she would sacrifice whatever was necessary.

Had Clarissa been able to see behind her in the shadows beyond the candle as she dropped her clothing to the floor, still following the instructions, she would have screamed in terror and fled from the subbasement, never again to enter the darkness.

Within the shadows beyond the candlelight lurked another shadow of a darker and deeper black—a cloak, a hooded cloak with only a minuscule trace of coloring beneath reflecting the light of the candle. A gnarled hand curved over the ornate head of a cane.

Clarissa stood naked in the light of the candle, unsure whether or not she should continue. All at once she felt stupid for trying such a thing. Black magic, BAH! Foolishness! She turned her body to reach for her clothing, but stopped—

Her life, alone and desperate, was reflected in the pile of clothes on the floor. To such lengths she had been driven, forced to turn to things she had never believed in . . . and for what? For what? But she was unable to dress. She was unable to turn back. She knew what awaited her in the light. Clarissa didn't know what awaited her in the shadows of this room. Perhaps it was love.

He swung his legs over the side of the bed and stood, removing the cream-colored sheet from Clarissa's naked body. She felt the chill of the early fall descend upon her and reached down, pulling the covers back over herself as he walked across the room.

She never grew tired of watching him. With his every

movement, his muscles rippled beneath the dark olive skin. Almost hairless, his smooth body was electrifying to touch.

He turned back to look at her. His large black eyes were moist and gentle. He smiled, his rose lips elegantly framing his perfect white teeth.

"Oh, do you have to go?"

"Clarissa . . ."

She melted. Whenever he spoke her name, she was lost. The deep, soothing tones of his voice always quieted her and made her acquiesce to his will.

"I know; we agreed not to discuss it. It's fine. I know you will be back soon. I shall wait for you here."

He flashed her another smile and slipped on his pants. A moment later he pulled on a shirt, open at the throat, and walked out of the door—barefoot.

She glanced at the clock on the nightstand. 2:15 A.M. Fifteen minutes before, they had been making love—and now he was gone. A tear formed in her eye, but it didn't fall. She wouldn't allow it; she knew he would be back. She knew that it was she who had the power, it was she who had summoned him and it was to her that he must return.

Bargolas padded down the stairs of Clarissa's building. Few people were about at this time of night. No one saw him leave her apartment barefoot and hurry outside.

As soon as he stepped out the front door, he searched the street for anyone coming his way. Satisfied that the streets were empty, he slid into the dark space between the buildings. As the darkness hid him, he slipped out of his clothing and in one easy leap he bounded over five garbage cans, then ran to the alley behind the building. The talons on his feet made a clicking sound as he crossed the concrete—a sound that was all but lost in the rustle of leaves blowing through the streets.

Bargolas stayed in the shadows of the alleys and dark streets. His color had changed: he was black as the night.

Wrapping the darkness around his body like a familiar old cloak, he darted through the streets. He crushed multicolored autumn leaves blown up in drifts and piles. Once in a while, on a sudden impulse, he stopped in an alley and stood there motionless, watching and waiting. People passed, and Bargolas considered them. Sometimes he cast out his illusions like a fine-meshed net to snarl his prey for the evening, but so far, he had not taken anyone from the street. No, he preferred the solitude and privacy of homes and apartments.

His powerful lungs heaved, and he tried to judge how far away he was from Clarissa, but he could not. He could not tell where he was because his lust for blood was too strong, it blinded him to all else. He looked up into a dark sky with low clouds reflecting the city's lights, drifting, drifting. His eyes followed the clouds for a minute, then settled on the side of a building.

Movement in a window caught his attention, lace curtains fluttering. Bargolas shifted his gaze to the fire escape a short distance from the open window. Driven by his excitement, he didn't bother to look around to see if anyone was watching him as he ran across the street. Scarring the wall with his talons, he scrambled up the brick face until he reached the first rung of the fire escape.

His smaller arms snaked out, grabbing hold of the rungs to steady himself as his longer arms drew him up the steel ladder toward the open window. When he had reached the level of the open window, he stretched out one powerful arm and dug his talons into the mortar of the building. Slowly, he extended his leg and plunged the talons of his foot into the mortar. He inched his way across the face of the building until he had covered the ten feet between the fire escape and the window.

Peering in, he saw a young man and his wife cradled in each other's arms. The woman's face was nestled under her husband's chin, her fine blond hair fell in waves down her back. The streetlight flowed in through the window and picked out highlights in her hair.

Bargolas' shadow fell across the sleeping couple. The creature hauled himself through the window and stepped lightly upon the wooden floor. His talons made a clickety-click sound as he walked to the foot of the bed.

Tom Norton stirred. He looked to his side for Mina. She was nowhere to be found. Suddenly, he saw something move at the foot of his bed, and he shifted his sleepy eyes. Mina stood at the foot of the bed, gazing at him. Her eyes were darker and more sultry than Tom had ever seen them. He watched dreamily as she slipped out of her sheer nightgown.

Tom felt himself becoming aroused. He pulled the covers aside and let the cool breeze wash over his naked body, warmed by his anticipation. Mina stepped over to his side and reached down with her long, lovely fingernails to caress his firm manhood. Leaning over him, she covered his mouth with hers and pushed her tongue inside.

Pulling his lips from Tom's mouth, Bargolas moved down to his neck. He closed his powerful grip on Tom's genitals and ripped them from his body. Tom's aborted scream gurgled in Bargolas' mouth as his teeth tore away Tom's throat. Blood sprayed all over the sleeping Mina.

Mina jerked her head away when she felt the hot liquid on her face. She wiped the blood from her eyes. It was then that she looked into the face of Evil, and a moment passed before she found the breath to scream.

Just as Mina opened her mouth, Bargolas brought up the bloody mass that he still held in his hand and shoved it down her throat, stuffing it deeply inside her. She gagged for air as the blood ran into her lungs. She flailed about on the bed, convulsing violently. Bargolas caught her by the wrists.

While Mina struggled beneath him, Bargolas looked up into the space between himself and the ceiling and remembered the older nun who had hurt his mother. His arousal was complete as he plunged himself deep into Mina's bowels. She died a moment later. Bargolas stood upon his knees and looked down at all the blood. Slowly he began to feed his hunger.

Clarence turned over in his sleep, pulling the sheet and blankets with him. Nelda felt the familiar chill; her husband had stolen the covers every night of their forty-eight-year marriage, and, as usual, she reached automatically to pull them back. This time, however, liquid dripped upon her arm. Damn, she thought to herself, the kids upstairs have let the tub run over again and it's dripping through the ceiling.

"Clarence! Clarence, wake up! The ceiling is leaking. Tom and Mina must have let the tub overflow again."

"Whaa . . . shit, not again. Goddammit all to hell! Irresponsible kids . . ." Angrily, he reached over to the nightstand and turned on the lamp.

The room was flooded by the warm light. Nelda put her

hand up to her eyes. As she got used to the glare, she heard a steady *plop-plop* of liquid dripping onto the sheet. Looking down at the sheet, her eyes widened.

"Oh, sweet Jesus!" she muttered hoarsely. "Clarence, it looks like blood!"

Minutes later, after repeated knocking on the door of the apartment above them, they woke up the building manager to check on the young couple. The lights to the bedroom were switched on, and the elderly couple's screams flooded the hallways.

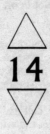

14

Othello, 1970

Mike pulled off his shirt, and Stan examined the deep claw mark on his shoulder. It gave him the creeps to wonder what kind of creature could do that. He was glad the two of them were safe in Mike's room where Mike had brought him directly after telling him the news.

"If I hadn't had my coat on, it probably would have torn my arm off."

Stan leaned back against the side of Mike's bed, staring at the pile of 45s on the floor. "Did you show your parents?"

"Are you out of your mind? What I am supposed to say? 'Oh yeah, it's just a flesh wound from this monster that Stan conjured up one night when he was bored.' "

Stan's face flushed in both embarrassment and anger. "Okay, so what do we do now?"

"You tell me. You conjured it up, you *un*conjure it. Send it back to where it came from while it's still light out."

"I don't know if I can do anything in the daytime."

"Come on, give it a try. I'll get you whatever you need."

"Do it where?"

"Here. My parents are gone for the day. Come on, do it— I'm desperate as hell."

Stan thought about it for a minute. Mike was right—it did

seem safer during the day. "Okay," he said, "let's push the
bed back."

"Whoa there, buddy. Not in my bedroom. We can do it in
Lea's room."

"Who's Lea?" asked Stan.

"Didn't I ever mention her? She's my older sister. She's
been away at college the last two years. Believe me, she'll
never miss the bedroom, haunted or otherwise."

"Okay," sighed Stan. "The first thing I'll need is a bag
of salt and some candles."

They walked down the hall and into Lea's room. The afternoon light lay pale upon the satin pink coverlet. The faint
odor of perfume still lingered in the room though Lea had
been gone for two years. Both looked around, then Mike left
Stan to move the furniture while he rummaged around the
kitchen for salt and candles. When he returned, Stan had
pushed the bed flush against the wall and set the chair on top
of the desk. Stan appeared to be lost within himself, and after
waiting for half a minute, Mike thrust the candles and salt
out in front of him and said, "Here, it's all I could find."

Stan blinked his eyes a couple times at Mike. "It's weird,"
he said. It was, Stan felt—but he did not say this—as if the
spell had begun just by his thinking about it. Weakly, he took
the candles and salt from Mike and squatted on the floor.

He ran his hand over the orange shag carpet and said, "It
would be hard to get the salt out of this rug. We're gonna
have to roll it back or put plywood or something down, so I
can pour out a circle of salt."

"We don't have any plywood, so let's roll the carpet
back."

The carpet was pressed down firmly, and the boys struggled with it before they got it out of the way. Then Mike sat
down on the bed as Stan began to pour a circle of salt, eight
feet in diameter, on the hardwood floor. He left an opening
at one spot along the circumference, as an entrance to the
space within.

"I need some saucers and matches."

Mike walked out of the room to fetch the items. Stan stood
outside the circle and looked at the salt. It already seemed to
have taken on a bluish cast. Stan noticed an odd tingle in his
hands and behind his ears, then down his spine. He wondered

if he was just excited or if this was an indication of his personal power. Mike returned then and handed him the matches and saucers.

Stan stepped back into the circle and lit the candles, dribbling hot wax on the saucers to stand the candles upright. Soon he had four of the candles going. He stood and looked over at Mike, lazing comfortably on the bed.

"Well . . . ?" Stan said.

"Well, what?"

"Well, get in the circle so I can close it up."

"You are outa your fuckin' gourd! I ain't gettin' in that circle with you."

"I'm not doing this alone."

"Why not? You started this whole damn thing by yourself; you're gonna have to fix it by yourself."

"You mean you don't have the guts to see it through. Look, probably nothing is gonna happen. I don't have my books or my *Athame* or any of the other stuff I used before."

"I don't give a rat's ass. You've always said it was just the power of the mind, and the rest of the ritual was window dressing. So go to it. You got yourself into all this, now you gotta get yourself out of it."

"Come on, who was it that wanted some excitement in his life? Who thought he could just lead the—what was it you called me?—the social misfit, just lead the social misfit around by his nose because nobody liked him, because you figured he would do anything just to have a friend?"

"Ah, shut the fuck up. You're makin' me out to be some sort of heartless monster, well I ain't the monster you gotta worry about. I ain't goin' on your little ride. You fucked up and brought something here. Now you send it back!"

Stan glared back at Mike, knowing that it was no use to argue. He picked up the salt and closed the circle.

In the same instant, Stan saw the faint blue glow of the salt becoming brighter. Mike, too, was looking down at the circle of salt. Could it be he also saw the bluish glow?

"Jesus Christ!" Stan heard Mike say, under his breath.

Stan stood up straight and stared into the candlelight, not knowing what to do next. Slowly, instinctively, he sank to his knees. He reached out with one hand, cautiously, and touched the flame of one candle, feeling the heat between his fingers as the flame went out. With his fingers still burning, he brought them to his forehead, to the place he had burned with his red-hot *Athame*. Instantly he felt the heat flow to his body. The hair on the back of his neck stood up, and he heard Mike draw in his breath sharply.

"Shit," Mike said softly, as he watched the flames grow brighter. At least, that's what he first thought was happening; but then he realized that it was rapidly growing darker outside. He was amazed. It was just barely afternoon on a Saturday—and it was getting dark.

Stan turned to look over his shoulder at Mike. The look of shock on Mike's face made him feel uncomfortable. Stan knew there was no turning back.

"I can't explain it," he said, his voice sounding hoarse, "but it's like I don't really need to do this. It's like I've already set all this into motion and something else has taken over. It's beyond my control."

"Well, I suggest you find some control, 'cause I think we're in a world of hurt. Somethin' tells me we ain't got no solar eclipse outside."

Mike tried to sound angry, but he was aware of the fear creeping into his voice. He glanced quickly out the window again to see if it was getting any darker—and noticed something very strange. It seemed like the wooden window frame was shimmering, sort of, like an image seen through a hot summer day. He stood and looked at Stan, who was returning his glance, and walked over to the window. He reached out and tried to touch the window frame—but could not.

It was as if he was looking at the afterimage from a bright flash, as if the image of the window frame was burned into his memory but didn't actually exist now. If he stared hard, he could almost make out the shape of the window, but not quite. Frightened, he turned toward the door—but the door was no longer there. Suddenly, Mike felt that he might be safer in the circle with Stan, after all. He crossed the floor in two strides, preparing to step over the line of salt.

"Stop!" Stan said, without looking up from the candles. "Don't even think about stepping over the circle. It might kill you—and if it didn't, it would probably make the circle useless. The circle is for protection against . . . whatever is out there."

Mike looked around himself. He could see nothing of the room now. It was all darkness except the safe and warm interior of the circle of salt.

"Let me the fuck in there or I'll break my way in!"

Stan looked at him and nodded his understanding. Cautiously, he swept a bit of the salt away to see what would happen. Nothing did, so he moved another small patch. This time, a high-pitched sound shrieked through their ears and the room suddenly became icy cold.

Stan waited for a moment to see if the sound continued. It did; in fact, the sound grew in intensity, indicating that it was approaching, whatever it was, and the salt wasn't stopping it. With a quick sweep of his hand, Stan opened the circle; Mike immediately stepped inside. The wail sounded very near, the pitch piercing their ears. Stan grabbed the bag of salt and filled in the gap. Where he poured the salt, there was a bright flash and a terrific boom.

The boys were jolted backward to the edge of the circle. They rolled against each other groaning, almost deafened and blinded by the explosion. After some time passed—they had no idea how long—they got to their feet and looked around. There wasn't much to see. Outside the circle, darkness stretched in all directions, a strange, objectionable darkness. Chunky. The darkness seemed to be made up of densely packed matter, *things*, that would not let the light through. They had the impression of being surrounded by something that was closing in on them.

"What now?" Mike's voice quivered.

"I don't know. I'd settle for just getting your house back."

"Me, too. I suppose we could make a run for it. We know where the door is."

"I don't think we're in your sister's room anymore. Here, watch this."

Stan reached into his pocket and pulled out a quarter. He tossed it out of the circle and into the darkness. For a second, it glimmered in the candlelight as if suspended there, then fell . . . without a sound. The boys looked at each other fearfully when they realized that the coin never hit the floor.

"I guess there is no turning back now," said Mike.

Stan nodded wordlessly.

Suddenly they heard a scraping sound, and both of them

turned their heads toward it. The inky darkness seemed to move aside, and a dark glow replaced it. As the glow brightened and widened out, they heard footsteps. A moment later, a silhouette appeared in the middle of the reddish glow. Their hearts pounded as the footsteps drew nearer. They felt themselves pushed over the edge into raw panic.

15

Baltimore, 1925

Clarissa heard the door open. She peered over the covers, expecting Bargolas. For an instant, it appeared as though there was someone—or something—else standing at the foot of her bed, something deformed, horrible, but the image quickly cleared as Bargolas cast out his illusion and transformed himself back into the ideal of her longing.

"Go back to sleep, Clarissa," he said softly. She looked over at the clock on the nightstand. It was a quarter of four.

Bargolas and Clarissa sat together over breakfast. He hadn't touched his eggs and toast. In the two months that Bargolas had shared her apartment, he had eaten very little. She wondered how he found nourishment. The question made her nervous, so, as usual, she put it out of her mind. She looked across the table at the beautiful man whom she had grown so to need. He was watching her with moist eyes that seemed to beckon her. The dark hair curled down upon his forehead like that of an ancient god. His flawless, olive-colored skin glowed with a warmth that made her heart pound furiously. Again she was tempted to call in sick at the library, but she had already done so five times this month; she must go to work this day, even though it was difficult.

Clarissa stood up. It was an effort. It was difficult to leave the beauty and love of this man-creature that she had sum-

moned from a place she dared not to imagine. As she pulled
her eyes from him and focused on the kitchen doorway, she
felt as though she had been released from a powerful grip.
On the one hand, she felt free; but on the other, she felt
vulnerable and weak.

She walked into her bedroom to dress for work. She pulled
her hair back into her customary bun and slipped on her warm
gray coat. She did not see Bargolas as she left the apartment,
but she knew that he was there. She hurried down the stairs
and just caught the #4 bus that took her to the front steps of
the library.

As she unlocked the door, she gathered up all the local
newspapers that had been left at the entrance and set them on
the front desk. She removed the previous day's papers from
their split wooden canes and began slipping today's newspapers onto the loose slats. As she finished arranging them, she
noticed the all-too-familiar headlines.

BRUTAL SEX MURDERS, #14 AND #15

and:

SERIAL MURDERS CONTINUE: VICTIMS #14 AND #15

Clarissa read the words over and over. Of course, she was
horrified by the terrible crimes. But she felt a strange connection to them. Something was unsettlingly familiar about
the feeling that came over her as she read the stories. She
tried to keep Bargolas out of her mind, but she knew the
murders had started shortly after she had summoned him. In
a daze, she returned to the front desk and sat down. A wave
of nausea churned away in her stomach, and she neglected
her duties for the next two hours—that is, until the rest of the
employees arrived for work.

When Clarissa walked into her apartment that evening, she
was determined to find out from Bargolas if he had anything
to do with the murders. But as soon as her eyes met his, her
determination vanished as if it were last night's dream. She
was overcome by his beauty and believed only in his ability
to light up the dark cavern of her aloneness.

Tenderly he laid her upon the smooth coverlet of the bed.

He traced the edge of her lips with his hot breath and grasped the tight bun of hair, then loosened it, arranging the hair loosely about her shoulders. Seizing the whiteness of her blouse, he pulled strongly until the buttons popped from the material—just before the fabric shredded in his hands. Clarissa gasped as he pulled the blouse from her body and flung it away.

Clarissa's head felt as if it were exploding. All light seemed to leave her, and a dark-red glow started in the back of her head, growing and growing until it spiraled out of control. She surrendered totally: her body quivered beneath Bargolas' strength, and, impaled in ecstasy, she screamed, finding her release.

Gently, Bargolas pulled the damp strands of hair from her face. He bent down, touching the beads of perspiration on her face with his tongue. Once again he sought her mouth and plunged into it. And again, only minutes later, she screamed the passionate screams of total ecstasy.

When she awoke, it was half past seven, and hunger pinched at her stomach. She looked around for Bargolas; he was nowhere to be found. She lay in the darkness for a long time, unable to sleep. She wondered if tomorrow's headlines would announce more murders. But could she blame Bargolas for them without proof? she asked herself. She could find no answer. She was painfully, hopelessly torn between her need for him and what her brain told her she must do.

It was still hard for her to understand what had happened, intellectually. She knew that she had summoned the creature. But until she had felt overwhelmed by loneliness, she had never considered such an act possible. She had never believed in the occult, and now she had to accept it as fact.

A thought occurred to her. Perhaps she should turn her question over to people who dealt with just such matters. Her hair rustled on the cool white pillow as she nodded to herself. Yes, she thought, I think I know just where to begin.

Flinging back the covers from her bed, she scurried across the cold wooden floor to her clothes. She dressed hastily, snuggled into her coat, and rushed out of the apartment and down into the street. After a few minutes of enduring the bitter cold, she was finally able to hail a cab.

"Where to, lady?"

"Downtown . . . Greene Street."

"No place in particular?"

"Somewhere near Mulberry. It's a gypsy place. I can't remember what it's called."

"Madame Rosa's?"

"Yes, that is the place. I'll start there."

The driver fell silent as he drove across Jones Falls and turned down Greene. He left Clarissa off in front of a gaudy façade with a hand-lettered sign that read: MADAME ROSA'S.

For a few cold minutes, Clarissa stood in front of the door, working up the courage to walk in. At last, feeling stupid just standing outside in the darkness, she walked through the door. The first thing she noticed was the odor: onions, garlic, human perspiration. It was, on the one hand, offensive and, on the other, strangely reassuring.

She heard the bells above the door tinkle a second time as the door closed, and she stood there listening to the background sound of a radio. A moment later, a stocky dark-skinned woman, white hair escaping in disarray from an old headcloth, walked out of the darkness to greet her.

Madame Rosa wore a smile on her brightly painted lips, and her eyebrows were blackened almost theatrically. Her eyes, dark and bloodshot, bore into Clarissa's as she greeted her with a pseudoelegance.

"Ah, I see you are in trouble. Please come this way."

Clarissa jerked her head backward from the strong stench of alcohol on Madame Rosa's breath, but she nevertheless followed the fortune-teller into a dimly lit parlor. Madame Rosa motioned for Clarissa to be seated opposite her.

"What makes you think that I am in trouble?"

Madame Rosa chuckled, looking deep into Clarissa's eyes. "I needed no special powers to tell. You are a woman out alone on a cold night. You are hastily dressed, and your hair is uncombed. All one has to do is use the eyes. Yes, you are a woman in trouble. But I can also tell you that it has to do with . . . with . . . but first, before we continue, let us settle on a fee."

Clarissa nodded her head and opened her purse. She took out a two-dollar bill and a one-dollar piece—her grocery money for the next week. She laid it on the table, and Madame Rosa instantly scooped it up.

"Now let us get down to business. Your trouble has to do with your husband. He is being unfaithful to you. Is that not correct?"

Clarissa's heart fell into the well of disappointment; her hopes for being helped by this woman were shattered. "No, it does not have anything to do with my husband; I am unmarried. Does . . . does the name Bargolas mean anything to you?"

Madame Rosa looked down at the table as she searched her memory. She glanced back up at Clarissa and shook her head slowly.

"No, I am sorry. The name means nothing to me."

Clarissa took a deep breath to steady herself. She needed to ask questions, and this was a place to start. She must try, even if the woman was a charlatan.

"Do you know of special, uh, ceremonies in which one can call up . . . creatures of . . . substance?"

Madame Rosa again looked deep into Clarissa's eyes, and a frown creased her forehead. It was a moment before she responded.

"You speak of black magic, do you not?"

"I'm not sure what I'm speaking of."

"You wish to know how to summon up such creatures?"

"No," she answered quietly and paused before going on. "I wish to know how to send one back."

Madame Rosa's eyes grew wide in fear and shock. She searched Clarissa's face, and her expression told Clarissa she believed her. Madame Rosa then held her hand over the table and dropped the money Clarissa had given her.

Clarissa looked at the pile of assorted coins and paper on the dark velvety surface and felt that her hopes were as good as destroyed.

"So this means you will not help me?"

Rosa stood up from the table, pulled back the dark curtain, and walked into the back. Clarissa waited for a few minutes and, when she was convinced that the gypsy woman would not return, she stood up and prepared herself to leave. Her knees wobbled, and she felt herself to be on the darkest side of despair. She didn't know where else to turn. She left the money on the table and turned to walk out of the shop. She didn't even hear the little silver bell ring above the door as she opened it and stepped outside. Just before the door closed, a hand reached out and grasped Clarissa by the arm.

Startled, Clarissa spun around. Madame Rosa placed a small piece of paper in her hand. The door closed, and Clarissa was standing on the dark street all alone.

She walked for a few minutes, then stopped beneath a streetlight and unfolded the piece of paper. It read: P. N. Bellcoda, 114 November Heights.

A chill settled over Clarissa as she walked to Mulberry Street to look for a cab. Could this Bellcoda be someone who could help her? She didn't know. She knew only that she was desperate enough to try almost anything.

As she crossed a street empty of motor traffic, she suddenly heard something behind her. She turned around and saw two unsavory men hurrying toward her. A rush of panic caught her and propelled her forward. As she ran, she heard the men behind her break into a run as well. She feared to look back as she heard them growing closer. She tried to run faster but she was no longer a young girl. Her running footfalls echoed loudly in the darkness, but there was something else. She could hear her own footsteps, the footsteps of the other men but also a rapid clicking sound becoming louder and louder by the moment. Crossing into still another dark empty street, she began to gasp heavily. Her instincts told her she could not outrun them, she must either get help or hide. She saw an alley on the other side of the street—enveloped in the darkest shadows—and ran toward it.

She ducked into the alley and turned to see if the two men were still chasing her. She heard their footsteps before she saw them. Her hopes fell as she realized they had seen her run into the alley. She was trapped. She began to shiver with fear as the men cautiously approached her hiding place.

Crouching behind some dark oil containers that smelled dark and musky, she suppressed the whimper she felt building in her throat. Panic blocked the sound of sharp talons against the cobblestones. On the verge of screaming she watched as the two men's silhouettes drew nearer, searching. As they drew close, she saw another figure enter the alley. Just as the thugs loomed above her, she heard a scuffle in the darkness and closed her eyes tightly.

Sitting in the darkness of the filthy alley, she heard horrible sounds—a gurgle, and then a crash of garbage cans. She could feel hot tears sliding down her face. She felt her lips quivering and, although she wanted to open her eyes and look, although she wanted to stand up and run, she could not beat down the fear that had invaded her very soul.

Quivering, she listened in the darkness and heard nothing now save for the scraping sound of an automobile horn in the distance. With her eyes squeezed shut, she listened hard for any indication of movement—and still heard nothing. A moment later, however, that familiar clickety-clicking sound drew nearer the woman. Then, words whispered, feather-light but as clear and sharp as crystal, came to her ear. Words rang in her head like a distant Chinese gong.

She jumped to her feet and dashed out of the alley, growling like a trapped animal. She ran down the street—and the words now clanged about loudly in her head: *RUN, CLARISSA!*

Her keys rattled noisily through the hallway as she fumbled with them, trying to open the door to her apartment. She knew Bargolas would not be there. She knew that he might not come back to her for a long time, but she also knew, just as she knew the sun would rise in the morning, that Bargolas *would* come back to her.

Clarissa pulled the multicolored quilt back, then the crisp white sheet. White sheets, clean and cold, always reminded her of ice, and they especially felt that way now when she slipped in between them. She glanced at the clock. It was only slightly after nine P.M., but all she wanted to do was sleep. She had felt that way for the last three nights, three nights during which Bargolas had not returned.

Sliding her hands under her feather pillows, she buried her sobs in the icy cold. She could not help it—she needed him. After she had purged herself, after she had almost drowned in her own self-pity, she turned over onto her back, sniffing loudly, and watched the changing patterns of light on the ceiling.

The patterns of light spoke to her, silently. In them she saw the future. It was the only possible future if she did not send Bargolas back. Swirling upon the ceiling were all the recent headlines. Over the past three days, the number of killings had tripled. The citizens of Baltimore were afraid to step outside their own homes. Clarissa saw in the patterns her own responsibility. The patterns . . .

She heard the creaking of the bedroom floor. Again the sound. She looked toward the door. He was there. Naked, beautiful, and aroused. As he moved slowly toward her, she focused on the smoothness of his skin, the oily black curls almost touching his shoulders, and she felt his spell dissolve the painful responsibility which had been torturing her, her guilt melted away in a wave of need and passion.

When Bargolas touched her breast, all she felt was the burning passion that he had kindled in her two months ago, desire that had lain dormant all her life. How could she give up something that she needed so much—someone that she loved?

Clarissa buried her trembling head in the sweet hollow of his neck and tasted his passion. He pulled her head away and knelt over her. He caressed her breasts for a moment, then he slipped abruptly, deeply into her. A gasp of pain mingled with pleasure caught in her throat, and before she was able to release that imprisoned moan of delight, he withdrew and thrust again, this time with more urgency.

It seemed that she had never been alive before. Every inch of her body tingled. As she lay there looking into the shadowy eyes of Bargolas, she heard every sound and smelled every odor. His throaty animal growl of release was still ringing in her ears. She wished to have him again, but she knew she did not possess the strength. Unwillingly, she climbed from the bed and walked into the kitchen for a glass of water to relieve the stickiness in her throat.

As she walked from the bedroom, she felt the spell dissipate. She felt pain deep in her loins, and an unbearable guilt in her heart. Her instincts told her to run, run and never look back—but she could not. Struggling against the panic of remorse, she walked into the kitchen and drew herself a glass of water.

The water was not enough. She needed more time. She

made herself a pot of strong tea, determined not to return to
the bedroom. Sitting at her small kitchen table, she drank her
tea and nibbled at stale cookies. It was past two A.M. Over
the next hour, she built up the courage to return to the bedroom while Bargolas slept. She felt sure that he was indeed
sleeping, otherwise he would have come out looking for her.
She suspected that, between making love to her and the un-
thinkable things he had done during the past three days, he
was exhausted—if indeed such creatures could become exhausted.

Quietly, she pushed herself from the table and crept upon
feet clothed in slippers to the door of her bedroom. She peeped
inside, cautiously—to be sure that Bargolas was not affecting
her. She felt nothing, so she ventured into the bedroom a step
and allowed her eyes to adjust to the darkness.

Muted light from the street illuminated the room. She stared
for some moments before she realized what she was seeing.
Bargolas had thrown back the bedclothes and lay open and
naked in the diffuse light. She saw him, for the first time, as
the terrible monster he was, and put her hand to her mouth
to quell the scream that threatened to escape.

She stared, unbelievingly. Gone were the sultry black curls
atop his head. Gone was the flawlessly smooth skin of a
youth. And folded across his chest was—*my God*, Clarissa
thought—another pair of . . . *arms*. The image of Bargolas'
ugly scarred head remained in her mind as she quietly backed
out of the bedroom and into partial sanity. She crossed to the
door and threw on her coat.

As she grasped the knob, she hesitated, wondering where
she could go. She had no friends, and her family was beyond
the city limits. She had only the library. Yes, the library, she
thought, she would be safe there. She stepped into the corridor; the door closed behind her with a low click. She dashed
down the stairs, into the street, and to a phone booth to call
a taxi.

For several minutes she stood in the darkness, watching for
the telltale black and red car of the Baltimore Cab Company.
At last, headlights flashed; the car rattled up to the phone
booth as Clarissa stepped out. She grasped the door handle
just as she caught a bit of movement from the corner of her
eye. Jerking her head around, she saw him. He had run from

the front door of her building and was speeding toward her. She flung the door open and fell inside, screaming, "Drive! Quickly!"

Clarissa was driven around the city for almost twenty minutes before she told the driver to drop her off at the library. Her heart had stopped racing by the time she paid him and began walking up the front steps of the Baltimore Public Library.

She locked the door behind herself and went over to the main desk. She started to remove her coat but decided to leave it on when she realized she was still in her nightgown. Reaching under her desk into a box, she pulled out a pair of shoes that she kept there to wear when her dress shoes became too uncomfortable. Slipping them on, she sat down at the huge desk and removed the folded sheet of paper in her purse. She smoothed the paper with the flat of her hand and read the name over and over again. P. N. Bellcoda.

Suddenly she heard a sound—an odd clicking, like fingernails upon a hard surface. Then it sounded more like a dog crossing a hardwood floor. Looking up, she saw him—tall, beautiful, and fully aroused.

She gripped the side of the desk and forced herself to look away. How had he gotten in? She stared down at the piece of paper, then slid it under the side of the blotter. She could feel herself being overcome by his spell.

"Please . . ." she cried hoarsely, still looking down at the desk. "Stop. Please stop. I want to talk to you."

Clarissa felt a lessening of that powerful sensation that had always given her such pleasure, that warm wave of air rushing over her, healing and accepting her, loving her . . . yes, now it was diminishing. She looked up at Bargolas. His image wavered in the air before her. He backed out of the light and into the shadow of a bookshelf.

"Why stop?"

The words rang strangely in her head. It was as if she were not hearing his words but rather thinking them. "Stop talking in my head," she commanded with firmness.

"I stop," said the gravelly voice in the shadow.

"I want you to go back, back to whence you came, back from where I summoned you!" Clarissa shrieked, and her words echoed in the darkness.

"No. I stay with Colizza. Love Colizza. Not go back."

Clarissa was struck by the childishness of his voice and the menace of his words. This is what had been her lover? This is what had led her down a path of self-deception? This is the Baltimore Monster, the Baltimore Slasher?

"You are MURDERING people! You are an evil creature! And now I am evil, too, for it was I who brought you back to this world."

"Need food," he croaked from the shadows. His talons clicked impatiently against the floor.

Clarissa felt a dagger of ice plunge into her heart. What had she done? Oh, dear God, what had she done!?

"Clarissa, my love. I need you." The voice, now deep and mellow, drifted across the floor.

She knew he was working his spell. His voice had changed, and she knew now he would become the beautiful man she loved. Slowly she brought her head up. Looking into his dark eyes, she was lost in a storm of passion. She felt every inch of her body ache for his touch. Pleading with him, she begged him to possess her.

"Please, please . . ." she moaned, caressing her thighs and breasts in slow, sensual arches.

Still Bargolas would come no closer to her. He waited until her passion built up. Her insistent pleas served only to excite him more. Then, in a dark commanding voice, he spoke to her. She could not resist.

"Clarissa . . . come to me, come to me—now . . ."

Vanished was the illusion, gone with the creature. He had gone back into the night leaving Clarissa, spent and exhausted, on the hard cold floor. The first rays of dawn had replaced the streetlight flowing through the windows and sky-lights. She could do nothing but weep.

Her tears cleansed her, however. They wiped away some of her shame and powerlessness. Moving against the soreness of her body, she walked slowly to the main desk and removed the piece of paper from under the blotter. She then pulled out the telephone directory and looked up the name Bellcoda. There was only one. Her desperation forced her to dial the number despite the early hour.

"Yes?"

"I would like to speak to Mr. Bellcoda, please."

"It is rather early, don't you think, madame?" The accent in the soft masculine voice was English.

"Yes, I'm sorry. I know it is early, but I am desperate. I need help."

"And might I inquire as to the nature of your request?"

"Well, it has to do with the . . . supernatural."

"Are you with the police or the newspapers?"

"No, I am in trouble. I need to talk to someone who knows—"

"Madame, excuse me for interrupting, but would you please tell me who gave you Mr. Bellcoda's name."

Clarissa paused before speaking.

"Madame Rosa."

"Please hold the line a moment, madame."

Spots swam before Clarissa's eyes as she walked up the slate-gray walk past slate-gray walls into a bare slate-gray courtyard. The house itself, although large and imposing, was predictably slate-gray. She wondered if the sudden absence of color had been too much of a shock to her vision, and her imagination was coloring it all gray.

Pressing the doorbell button produced no sound, so she used the heavy knocker on the plain slate-gray wooden door.

An Englishman, surprisingly young, answered. "Yes, Mr. Bellcoda is expecting you. Please step this way."

The servant led Clarissa into a sitting room. The inside of the house was not as colorless as the outside, but it was no more highly decorated. There were only the necessary furnishings, nothing that would betray the personality of the owner. After a few minutes, a stately woman walked into the sitting room.

Clarissa took note that she wore an excess of makeup. Her eyelids were painted blue and her lips an absolute red. Rouge extended upward from her cheeks almost to her temples, where it met her heavily penciled-in eyebrows. Her wrists were heavy with bracelets of varying widths and colors, some metal, some of woven materials, and her hands terminated in extraordinarily long fingers tipped with nails painted the same red as her lips.

As the woman flowed gracefully into the room in her long white gown, Clarissa stood.

"Good morning," the person said in a deep bass, "I am *Mr.* Bellcoda."

Clarissa swallowed hard and tried to mask the shock she felt at seeing this unusual personage. "Hello . . . I am Miss Arbor. I—"

"Sshhh . . ." Bellcoda hissed, silencing Clarissa as he floated over to her.

Clarissa felt beads of perspiration forming above her lip as she tried not to be put off by this person's appearance. Surely after what she had seen in the last few days, the sight of a man dressed as a woman was not going to unnerve her. But still, he was in such absolute contrast with his environment—ah, she realized, that is why everything is so plain and colorless. Mr. Bellcoda had to dominate his surroundings, she reasoned, he had to have no competition.

Bellcoda took her hand in his and looked deeply into her eyes. Then, slowly, his breathing became shallow and his eyelids grew heavy. Suddenly, his eyes widened and dilated completely. A smirk formed beneath Bellcoda's makeup, and then a smile split his face.

"Ha, ha, ha—pay no mind to the appearance of the man. It is his emptiness that is useful, just as it was your emptiness that has been useful to . . . the incubus."

Clarissa was shocked. Bellcoda knew! Perhaps Bellcoda could help.

"No, it is not Bellcoda that knows," the strange person said. "It is I that know. I look into your soul and your *karma*, and I know. Bellcoda is only a shell."

"Who . . . are you then?"

"That is a question I shall not answer. Bellcoda is so generous as to lend me the use of his body. My dear Clarissa, you have more urgent things to discover than my name."

"Yes, the incubus—his name is Bargolas—"

"Do not speak his name. His powers are lowly, but he does have ears, and for all eternity, death and bloodlust are his pursuit. And you, my dear Clarissa, have unleashed him upon the world once again. Murder is all around you, death and blood—all for the desperate craving of your loins."

Clarissa could not stop the hot tears running down her cheeks. They flowed into sobs that wracked her body.

"Silence! Do you come here to wallow in self-pity, or do you come for a knowledge that you do not have?"

She nodded her head, saying, "Yes, I need help. Please help me."

"The stones. The possessor of the stones can send him back. But only with the promise of his return—and a sacrifice. He will not return alone to his place of darkness. Only the force of your will is needed."

"What do you mean, a sacrifice?" stammered Clarissa.

"Only his father has the power to send him back without compromising. I repeat, this evil creature will return to darkness only under the condition that he does not go back alone. I can be no more explicit: who possesses the stones can send the incubus back to the darkness, providing the person who summoned this evil agrees to return with him."

"No, oh dear God, no . . . NO!"

"Silence! You are not the first to summon the incubus. Six times he has returned to this level of existence, six times I have foretold the misery . . . and six times he has been compelled to return. It will be many lives before you erase the traces of your deeds from this level of existence; your *karma* is very heavy. Your crime consists not in the thirst of your loneliness, but in the way you chose to quench it. The stones are a gift; they are also the key."

"I cannot do it, I cannot!"

"You can and you will. You are not an evil woman. You will not allow the death around you to continue while your lust is satisfied." The speaker paused for a few seconds. "Now I must leave. This silly shell grows weary with the strength of my presence. Bellcoda must rest. Leave here and do not return."

A moment later, Clarissa continued to look into Mr. Bellcoda's eyes as his pupils shrank to the size of a pin. His luminous blue irises shone through again, and he smiled a great crooked smile.

"I hope you got what you came here for, lady. I'll bet you did. I feel like I could sleep for a week."

"I—" Clarissa started to respond but was unable to finish

the thought. She brushed her hair back over her shoulders and walked toward the door.

"Wait a second, lady. Did the guide that talked to you tell you his name?"

Clarissa shook her head and walked out the door into the chill of the winter morning. There was no one to turn to for help except Bonnie. It was a horrible thing to ask of anyone but if she was going to stop the horrible killings someone had to help her.

Bonnie stood, staring at the creature. Clarissa watched her, aware of Bonnie's terror. She could see her friend trembling as she held out her hands. The Carnelian and Peridot were in plain sight. Bonnie bowed her head and gazed into the candle flame just as Clarissa had instructed her.

Crouching in the circle of salt drawn upon the floor of Clarissa's bedroom floor, Bonnie was frightened. Clarissa had told her everything, and Bonnie had not believed her until she had seen the creature. Then she had believed. But with that belief came the terror.

Bonnie looked back up at Clarissa, whose hand was folded tightly in that of the creature. A strange whimper came from the beast. It appeared to know what was happening, but it was powerless as long as Clarissa commanded it while holding the stones.

"Remember what I told you, Bonnie, remember . . ."

After a while, Bonnie looked up and saw that both the creature and Clarissa were gone. She had neither seen nor heard them go, but she knew that they would not return—at least, not Clarissa. Suddenly the candlelight reflected from the two stones on the floor where Bargolas and Clarissa had been moments before.

Stiffly, Bonnie stood and walked over to the stones. She picked them up and put them in a large leather bag together with *The Maleficuarm*.

For poor Bonnie, several weeks of torturous nightmares followed the disappearance of Clarissa and the creature she had . . . But Bonnie remembered Clarissa's instructions clearly. After a while, as the nightmares continued, she realized the only way she was gong to find peace was to get rid of that evil book.

Several times she considered burning the book. However, each time she did so, she would get such an agonizing headache that she would be unable to continue.

Then one day, as her friend Emma sat with her in her kitchen drinking tea and excitedly telling her of her plans to move out West, Bonnie suddenly stood and stepped to the counter. She knew the book was buried amid the junk piled in the drawers. She was torn between not wanting to touch it and desperately wanting to get rid of it. She turned back around to Emma, the confusion easily read in her face.

"I have something I have to give you, Emma."

Months later, in Gresham, Oregon, when Emma finally unpacked the remainder of her boxes, she came upon the package Bonnie had given her. Emma remembered the warning Bonnie had given her and she simply slipped the package onto the top shelf of a closet.

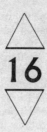

16

Othello, 1970

Mike lay on his belly within the illuminated golden circle of salt and squeezed his eyes shut. He began to pray to God and Jesus Christ. He bartered—a lifetime of good deeds if they would just spare him this horrible fate. Stan listened to him pray, sniffling and sobbing, and then turned his attention to the approaching menace.

Watching the shadow grow closer and hearing the din grow louder, Stan began to crack under the strain. He fell and landed on Mike, who shook violently as he prayed. Believing these moments to be the last of his life, Stan felt a desperate need for physical contact with his friend, and he grabbed a handful of Mike's shirt.

The sound was unbearable. To Stan, it seemed to be rapidly disintegrating his brain. Suddenly it took on the qualities of a voice speaking. The intense loudness of the voice made it impossible to make out the words, if indeed words were being spoken. The voice was like a storm, like a tornado that sucked and tore at their clothing as it blew across them. The force of this storm threatened to uproot them from their prone positions and toss them into the abyss outside the circle.

The two boys flailed about; they grabbed onto one another, they groped for something on the bare floor to anchor to, they grasped in desperation at the candles. Mike knocked one over, extinguishing its flame. Instantly, there was a change. The roaring diminished and the darkness around them seemed to lessen a bit.

Mike was too much in panic to make any connection, but Stan seized upon the situation and began extinguishing the other candles. One by one, as the candles were snuffed out, the brightness of the winter afternoon returned and the horrible noise left their heads. Soon it was over.

Stan knelt in front of the candles, graceful wisps of smoke still curving and twisting in the air, as Mike pushed himself off the floor with his hand. He looked around the room and saw the security of the door and the window and a dirty wooden floor beneath them.

"It's over . . . I think," said Stan, cautiously.

Mike made no response; he wiped the tears from his face and took a deep breath, silently thanking God for his life.

Without a word, Stan pushed away a patch of salt and stepped unsteadily out of the circle. He stumbled to the door, feeling numb and cold. He turned back to the circle to see Mike standing up. The front of his light-blue cords was wet, but Mike didn't seem to notice. With difficulty, he walked out of the circle. He pushed past Stan and, with sudden energy, dashed from the room. As Stan himself left the bedroom, he saw the door to the bathroom close; shortly after, he heard the sounds of vomiting.

Mike knelt over the white porcelain toilet and stared into the fresh water, rising to fill the bowl again. The water's clarity seemed somehow comforting. It was transparent, Mike thought to himself, there was nothing hidden in it. For a moment, he felt as though he might vomit again; the feeling subsided, and he released his death grip on the toilet.

"Damn the fuckin' day I ever laid eyes on Stan Fuller." He spoke into the white cavern, smelling the strong odor of disinfectant and feeling the echo of his words bang against his eardrums.

Stan, meanwhile, could not stop shivering, though he concentrated as hard as he could. His hands were vibrating so fast they appeared out of focus. He realized that he had never been so scared in his entire life. Swallowing hard, he tried to suppress the urge to throw up like Mike had been doing the past several minutes. But the harder his heart pounded, the queasier his stomach felt.

The bathroom door opened, and Stan heard soft footsteps padding toward Mike's bedroom. Stan waited several minutes for Mike to come back out, but he didn't. Stan decided to venture into Mike's room and see if he was okay. He knew Mike was not feeling especially friendly toward him at the moment, but he believed the two of them had to work together to find an answer to their horrible problem—and soon.

Stan rapped lightly on Mike's bedroom door. There was no answer, so he opened it a crack. Mike had gotten as far as changing his pants, but then he had apparently lain down on his bed and fallen fast asleep. Stan wondered how Mike could sleep after all he had been through in the last hour. God, had it been only an hour? It had seemed like half their lifetimes. Stan couldn't believe it, but he too felt exhausted. Now he knew how Mike could go to sleep—it sounded like such a good idea. Quietly closing the door behind him, Stan walked into the living room, slumped down in a chair, and fell asleep.

Mike looked on in horror at the angry red glow. A hand, thorny and covered with a stench of slime, reached out for him and caught him by the arm. Mike screamed, his voice cracking loudly with adolescence, and fought against the powerful grip. Stan also pounded upon the grotesque hand, but they were unable to loosen its grip on Mike. It squeezed and squeezed, with superhuman pressure, until Mike could feel blood squirting from his arm. He could see his own blood running down his arms and face. His tongue and eyes began to swell under the grip of doom, and he screamed again, this time a scream of death.

"Mike, Mike . . ."

Mike's eyes fluttered open and he flung his arm up, catching Stan across the face and knocking him into the closet door. Stan put his hand up to his mouth and felt the blood beginning to escape from the gash. Deciding not to get too close again, he yelled, "Wake up, Mike! You're dreamin'!"

Mike weaved, then leaned over the side of the bed and vomited again. He heaved and heaved until there was nothing left in his stomach. The acrid odor of bile and partially digested food filled the room, and Stan jumped to his feet, overcome by the smell. He barely made it into the bathroom before his own stomach followed suit and emptied itself into the toilet.

Later, after the boys had cleaned themselves up, they sat at the counter in the kitchen and drank hot tea. Both of them drank it without their usual sugar; they craved the bitterness of the dark tea, prayed to God that it would settle their stomachs. Neither of them spoke or even looked at the other for a long time.

Eventually, they agreed to go back to Lea's bedroom and investigate. They entered cautiously, turning on the bright ceiling light. It seemed all too normal. Stan swept up the salt, and they rolled back the rug. After arranging the furniture, they were beginning to feel better. Mike, trying to relieve the stress of the situation, commented in a Groucho Marx voice that things were beginning to get out of hand. Then he mimed a cigar in his hand and wiggled his eyebrows up and down; Stan laughed a bit self-consciously, but laughed nonetheless.

When Mike opened the front door and the blast of freezing night air slammed into their faces, they knew that taking a walk would do more for them than twenty cups of tea. The wind bit sharply at their ears and noses. Their moist lips dried and felt the beginnings of splitting. Crunch. CRUNCH. CRUNCH. The icy snow resisted, then gave way beneath their weight.

Suddenly Stan broke away and ran down the street. He stopped abruptly, only to slide ten more feet on the shiny surface. He turned around to look at Mike, who was lighting a cigarette. Quickly, Stan reached down and formed a snowball, the ice jabbing his bare hands painfully, and, laughing, threw it at Mike. It fell several feet to Mike's left.

"You throw like a girl, Fuller."

Before Mike could even finish his accusation, Stan had launched another snowball at him. This one caught Mike square on the thigh.

"Ouch! You asshole!"

"I may throw like a girl, but I still gotcha!" Stan laughed as he watched Mike reaching down to construct his own snowy projectile. Before Mike could send his through the air, Stan was off and running down the icy streets, laughing like a maniac. Mike took off after him, slipping and sliding, also laughing.

From the shadows, a strange sound stopped Mike in his tracks. A clickety-clicking echoed in the icy streets, and then the whoosh of some snow sliding from a warm roof. Mike's alarm subsided as he looked all around his neighborhood, the ice and snow so beautiful that he wished the time would stand still. He looked up into the bright sky. The low clouds were illuminated by the lights of the town, and the first flakes of another snowfall were floating down.

Pow! Another missile hit him on the back of his coat. He looked around at Stan, who had doubled back around a house and lobbed another one at him. Mike flipped him the finger, and Stan smiled back wickedly.

After the boys had gotten rid of some the tremendous stress and tension from the recent events, they climbed into Mike's truck and headed for the hospital to see Pam.

17

Pam looked around the room for some water. Her throat was dry and sore. Her head ached, and her eyes burned from crying. The ankle hurt only a little bit now, sending a dull throbbing up her leg.

She hadn't answered any questions. She would have told them everything, but something prevented her from talking. Every time she tried to speak, it felt as though worms were crawling in her brain and around her heart, squeezing her lungs and constricting her breathing. If she didn't talk, and didn't think about the previous night, she would begin to calm down and feel almost peaceful.

Rachel, the floor nurse, walked into the room. She glanced down at Pam with a quizzical expression and refilled the water jug. Pam leaned across the bed and poured herself a glass of water, then drank it down in two noisy gulps.

Rachel watched her, a bit confused. Rachel couldn't understand why she had felt compelled to come in here and fill the water jug; she had been on her way to relieve Kelly. She shook her head and quietly left the room.

A few minutes later, Mike and Stan entered Room 112. Quickly they closed the door behind them, hoping to get enough time with Pam before they got caught; the last thing they wanted to do was make explanations. They stood at the foot of her bed and said hello. Pam turned her head away from them and refused to respond.

While staring at Pam, Stan all of a sudden had the impression that there was something moving around her head, something translucent. It moved weirdly, slithering around Pam's head and shoulders, now appearing to divide into numerous wormlike shapes. Stan slipped into a trance, momentarily hypnotized by the shapes grouping above Pam's head. There appeared to be five or six of them. Slowly, two of them separated from the others and drifted away from the girl. Soon they began to close in on the two boys.

"Hey! Hey, man, what are you doin' now?" growled Mike.

Stan shifted his eyes from the approaching menace to Mike and then back. Looking back at Mike again, he snapped out of it and grabbed Mike's coat sleeve, pulling him from the room saying, "We got to get out of here, fast!"

At the doorway, Stan turned and looked back. The strange shapes seemed to be picking up speed and were drawing still nearer.

"Come on, come on, come on," chanted Stan, urgently, as the two hurried along the brightly waxed linoleum to the end of the hall. There, Stan turned to check once again.

"What the fuck, Fuller? I know you see something—what the hell is it?"

"Wait," Stand said harshly.

Mike felt resentful as he followed Stan's gaze toward Pam's door. When he saw the wormlike shapes hovering in the hallway, however, he caught his breath and whispered, "Holy fucking shit!"

The shapes had stopped outside Pam's door. The two boys stood at the end of the hall with their mouths open as, some twenty feet beyond Room 112, Nurse Rachel stepped from another corridor into the hallway, carrying a tray of juice. She walked now in the direction of Mike and Stan, directly toward the wormlike shapes.

Rachel, age forty-three, had been working at Othello Hospital longer than anyone else on the staff. She wasn't head nurse—and she liked it that way; she didn't covet the aggravation that came with the extra responsibility. And today there had already been far too much aggravation.

Rachel wondered why the two young fellows standing at the end of the hall were staring at her; then she realized, as she drew nearer, that they were actually looking off to the side, toward one of the rooms. She turned her eyes to her right and saw what the kids were staring at—fat, ghostly worms floating in midair. She stopped and opened her mouth to scream but stopped short, instead bravely creeping closer to the strange sight.

Stan and Mike watched with fear and curiosity as Rachel drew closer to the ectoplasm. When she stood two feet away from the floating creatures, she turned to set her tray down on the floor. As she tilted her head sideways, the worms coiled around it, and, before she knew what was happening, they had penetrated her and vanished from sight.

"Shit!" exclaimed Mike, dumbfoundedly.

"Yeah," Stan muttered. He started to walk toward the nurse, but Mike grabbed him by the shoulder.

"Don't be stupid!"

Stan didn't respond, but neither did he go any closer.

Rachel just stood there, wearing a dazed expression. Then suddenly a wide smile split her face and she hugged herself tightly. Slowly at first, then faster and faster, she began to spin around and around, singing in a strange, harsh voice that made the boys' blood run cold. "Oh, pretty pretty Pam . . . here I come my pretty pretty . . . oh, my pretty pretty Pam . . ."

"Shouldn't we have told someone?" Stan looked out the cracked window of the Ranchero as it sped down Seventh Street toward Mike's house. The cracked glass defracted the light and centered Stan's concentration.

"Yeah, sure! Sure as shit, we're gonna tell someone we saw a ghost possess that nurse. Yeah, right—they'd stick us in the bug-house just like that." Mike snapped his fingers for emphasis.

"What are we gonna do about Cliff and Peggy? It was a good idea to come and see Pam first, but now it's almost seven-thirty. It's already dark, and God knows I don't want to go back out there in the dark." Stan continued to stare out the window at the passing scenery.

"Shit! I don't want to go back out there at all. Why don't

we just tell the sheriff they're out at the house, and let him go check?'' Mike glanced across the cab to Stan, who was now looking down at the floor with his hands tucked into his crotch.

''You know we can't,'' Stan said slowly. ''If we tell him that, we'll get caught up in trying to avoid telling him the reason *we* were out there.''

''Why? Kids have been goin' out there for years. He won't think there's anything special going on.''

Mike blew cigarette smoke out the window. Neither boy spoke for a minute.

Finally, Stan broke the silence. ''Yeah, maybe it does make sense. Okay, let's go talk to the cops.''

''Well, it don't look like we'll have to wait long,'' Mike remarked as he turned the corner from Hemlock onto Main Street. ''There's Johnston parked in front of Koster Realty.'' Mike slowed the Ranchero and turned into the parking lot of the realty.

Sheriff Johnston had parked his brand-new patrol car ''nose in'' and was pouring himself a cup of coffee from his thermos as Mike swung the Ranchero around to back in beside him. The sheriff rolled his window down and greeted Mike.

''Hey, Mike! How you doin'?''

''Okay.''

''Did you think of somethin' that might help us figure out where Cliff and Peggy have gotten off to?''

''Might've. I'm not sure. Think I heard him talkin' one day 'bout goin' out to that old haunted house on the highway, five miles past Killer Corner. You know where Williamson chopped up his wife in the '50s.''

Sheriff Johnston looked Mike in the eye and knew that the boy had known this all along. He took a deep breath and calmed himself. There was something pretty peculiar going on, and if this kid was going to be any help, he'd have to stay on good terms with him.

''Ya know,'' the sheriff began, ''I should have thought of that myself. A lot of you kids go out there to try to scare the shit out of each other. Been a lot of people, both kids and adults, who have used that old house out there to test their courage. I remember when Mr. Williamson was a preacher, well respected and all that and then all of a sudden . . .''

Johnston slurped loudly from his plastic cup. "Yep, ever since the tragedy, people been going out there for excitement, tryin' to throw a good scare into themselves." He paused to take another mouthful. "Yep, I should have guessed it myself."

Mike looked away and pretended to watch the traffic on Main Street. He was sure the sheriff knew he'd been holding out on him. He also knew Johnston was trying to get more information out of him.

"Say, Mike, you and your friend there feel like takin' a little ride with me to check it out?"

"I'd like to, Sheriff, but it's past dinner time and my parents are gonna kick my tail if I don't show up soon. But I'd appreciate it if you'd let me know when you find out anything."

"Yeah, I'll do that," the sheriff answered curtly, annoyed at Mike's fake deference.

"Uh . . . ya know what happened with Pam's leg," Mike ventured cautiously. "There might be some sort of wild animal out there—" Mike stopped abruptly. He wanted to warn the sheriff but still didn't want to involve himself any more than he already was. "Well, you got a gun so I s'pose you probably ain't too worried. I gotta get goin'. See ya." Mike shifted the Ranchero into low and pulled out.

Johnston picked up his radio microphone and called in to the station. After three attempts, he threw the mike across the seat and growled. "Damned Milly. Probably on another one of her coffee breaks."

He eased the police car into gear and pulled onto Main Street, heading out of town toward Killer Corner.

The incubus perched on top of the house like an ancient gargoyle, gently clicking his talons against his teeth. He turned his empty eyes toward the dark sky. Soon he would follow his obsession back into Othello. He smiled to himself, drooling in anticipation and muttering incessantly, "Ohhhoooo, pretty pretty Pam . . . pretty pretty . . ."

The dusky winter light made it difficult for Sheriff Johnston to maneuver the car up the snow-frozen drive to the old Williamson place. The route was a familiar one to him. Over the years he had checked the place out many a time, hoping to

catch some of the vandals who were demolishing the house
bit by bit.

He frowned, peering through the hazy light, and blinked a
couple of times. It was hard to tell for sure, but it looked like
something was sitting on top of the house. Who or what could
be up there? What . . . ? Now it was gone. The sheriff wondered if the light was playing tricks on him—or maybe Cliff
and Peggy were here after all. But it just didn't figure. This
wasn't exactly the sort of place you'd use as a love nest. And
what would they be doing on the roof?

His tires crunched loudly against the snow. Details were
difficult to make out against the light; the house was a blocky
shadow as he pulled up in front of it, made a wide circle,
and checked the place out thoroughly before backing up to
the steps and parking.

Johnston left the car running as he stepped out and shut the
door, the sound carrying like a gunshot across the frozen
landscape. An image of Pam with the claw marks on her
ankle shot through his mind. He reached down, unsnapped
his holster strap, and removed his revolver. It felt heavy and
secure in his hand.

Looking down near the stairs he saw the frozen drops of
blood. Fresh tire tracks crisscrossed the area as well as footprints. The sheriff even noticed the coyote tracks leading up
to the stairs, but he missed the inhuman tracks just on the
other side of the snowy ruts.

Johnston walked up the stairs and along the perimeter of
the porch to the front door, his boots echoing with authority.
The door stood ajar, and he walked in unhesitantly.

Without the slightest warning, talons came down across
Johnston's face, tearing an eye from its socket and sending it
across the room to land in a bloody mass on the floor. The
gun fell from his hand and slid, spinning, under the staircase.
The sheriff fell unconscious.

The incubus, Bargolas, stood above the sheriff with his
head cocked sideways and his black eyes glittering in the last
light of the day. Reaching down with his powerful arm, he
grabbed the man by the leg and dragged him from the living
room, through the kitchen, and down the stairs into the basement. The sheriff's head bounced against the steps, and a
dark-red stain trailed behind him.

Once in the basement, Bargolas gingerly pushed the man into a heap in the corner and stepped back to look at his victim and chant again: "Pretty pretty Pam . . . eat pretty pretty Pam . . ."

His face split by the evil broken-tooth grin, he turned away from his victim and started to bound up the stairs. He stopped before he reached the top, however, and slowly climbed back down. He stood once more in front of the cop. All at once he crouched and yanked one of the man's legs off the floor.

The incubus held the leg tightly with his short arms and brought his powerful jaws together. The moist crunch told him that he had crushed the sheriff's tibia. With the metallic taste of the blood still in his mouth, he picked up the other leg to do the same. This time, as the monster closed his jaw around muscle and bone, Johnston groaned. Bargolas smiled, knowing that his prey would still be alive and fresh when he returned.

Emerging into the evening, the incubus saw a disturbing sight. The sheriff's car was parked outside the house with its engine growling threateningly. Cautiously, the incubus approached the car. He peered into the windows and drummed his talons upon the roof. He tried the door, fumbling with the shiny handle; after a few minutes, the door opened and he crawled in.

At first, he scrambled straight across the seat, ending up on the passenger side, but eventually he turned his body around and squeezed his powerful torso behind the steering wheel. He gripped the wheel with his short arms while his longer arms explored the dash controls. While he was thrashing about, his foot fell heavily upon the gas pedal and the engine roared like an angry animal. The windshield wipers flipped back and forth, the radio blared, and the siren began to wail. In panic, the monster grabbed the gearshift lever, and the transmission dropped into reverse. The car lurched backward and crashed into the porch stairs, killing the engine. The siren continued its shrill cry until an accidental brush of the creature's hand flipped the switch off.

Fury gripped the incubus, and he screamed his rage. He lowered his head and began to gnaw on the steering wheel with his powerful teeth. The hard plastic began to peel away in shards, and a moment later the wheel snapped, leaving a large chunk of fiberglass in the creature's mouth. He spit it out angrily and began raking his talons across the seat of the patrol car. Within seconds, he had shredded the fabric, and bits of it clung to his hands and arms.

Clumsily pulling on the door handle, the creature tried to open the car door. However, the door was jammed against the side of the porch and would not budge. In an insane fury, he bashed his head and fists against the windows. Even the tempered safety-glass cracked under the attack. Finally, the window on the passenger side shattered, and a million pieces of glass sprayed across the frozen snow, looking like ice crystals.

Bargolas crawled through the broken window. It was a tight fit, and the remaining shards of glass cut his skin. Rivulets of black-red blood dripped down his thighs as he stood upon the snow. Suddenly, he became as still as the winter night. He looked up into the cloudless sky and bathed himself in the bright moonlight.

Now he began to move slowly across the white expanse, his color gradually lightening. After a few minutes of walking, he blended into the snow. Standing on top of the knoll, he looked down upon the lights of Othello and once again muttered to himself, "Pretty pretty Pam . . ."

"Hello. I'm calling about one of your patients. Her name is Pam Getner, in Room 112 . . ."

"Yes, are you related to her?"

"No, I'm just a friend . . ."

"What can I do for you?"

"I was just wondering how she's doing. Is her ankle better? Has she started talking?" Stan's hand was sweating as he held the receiver and waited for an answer. He looked over at Mike, sitting in the Ranchero. Slowly Stan exhaled a cloud of steam in the harsh light of the phone booth.

"Well, it took a few stitches, but her ankle is just fine. I'm sorry to say that she hasn't begun to talk yet. I'm sure it's just shock; she should be fine in a few days. I wouldn't worry."

"Uh . . . how's the nurse?"

"What do you mean?"

"Well, uh . . . when we were visiting this afternoon, the nurse that was looking in on Pam seemed kinda sick."

"Oh, you must mean Rachel. Yes, she said she felt a bit queasy and took the rest of the day off."

"I see, well I'm glad she's okay. Yeah . . . well, thanks a lot."

Stan walked back to the warmth of the Ranchero. He closed the door behind himself and shrugged his shoulders.

"I guess nothin' happened to the nurse we saw flip out. She went home because she was feelin' sick."

"Yeah, I'll bet."

"She sure has been cryin' a lot lately," remarked Matt.

"She's teething," answered Trish. "I stuck my finger in her mouth and I could feel something on her bottom jaw—probably a tooth."

"Well, the main thing right now is that she's quiet for once." He looked up at Trish, standing over him as he enjoyed his favorite brown recliner. Reaching up, he grasped her firmly by the arm and pulled her down into the chair with him. She laughed as her soft brown hair fell across her face.

Matt combed her hair back with his fingers and traced the outline of her lips. Their foreheads touched as they looked into each other's eyes. Trish looped her hands around her husband's neck and kissed him on the lips. His hands flowed across her body, lingering at the nape of her neck. He grabbed a handful of her beautiful long hair and pulled himself lower, nuzzling his face into her breasts. Gently he slid the two of them from the chair to the carpet. Trish laughed as his body pressed urgently onto hers. But her laugh was drowned in his passion.

From outside the family room window, the incubus watched them through a crack in the drapes. His eyes caught the soft light of the fireplace and noted the passion that culminated not in destruction but in love—a love he had known once but could never know again. His loins ached unbearably; he bit his lip.

His talons skittered across the surface of the frozen snow as he circled the house looking for a way in. A smile crept across his face when he spied a narrow opaque window cracked open a few inches.

His talons clicked against the aluminum window frame as he raised his powerful body up to its level. The claws of his feet dug into the metal while his hands pried the opening wider. He dropped into the bathroom and immediately began a color shift. Soon he was the gray-black of shadows.

He clicked softly across the linoleum and peered into the hall. Just outside the doorway, he stopped. Listening carefully, he could hear delicate breathing. The sound aroused him, and he traced it to a darkened room with the door standing ajar.

He entered the room cautiously and approached the crib. He was overcome by the beauty of the sleeping child. She was female—he could see it in her aura. He was so engrossed by the baby girl that he forgot about the couple in the other room and the spell he had begun to weave.

Gripping the edge of the crib with the hands of his short arms, he lay his chin down upon his hands and gazed longingly at the child. She sparked a memory . . .

Reaching into the crib with his longer left arm, he tenderly pulled the blankets from the sleeping baby's body. She shivered once and then sighed deeply. The cold eyes of the incubus traveled the length of her body. Its plumpness, its smooth softness, aroused him deeply. Slimy brown strings of drool ran from his mouth onto the child's arm as his outstretched hand touched her diaper. A filthy, blood-stained talon sliced through the cloth, leaving her innocent body exposed.

"Ahhh . . ." Matt released, quivering over Trish. She loosened her grip on his arms as he slid gently out of her. He kissed her neck and rolled over onto the floor beside her, his heart still pounding in his ears.

Trish arranged her clothing and sat up. She threw back her hair with a flick of her head and stood up, smiling. "I need to go check on Laura."

Matt watched her walk from the room, wiping the sweat from her temples onto her sleeve, then he lay his head back on the floor, but just as it touched the nubby carpet, he heard a terrifying scream from Laura's bedroom. Matt bounded to his feet and dashed through the house, hearing a crash and another scream.

The room was flooded with light, and an icy draft was coming in through a large, jagged hole in the window near the foot of Laura's crib. Trish stood with her hands to her mouth, staring toward the window. In the next instant, she bounded to the crib and swept Laura into her arms. The baby, stark naked, sputtered and began to wail loudly. Trish grabbed a blanket and wrapped it around Laura, then began to cry spasmodically.

"Oh, Matt . . . somebody was here . . . the window," she sobbed, barely able to get her breath as Matt encircled both of them within his strong arms.

After a few seconds, Matt released them and walked aggressively over to the smashed window. He surveyed the area outside but could see no sign of the intruder. He returned to Trish and led her into their bedroom, where he called the police from the extension phone on the nightstand. He noticed then the blood seeping through the baby blanket from Laura's leg. He took the child from Trish. A terrible smell assulted him as he pulled his hand away from some sort of sticky slime. For a moment he just stood there wondering with pent-up terror just what the hell had been in there.

Twenty minutes later, Matt greeted Deputy Hastings at the front door. "Where's Sheriff Johnston?"

Hastings stammered, "Uh . . . he's, uh, tracking down a lead on something else. How's your wife doing?"

"Okay. It looks like the baby took a scratch on her leg when Trish grabbed her from the crib. Let me show you the room where the guy jumped out the window."

Laura's room was cold, and the sheer curtains fluttered lightly. There were a few pieces of glass on the floor, but most had fallen outside.

"How do you think he got in, Matt?"

Matt shook his head.

"I'm gonna go outside and take a look around. You just stay in here with your wife and keep the door locked. Don't open it for anyone except me. Okay?"

"Okay."

Hastings took his gun from the holster and walked out into the bright winter moonlight. Looking across the front of the house, he saw nothing unusual. He turned around and glanced toward the road. It was a good quarter of a mile to the highway, but it was flat and unbroken—not a tree or even a rock sticking up. Just flat snow, all the way to the road. Hastings walked cautiously along the side of the house and peered around the corner into the backyard. He saw the lights of Othello about half a mile away.

He examined the ground near the broken window and frowned when he spotted what looked like deep impressions in the snow. He couldn't tell what they were, however, because of all the foot traffic that had been around the house, leaving boot tracks. Then he saw the smaller window standing open. He dragged a garbage can over and stood on it to inspect the opaque bathroom window. In the moonlight, he could see deep scars in the window's metal frame.

"Now what the fuck could have done that?" Hastings said to himself.

18

Othello, 1951

Footsteps echoed from the stairway. Lydia scrambled out of bed, the old book in her hand, and lifted up the corner of the mattress. She virtually threw the book between the box spring and mattress, dropped the corner, and hurriedly crawled back into bed, pulling the covers up around her neck—just before Seth walked into the room. He stood for a minute, looking around.

"Did you forget something?" Lydia asked sweetly.

"My watch," Seth remarked offhandedly.

"Are you sure you don't want me to get up and fix you some breakfast?"

"No." Seth seemed distracted. "I'm probably going to be late for the train as it is."

Lydia nodded her head in agreement, wanting to stay in bed, anyway. In fact, she was anxious for him to be gone. She had been planning this weekend for a month, ever since she had found out that Seth's brother was getting married. Seth had to go back to Georgia for the wedding, just as she had to be the dutiful wife and stay home. After all, they didn't have enough money for both of them to go. At least, that was what Seth told his father.

Lydia knew better: Seth was ashamed to take her home to

his folks. She had never met them, and she doubted that she
ever would. But at this point, it didn't matter much anymore.

"I'll be home late Saturday evening," he said, walking
from the room without so much as a goodbye.

Lydia heard Seth's leather shoes slap loudly against the
wood again as he hurried down the stairs and out the door.
She heard the car engine rumble beneath her window, and
she felt a growing sense of excitement.

Gone, she thought happily. Four whole days to myself.
Grinning, she slipped out of bed once again and lifted the
corner of her mattress. She pulled the worn book from its
hiding place and ran her hand over its surface, wondering if
she wasn't just a little bit crazy to believe that old hag. But
the idea excited her. She knew, once she heard the story, that
she had to give it a try.

Lydia had spent the last two weeks preparing for this day.
She had spared no effort to bring together all the elements to
make the magic work. She started by making all of her own
candles. She had scented them with rosemary and lilac, sprinkled them with water she herself had blessed under the full
moon a week earlier, wrapped them in a silk scarf, placed
them in a box, and buried them in the backyard.

The old woman told her she would need some special stones
that were hard to find in these parts. It turned out the woman
had them, so she gave them to Lydia with the express instruc-
tion to place them in linen and put them under her pillow.
One of them, called Peridot, was green and translucent. The
other, Carnelian, was a reddish stone. The old woman had
said these were "his" favorite stones, and when they were
together in the same circle, they provided an irresistible at-
traction.

It was really a simple matter, she had said. You perform
the ceremony at his favorite time of the night, and use all his
favorite things—his favorite stones, scents, colors, and
sounds—and then ask him to come to you. If you do everything right, it's a sure bet.

Lydia opened the book. *The Maleficuarm* had originally
been written in 1603. It had been translated from the Latin
in 1845, and the edition that Lydia held in her hands was the
1864 printing by Triton Publishing, Inc., London. The book,
smelling moldy, seemed even older.

Lydia's stomach growled with hunger. She looked at the clock. It was nearly 9:00 A.M., well past the time that she and Seth usually ate breakfast. This was a special day, however; she could have no food or drink save water. She raised one of her eyebrows and said to herself, "It's gonna be a long day."

She walked into the bathroom and turned the water on to prepare her special bath. Into the steaming water she poured a mixture of olive oil, honey, red wine, and her own blood and urine, all of which she had mixed earlier with a knife—a special knife, called an *Athame*. Actually, it had been just a regular hunting knife, but it too underwent a transformation at the time of the last full moon. Lydia had painted runes on the handle and then buried it, point down, in the backyard.

She returned to the bedroom and retrieved *The Maleficuarm*. She set it on the rim of the bathtub, making sure that it would not tip over into the water. Then she stepped into the hot liquid and uttered a quiet sigh.

After a few minutes of relaxing, she leaned over the book and began to recite the purification spell. The words echoed in the bathroom and seemed to fill the whole house. The sound expanded and compressed in regular patterns of waves, waves that rolled over her and made her feel both powerful and pure. All fear, all hesitation washed away like the soil from her skin.

> WATER AND SALT
> PURE AND POWERFUL
> WASH AWAY THE STAINS
> OF PANITACAS AND WOE
> CLEAN MY POWER AS I
> CLEAN MY WORTHLESS SHELL . . .

Suddenly she was standing in the bathtub, water dripping from her skin onto empty white enamel. For a moment she was frightened. She didn't remember finishing the spell, nor did she recall pulling the plug. She took a deep breath, and a feeling of calmness spread throughout her being. She stepped from the tub to the sink and wiped off the steamy mirror with a towel, then filled a glass with water. The water had barely touched her lips when she felt a warm glow spread across her body. She stared into the mirror and saw an odd radiance streaming from her eyes. She knew she was opening parts of herself that she had only guessed about. She also knew there was no turning back now.

Back in the bedroom, Lydia slipped on her robe. She made her way down to the kitchen and, once again, stopped for a drink from the faucet; as before, the very contact of water on her lips gave her a feeling of warmth and well-being throughout. Elated, she walked to the basement door and flipped on the light. Once down the steep wooden stairs, she stepped into a corner where a stack of broken-down cardboard boxes stood. Digging down into the cardboard pile, she removed a blue cotton bag.

From this bag she extracted four of her handmade candles, her *Athame*, and the two power stones, and set them on the dirt floor. From the corner under the stairs she retrieved a bag of salt and began pouring it out upon the floor in the form of a circle, leaving one section of the circle broken by a space about a foot wide. She entered the circle through this space and placed the four candles according to the directions. After lighting the candles, she walked back up to the top of the stairs and turned off the light. Slowly descending the stairs, she looked suspiciously into the shadows created by the hissing candle flames.

She felt a rush of excitement. One part of her wanted to stop this madness, go back upstairs, and just forget the whole thing. However, another part of her wanted to continue and didn't really care about the consequences. Even eternal damnation had to be more interesting than the life she had now.

Lydia picked up the two power stones and her *Athame*. Then she let her robe fall to the floor. Walking back into the circle, she lifted the bag of salt, poured from it to close the entrance, and set the bag outside the circle. Placing the Carnelian in her right hand and the Peridot in her left, she lay her naked body on the cold dirt floor. She arranged her hair so that it flowed out from her head in a golden halo. Then she placed the *Athame* on the milky skin of her abdomen. The knife was arranged so that the point just touched her pubic hair and the handle rested just below her breasts.

Closing her eyes, she felt a flush spreading up from her feet. When it reached her stomach where the *Athame* lay, it felt as if the knife was on fire. She resisted the temptation to look. Suddenly, the stones in her hand began to feel like lumps of ice. The more they numbed her hands, the tighter she squeezed. Freezing water crawled rapidly up her arms and began to seek the heat on her abdomen. She knew she must call his name now before she became lost in the imminent explosion of fire and ice. The cold seized her lungs; almost unable to draw a breath, she screamed out: "BAR-GOLAS!" Then she lost consciousness.

Lydia opened her eyes and saw only blackness. She suffered a moment of panic, fearing she might have died, before she became conscious of the weight of the knife still resting upon the altar of her belly. The stones were hard sweaty lumps in her hands; she relaxed her grip and let them fall into the dirt. She carefully removed the knife and set it aside, then stood up in the darkness.

She could make out a tiny sliver of light under the closed basement door at the top of the stairs. Using it as her beacon, she stepped out of the circle and up the stairs. Upon opening the door, she discovered that the light was not the light of day but the outside porch light which she left on all the time. Evening had come. She had spent the entire day in the grip of the first part of the summoning.

Still naked, she entered the living room and looked at the clock on the wall. It was a quarter after seven. She shook her head in disbelief. The emptiness in her stomach gnawed at her, but she was determined to finish this. She must not eat, but she could have water. Back in the kitchen, she turned on the tap and let the water run until it was ice-cold. She filled a glass and brought it to her lips. The instant the water touched her lips, she reeled and began to vomit violently from an empty stomach. Her sides ached with the wracking pain of dry heaves. Momentarily, the wave of sickness left her and she walked weakly upstairs to her bedroom.

Glancing in the mirror, she was shocked by her appearance. Her face was pale and her lips bloodless. Her hair was tangled and caked with dirt—as was her skin. Disgusted, she walked into the bathroom to run herself another bath. She

still had three hours before it was time for the final part of
the summoning.

When she emerged from her bath she felt refreshed, if still
somewhat hungry. She put on a clean robe and brought *The
Maleficuarm* downstairs with her. It was a deep, moonless
night. All the windows in the house reflected her own image
back to her. She was aware of a strange contrast between
what she saw and how she felt inside. Sitting down on the
worn couch, she opened the book to a place she had marked
with a dog-ear and began to memorize the invocation. Twenty
minutes later, she felt confident with the passage and, her
mind resolved, headed for the basement. She felt a power she
hadn't known before. She was excited by the possibilities as
she closed the door to the basement and began climbing down
the stairs.

The ceiling light still shone dimly as she once again
rummaged around in the blue cotton bag for candles. This
time, she took out twenty-four, one for each house of the
zodiac and one for each halfway marker. Next, she pulled
out a large, moist chunk of clay, which she fashioned into
makeshift candle holders, and arranged the candles in a
circle.

From the pile of cardboard, she removed one sheet onto
which she had copied the designs directly and as accurately
as she could from *The Maleficuarm*. She set this design into
the center of the circle and proceeded to light all the candles.
Once they were lit, she hurried up the steps to switch the
basement light off. Walking carefully back down the stairs,
she was awed by the dramatic sight of all twenty-four candles
alive with brightness. It gave the whole scene a truly religious
feel. Standing there in a tremble, she knew, for the first time
really knew, that she was going to succeed.

She retrieved the Carnelian and Peridot and placed them in
the center of the circle, along with her *Athame*. Then she
added a small silver bell with the name BARGOLAS in-
scribed across the side. Finally, she removed a small bowl,
filled it with alcohol, placed the bowl into the circle, and set
the alcohol on fire. She sprinkled lavender and vervain into
the flame, bringing forth a pungent aroma that filled the cool
basement.

She removed her robe and grabbed the bag of salt to pour

a circle around the candles. Once she had stepped inside and closed the circle of salt, she began the ceremony. Raising the *Athame* high above her head, she muttered:

Bargolas, I summon you from the bowels of darkness to my service.

She felt a rush of energy as she thrust the *Athame* through the cardboard, driving it into the dirt floor of the basement. She picked up the Carnelian and the Peridot; holding them together in her left hand, she then picked up the bell with her right. Slowly, she began to ring the bell. Its bright chime seemed to increase the burning glow of the candles. She took note of this, considered it a favorable sign, and continued with increasing fervor, speaking the words of the summoning incantation with speed and strength:

ETCHO; ETCHO AZARAK! ETCHO ETCHO ZOME-
LAK!
BARGOLAS ETCHO BARGOLAS CHENUNNON!
ETCHO!
AGABE CHAHI BACHABE
KARELYOS!
LOGOZ ATHA FEMYOLAS; BARGOLAS
ETCHO; ETCHO AZARAK!
BARGOLAS ETCHO BARGOLAS!

LORD BARGOLAS, I ASK OF THEE
FOR ME NO PLEASURE, SLEEP NOR SOLACE SEE,
TILL YOUR HEART AND LOINS BE TURNED TO ME!

URE SPIRITUS IGNE
RENES NOSTROS ET COR NOSTRUN
FIAT, FIAT, FIAT!

BARGOLAS ETCHO BARGOLAS CHENUNNON!
ETCHO!
ETCHO; ETCHO AZARAK!
BARGOLAS ETCHO BARGOLAS!

As she spoke these words, bile rose up in her throat. The chiming of the silver bell echoed in her ears; the brightness of the candles blinded her. The burnt scent of lavender and vervain were pungent and rich, and she felt herself beginning to swoon. She fought for control; she must complete the last part. She had to hang on that long.

She separated the Carnelian and Peridot, holding one in each hand, and spoke again, her voice cracking and fading:

> BY THE STRENGTH OF MY WILL
> BY THE NEED IN MY LOINS
> BY THE PURPOSE IN MY HEART
> BY THE FIRE IN MY SOUL
> I COMMAND THEE
> APPEAR, AND CLAIM YOUR TREASURE
> APPEAR BEFORE ME
> OBEY ME AND SERVE ONLY ME
> I COMMAND THEE
> BARGOLAS! BARGOLAS!
> BY THIS POWER
> AS MY WORD
> SO MOTE IT BE!

Lydia's voice died away, leaving only the bright candlelight and the flickering shadows. Exhausted, she searched the pockets of darkness for . . . anything. She had not realized until now just what this meant to her.

Damn that old woman, when she had told Lydia about her lover she had given her hope for overcoming the loneliness of her life with Seth. The hope had given her strength. She needed this to stay alive. Without this, she would die. Painfully, she looked out into the shadows again, searching until her eyes burned from the strain. Tears began to well up and spill over onto her face. In anger and sorrow, she flung the stones into the darkness, screaming, "Fuck you!"

Exhausted, Lydia slumped forward, thrusting her hands into her lap and sobbing. Her failure had sapped her strength, and she felt as if she couldn't move from the spot. Suddenly, she heard a strange clicking from the shadows. It reminded her of fingernails drumming on a hard surface. "Damn rats," she said to herself.

Tears streamed down her cheeks and dripped from her chin onto the diagram. She was angry and desperate. Weakly she stood and started to step over the circle of candles.

Then she heard him. She saw nothing, but a voice as soft as a butterfly touched her ear, whispering urgently.

"Lydia . . . Lydia, wait!"

It seemed to Bargolas that he had lived in darkness forever, but the memory of his last love still haunted him. He had indeed lived in hellish agony with the memory of the scent and the heat, but he had been relegated to darkness, bound by frustration and impotence stronger than chains. So long ago—but now it was over!

He examined his skin, glistening blue-black, and touched the talons of his longer arms to the slick surface. Glancing down, he caught sight of the precious Carnelian and Peridot lying at his feet. He picked up the stones and clasped them to his chest just as the darkness was split open by the circle of golden candlelight. Then he saw her. He was being freed by this beautiful woman!

Her cheeks were moist with tears; her body trembled. Highlights streaked her hair, and her perfect nude body called out to every fiber of his being. Her every request, her every desire would be his desire. But wait! He was not yet complete. *He* was not yet *her* desire, her dream.

He bowed his head slightly, and ethereal—almost transparent—wisps drifted from his ear holes toward the woman standing in the circle. A moment later, they penetrated, and Bargolas knew her name.

He called out for her to wait and she stopped, shaking violently from fear and excitement. Bargolas lowered his shiny black eyes and began to weave his spell. Moments later, he stepped into the candlelight for Lydia to see.

Lydia stood her ground, trying to put on a brave face, but her heart threatened to burst from her breast. She felt so naked and so vulnerable. She wished for her robe to cover herself. Glancing sideways, she saw the sleeve of her robe; she bent down, reaching over the ring of candles to pick it up, but stopped at the request of the creature she had just summoned.

"Lydia, don't—please don't hide yourself. You are so beautiful."

His voice soothed her with its deep, mellow tone, and her fear lessened. Excited, she stood upright again. She inhaled the rich aroma of her lover. It was like crushed ripe olives, like warm oil. Even though she could not see him, the scent made her long to touch him, to feel the contours of his body.

She peered into the shadows, desperately seeking some small physical indication of his presence. Her fear was now gone, evaporated into the darkness by the heat of her longing. A moment later, he stepped out of the oily shadows.

The candlelight illuminated only a small portion of Bargolas, but it was enough to send Lydia's heart racing. She trembled and took a step toward him, but he stopped her.

"No, Lydia, not yet. First you must finish the ceremony. You have summoned me, but until the ceremony is complete, I cannot remain here with you. If you step out of the circle before you have finished, you will die—and I will be hurtled back into unspeakable loneliness."

"But I don't know what to finish. There is no more in the book. What should I do?"

"Lydia, be calm. I shall tell you what to do. First you must remove some of the candles. Point to each one, and I shall tell you if you must remove it. When you remove a candle from the circle, you must not extinguish the flame. Instead, you must begin to build a smaller circle of candles in front of you. Let us begin."

As Lydia pointed to the candles in order, the incubus told her which ones to remove. In the end, she had removed seven candles and constructed a circle with them in front of her. Suddenly, the Carnelian and Peridot were tossed back into the circle.

"Now, my dearest," Bargolas began, "you must take your incense bowl and empty the alcohol from it. You must then place the two stones in the bowl and put the bowl inside the circle of seven candles."

He waited for her to finish, then continued his instructions. "Good, my love, very good. I cannot yet move into the circle of protection, but I want you now to lean across the circle with your *Athame* and cut my hand."

Bargolas extended his hand for Lydia to cut. She looked into the shadows to see his face, but he cried out and asked her not to look. She extended the *Athame* and held the blade over his palm, but she could not bring herself to make the cut.

"Lydia, do not fear. You will not hurt me any more than you will hurt yourself. You must cut me."

Lydia took a deep breath and drew the knife quickly over his palm. Red-black blood immediately oozed out and began dripping down the side of his hand.

"Now, Lydia, remove the bowl from the circle and catch some drops of my blood in the bowl."

She did so, knowing, even before he instructed her in the next step, what was to follow. She drew the knife now sharply across her own palm and mingled her blood with that of the incubus.

"Very good. Now you must change the polarity of the circle of protection. Remove the candle directly behind you—no, not that one . . . yes, that's right. Now pick up the candle closest to the bell. Yes. Now put that one exactly in the spot from where you took the one behind you, and put the other in its place. Ahhh, very good! Now fill the bowl to the top with salt."

Bargolas waited for her to finish and then stepped farther into the light. Lydia looked up from her crouching position and was unable to breathe. In a moment she found her breath and whispered, "You are so . . . beautiful."

The incubus stood before her, naked. His burnished skin reflected the gold of the candlelight. Black hair crowned his head with tight curls. His deep piercing eyes were framed by thick, dark eyebrows. The tips of his long elegant fingers rested lightly against his muscular thighs. As he shifted his weight nervously from foot to foot, his leg muscles rippled, catching the light and reflecting it back to Lydia in a wave of sensuality.

The tight dark curls atop his head barely touched his shoulders. Lydia's eyes caressed the rounded muscularity of his arms as they flowed powerfully into his shoulders and chest. His breathing was deep and rhythmic, and each breath contributed to the slow heaving of his abdomen, which ended mysteriously at his loins.

Lydia's thoughts were confused as she gazed upon a man that she had seen only in her dreams. She knew he was not truly a man, he was something else—but she didn't care. He came because she had called out of desperation and need.

She longed for the quickening heat that the touch of a man could bring to her. Still, part of her feared . . .

"Lydia, please do not be afraid. I love you."

At his words, whatever hesitation had lurked in the corners of her common sense vanished. She stood again and moved toward him. But once more he stopped her.

"Stop. Soon, my dear Lydia, soon. But we must first complete the ceremony."

The yearning in Lydia's heart was almost unbearable. She almost could not resist the desire to run to him. Only his insistence halted her; the conflict set her body trembling once again. She stood, looking into his eyes, and asked, "What must I do? I will do anything."

"Leave the bowl in the circle and pick up the candles one by one. Allow the hot wax from each to fall upon the salt in the bowl. After you seal the stones in this manner, extinguish the candle."

Lydia did as she was told and then looked back up into his beautiful face. He smiled at her, his straight white teeth reflecting the candlelight. He continued with the instructions.

"Now take the *Athame* and cut a hole in the cardboard that you knelt upon. Cut exactly around the center pentagram. When you have done this, dig into the earth until you have a space large enough to place the bowl—and then cover it with soil."

Quickly, almost violently, Lydia dug with the *Athame*. In a few minutes she was finished. With dirt and sweat smudging her face and grit on her hands, she looked back to Bargolas.

"Now," he said gently, "scoop away some of the circle of salt . . . break the circle."

Without hesitation she scraped away, the salt scattering across the dirt floor. The moment she broke the circle, he stepped into it with her. She gazed at his perfect feet, almost embarrassed to look upward into his beauty. But slowly she raised her head. He was standing so near that when she raised her head, her hair brushed against his partially aroused manhood.

Lydia looked into his eyes, her very soul overflowing with desire for this creature. But she could not move; she had lost the will to direct her movement. She ached to touch him but could not even raise her hand.

Gently he reached down and, grasping her firmly beneath the arms, lifted her to her feet. Her knees were weak and she started to falter. Immediately, he scooped her up into his arms. She rolled her face against his skin and inhaled the deep musk, the scent arousing her even more.

With long, powerful strides, Bargolas climbed the stairs, Lydia in his arms.

19

Othello, 1970

"Where are you goin'?"

"I'm headin' for the Potholes. We can lose Zeke and his asshole friends out there!" Mike growled as he cranked the steering wheel in the direction of the truck's skid. The Ranchero straightened out and resumed speed.

Stan held onto the armrest with his feet spread wide on the wet floor, trying to keep his balance. Not daring to turn around, he asked, "Do you see them behind us?"

"Not yet, but it's just a matter of—damn! There they are. They just turned down the road and they're comin' after us. Shit!"

Stan remained silent. The Ranchero bounced violently as they crossed the railroad track and half-slid down the hill into the snowy darkness. Just before Mike turned onto the Goose Lake road, he turned off his headlights. But as soon as they hit the snow, Zeke's headlights peeked out over the hill, followed by the car with Zeke and his companions.

"Look at those assholes!" screamed Peterson. "They turned their lights off. Ha! Why the fuck bother? You can see that red piece of shit against the snow as plain as day!"

Peterson handed the bottle of Jack Daniels over to Zeke. Zeke removed one hand from the wheel and took the bottle, pulling hard on it. "Whew! Good stuff!" he exclaimed, keep-

ing an eye on the little red truck. "I bet they're headin' for
Goose Lake. Why don't we just take the lower road and surprise the shit out of them?"

All three of the boys laughed as Zeke turned his own lights
off and steered right, driving into the Ranchero's tracks. Then
he made a hard left that took them around a large rock out-
cropping and headed them toward the north side of Goose
Lake.

The surreal landscape of the Potholes, now bright with
snow, had been formed by glaciers millions of years ago. The
contrast between this area and the surrounding desert was like
that between night and day. The sagebrush plains, broken
only by an occasional rolling hill, reached to the Saddle
Mountains, themselves really just hills. In the opposite direction, where the drab flatness of the desert ended in an abrupt
escarpment, it was like the edge of one world and the beginning of another, dropped from the edge of that first world, a
world of sage and rattlesnakes and blowing sands into one of
lakes and marshes, bulrush and waterfowl.

Back on the upper road, Mike pointed the Ranchero as
straight as he could, sliding it down the snowy road. That
was the easy part. Now he decided to take advantage of his
momentum to help him get up the next grade. It almost
worked; two-thirds of the way up, however, the wheels began
to spin. Knowing his back end was too light, he set his mind
on just getting back down the hill. The problem was that he
had to do it backward, and without using brakes.

Stan gripped the armrest as Mike turned around to view
the return path. Stan could feel something was going wrong
a split second before Mike groaned and exclaimed, "Shit!"

The little truck listed sideways and slipped off the edge of
the road into a deep snowdrift. Swearing, Mike tried to rock
backward and forward but was unable to gain any headway.
The two boys stepped out into the cold night and looked at
the truck. Mike took the shovel from the truck bed and said,
"Well, not much else we can do except dig . . . and hope
we fuckin' lost Zeke."

Stan stood, looking at Mike with the shovel poised above
the back tire buried deep in snow. Stan shook his head and
said in a low scared voice, "We haven't lost them. They're
comin' from another direction. They'll come from . . .

there." He pointed ahead to the top of the hill they had just slid down.

Pam turned her head toward the window. "Was that clicking sound coming from there?" she said to herself. Once again she heard it. It did indeed seem to be coming from the window. Cautiously she threw her feet over the side of the hospital bed, but they didn't reach the floor. She had to slide down the side of the bed, dragging the sheets with her.

She hobbled over to the window and listened for the strange clicking sound; she didn't hear it anymore. Slowly she parted the cheap plastic drapes with her hand. She couldn't see anything outside because of the bright light inside, so she slid behind the drapes to block out the room light. After a moment, her eyes adjusted and she was able to see into the hospital's backyard.

Heat rose from the baseboard heater directly below the window, but the window radiated the outside chill. Hot and cold met on her face. Her eyes searched the snow outside her window. The snowman that some children had made the day before had been knocked down by the same children today. But she saw nothing that could be causing such an odd noise. As she turned to get back to her bed, she noticed, in the very corner of her window view, a dull white shape almost blending in with the background.

It looked like a child crouched in the snow wearing an odd white snowsuit, its head covered by a close-fitting scarf or hat. Then suddenly, from under the scarf, black bulbous eyes opened, slapping Pam with a terrifying memory. Pam inhaled sharply, staring at the monster as it now began to move toward her. She stumbled back, holding her stomach as if someone had punched her.

"What are you dong out of bed, dear?" demanded the night nurse, who had come into the room for the evening bed check. She hurried over to Pam and took her by the arm.

Instantly, Pam broke away from the nurse's grip and broke for the door. Still weak, she fell against the wall and slid to the floor. The nurse locked her hands around the girl's arms and pulled her toward the bed. Pam shook her head violently, her carrot-colored hair flying into the nurse's face.

Pam could not scream, though she wished to do so with all

her soul. The only sounds she could make were shallow gasps. She punched the nurse sharply in the abdomen. The nurse spun away and fell against the metal bed as Pam limped toward the door. The nurse pushed the call button clipped to the bedsheet.

Pam stumbled down the hall a few feet before another nurse grabbed her by the arm. A half-minute later the first one joined in the struggle, while calling to the nurse at the hall station, "Sara! Get Dr. Masters. He's in 108."

The two women dragged Pam back into her room and lifted her onto the bed. Dr. Masters and Sara dashed into the room, and together they secured the hysterical girl to the bed with canvas straps around her wrists and ankles, and across the top of her chest.

"When was the last time she had a sedative?"

"Only about half an hour ago, Doctor."

"Hell, we can't give her another one so soon. She's scared out of her wits. What set her off?"

"It's the same way she looked when they brought her in yesterday," said Sara.

"Keep an eye on her, and if she hasn't calmed down in an hour, give her doctor a call at home."

"Yes, Doctor."

"Poor thing, she looks so pitiful. I wonder what in the world could have scared her so."

Pam's body lay stiffly against the bed. All of her muscles strained against the straps as she watched the doctor and nurses leave the room. She took several deep breaths and gazed up at the ceiling. Then she heard it again. Click . . . click . . . click . . .

This time she knew what was making the sound. She stared at the window in terror, expecting the monster to break through at any moment.

Mike exhaled the acrid cigarette smoke into the cold night air. He took a break from digging, and Stan took a turn with the shovel. They had been stuck here for at least ten minutes—certainly long enough for Zeke and his buddies to have caught up with them if they were coming.

Asshole here is probably just runnin' off at the mouth with more of his psychic bullshit, thought Mike as he trudged up the snowy embankment for the second time to make sure they hadn't been followed. He looked back at Stan, hard at work, and called out to him. "That's probably good enough. Get in the back of the truck; I'll need your weight for traction."

Mike looked all around. In the distance, he saw the edge of Goose Lake. The sky had begun clearing of the dense snow clouds and the water shimmered a cold bright silver, reflecting the moon peeking out from the clouds. The surrounding area rose up in dark rocks capped with snow. Snow had also drifted between the rock outcroppings, forming whorls and white valleys. The scene was quiet and motionless; the wildlife that populated this area during the summertime slept now safely below ground.

Satisfied that they were alone, Mike slid down the hill back to the car. He stamped his feet, freeing his loafers from the clinging snow. Carefully, he climbed into the truck and started the engine. He just barely gave it gas in second gear, rocking forward, and then slammed it into reverse and rocked backward. The truck eased out of the hole. Mike smiled to himself. He wasn't completely out yet, but it was just a matter of time.

Looking into the rearview mirror, he watched Stan, who squatted in the bed of the truck holding onto the sides. A deep frown creased his boyish face.

"What now?" Mike called out the window as he put the transmission into neutral and set the brake.

"I think they're here," said Stan, shaking his head.

"Bullshit!" exclaimed Mike angrily, as he stepped out of the cab and over to the side of the truck below Stan. "I was just up on the hill and couldn't see nobody out there. Zeke didn't see us turn off, so just relax."

Stan looked stubbornly away. "I know what I know."

"Oh, fuck! There you go with that crap again. I don't think you know when you're dreamin' or awake. Haven't you already got us in deep enough shit with this mumbo jumbo?" Mike turned away from Stan before he said something he might regret.

"Well," came an unexpected voice, "it looks like the two lovebirds got a little teensy-weensy stuck in the snow."

Peterson laughed at Zeke's taunting remark as they surprised the two teenagers. He grabbed the bottle of Jack Daniels from Hampton. Peterson and Hampton stood on opposite sides of Zeke like honor guards.

Mike looked up at them. His heart caught in his throat as he spoke. "Now, we don't want no trouble." Mike's voice cracked with fear; he saw the sawed-off shovel handles that Zeke and his friends were carrying.

"But *we do*," said Peterson.

"Yeah," piped Hampton.

"Actually, we got no beef with you, Kawaguchi, we just wanna make sure ol' Fuller here never fucks with us again," declared Zeke. He spread his legs in an aggressive stance.

Mike looked back at Stan, whose eyes were huge with fear. He had one hand up to his mouth and bit absentmindedly against his thumb. His eyes darted back and forth, searching for an escape route.

"I think you ought to leave him the fuck alone," Mike said bravely. "You know he's half-crazy as it is, it ain't really worth your time." He edged his way along the side of the truck back to the cab.

"Man, I think you ought to shut the fuck up and stay out of it!"

Mike leaned inside the cab and pulled the hunting rifle from behind the seat. "I ain't gonna stay out of it. YOU are, asshole!" Brandishing the rifle, Mike stepped back to Stan and said in a low voice, hoping the others couldn't hear, "Take off! Head for the end of the road and wait for me there."

"Who the fuck do you think you're kiddin'? You ain't gonna shoot nobody. Shit, what a dick-brain!"

Stan still crouched in the back of the pickup. Mike glared back at him and yelled, "I told you to RUN, asshole!" Stan looked as if he were just waking up from a dream. Suddenly, he came alive. He hopped out of the truck and began to run along the road. Zeke and the boys began to slide down the hill toward Mike.

"Come on, asshole, shoot me!" screamed Zeke. "Let's see if you got any balls . . . SHOOT!"

Mike aimed the gun high and to the left, and fired.

The sound of the discharge scared the three aggressors, but only slightly. Zeke narrowed his eyes and slowed his descent toward Mike. He knew Mike wasn't going to shoot them, but there wasn't any reason to spook him, either. Cool it, he told himself; accidents happen in situations just like this. Peterson and Hampton slid the rest of the way down the hill and joined Zeke, standing in front of Mike, who now pointed the gun down at the ground with a look of defeat set deeply in his face.

"So you got no guts, huh?" taunted Zeke.

"Blow it out your ass. Why don't you just go the fuck home and leave us alone?"

"Why don't you try to make me? Shouldn't be too hard for you—you with a gun an' all." Zeke took another step forward, closing the gap between him and Mike to only a couple of feet. Suddenly, Mike brought the barrel of the rifle up between Zeke's legs and slammed it into his testicles. Zeke fell to his knees and rolled forward in pain. Peterson raised his sawed-off shovel handle and hit Mike across the arm with it. A second later, Hampton brought his club down across Mike's back.

Mike groaned as he fell into the cold snow. Slowly and in great pain, he rolled over onto his back. Peterson helped Zeke to his feet, and the two stood over Mike. Zeke kicked his boot hard into Mike's groin, and Hampton kicked him in the side of the face. A split appeared above Mike's eye, and blood flowed onto the snow. Mike's arm slowly slid from his chest down to the snowy ground; his breathing became shallow and irregular.

"Come on, guys, let's go kick the shit out of the warlock!" ordered Zeke, mostly recovered from his own pain.

Pam stared wide-eyed at the window. The clicking had stopped. Still straining against her bonds, she was far past a state of panic.

Evil, the color of snow, lurked outside the hospital's kitchen door. He had watched while the janitor threw trash into the cans and then returned inside. Instinct told him the janitor would be back, so Bargolas just waited, softly singing to himself, "Pretty pretty Pam, pretty pretty . . ."

A scraping sound preceded the opening of the door, and instantly the incubus vaulted over to it. The janitor had barely taken a step onto the black ice when razor-sharp talons tore away most of his face and neck, spraying hot blood across the side of the beige outside wall.

The creature looked both ways down the darkened hall and
then set his eyes upon the door he knew was Pam's. As he
crept toward it, his color changed to a shadowy black. The
only sound from him was the regular click-click-click from
the talons on his feet as he crossed the expanse of brightly
waxed linoleum. Pausing momentarily at Pam's door, he
checked again to make sure no one was watching. He then
opened the door slowly and slithered into her room.

Half mad with fear, Pam continued to stare at the window.
Then, however, she heard the clicking sound. She twisted her
head sideways and looked with horror into the face of Evil.

"Pretty pretty Pam. Oh-ho-ho-ho-tee-hee-hee, I found you,
my pretty pretty Pam, now—just for me!"

The small hands, jutting from his upper chest, milked each
other in anticipation. His mouth was open in a cruel smile,
with saliva dripping from one side down his longer right arm.
With that hand, he fondled his oversized genitals, caressing
them into fullness. He raised his face toward the ceiling but
kept his eyes on Pam and hissed loudly, "Mine . . . all
mine!"

Pam began to buck in her bed. She convulsed as if receiv-
ing an electroshock treatment. Her eyes rolled back in their
sockets and foam gathered at the corners of her mouth. The
only sounds she could manage were low grunts.

The incubus slowly walked over to the foot of her bed and,
with the very tips of two talons, grasped the sheet covering
the strapped down girl. Gingerly, he pulled the sheet to the
floor and then looked at the girl, clothed in just her loose
hospital gown, firmly restrained by her straps. Slowly he
reached under her gown, sliding his fingers along the smooth
flesh of her inner thighs. The talons extended to rip flesh—
but then he stopped.

He looked at the sheet on the floor, remembering the boy
who had called him just three days ago. He remembered pulling the sheet from his bed, remembered the feel of his skin.
But then there was something more . . . The evil face of
Bargolas grew solemn. The opaque membrane slid over his
eyes, and he shut his lids in concentration.

He saw snow. He saw breath coming in ragged gasps. He
saw danger. Without the boy, he would be flung back into
that place of unbearable loneliness.

He walked quickly to the window. He pulled the curtains aside and fumbled with the latch, unlocked the window, and flung it open. Moments later, he raced across the snow, his color again lightening.

Stan stood freezing in a snowdrift almost up to his knees. He peered out from behind a snowcapped boulder at the three angry teenagers coming up out of the dip in the road where the Ranchero had gotten stuck.

Mike had told him to run down the road and wait, but his own instincts told him to hide. So he had run only a short distance, looking for an area where his footprints would not give him away when he left the road. Unable to find a good place, he ran as hard as he could on the slippery white—and jumped out into the snow. Then, slowly he began to trudge his way down the side of the road back toward Mike. He figured when he saw Mike's headlights he would be close enough to the road that he could get out to him before he passed by.

As he made his way back toward the dip in the road, Stan heard yelling. He positioned himself behind a boulder and peeked around to see what was going on. As Zeke and his cronies emerged, Stan hugged the cold stone and held his breath lest the plume of steam give him away. He listened to them as they passed his hiding place.

"I'm gonna pound that fucker into hamburger!" growled Hampton loudly.

"Fuckin' A, man, let's git the little prick!"

They broke into a trot down the road, all three carrying clubs meant for Stan. A chill, colder than the snow he stood in, shook his body. He continued to watch until he was sure they would not be able to hear the crunching of his steps on the hard surface. He ran back to the road and down the grade where he had left Mike. By now he was a little concerned that he hadn't seen the Ranchero's headlights. Suddenly a sharp pain tightened his chest, and he knew something had happened to Mike.

Crossing over the ridge, Stan could see his worst fears were realized. Mike lay motionless. Even from this distance, Stan was able to see the dark red stains upon the snow. Stan fell twice, scrambling down the icy road to his friend. Mike's image was blurred by the rush of tears. Stan knelt beside him.

"Mike, oh Mike, they killed you!" Stan wailed, forgetting that Zeke and the others were looking for him. Stan grabbed a handful of Mike's jacket and pulled him over on his back. Mike moaned.

"Mike! Mike! You're not dead!"

"Jesus . . ." groaned Mike. "Are they gone?"

"Nah, I don't think so. I doubled back and they passed me while I was hiding."

Stan reached under Mike and helped him sit up. Wiping the blood out of his eyes with the back of his hand, Mike looked at Stan and said, "We gotta get out of here before they come back. They're probably on their way right now. Climb up there and take a look. I'll start the truck to get us the fuck out of here."

Stan obliged and climbed back up the snowy incline to take a look. Zeke and the other two had indeed turned around and were running back toward them at top speed. Scrambling down the road, Stan crouched beside Mike.

"They're comin' back. Pretend you're still out. I'll go the other way, toward the falls, and see if I can lose them. When they leave, try to get the truck out and I'll come back. If I don't get back, I'll be hidin' somewhere near the falls."

Stan scampered up the embankment opposite the road and ran across the snow in the direction of the falls as voices sounded behind him.

"I see the motherfucker!"

"Over there!"

Stan's dark coat stood out plainly against the white background. The group of boys ran down the slick slope of the road, passing Mike without a glance. Alcohol-scented vapor ran like white rivers from their mouths as they climbed up the embankment and chased after Stan, their progress impeded by the Jack Daniels in their bloodstream. Waving their clubs in the air and shouting threats, they thrilled to the excitement of the hunt.

Mike lifted his head and watched them slip and slide while trying to climb the embankment. He flexed the fingers of his hand and raised and lowered his arm. His heavy winter coat had kept it from breaking, but blood still flowed freely from his eye and neck where they had kicked him. He could taste blood in his mouth while he tried to think rationally.

He was past anger. His survival, and Stan's, depended upon more than just his anger. In the darker corners of his mind, revenge lurked. The sensible course of action might be to report them to the police for assault. But then he would have to explain about the rifle . . . But that was self-defense, wasn't it? He wondered if the cops would see it that way.

While these questions raced through his mind, a sound reached him from somewhere off to his right. He looked in that direction and thought he saw something move near a patch of ice-encrusted sagebrush. Everything was so white. He scanned the area, seeing nothing out of the ordinary, then limped stiffly to the door of his truck. He eased himself onto the driver's seat and started to turn the ignition key, but stopped to look around once more, quickly snapping his head back and forth. He didn't see anything, but he heard a distinctive clicking sound followed by a crackling, like a dog skittering across the frozen surface of the snow.

Frowning, he tried to remember where he had heard that sound before, but the more he concentrated, the further away he seemed to be from recalling. It was as if he'd heard it in a dream. Dread crept over him; trying to ignore it, he turned the key and the Ranchero purred to life.

Peterson had had more to drink than his two friends, and now, with all this running, his stomach seemed to be turning inside out. He quickly fell behind and soon stopped.

"Hey, man, what's with you?" hollered Zeke, thirty yards ahead of Peterson.

"I think I'm gonna puke."

"You want us to wait? We can catch up to that shithead later."

"Nah, go ahead and catch the little fucker. I'll be okay; I'll catch up to you."

Zeke and Hampton turned their backs on Peterson and continued running in the direction of the falls.

Peterson hunched over, fighting an intense wave of nausea. Finally he just decided to give in and get it over with. He opened his mouth and stuck two of his fingers clear to the back of his throat. It worked. Before he was even able to get his fingers out of his mouth, he vomited.

He felt much better. He stuck his foul-smelling hand into the snow to clean it off, then scraped some of the white stuff together and popped it into his mouth. It soothed his stomach. He straightened up and looked off into the bright, white night.

He blinked a couple of times trying to focus, for something appeared to be approaching. It was hard to tell, because whatever it was looked almost the same color as the snow. Peterson cocked his head and tightened his grip on his club as he watched. The closer the thing got, the more it looked like a man dressed in a white coat and wearing large sunglasses.

A feeling of dread mixed with fear began to rise from Peterson's groin and travel up toward his chest. The tightness spread across his shoulders, and his breath came in shallow gasps as he watched the thing take on a distinct form.

"Oh God," Peterson muttered, stumbling backward onto his butt.

The bulbous, glossy black eyes of the incubus stared unblinkingly at the boy who had fallen backward. As the creature's white skin began to darken, the boy began to wail like a baby. The incubus raised his talons to his mouth and tapped them against his stained and cracked teeth, thinking. Click-click-click. He took another step closer.

Peterson began to emit the low growls of a trapped animal. As the incubus stepped forward again, Peterson swung his club with all his strength against the monster's knee. A loud crack sounded. The incubus jumped back in pain, hissing loudly and waving his two short arms in a slow, hypnotic motion. One of his longer arms grasped his knee and rubbed it gently.

"Oh . . . bad bad boy. Bad . . . terrible boy."

The incubus again approached the boy, more quickly this time, trying to come in on the side away from the club. But Peterson was quicker than his foe and brought the sawed-off shovel handle hard against the creature's hand. Bargolas screamed a gravelly cry of pain, hopping around on one foot while his other three hands held the injured one.

Taking advantage of the moment, Peterson jumped to his feet and began to run for his friends, screaming at the top of his lungs. He got about sixty yards before he heard the skit-

tering of talons against the snow. Just as he started to turn
around to see how close the monster was, those talons dug
deeply into his shoulder, twisted his arm right out of the
socket, and flung it ten feet away.

Agony threw Peterson to the snow, where he flopped about
like a fish on the wharf, each frantic heartbeat spraying the
snow with blood. Suddenly the incubus climbed on top of the
boy and pinned his remaining arm down. Leaning forward,
Bargolas grasped the boy's head with the hands of his short
arms and brought his face down close to listen to the screams.
Slowly the creature placed his lips over the screams and let
them fill his mouth. Then he snaked his tongue into the boy's
throat, pushing it far down and muffling the screams.

The incubus began to rock slowly back and forth on the
struggling boy, the motion arousing his sex organ. Then the
creature sat up and withdrew his tongue, savoring the taste
of the boy's terror upon it. Shifting his weight forward onto
the boy's chest, Bargolas held his face in two powerful hands
and began applying pressure, his own arousal intensified. The
boy began to blubber insanely, his terror and agony melting
into death. Evil pressed himself against the boy, seeking his
lustful release in the boy's final moments of life. Before that
could happen, bones cracked and the boy's skull caved in.

Evil rocked back and forth for a few moments. He wished
to savor the moment, wanted to find his release, but he knew
there was still danger. With a moist sucking sound, he withdrew from the now lifeless boy and stood up. He cocked his
head slightly, as a dog might, while he listened to the night.
He heard running and breathing, felt the fear and desperation
of other creatures. With long strides, he turned in the direction of the sounds and began to change color once again.

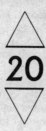

20

Despite the cold, sweat ran down the small of Stan's back. With his heart pounding in his ears, he rested his head in the cradle of his arms. The sour odor of his breath betrayed his fear. The last few days' events swam in his mind—the house, the disappearance of Cliff and Peggy, Pam in the hospital, and God knows *what* in his room—and made him feel like crawling into bed to sleep for a hundred years.

Shouts broke through Stan's reverie.

"Look here!" It was Zeke's voice, not far away. "The dumb shit's leaving us a clear trail through the snow. Hot damn—we got him now!"

Stan raised his head from the boulder and looked off in the direction of the shouts. His two pursuers broke into view. Stan turned and began crunching through the snow as hard as he could run.

"There he goes, headin' for the falls!"

"Wooo . . . shit!" yelled Hampton as he tripped on a snow-covered rock and fell headlong into a deep drift.

Zeke paused and looked back at his friend. He laughed and continued to run, shouting over his shoulder, "Come on, asshole, we ain't got time to build snowmen!"

"Shit, I got snow down my shirt!" Hampton yelled loudly as Zeke closed the distance between himself and Stan.

Hampton stood up and stamped his feet vigorously; he pulled his shirttails from his pants to free the snow trapped against his bare skin. Suddenly, he heard a hissing sound behind him. He turned around and, even before a look of surprise could register on his face, sharp black talons ripped through his throat and down his chest. Hitting the blood-covered snow, the mangled body twitched violently—then was still.

Meanwhile, Stan glanced back to see how close his pursuers were. He saw only Zeke, gaining on him quickly with his club waving. Unable to see any place to run, Stan clawed his way up the slope to the top of the falls with Zeke almost at his heels.

The falls were about eight feet across at the top, widening out as they dropped thirty feet into a small rock pond originally carved by a glacier. The pond drained out the side opposite the falls into a stream that ran through a mosquito-infested marsh during the summertime.

Zeke, drunk and half-crazed with the excitement of the chase, caught up to Stan and swung the shovel handle at him. Stan heard it slice the air near his head and jumped sideways to avoid the anticipated next blow. It didn't come. He rolled over on his back with his feet in the air to protect himself. The hard wooden club smacked him sharply across the ankle; Stan howled as he got to his feet, hoping he could escape by jumping the narrow falls.

Just as Stan pushed off, using the injured ankle so he would land on the good one, he felt the third blow from Zeke catch him at the base of the neck. Stan crumpled in the middle of his jump and fell into the icy rushing water. At first, he had the impression he was standing still in the falls, but then the full force of the water hit him in the chest, propelling him down, down into the pond below.

Above him, Zeke frowned. He hadn't really meant to knock Stan into the water. He'd just wanted to hurt him a little. Now, as he began thinking about what he'd done, a strange feeling took hold of his gut. He turned around, expecting to see Peterson and Hampton approaching by now. Instead, what he saw plunged him into absolute terror. His screams of protest stuck in his throat, gagging him, stealing his breath.

The incubus stood a few feet away, but he wasn't looking

at Zeke—his eyes were turned downward, toward the pond at the bottom of the falls. His shorter arms flailed about in confusion while the hands of his longer arms were tensed in fists. Suddenly he shifted his eyes to Zeke and said in a deep and gravelly voice, "Bad bad little boy."

On the word "boy," the incubus leapt powerfully, and in three bounds he was down the side of the falls to the snow-dusted, craggy bank of the pond. He searched the surface of the water for the one who had summoned him back into this world.

Zeke stood on the bank above, staring after the creature that had just jumped a distance no human ever could. Zeke's whole body shook in fear, and urine spread hotly across the front of his jeans. He began to stumble away in a daze of terror, but within a few steps he was running back toward his car as fast as his legs would carry him, screaming at the top of his lungs for his friends.

Stan, meanwhile, was curled forward like a fetus. Miraculously, he was still conscious, but the intense cold of the water had dulled his reason. He had enough strength to hold his breath as he was thrown against the rock walls of the pond, waiting to rise to the surface. The force of the water, however, was churning him in a vortex and the freezing temperatures had already numbed his limbs so that he couldn't swim. His mind casually pictured unrelated things—apple pie, his bicycle on a hot summer day, his mother. Just before he blacked out, he knew that he had to breathe—and he knew that his next breath would be the cold dark water of his death.

"Why have you got her strapped down?" shrieked Pam's mother in a raspy, half-sober voice.

"We restrained her because she was hysterical. We feared she would injure either herself or someone else." The head nurse spoke firmly, trying to avoid the woman's rank breath.

"Well, I wanna take her home. It costs too gall-darn much money to keep her in here. I can take care of her at home."

"You have that right, of course, but we strongly advise that you leave her here for observation—"

"I don't give a damn what you think!" she shrieked. "I want her untied and out of here right now. I'm gonna take her home."

The nurse turned around and walked back to her desk, wrote something on a chart, and then responded to the angry woman. "Okay. She will be ready in a few minutes, if you'll just have a seat in the waiting room."

"No way, dearie. I'm gonna get my daughter dressed and out of here. This is supposed to be a hospital, not a prison!"

The head nurse's face reddened, but she decided not to say anything more and, instead, led the way back to Pam's room. The instant the restraints were loosened, Pam jumped from the bed and fled to her mother's arms. Her mother stroked her tangled hair.

"There, there, honey, I'm here now and we're going home. Come on, let's get you dressed."

After Pam was dressed, her mother helped her walk out of the hospital room. Pam's eyes were on the floor, her head slowly shaking from side to side, her hands clutching her mother. At the front desk, the head nurse held out two pieces of paper.

"I will need you to sign these release forms, please."

The elderly woman let go of her daughter's hand and started to sign the papers. The nurse, looking on, tapped her fingernails lightly on the countertop.

Pam's eyes widened in terror. She opened her mouth and her breathing came in gasps. Her mother looked down at her and saw the crazed look of fear in her eyes. Pam broke away and began to stagger down the hall, crashing into a laundry cart. She picked herself up and flung the cart out of the way in a blind panic, lurching down the hall.

Immediately, the head nurse was on the intercom calling for help. A few seconds later, two male orderlies appeared and ran after the girl. Pam's mother looked on in sorrow and confusion.

"What's happening? What is wrong with my little girl?" she screamed at the head nurse.

A few minutes later, the orderlies returned with Pam, half-carrying her. "We found her in the kitchen, hiding under the sink," one of them said. "She sure is scared of something, but she won't tell us what."

The head nurse turned to the girl's mother and said calmly, "I would really advise against taking her home. She would be too much for you to handle by yourself. Let us keep her here until we find out what is wrong with her."

Pam's mother, who had buried her face in her hands, looked into the eyes of the head nurse and nodded in agreement.

The head nurse stepped over to the two men holding Pam and said in a low voice so that her mother couldn't hear, "Take her back to her room and restrain her."

Bargolas searched the surface of the rolling black water. After a minute, he saw an arm. He jumped in and, even before he sank beneath the waves caused by his impact, he had one of his taloned hands locked around Stan's arm. Three strokes, awkward but powerful, brought the pair to the edge of the pond.

The incubus draped Stan's unconscious body over a half-submerged rock, then he pulled himself out of the water. For a moment he just sat and stared at the unmoving body. He was confused. The bloodlust was as tumultuous inside his soul as the black water before him. But Stan was like Lydia. Bargolas knew he must serve the desire of this boy. Deep inside him, he knew Stan would die soon if he did not help him. Now he scooped the cold, limp body into his arms and began running back toward the little red truck. He could hear the roar of the engine even this far away.

As the creature ran, the vibration started to revive Stan. His teeth began to chatter and he hugged closer to the odd vibration. Forcing his eyes open, he looked up into the gentle face of a young woman. She smiled at him and spoke, "Rest, my lover, you will soon be safe."

Stan passed out again. The incubus watched as the Ranchero drove carefully up the road toward them. Running out to intercept the truck, the creature laid Stan on the snow in plain view. Then he bounded away several feet and leapt into the air, forming himself into a ball; he fell silently into the snow without a trace of movement.

As Mike drove around the corner looking for Stan, his eyes were drawn to a dark patch beside the road ahead of him. Slowing up, he allowed the headlights to fall upon the patch and recognized it as Stan. Mike jumped out of the truck, wincing at the pain of his own injuries, and ran to his friend.

He grabbed Stan by the coat and discovered that he was

soaking wet, with a layer of ice forming. He knew that if he
didn't get the wet clothes off him right away, Stan would be
in big trouble. Grasping him under his arms, Mike dragged
Stan through the snow to the Ranchero and painfully maneuvered him up onto the seat. He removed Stan's shoes, then
his coat. Within a few minutes Mike had stripped Stan naked
and tossed his wet clothes into the truck bed.

He propped Stan against the passenger door and turned the
heater on full blast. Stan began to squirm. Mike maneuvered
the Ranchero back down the road and decided to take the
long way around the lake back to the main highway.

Minutes later, he came upon Zeke's white Corvette. His
first inclination was to turn around and run the other way.
However, there didn't seem to be anyone in the car, or even
nearby. Quickly Mike drove around the car and headed for
the highway.

Zeke, in panic, had just struggled out of a waist-high snowdrift. A moment later, he climbed to the top of the ridge—in
time to see the red Ranchero driving around his car and back
toward the safety of town. Stumbling down the small hill,
Zeke waved his hands and yelled hoarsely for Mike to stop,
but his words were lost in the snow-covered expanse.

Zeke ran to his car and grabbed blindly for the door handle.
He froze when he heard the sharp clicking of talons on frozen
snow. Zeke heard the creature panting behind him, but fear
kept him from turning around. The vision of the creature he
had seen at the falls swam before his eyes. Zeke's hand tightened around the door handle, though he knew he would never
open it. He started to whimper, and tears ran down his cheeks
in the cold empty night. His knees started to sag; all he wanted
to think about was being safe at home, tucked warmly into
bed. He smelled the putrid breath from behind him, and his
stomach tightened. From deep in his soul, sobs erupted and
poured forth, gurgling and tearing sharply at his mouth.

The incubus stood little more than a foot from the terrified
boy. The delicious scent of fear radiated from the boy like
heat. He drank it in, feeling it nourish him and make him
stronger. The bellows of his hate fed the fire of his lust. Heat
filled his loins and his member stood erect. Bargolas stepped
closer, cradling his body against the trembling boy. His wide

nostrils flared, catching a rich, fetid odor as the boy lost control of his bowels.

Zeke felt small hands upon his neck, snaking slowly into his hair. A hand the color of snow inched over his shoulder. Zeke stared at it in wide-eyed horror. The black talons gleamed. Teardrops flowed down Zeke's face, filling his open, twisted mouth with the final tears of his life. He felt the creature's sexual urgency, and it touched the most primal of his terrors. He felt the incubus growing harder as it pressed down upon him. Then, softly in his ear, he heard, "Oooo, my pretty pretty little boy . . . oooo, yes, pretty . . ."

Black claws tore through the weak material of Zeke's clothing, reducing them to shreds, the skin beneath flayed and bleeding. Bargolas thrust suddenly forward and Zeke cried out in agony, the pain tearing away his vision. The creature's teeth sank into the back of the boy's neck and tore away small pieces of flesh. Bargolas slowly devoured them while the boy suffered his last few moments.

Minutes after the boy had died, the creature continued to rock back and forth, savoring his pleasure. Blood covered the white Corvette's hood and ran down one fender into the snow. Slowly the incubus pushed the limp body away and licked the slime from his own hands and body. He looked down at Zeke, who lay in a heap on the snow. His luminous black eyes searched the boy's lifeless form, trying to recall something. Then, remembering, he smiled his broken-toothed grin.

"Pretty pretty Pam . . ." He repeated this, chiming it over and over as he spun about, hugging himself. Finally, without the slightest backward glance, he skittered across the snow.

Bev and Dale turned the corner as lights approached them. Whoever was coming up the hill was hogging the whole road, and Dale had to do some fancy driving to keep from hitting the little truck while staying on the road himself. Swearing at the careless driver, Dale continued on to the Potholes and turned onto the road to Goose Lake.

Bev laid her hand on Dale's leg and her head on his shoulder as they drove the long way around to the lake. This had been their favorite parking place ever since they had started going together a year and a half before, when they were both freshmen. On this particular night they were both silent. They listened to the rock 'n' roll on the radio with the volume set low, and felt content just to be in each other's company.

Suddenly Dale saw something run across the road, and he applied the brakes in short pumps. His heart raced; the image still burned in his memory—a naked man, it had looked like, running through the snow. Nah, he thought to himself, must be a coyote or something.

A few minutes later, he rounded a corner and his headlight glinted off the shiny surface of a white sports car. "Hey," he exclaimed, "that looks like Zeke's 'Vette."

The next moment the inside of the car began to reverberate with the sound of Bev's terrified screams.

Pam's breathing was slow and easy. She had calmed down and now slept lightly. Her eyes darted back and forth under her closed lids as if searching for something. Every couple of minutes she would sigh deeply, and then her breathing would return to normal.

The restraints held her firmly, and her left hand felt the effect of a strap that was too tight. Without waking, she flexed her fingers. The curtains of her room fluttered, and a hand gripped the side of the window frame. Talons clicked softly against the polished linoleum as the incubus settled his weight onto the floor.

Pam sighed loudly again and rolled her head away from the window, settling deeper into slumber as the creature walked slowly toward her. The click-click-click of talons seeped into her subconscious, and although she remained asleep, her eyes again flickered under her lids. The evil creature stood over her, looking directly into her face. He smiled slowly and, as his lips parted, stringy brown slime still stained with the blood of his recent feast, dripped down upon Pam's fair cheek.

Bargolas lowered his head down to Pam's ear and whispered, "Pretty pretty Pam, I am . . . here."

A frown creased her forehead and she exhaled sharply. Bargolas opened his mouth above hers and inhaled her breath. Suddenly Pam's eyes flickered open and she stared directly into the eyes of the incubus, only a few inches from her own.

From the depth of her soul, a scream began. It snaked up her spine and exploded in her head—but found no release through her voice. Only a low growl passed her lips as she tossed her head back and forth, fighting against the restraining straps.

Bargolas folded his short arms together and rested his chin in their cradle. With his longer arms, he grasped her head and held it still. Lowering his face, he covered her mouth with his own cracked, foul lips. Pam's breasts began to heave. She thought of the nurse's call button clipped to her bed and pulled at the straps, but her arms would not budge. Tears ran down her cheeks, wetting her pillow.

Standing up now, the incubus grasped the white sheet and pulled it slowly from her body. With the sharp tips of his claws, he methodically began to shred the girl's nightgown. Soon her young white flesh shone through the remaining pieces of cloth. The creature looked down upon his helpless victim and shuddered with excitement. Once again, he lowered his head; with his swollen tongue, he flicked at the dark red nipples of her breasts as, with one hand, he stroked his member into a state of readiness. When he raised his head, blood dripped from his lips.

Pam, convulsing wildly in pain, somehow managed to raise her head and look down. Blood was flowing in a wide river from where her nipple had been. She watched in agony as the creature slowly chewed her flesh and swallowed.

Bargolas now walked to the foot of the bed, his talons clicking. He extended his longer arms and thrust both hands into the girl's bright red pubic hair. Then, positioning his talons on the insides of her thighs, he began to draw the sharp points slowly downward. He watched in absolute delight as the milky-white skin tore away and curled under his black talons. By the time he had finished, the girl lay in a pool of her own blood.

Pam's eyeballs had rolled back into her head and the veins, ruptured from the intense pain, bathed the whites of both her eyes in red. Her mouth, too, was a basin of blood as her teeth bit through her tongue.

The incubus now climbed on top of her, and, as he positioned his erect penis at the mouth of her vagina, he leaned forward and licked the blood from her lips. Its taste, combined with his own sexual urgency, allowed him no more restraint. He reached forward and sank his talons deep into

Pam's breasts, thrusting with all of his might into her trapped body. While she convulsed with the last flicker of life, the creature remained embedded in her, savoring the transition of life becoming death as Pam's torn membrane, gripping the length of his sex, vibrated and then became still. Closing his eyes, the beast whispered one final time, ''Oh, pretty pretty Pam.''

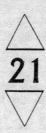

21

Stamping his feet restlessly, Dale watched Deputy Hastings from the corner of his eye. He maintained a respectful distance from the lawman and allowed him his privacy while he bent double, throwing up his dinner. Dale looked over to the white Corvette and shook his head in disbelief. Goose Lake would never be the same.

We interrupt our regularly scheduled program for an important announcement. A spokesman for the Adams County Sheriff's Department has just issued a warning about one or more dangerous animals believed to be running loose in areas of both Adams and Franklin Counties. The animal, or animals, believed to be a wolf, or perhaps a pack of wild dogs, attacked and killed five persons last night. All persons in Adams and Franklin Counties are strongly urged by the Sheriff's Department to stay indoors after sunset until the animal is disposed of. The Fish and Game Department has been called in to aid in this serious crisis. We repeat, residents are strongly urged . . .

Stan looked up from the cold bowl of oatmeal in front of him and stared at the radio as if he could see the announcer. Shifting his gaze to his mother sitting across from him, also listening to the radio, he could see the shock in her face. He flushed; he thought that she must know her son was connected to the terrible event.

"Oh, my Lord! It's probably a bear or something. Well, that settles it. You boys are not to be out at night until they kill whatever it is."

Stan stood up in his brown bathrobe and walked from the room, regaining a bit of his composure. He wondered if Cliff and Peggy were among those killed. He felt a pain in his stomach and knew in his gut that the whole thing was about to explode in his face.

"Mom? I'm going to stay home from school today. I think I caught a head cold last night."

Upon returning from the Potholes, his mother had been asleep but his father had not. He had told his father that he and Mike had been ice skating at Scootney and he had fallen through thin ice. After all, it was pretty hard to tell them nothing had happened when he walked into the house wearing Mike's clothes. In addition, he had told them that while Mike had helped him out of the water, Mike had slipped and scraped the side of his head on the ice. That way both sets of injuries were covered with explanations.

"Well, honey, if you stay home I won't be here to look after you. I promised Betty Mastie I'd take her to Moses Lake today to do some shopping."

"That's fine. I'll just curl up in front of the TV with some tea and soup," Stan called over his shoulder as he shuffled into his room and crawled into bed.

Stan went back to sleep and didn't even hear his mother leave an hour later. He did hear the phone at ten o'clock, however. He stumbled out into the dining room and picked up the receiver.

"Hullo?"

"Why the fuck aren't you in school today? Did you hear the news? Man, we are in shit up to our necks."

"Oh, it's you . . . I was asleep."

"Fuck you! Get your ass over here. We got a lot to talk about."

"I told my mother I was staying home today because I'm coming down with a cold from last night. And I think I really might be."

"Oh, cut the crap! What are we gonna do? If anyone saw Zeke chasing us or Zeke told someone he was after us, the cops are gonna be on us like stink on shit."

"What's Zeke got to do with it?" Stan's legs began to wobble a bit.

"I thought you said you heard the news."

"I heard that some wild animals killed five people last night, but—"

"Christ on a crutch, it's all over school. The people killed last night were Zeke, Hampton, Peterson, and Pam! And a janitor at the hospital. They were all ripped to shreds. Some people are saying they were raped as well. Everyone is saying that it was just like the killings twenty years ago."

Mike listened for some response on the other end of the line, but there was only silence. He couldn't even hear the sound of Stan's breathing.

Stan stared at the family photos around the telephone, trying not to think of what Mike had just told him; but he couldn't *stop* thinking about it. It implied that all this stuff was connected to him. And he knew . . . he knew deep in his heart, it *did* have to do with the ceremony he had performed several nights ago.

"Hey! Hey, you! Snap out of it!" screamed Mike over the phone. "We gotta talk, and we gotta talk NOW!"

"Yeah, okay," Stan replied meekly. "My mom's gone till late afternoon. Why don't you cut class and come over here. That way we don't have to worry about other people hearing us—*or* you being seen with me," added Stan, with a slight bite in his voice.

"Okay, I'll be right there."

Stan hung up the receiver and walked back to his bedroom. Slowly, almost in a daze, he removed his robe and pulled on his jeans. He thought back to the house and how confused he had been there. He knew that the source of the problem was there, in that house.

Half an hour later, Mike rang the doorbell and Stan let him in; neither one said a word. Mike walked over to the couch and sat down, brushing his shiny black hair out of his eyes. He glared at Stan and shook his head. Stan looked away.

"You know this is all your fault, don't you, Fuller? You can feel it, can't you?"

"It's your fault, too. You were the one who wanted me to do the ceremonies. You didn't think I could really do anything. Well, you got a surprise. You wanted some excitement—and here it is. You've got to take some responsibility for it, too."

Mike was silent for a few minutes. Then he spoke again. "Just how much do you know that you aren't telling me? Huh? A whole shitload, I'll bet."

"Uh, yeah. I might have caused some of it . . . but I'm not really sure."

"Oh, gimme a break. You know what happened last night. What did you see? Did you know that those assholes were killed? Was it really wild dogs? Or is it . . ."

"NO! I didn't know they were dead. But there was more than I told you. Zeke *did* knock me into the waterfall. But I didn't get out by myself."

Stan paused and looked Mike in the eye. Mike narrowed his dark Japanese eyes in suspicion and said, "So who helped you out? Zeke?"

Stan shook his head and looked down at the floor.

Mike leaned forward and raised his voice. "Well, what the fuck happened? Just stop with this mysterious bullshit and tell me what happened!"

"Honestly, I don't really know. I—"

"Fuck! Give me a goddamn break. I'm really gettin' sick of your stupid—"

"I WAS DROWNING! I WAS ALMOST DEAD!" screamed Stan, his face discoloring with anger and fear. He turned his back on Mike and took a few deep breaths, then closed his eyes before continuing in a calmer voice. "I was knocked around on the bottom of the pond. I was too numb to swim. I was barely able to hold my breath. I thought I was going to die—knew that the next breath I took would be water, not air. Then, just when I was sure I was dead, I felt a hand around my arm. I was raised out of the water and got a breath of air. Then I blacked out."

"So then you walked to the road and collapsed where I found you."

"No."

"Whadda ya mean, no?"

"I was carried. Someone carried me from the falls to the road."

"That's almost half a mile! Who could have gone swimmin' with you and then carried you that far? Anyway, I thought you were out."

"I came to for a second, and I saw someone . . . it was a . . . a woman. A beautiful woman with dark hair and dark eyes and a pink mouth. And she said something to me."

"Jesus fucking Christ!" exclaimed Mike, throwing himself back against the couch in frustration. "Am I supposed to believe a woman jumped into freezing water, saved your ass, and then carried you half a mile to the road? And how could I miss that trick? I didn't see any women out there. There wasn't anyone out there except us crazy assholes!"

"I said I *saw* a woman. I didn't say she carried me back. And if you had any sense you'd know what I'm talking about. Two days ago we saw people that weren't there!"

"What are you talking about now?"

"Don't play dumb! You were there—the house. Or do you let just anyone give you a blow job?"

Mike blushed deeply and sat there for a minute before saying anything else.

"So what was it?"

"I don't know. But it was in my bedroom the night before we went to the house. I was asleep. The 'something' pulled the covers off my bed and . . . and . . ." Stan's voice trailed off into silence.

"And what?" Mike asked as he leaned forward.

Stan shook his head as if confused about something.

"Nothing," he mumbled.

Mike stood up and looked compassionately at Stan. He was crazy, probably, and dangerous to boot. And he just didn't seem to know right from wrong, as though no one had ever sat down with him and explained what was good and what was bad. He acted like the whole world was a lab for him to conduct experiments in, and the people he knew were white rats to use as he saw fit. In spite of everything that had happened, though, Mike still liked the guy.

He walked past Stan, thinking better of his inclination to put his hand on the confused boy's shoulder. He walked into

the kitchen and opened the fridge. He took out a Coke, pulled
the ring sharply, and threw the metal tab into the sink. Standing under the archway between the living room and the
kitchen, he looked back at Stan, who had still not moved,
and asked, "So hey, ol' Stan, ol' buddy, ol' pal . . . what
the fuck are we gonna do?"

Stan tilted his head and shot a sharp glance at Mike. "We're
gonna do what we should have done yesterday but were too
scared to do. We're going back to that house and see if we
can find Cliff and Peggy."

"You're fuckin' out of your mind! Do you know what
you're sayin'!? You're tellin' me that what killed Zeke,
Hampton, Peterson, and Pam is in that house! And you want
US to go back out there and git our asses killed, too? Fuck
you! I didn't sign on to be no hero!"

"Then I'll go alone."

Mike continued to stare at Stan and grew still angrier. Deep
inside, he realized that if there was something psychic or
conjured killing people, and that if Stan had anything to do
with it, he himself was partly responsible. And if Stan got
killed, there wouldn't be anyone who could help. Mike also
knew, deep in the most secret parts of his mind, that it would
come after him, too—it already had once, when he crashed
the Ranchero. He shuddered as he remembered the night-
marelike events in the house. Mike sighed deeply and then
responded in a low voice, "No. You can't go by yourself.
You're probably the only one that has any idea what we are
dealing with. I also know there's still more to all of this than
you're tellin' me. You have got to realize that unless you tell
me what is goin' on I can't really help you, and in the end
that's going to git us both . . ."

"We could take Maria with us."

"Who's Maria?"

"She is *la bruja*—a witch."

"Good Christ—a cast of thousands. Okay, so she's a witch.
What does she have to do with all this?"

"She helps me with the ceremonies. She's like my teacher,
sort of. But she doesn't speak any English. My Spanish is
okay to get by with, but I have trouble understanding her.
Still, at this point we need all the help we can get."

"God," moaned Mike. "What we need is someone to

wake us up from this nightmare. Okay, so call her. If we're going to our graves, it might as well be a party.''

"I can't call her. She's staying at that old run-down motel on the other side of the tracks."

"Shit. I should have guessed. Okay, let's go.''

Stan put his brother's wool coat on, since his own was still wet. Together they walked out the front door of the Fullers' house and got inside the Ranchero.

A few minutes later, they were parked outside the Casaita. Mike watched as Stan stood in the open doorway of a room, nodding his head and waving his arms about. After a moment's delay, Stan came out with an old Mexican woman.

Stan opened the door and slid in first, next to Mike. As the old woman stooped awkwardly, sliding onto the seat, Stan looked at Mike and said, in an ominous voice, "She told me she was expecting me. She said that I triggered something the other night with a ceremony . . . that she had been able to feel it. But she doesn't really know what was triggered, or if she does know, she isn't tellin'. But I can tell you, she isn't very happy about coming with us. I had to promise her that I would go back to L.A. with her and be her student. She said I would have to sweep the floor and do chores as well. But I ain't gonna go with her, I just said . . .''

"So I guess it's the house now, right?" interrupted Mike as he shifted the truck into gear.

Stan nodded his head, and Maria stared straight out the front window. None of them spoke another word until they pulled into the driveway of the house, where, to their horror, they caught sight of the sheriff's car, rammed into the side of the porch.

"Oh my God," said Mike. "This is crazy, he's been missin'. We should just haul our asses back to town and let someone else handle it.''

Evil poked around in the bloody remains of Sheriff Johnston. His short arms waved around, the little fingers scrubbing his face clean, while the blood-stained hands of his longer arms picked the corpse for remaining morsels. Loudly he belched, filling the dark basement with the foul odor of his stomach, laced with the scent of fresh blood.

Suddenly the incubus looked from side to side. He'd detected something—sensed it more than heard it. He jumped to his feet and ran up the stairs in such haste that his talons scarred the steps. Seconds later, he passed through the odd little room upstairs and into the rafters.

Peering out from a crack in the deteriorating wood, Bargolas watched the little red truck come up the driveway and park. An instant later, a dark old woman got out of the truck and looked up at the house. It seemed to Bargolas that she looked directly into his eyes. Smiling to himself, he muttered, "Oh, goody goody—play, ha-ha-ha, play . . ."

Mike and Stan remained in the truck as Maria stood outside, looking up at the house. She seemed to be staring up at the top floor as if she could see something.

"God, more mumbo jumbo," said Mike quietly, though he fell silent after that and waited for a cue from either Stan or the old woman as to what to do. Maria spoke for a few seconds; Stan slid out of the truck and stood beside her. Mike, too, climbed out of the truck and said to Stan over the top of the hood, "So you want to tell the *gringo* what she said?"

Stan shrugged. "She said something about the house having two different spirits. I didn't really understand the main part."

Maria spoke again, this time for much longer.

Stan looked over to Mike and shrugged once again. "I didn't really get any of that . . . sorry."

Slowly, as if in a trance, Maria moved toward the house. She crossed herself in the Catholic manner several times, and then did the same thing using the pentacle of protection. Stan walked beside her, and together they entered the house. Mike pulled his rifle from behind his seat and checked to see if it was loaded. Satisfied that it was, he followed Stan and Maria up the steps to the porch and into the house.

Maria stood quietly and half-closed her eyes; Stan did the same, looking off to the side, but his eyes widened as he focused on the handgun at the base of the stairs leading to the second floor.

Mike watched Stan as he walked over to the stairs and started to bend down and pick up the handgun. The second he recognized the gun he called out to Stan, quietly but urgently, "Don't touch it! It's the sheriff's and you don't want your fingerprints on it."

Stan stopped abruptly. Both of them knew what the gun meant. The sheriff had drawn the gun and then lost it. Both of them knew he was dead. And if Cliff and Peggy had come out here, they were sure to have gotten the same treatment or worse.

"Let's just go back into town and report this whole thing. We're in way over our heads—" said Mike.

"Shhh!" hissed Maria.

Maria walked around the room, her brow furrowed. She'd obviously detected something that she didn't like. She turned to Stan and spoke for a minute, then fell silent again.

"She said that there were two forces in the house, one good and one evil—very, very evil. She said that the evil is very strong and that the good is almost dead. I think she also said something about the good force being the force of the house."

Maria now crossed the floor quickly and grabbed hold of Mike's arm; looking over her shoulder to Stan, she spoke. After a moment she finished, but she maintained a tight grip on Mike's arm. Mike looked over to Stan questioningly, but Stan just turned away.

"Well, what did she say?"

"Uh, I don't know . . . I couldn't understand."

Mike shook himself from Maria's grip and shot across the floor. He grabbed a handful of Stan's jacket and spun him around. "You asshole! I got the shit kicked out of me for you, so don't stand there and lie to me. You know what she said . . . what the fuck was it?"

Stan look Mike directly in the eyes and spoke quietly. "She said that I was connected to the evil force, that I was a . . . a bridge for it between here and hell."

Mike released his grip on Stan and walked over to a broken window. For a moment he just stared out the window at the cold white winter. Still facing away from Stan and Maria, he spoke loudly enough for them both to hear. "This is what you've brought on with your fuckin' around—death!" Mike cocked his rifle. "Well, if this evil is flesh and blood enough to kill people, it is flesh and blood enough to git its ass shot off. Come on!"

Mike wheeled around and, with two strides, stood directly

in front of Stan. He grabbed at Stan roughly and caught his
coat, pulling Stan along behind him toward the kitchen. Stan
put up no resistance; he followed Mike to the basement door,
where Mike pulled his flashlight from his coat pocket.

Mike opened the basement door cautiously with his foot,
pointing the barrel of the gun into the darkness. He handed
the flashlight to Stan and said, "Stand behind, but to the side
of me, and shine the light in front of me. Make sure that you
keep the light in front of me . . ."

Together they descended the stairs. Before they got halfway
down, the stench wafted up and slapped them across their
faces, making them nauseated.

Maria, who had felt that something more important was
upstairs, followed them angrily across the kitchen and stopped
at the top of the basement stairs. She had heard a noise overhead. Not sure whether it was the wind or something more
sinister, she walked back into the living room and stood at
the bottom of the staircase leading to the second story.

She noticed the handgun lying at the bottom of the steps
and reached down to pick it up. The gun boosted her courage,
and she took her first step up the stairs. One by one she
climbed, pausing on each stair to listen for any signs of danger.

By the time Maria reached the top landing, her heart was
pounding and she could feel the pulse in her throat. Again
she crossed herself, and in the midst of the act, she heard the
sound again. It came from the room down at the end of the
hall, the one with a small window in the door. Then she heard
it again, a click-click-clicking sound.

Cautiously, Maria thrust the handgun out in front of her
and walked toward the room. The floor creaked under her
tread as she neared the doorway, and an icy draft made
her wish for the heat of Mexico. Slowly she pulled the door
open and walked in.

Bargolas heard the approach of the old *bruja*. Her steps
were noisy and her crosses of protection useless. As he heard
her approach, he lowered himself a little, headfirst, through
the access panel in the ceiling so just his head and a bit of
his shoulders poked downward. As the old woman approached, he watched her through the small glass window set

in the door. Brown, stringy slime began to fall from his open mouth as she pulled the door open. He extended one of his powerful arms in readiness.

Tears stung Mike's and Stan's eyes as they looked down at the pants encrusted with blood and gore. Looped around the pants was a leather belt with the familiar buckle of polished lapis lazuli. Cliff had often bragged about how his grandfather had given him the belt buckle when he shot his first buck.

The boys' sense of danger prevailed over their urge to cry. Waving the rifle, Mike instructed Stan to shine the light around the basement slowly. As the dim yellow circle panned across the room, Mike followed it with the rifle barrel. Suddenly something glimmered in the light, and Mike and Stan inched their way over to the spot, listening for any sound that meant danger.

A moment later they realized what they were looking at, and Mike vomited. Stan stared in horror at the puddle of slime and bloody bones lying on Sheriff Johnston's uniform shirt. Slowly Stan began to back away, the smell and the sight finally wrenching the last bit of control from him. Stumbling backward, he fell onto something moist and slick. The flashlight spun from his grasp, plunging them into darkness. Mike began cursing as he and Stan felt their way around until they found the bottom of the stairs.

Maria examined the outside of the odd door for a moment before she slowly pushed it open. Suspiciously, she scanned the room for some sign of danger. Suddenly she caught some movement out of the corner of her eye and jumped back just in time to avoid the decapitating swing of a taloned hand.

When Maria turned full to view the monster, she was for a moment stunned by its grotesqueness. The creature hung from the ceiling access panel with one muscular arm swinging freely. His eyes glittered with menace as he opened his mouth. His stench filled the room as he spoke.

"Ooohh, Maria, play play . . ."

Maria stared the beast down, crossing herself several times, and then she screamed in Spanish, "Back to hell, demon!"

She stepped forward, pointing the gun at the creature; she

screamed, *"Diablo! Diablo!"* at the top of her lungs and
pulled the trigger.

Bargolas, however, swiped his arm at the gun and deflected
it just as it went off. Quickly, he brought his hand back down
and grasped Maria by the back of her neck, digging his talons
deep into her spinal cord. For a moment she writhed, suspended in the air like a snake caught by a stork. Then, slowly,
the incubus licked at her face with his swollen tongue. After
a few moments he flicked at her eyes lightly, then progres-
sively with more strength as the intensity of his lust increased.

Mike and Stan had clambered to the top of the stairs just
in time to hear Maria scream, and felt the dread of the exploding gun. Stan screamed out for Maria and ran through
the house and up the stairs. Mike followed as fast as he could,
taking care not to trip on anything lest he fall and discharge
the rifle. He was not yet to the top landing when he saw Stan
rush into the odd little room without the slightest precaution.

Mike burst in behind him. Stan stood plastered against the
wall, staring bug-eyed at something. Mike quickly turned to
follow Stan's stare, aiming his rifle in the same direction. He
saw Maria, suspended from the arm of hideous monster from
the ceiling. Most of Maria's face was gone, and her head was
connected to her body by only a few tendons. Blood dripped
from the creature's lips, which were twisted into a grisly
smile. Mike aimed and fired. Simultaneously, Stan and the
creature screamed in pain.

Mike had missed the creature's head and hit his shoulder.
The incubus dropped the lifeless Maria to the floor and pulled
itself back up into the rafters. With the rifle still pointed at
the ceiling access panel, Mike backed up a couple of steps
and bent down to look at Stan.

Stan had collapsed against the wall, holding his shoulder.
Stan's eyes were clenched in pain as Mike pried his hands
away to see how Stan was injured. "What's wrong?" Mike
asked. "Where are you hurt? What happened?" Mike thought
that the shot had somehow ricocheted and hit Stan. However,
he could find no injury, nor any blood. Mike pushed his
thumb against several places on Stan's shoulder. On the third

try, Stan winced—and from the attic above there came a wail of agony. Understanding the connection, Mike struggled against an urge to panic; he helped Stan to his feet and got him started down the stairs, saying, "Come on, you asshole, let's get the fuck out of here!"

22

Othello, 1951

As gently as an autumn leaf drifting from the upper reaches of a tree, blown free by the changing winds, he laid her upon the coverlet. The bed moaned slightly as he took his place beside her, and she in turn echoed the moan with one of her own. He looked deep into her eyes, seeking the dreams and desires of this woman named Lydia. Easily, he breathed in her wants and needs, knowing exactly how he would become her perfect lover. He would make no mistakes this time; this time he would never, never go back to the suffocating darkness.

Lydia melted under the heat of his lips, their urgent pressure molding her passion into a temple, a sanctuary where she could make love with this man, who was everything she had ever desired. His hands touched her lightly—everywhere— exploring, teasing her into pure, ruby-red lust.

His tongue washed over her like that of a serpent seeking heat, finding it, lingering a moment, then moving on, leaving behind a cool, moist trail. He played her body with hot and cold, with bone-crushing pressure and feather-light touches. He awakened her awareness of places long forgotten—buried away in the painful rubble of a neglected marriage.

In turn, she devoured him. Her teeth bit into his flawless skin. Her hands alternately caressed, then dug frantically at his body. Her fingernails drew blood, which meandered in rivulets down the sculptured hills of his physique, as her passion and heat kept rising. She drank him like water, quenching the thirst of a lifetime. She drank him like gasoline poured onto a fire, exploding in a blur of heat and motion. She rubbed her body against his, finding in some places a magical slickness and in others, a bleak friction; the contrast made her ache in excitement.

When he found the tender hollow of her neck, she felt his searing breath on her skin. Bending slightly, she inhaled the sweetness of his oily black hair. She smelled the azure skies of Greece, the rolling hills of olive trees, wild rosemary, and clusters of basil. When, suddenly, he entered her, she thought the pain might kill her.

The pain returned her to the little house outside Othello. She returned to the trancelike stare of Bargolas, looming over her while he began to move inside her. She was there on the bed, beneath a man who looked like a god. His passion became her pain, queerly mixed with pleasure. Tears streamed in hot rivers down the sides of her face as she reached up to touch his chest. He caught her hands and pulled them gently, but forcefully, down to her side, to pin them beneath his powerful hands.

He quickened; she screamed. She was suspended forever, praying that it would never end—yet not sure she could endure another moment. She screamed again and again.

The screams excited him—his arousal was complete. But he knew he must restrain himself with this fragile creature who brought him back from the darkness. He would make no more mistakes. He held himself back, concentrating as best he could . . . He felt the spark tickle deep within the heat of his loins, and suddenly he exploded with white-hot fire boiling up from the depth of his bloodlust.

Lydia's eyes rolled back into her head as she tried to force herself to remain conscious, but huge black suns with red centers flashed before her eyes and her breathing came in ragged gasps. Her body heaved upward, her breasts quivering, as she tried to hang on. The welling up of her own passion shook her in savage release.

Bargolas' breathing was rasping and violent. The room

shook with the force of a summer thunderstorm as his sudden scream filled the room. The bed was buffeted by desperate penetrating lust. Then he stopped.

The storm passed over them, leaving only the exhausted gasps of spent passion behind. Bargolas withdrew, and instantly Lydia felt that part of her had been stolen. Softly, she cried for her loss as he covered her cheeks in soft kisses. He cradled her in his arms, and she slept.

23

Othello, 1970

Panic devoured reason. Nothing mattered, neither the cold nor the location. The only focus was the car—and running, running as fast as they could get away.

Mike threw the gearshift lever into low and gave the little red truck too much gas. The tires spun on the icy surface, then began to dig through the hard-packed snow, unable to gain traction. The cab of the truck was filled with the boys' screams. Mike pulled on the steering wheel hard and then released it, slamming the palms of his hands on the rim repeatedly, swearing oaths at the truck, at Stan, and at their horrible predicament.

Suddenly, without having been turned on, the radio began to blare at top volume. The hysterical laugh at the beginning of The Moody Blues' "Ride My See-Saw" only heightened the boys' panic. Stan trembled and crossed himself every few seconds with the pentacle of protection, tormented by the image of Maria, dangling and faceless.

Mike turned on himself, biting into his knuckles like an animal frightened beyond the reason of instinct. The pain brought him out of his panic. He took a deep breath and tried to concentrate, now depressing the clutch pedal once again and pulling the gearshift into second to generate less torque;

methodically, he released the clutch and increased the steady pressure of the gas pedal.

The little red Ranchero inched forward, trying to get out of the hole it had dug itself into. The wheels started to spin again. This time, Mike eased off on the gas and the truck slid back into the hole. Then, as it reached its farthest backward position, Mike applied the gas again and the truck lurched forward, just a bit farther than on the previous try. Mike rocked it back and forth several more times, trying not to think about the monster in the house, but he reached a point where he gained no more ground and only slid back into the depression again.

Stan found some comfort in Mike's calmer attitude. As the stinging in his shoulder diminished, he reasoned out some of the connection between himself and the creature. Meanwhile, he turned off the radio and kept watch out the back window for any sign of the creature, reaching up to wipe the vapor from the window with the sleeve of his coat. He could smell his own fear as Mike rocked the truck back and forth.

Then he saw movement at the corner of the porch—a dark figure, he thought, though he wasn't sure. He started to say something to Mike and then caught the movement again out of the corner of his eye. It looked as if something had jumped over the side of the porch. Stan opened his mouth to warn Mike, but Mike spoke first.

"We ain't getting out of here unless we break open the sandbags in the back and pour it under the tires." Mike looked at Stan and saw the fear in his eyes. "Yeah, I'm scared shit-less too, but—"

"I just saw something out there. I think . . ."

Mike jerked his head around. Swiping at the vapor-covered windows, he looked out. "Fuck . . . We got no choice if we want to get out of here."

Stan said nothing as he turned around and unlocked his door. He felt it would fly open and the creature would leap in and kill the both of them, in the same horrible way it had killed Maria.

Mike also unlocked his door and grabbed his rifle again. He flung the door open and stepped out with the gun at the ready. Seconds later, Stan stood beside him.

"Where did you see it?" Mike asked softly.

"Over there." Stan pointed toward the corner of the house.

Mike aimed and fired. Splinters flew and dust rose from the corner of the porch where the bullet exploded. The echo reverberated across the snow, giving the two boys the courage to jump hurriedly into the back of the truck and haul out the sandbags. The one Mike took was already open. Stan's was still sealed; Mike tossed him his Buck knife, and he quickly sliced open the bag like a freshly killed animal, its dark guts spilling onto the trampled snow.

Stan saw blood covering his hands. Then he saw *her*, the deep slash across her breast exposing the individual layers of tissue, some white and some reddish-gray. He looked at the great knife in his hands and stepped back. The dark red liquid soaked into her blond hair, and he realized she would never move again. The blood ran down the slight slope of the linoleum floor, running into . . . forever, forever . . . He took another step back and raised the knife high above his head, screaming—

"Hey!" Mike said to him. "Stan! What the fuck—"

Stan shook his head, trying to clear the hallucination away. He hissed sharply, "IT is still around. It was putting images into my head again. I made me see—"

"Forget about it, we've got to get the fuck out of here. Dump the sand in front of the tire and get back in the truck."

Stan shook his head once more before he started pouring sand behind the rear tires. Just as he finished, he again caught some movement off to the side. Looking quickly, he saw nothing.

Mike had spotted it, though, too. He spun around in time to see the creature duck behind the corner of the porch. It was on the snow, sneaking up on them—stalking them. Mike realized they were now like wild animals that had become prey for this unholy creature.

"Mike," came a soft, soothing voice.

Mike jerked his head around and brought the gun sight to bear on the girl who had rounded the corner of the porch. It was Paula, barefoot, wearing only panties and a bra. Her dark hair flowed down over her shoulders. She smiled and held out her arms, inviting Mike to dash into them.

"SHOOT!" screamed Stan at the top of his voice. "SHOOT!"

Mike heard a voice in the background, but he couldn't make out the words and didn't even care to try. He took a step toward Paula. His foot crunched in the snow and his breath blew a plume in front of his face. It felt like he was walking through water. Suddenly, the whole world exploded in sharp ice crystals, obscuring his vision. He brought his hand up to feel the point of impact and pain on his cheek. Then he heard Stan screaming at the top of his lungs.

"Shoot! Mike, SHOOOOOT!"

Bargolas, his spell over Mike broken, lunged at the boy. Mike saw only white, but he could hear Stan screaming at him. He had a feeling that his life was ending. He could feel the rifle stock, smooth and heavy, the trigger hard. He squeezed the trigger, unseeing. He squeezed it again.

The incubus bounded toward Mike, grimacing with pain and anger, tasting blood in his mouth, lusting after the boy. His genitals were retracted up inside his body, but he could feel the blood coursing through them. Suddenly there was an explosion of noise from in front of the boy, and a flash of fire brighter than the snow that lay all around them. Pain, like an arrow, burned with searing intensity across the creature's cheek and back along his head. He howled and lurched sideways, angered even more, and he sprinted toward the boy, just as another eruption of fire and noise came from the boy's weapon.

This time, the snow in front of Bargolas puffed and he heard a slight sizzle where the hot bullet had entered the cold. He stopped, put his short arm up to his wound, and felt the blood running down his cheek and neck.

Stan stood, watching in terror, holding his cheek where there was the echo of pain from the incubus's wound. Mike was still aiming the gun toward the beast. But he seemed to be still caught up in the illusion the creature had cast. Then, to his relief, he saw Mike slowly come out of his trance. Stan had another snowball ready to hit him in the face again if Mike showed signs of falling back under the monster's spell. Then, as if the horrible creature recognized the danger, it started to retreat around the side of the porch, growling.

"Mike!"

Mike looked around, but not directly at Stan.

"Mike!"

This time Mike looked squarely into Stan's eyes.

"Mike, we've got to get this sand under the tires before the thing comes back!"

Mike nodded his head and picked up his bag of sand. He stood the rifle up against the truck within his reach and began dumping sand in front of the rear tire, keeping one eye out for the creature. Soon it was done and he yelled, "Let's go!"

The two boys leapt back into the truck and locked the doors. As soon as the engine started up, the supernatural creature attacked again.

A high-pitched wail keened over the white snow as the creature ran toward them. Stan yelled in a panic, "Here it comes again! GO . . . GO!"

The wheels spun uselessly for a second, then suddenly caught hold of sand. The truck lurched forward, and BLAM!—the beast hit the window on the driver's side, glass shattering into a thousand jagged pieces that sprayed the entire inside of the cab, some small pieces lodged themselves in Mike's cheek. Mike screamed in pain and anger as the impact knocked the creature backward into the snow. Mike reached frantically for the gun, but his hands couldn't find it. Stan, still writhing from the mirror image of Bargolas' agony, was unaware that the rifle was within his grasp.

Instantly, the unholy creature was back on its feet with a screech of rage, just as the Ranchero jumped out of the icy rut and onto hard snow. The beast leapt through the air and latched onto the side of the truck as it began to pick up speed, then quickly reached through the broken window and grabbed hold of Mike's coat. Its talons pierced the jacket and dug deeply into Mike's chest. He screamed in pain and panic, floored the gas pedal. The Ranchero slid sideways. Stan jumped over and tried to pry the creature's hand from Mike's shoulder, but he was unable to budge it. Remembering the knife, he dug into his coat pocket and pulled it out; his cold fingers fumbling, he pried open the blade.

Stan himself felt the excruciating pain as he repeatedly sliced through the beast's claw. Blood streamed from the horny flesh, covering Mike's coat. The monster shrieked increasingly louder and finally let go of Mike. He dropped from the boys' sight—but he retained his hold on the outside of the truck.

Mike had eased up on the gas, and the truck managed to straighten itself out; then he began to pick up speed again. "We'll lose him when we get on the road!" screamed Mike. "Pick up the fucking gun in case he comes back!" The icy wind blew through the broken window into his face, making him shiver even more.

Mike slowed for the turn onto the highway, and two-inch claws poked in through the window. Instantly, Stan was all over the leg with the Buck knife, trying at the same time to conquer the slicing pain he felt in his own legs. Just when the truck completed the turn, the creature's talons raked across Mike's face.

Pain flashed through his consciousness—the bright red flash-flash of a warning light, telling him his death was very near. His vocal cords were now raw from screaming. In a reflex, he twisted the steering wheel, and the truck veered first to one side, then the other. Through sheer willpower Mike maintained control, correcting the slide. A dull thump behind the truck drew Mike's eyes to his rearview mirror, where he saw the creature picking himself up from the road and running full speed behind them.

Stan saw him, too. "He's off! Drive! GO!" he yelled hoarsely.

"Yeah! Yeah, all fuckin' right. MAN!" gasped Mike. A smile began to creep across his face.

Stan looked at his own hands and leg. He saw no blood—no sign of injury at all, in fact. But the *pain* . . . he still felt the horrible pain that he'd shared with the creature while knifing him.

When he looked over at his friend, however, Stan could see that Mike was in much worse condition. Strings of loose flesh hung from the side of his cheek and neck. Mike continued to smile, even though his white teeth were swimming in his own blood and bloody spittle collected at the side of his mouth; his smile grew and grew, finally becoming a laugh.

Mike laughed and laughed, like a maniac, as Stan sat silently watching him. Stan tried to speak to him, but Mike only laughed, and tears squirted from his eyes.

Soon, Othello came into view; dusk was covering the area,

and a low haze was settling lightly upon the fresh snow. Mike drove home and parked on the street in front, in his usual place. He had stopped laughing, and now he just sat, making no movement to get out. Stan sat beside him for what seemed a long time. He was glad Mike's parents weren't home; he needed time to decide what to do next.

Finally, Stan stepped out of the Ranchero, walked around to the driver's side, and opened the door. Gently, he slid his hand under Mike's arm and helped him out of the truck. Supporting a lot of Mike's weight, he walked him across the slick road to the house. As he helped Mike put one foot in front of the other, he felt his own muscles and bones smart from the pain and stress. He, too, wanted to retreat into a world where he wouldn't have to cope with what was happening. That was what Pam had done, that was why she had ended up in the hospital. That was why she had been unable to tell people what had happened. If she had just fought against the blinding panic that caused her to retreat, perhaps she would have been able to tell someone how to help her— perhaps she would be alive today. But now it appeared that the path of blinding panic had led Mike, too, to the same place of false security.

24

Othello, 1951

He chuckled as he ate his beans and Dutch Oven corn bread. He was always smirking and posturing, as though some enormous practical joke had been played on someone, when none had; that was why they called him crazy—Crazy Ol' Tom. Giggling, he shoved another spoonful of beans into his mouth.

His teeth ground against some grit and he snarled, "Goddamn roof!"

Covering his plate with his hands, he looked up at the sod roof overhead, searching for more falling debris that might find its way into his food. Then, just as he expected, he heard a thump-thump across the roof. Dirt and chunks of sod pattered onto his old wooden table; some of it fell right through his fingers and into his food, while still more disappeared onto the dirt floor.

"Goddammit to hell! Jonny, you dumb fuckin' no-count worthless flea-ridden bag of bones! Get the fuck off o' the roof!" Ol' Tom screamed at the top of his lungs, trying to scare the mule off the sod roof before the weight of the beast caved it in.

He listened carefully but didn't hear anything more, so he continued with his dinner, satisfied that the mule had taken his advice. Turning around, he looked up the dirt slope at the cracks in the wooden door and was unable to see any daylight

through them. Shaking his head back and forth, he squinted
at his father's pocket watch.

"Shit! Ain't even five o'clock yet and it's dark a'ready.
Well, well, won't be long till Ol' Man Winter comes knockin'
on my door," he chanted in a singsong voice.

He cocked his head as he heard a thud and a honk from
his mule; then there was only silence. He considered whether
to go out there and kick the shit out of that mule and decided
he'd finish his beans and corn bread before moving Jonny for
the night.

"Shit," he mumbled into his beans, "gotta do everythin'
myself now."

He thought back on Gus, who had fallen down an old mine
shaft the summer before. It wasn't their shaft. Someone had
covered it with rotting planks and then thrown dirt on top of
'em. Looked for all the world like a trap. Tom spent the
better part of a day hauling Gus out, with both his legs broke
and several ribs caved in. It was a hellish ride for the poor
sucker on top of Jonny, down to Doc Weber's in Othello.
And now that it was fall, it didn't seem like Gus was comin'
back before next summer.

Ol' Tom got up and moseyed over to the makeshift stove.
The smoke pipe ran out the top of the fifty-five-gallon oil
drum and up through the sod roof. He poked a few more
pieces of dried sagebrush through the hole and watched it
catch on fire. It didn't really take too much to keep this little
dugout warm, he thought to himself, even in the dead o'
winter. There were no windows to let out the heat and only
the cracks in the door to worry about.

Tom daydreamed his way back to when he and Gus had
built the place. It had taken them one full day, one chilly
day, two springs ago—was that the spring of '50 or '51? He
just couldn't remember dates anymore—to dig the hole in the
ground that would be their mining camp. Then they needed
another day to lay planks and cut the sod to put over the
planks. They put tar paper between the sod and the planks,
but it tore in a lot of places and you could see bare sod all
over when you looked up. He remembered how funny it was
when they built the door. They'd remembered everything—
except nails . . .

Ol' Tom frowned as he heard the thump-thump above him

again. This time the weight of the mule made the roof planks sag and creak. "Goddamn rotten fucking mule!" Tom yelled at the top of his voice and grabbed his Coleman. He headed up the dirt ramp to the door.

He threw the door open and stepped into the chill of the autumn night. He held the lantern up over the flat roof but didn't see Jonny there—in fact he didn't see Jonny anywhere. It wasn't like that old varmint to wander off by its lonesome.

"Jonny . . . Jonny!"

Tom heard no response; no movement to indicate the mule's location. He swung the lantern first in one direction, then the other, casting eerie shadows in the darkening light. "Fuckin' MULE!" He growled loudly, walking over to the last place he had seen it.

The lantern light reflected off something on the ground. Tom thought at first it might be piss from the mule, but looking closer he discovered it wasn't. He dipped his finger into the liquid and felt that it was still warm. Examining it in the light, he realized it was blood. Tom's heart started to pound in his throat, and he hoped to God it wasn't old Jonny; he was a bothersome cuss, but he'd been Tom's companion nigh onto twenty-five years.

Instinct told Tom something was wrong, but it didn't make a whole lot of sense. There hadn't been any wildcats in this area for a long time, and that was just about the only thing that could attack an animal big as a mule.

In fact, as he continued to ponder the situation, he realized there wasn't much out here in the way of wild animals except a few badgers and coyotes. He picked up his lantern and followed the tracks of the mule; then he picked up the tracks of something else. He would have sworn they were the tracks of a full-grown man—and barefoot, at that—except that there were deep gouges in front of the toes: claw prints, they looked like.

Ol' Tom stood up. He'd never seen anything like this in the fifteen years he'd mined this area. He started toward the sod-covered dugout for his rifle when he heard something off to his left. He turned to hear better; concentrated.

It was a strange sound. Wet. Slick. Sometimes a slurping sound. Like old toothless Gus when he ate: he sort of inhaled his food and then gummed it. God, he thought, I wish Gus was here right now. Tom listened closely to the sound and began to walk silently toward it.

The blood now pumped loudly in his ears as he pushed the lantern out in front of him. He couldn't hear the slurping sound anymore but he didn't know if it was because he was scared or if it had really stopped.

Then Ol' Tom saw him. "Jesus Christ . . . Jonny." Tom's knees began to wobble. "Oh my God . . ." He felt hot tears run down through his whiskers and into his mouth, tasted salt. "Oh God, Jonny . . . what did they do to you?"

Jonny lay there on his side. His neck was doubled back onto itself and the top of his head rested against his spine. His throat was torn out. The dirt around Jonny's body was shiny with blood that had spread out in two or three main rivers and numerous small tributaries. One hind leg had been torn free from the old mule's flank and almost completely stripped of flesh. Guts lay strewn about; the pink and gray matter oozing from several rips in the stomach had been pulled up over the body. Tom gazed into the eyes of his old friend. They were wide with fear, and still moist, glistening in the light of the Coleman lantern.

Next thing Ol' Tom knew, he was down on his hands and knees, only a few yards from his sod cabin, puking up his beans and corn bread. He heaved and heaved until there was nothing left to puke up. After he stumbled back to his feet, he could again feel the tears wetting his face. He found the cabin door and pulled it open. He had barely set the lantern on the edge of the table before he fell over sideways onto his bunk.

He lay there in the light of the lantern with his arm thrown over his eyes to shield them, and felt more lonely than he ever had in his entire life. He so wished Gus was there. At least then they could drink some whiskey together.

"What . . . ?" He uncovered his eyes and squinted into the harsh lantern light. He had heard something. A clicking sound, and then a shuffle . . . then silence again. He looked all about the little dirt cabin but didn't see anything. But wait—what was that big sacklike shape beside the stove? That wasn't there before . . .

Ol' Tom sat up and looked more carefully into the corner. That baglike thing appeared to move. Sweat broke out on the palms of Tom's hands. He felt glued to the bed. He looked around the room for his rifle and saw it leaning against the dirt wall next to the box of potatoes—only a foot or so from the mysterious sack. Cautiously, Tom stood up. The bag moved again, and Tom's heart almost stopped. He crept around the side of the table. Standing only a few feet from the rifle, he watched the bag move again as he started to reach for the gun. He stopped, however, as a strange apparition appeared.

The bag grew larger, taller. It untwisted and uncoiled like a serpent. The bag, Tom suddenly realized, was some sort of man, black like shadows, who had been crouching in a tight ball. Now he stood, and his head almost touched the sod ceiling. The lantern light reflected from powerful back and leg muscles as this creature of darkness slowly turned to face Tom.

So terrified was Tom by the appearance of this hellish beast that he was unaware of himself making soft mewing sounds like a baby preparing to cry. Bulbous black eyes glared into Tom's fear; a mouth opened, revealing uneven rows of blood-stained teeth. Fresh blood glistened down the front of the creature. Jonny's blood, Tom realized with a sense of doom.

Tom had forgotten the gun and didn't even think of running. He stared in horror as this foul-smelling nightmare took a step toward him. The creature's short arms unfolded from its chest and snaked upward to wipe the blood from its mouth and ears.

Then there was darkness, and Tom was sure he had died. After a moment, a deep blue glow appeared before him, brightening bit by bit until he saw the light reflecting from the eyes of Rebecca Frist.

She was as beautiful as the first day he had laid eyes on her. He was eighteen, and they had met on the bank of the Columbia. She smiled at him then, just as she smiled at him now, and he could feel the heat building between his legs. She took a step toward him and pulled down the front of her red dress. Her white breasts quivered proudly, and he stepped forward to touch them. He buried his face in the soft mounds of flesh and inhaled their natural perfume. It felt as though his lust might burst through his pants. He crushed her to his chest and covered her pink mouth with his insistent kisses.

She ran her tongue over his ears and down the side of his neck. She ripped away at his shirt with her bloodred nails and then began tugging at his trousers. An instant later he felt her moist velvety tongue sliding down his belly to his erect flesh. He inhaled sharply as the ring of hot moistness covered his throbbing member. A small eternity later, he felt his release—and excruciating pain.

Tom glanced down to find the creature looking up at him, its lips gleaming with semen. Tom's chest and belly were covered with blood, running in rivulets that the creature now licked up greedily. Tom tried to push himself away, his screams echoing with the certainty of his own death. The creature brought up a taloned hand and ripped away his throat, silencing him.

Several minutes intervened—a lifetime and more of intolerable pain and the incapability of expressing it, time enough for what was left of Tom's spinal column to carry to his brain the consciousness of having his guts ripped from his body—before finally, mercifully, that tortured brain succumbed to the lack of oxygen. Ol' Tom died watching the creature from hell eat his flesh. It wasn't until late fall the next year that some hunters found his body.

Lydia bowed her head and leaned into the wind. It was the frigid autumn wind, laced with the dirt of the desert. This flat area was known for its windstorms, no matter what time of the year it was. She grabbed for her hat, catching it just as a strong gust tried to fling it into the dirty brown air.

It was probably a mistake to walk from Doc Weber's to the church. She should have just stayed put until Seth finished his business at the church and came to pick her up. But she hadn't, and now she was halfway there; it would be pointless to turn back now.

A few minutes later, she shut out the wind behind the double doors of the Mount Zion Baptist Church. She turned to face the empty rows of pews where she sat dutifully Sunday after Sunday while her husband, from the pulpit, preached the threat of hellfire from an uncompromising god.

Shaking her hair, she stirred up a terrible cloud of dust. She wiped at her face with her gloves and licked her lips. She could feel the grit, tasteless but uncomfortable, between her teeth. She listened to the howling wind and wondered what she was going to do about her predicament. Doc Weber had told her she was pregnant.

It had been well over four years since Seth had even touched her. That left only one possibility: Bargolas. She wanted to have the baby, but first she would have to get Seth to sleep with her—once more, just once more.

Lydia heard a chair slide across the floor in one of the outer rooms of the church and knew that Seth was still there. He had told her long ago that he didn't like for her to be back in the offices with him. He preferred her to wait outside, like the rest of his parishioners.

"Pregnant! My God! What am I going to do?" she whispered to herself in a mock prayer to a god she no longer believed in. For the hundredth time, she asked herself how this could have happened. Bargolas had told her he couldn't give her a child; his seed was worthless. Could he give her a child with the seed of another? Whose seed was it?

Together, Seth and Lydia drove back to the farmhouse. As usual, they were silent, with only the wind slamming at the car and churning up great clouds of dust.

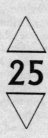

25

Othello, 1970

Stan leaned Mike against the doorway of his bedroom, and there Mike remained, zombielike, while Stan searched for old towels in the bathroom. He found some in the linen cabinet, at the bottom of a varicolored pile of terry cloth. He took three of them and, after pulling down the covers of Mike's bed, laid the towels across the pillow and over the sheets. Mike's chin appeared to rest upon his chest. Dried blood covered most of his face and neck, extending partway down his torso. Stan was silently thankful that Mike's parents had gone to visit friends in Pasco. There was just no way the two of them would have been able to cope with giving explanations at this point.

Stan surveyed Mike's wounds. They were ugly and needed attention quickly to ward off infection. He steered Mike over to the bed, helped him lie down, and pulled the blankets up over his chest.

Looking down at Mike's lacerated face, Stan felt very responsible—and sick to his stomach with guilt. He considered the possibility of taking Mike to the hospital, and the dilemma tormented him. What should he do? There would be so many questions, and even if he found the courage to tell the whole story, nobody would believe the answers: "That's

right, folks, my hobby is demonology and one of my projects
seems to have gotten carried away.''

Facing the questions was the least of his worries; more
important was Mike's safety. After all, had Pam been safe in
the hospital? On the radio, they had played the whole thing
down, as they had with the other deaths in the last few days,
yet all you had to do was look at Mike's face to imagine the
fate that everyone had suffered at the hands of this creature.

Stan could feel his guts churning over and over. He knew
he would have to make a trip to the bathroom soon, because
of stress and fear. But something else was upsetting him: the
creature had drawn Mike's blood, had tasted his youth and
warmth; he would be back, just as he had come back for
Pam. A cramping sensation started near his pelvis and grew
out in rings of discomfort. Stan headed for the bathroom,
undoing his pants as he ran.

A few minutes later he emerged, the sound of the toilet
refilling in the background. On his way out, he had taken a
moment to search the Kawaguchis' medicine cabinet and
found a bottle of hydrogen peroxide. Walking back into
Mike's room, he saw that Mike had turned slightly toward
the wall, his clawed face against the towel covering his pillow. Mike's right hand was clenched—that seemed to be a
good sign. Stan knew Mike wasn't the type to give up, even
if he was scared half out of his mind.

Carefully he rolled Mike onto his back. Mike stared toward
the ceiling. Suddenly, almost too fast for Stan to be certain,
Mike's eyes shifted to look at him and then quickly returned
to the ceiling. Stan believed the quick look said a great deal:
Mike was asking him to take over for a while, Mike needed
a break—but don't worry, it seemed to say, he'd be back.
Stan's heart thumped a couple times, and he hoped his feelings were at least partly true; he didn't really know if he
would be able to cope with what was to come without his
friend's help.

For the incubus, pain was a transformative force. He did
not like it—he recoiled from it, as all living, breathing beings
did—but it gave him something: it gave him purpose. Pain
concentrated his mind into a strength of will that could not
be opposed. Now, as he crouched among the shrubs in front

of the boy's house, he regained his breath and licked at the deep slices across the top of his hand until there was no more blood there—only the deep, throbbing slashes across his flesh. Still in his mouth was the taste of his own blood, mingled with the blood of the boy, which impelled him to the hunt.

The crunching of tires over the crusty snow stirred him from his lustful fantasies of revenge. He peered out from the snow-covered shrubs and watched an automobile pass by; then he shifted his gaze toward the little red truck sitting on the street. He could *feel* the two boys inside the house. He smiled a toothy grin, and saliva dripped from the side of his mouth. He was white as the snow, but he itched to change to the black of shadows in preparation for the evening of pleasure that lay ahead. His skin tingled with anticipation.

Stan poured hydrogen peroxide on the fluffy cotton. The cotton collapsed under the weight of the liquid and ran between his fingers onto the towels. He began to sponge the deep gouges in Mike's cheek; the jagged edges of the wounds gathered up the soft cotton like thorns. Trickles of blood-stained hydrogen peroxide ran down Mike's neck, cold and wet. Mike flinched. The gouges foamed white as the peroxide boiled away at the beginning infection. Mike rolled his eyes and blew his breath out between his lips, making a hissing sound.

Stan blinked at the staleness, the almost putrid odor of fear, on Mike's breath. Mike would not look at him; still, Stan felt reassured that he was going to be okay. After all, he was reacting to things—like the discomfort of the antiseptic. Now Mike was gritting his teeth. The muscles along his jaw flexed over and over in ripples. Stan returned to the bathroom and took out the bottle of aspirin. He ran a Dixie cup of water and took three of the white tablets, along with the water, back to Mike.

"Here, take these. They'll help with the pain."

For a moment, it appeared that Mike hadn't heard Stan. Then, slowly, he propped himself up on one elbow and held out his hand. Stan dropped the tablets into his palm and Mike threw them to the back of his throat. He reached for the water and washed them down. Still holding onto the Dixie cup, he fell back to the bed and closed his eyes.

Stan looked on in silence. Stray filaments of cotton, clinging to the ragged edges of skin, wafted gently in the air cur-
rents of the little bedroom. Stan returned again to the
bathroom and brought back a washcloth. After soaking the
cloth with peroxide, he tried again to clean Mike's wounds.
The cloth worked much better; soon Stan had cut away the
ragged flaps of skin and cleaned all of the wounds—the physical ones, at least.

Stan stood back, admiring his work. The wounds were devoid of dirt and blood, and in most, the antiseptic was still
boiling away at the bacteria.

Then a noise caught his attention, a soft clicking sound.
Stan turned his head, trying to locate the source, and heard
it again—a clicking against Mike's bedroom window.

Stan knew what it was, and his breath stopped. Finding the
courage from somewhere, he took a step toward the window,
waited, then took another. Slowly he crossed the five or six
feet to the window, then for another minute and more he just
stared at the curtains. He brought his hand up to push away
the fabric, then dropped it again. His mouth was dry. He
could feel beads of sweat forming above his lip. Once again
he brought his hand up, grasped the edge of the curtain, and
slowly lifted it.

All he could see was the shiny glass surface reflecting the
light of the room back at him. He saw his own reflection and
thought it looked like a stranger. He stepped forward and let
the cloth drop behind him, shielding some of the room light.

Stan could feel the cold from the glass as he put his nose
to the icy surface. He allowed his eyes to adjust to the dif-
ference in light. It was a moment before he realized he was
looking directly into the dark and loveless eyes of Evil.

Bargolas looked into the eyes of the man-child and began
to weave his spell of lust. His brain generated the image of
a girl, and he began to weave it into Stan's mind. The spell
danced across the foul breath of the incubus as he tapped
lightly at the window, begging—demanding—to be let in.

Bargolas felt the heat in his groin as his member became
engorged and began to emerge from within his body. His
teeth began to ache with the urge to tear flesh, to lather in
the warmth of fresh blood.

But restraint gradually overcame his lust. This boy Stan was special. He was to be served, to be loved. This boy would protect him, because this boy would need him; Bargolas would *make* the boy need him. He would take this Stan to unimaginable levels of pleasure. He would become anyone and everyone the boy had ever dreamed about—and then . . . then, the boy would need him.

Stan started to back away at the sight of the forsaken creature, but something kept him from it—a flicker of light and the pale scent of perfume. The endless black void of the evil eyes transformed into human orbs rimmed in pale blue. The face became feminine, mild and young, framed by blond hair; salmon-pink lips pouted seductively . . . Cynthia.

Slowly he reached up to the window latch. Cynthia looked as if she were freezing; must get her inside at once. The latch pushed upward and clicked. The window slid open and Stan could feel the wintry air scrub his face with icy fingers. Cynthia reached up with her long fingernails and slowly ripped the screen apart. She wore such a lovely smile. Stan had always loved her smile and her moist blue eyes . . .

Mike had ignored the clicking of the window latch, preferring the soft oblivion of his retreat. But the ripping sound carried with it a desperation and a danger. Mike wanted to stay in this state, in the soft, gauzy denial of his pain, wanted to remain out of that hopeless struggle against such a power—but his self-preservation instinct bubbled up from the thick soupiness of his shock. Slowly he opened his eyes. He saw the pale green of his wall, with the old paint crack spreading upward like the branches of a leafless tree. On the opposite side of the room the ripping continued; Mike slowly rotated his head toward the sound. At first all he could see was Stan, positioned in front of the window, with the curtain pulled over his head. Then, as the curtain parted and Stan took one step back, Mike saw a smoky-black foot with inch-long talons slither down from the window.

Stan took Cynthia's hand and helped her down from the windowsill. For a moment they stood still, looking into each other's eyes. Then Cynthia took a step forward and placed her talons within Stan's trembling hand. Reaching up with his other hand, he brushed back the sun-bleached strands of her hair. Ever so gently, he traced the curve of her brow and the outline of her lips. His hand fell to the swelling of her breast as he leaned forward and covered her mouth with his. The heat of her breath burned his cheek, and she wrapped her arms around him. Stan pressed his body closer to her, trying to ignore the screaming in the far corner of his mind.

Mike stood crouching at his bedroom door, his lungs burning from the heat of his screams. The thick soup of shock threatened to drown him once more; he knew if he went under again, he would never see the light of morning. He reeled from the obscene sight of Stan locked in a passionate embrace with the monster, and fought to steel himself by recalling the grotesque image of Maria.

"STAN . . . STAN! RUN—STAN—RUN!"

The embrace seemed to grow tighter. Desperate, Mike grabbed his clock radio and flung it across the room. It hit Stan square in the back, then fell loudly to the floor and broke into several pieces.

The impact against Stan's back registered, and he sucked his breath in sharply, freeing one hand to reach for the pain where the radio had hit. The spell broke as suddenly as a thunderstorm on a hot summer night. The hideous creature loomed, and Stan pushed himself back. Now he heard Mike's screams imploring him to run. He jumped backward and fell against the sliding doors of the closet.

Mike remained in the doorway. Now that Stan was on the floor and the spell had been broken, the creature turned his attention to Mike. The incubus lunged forward. Stan lunged at the same time, and wrapped his arms around the creature's legs. Bargolas had no time to correct for the lack of balance and fell forward, talons outstretched. Mike jumped out of the way and the creature hit the floor hard, knocking its head against the door frame.

Mike stared at the beast, now lying motionless on the floor, but only for a second. He scurried into the kitchen and opened the silverware drawer, in his haste pulling it out too far; the drawer and all of its contents were flung out onto the floor. Mike grabbed a carving knife and ran back to his bedroom with it.

Stan had rolled over on his back and was trying to get up. The creature still lay facedown but was starting to move, when Mike shrieked and plunged the knife into its back. Mike felt the blade deflect against the beast's rib cage and sink sickeningly into the body. Bloodlike red tar oozed from the wound, and screams echoed in his head.

Stan was on his hands and knees. He stopped screaming, but his face was contorted in pain. He crawled a step toward Mike, his knee feeling the hard bones in the beast's hand. Slowly he lifted up one of his own hands toward Mike.

Mike saw his friend pleading for help but was unable to move toward him. He watched as Stan dropped his hand in resignation, the hand hitting the floor with a thump. Stan fell over to one side and lay there, his eyes closed, his breathing quick and violent. Finding some small measure of courage, Mike stepped forward and grasped the handle of the knife sticking from the incubus's back. Flexing his arm and shoulder, he tugged at the knife. At first it would not move, but suddenly it came free, sliding out of the wound with a sucking sound.

Instantly, a gusher of blood blew from the wound, spraying the dark fluid over the carpet. Mike jumped back, his shoes and pant legs getting caught in the spray. The creature's hand swung back, claws extended. A throaty growl began, almost a purr, in time with the creature's breathing.

Then Stan sat up, the pain still apparent in his twisted face. But it was waning. He turned his head to look at Mike, standing with the blood-covered knife in his hand, his eyes darting back and forth between Stan and the creature. The beast now moved again. Its knee inched its way up toward its chest, as if it was preparing to stand up.

Stan screamed, "Mike . . . RUN!"

The creature crawled to its hands and knees.

"RUN," Stan repeated, "GET OUT OF HERE!"

Mike bolted for the front door. Coatless and with the knife still clenched in his hand, he dashed out the front door and into the wintry night. He sprinted down the icy sidewalk into the driveway. Suddenly he realized he didn't have the keys and tried to turn back on the ice to get them. His feet flew up in front of him and he twisted in midair, coming down hard on the point of the knife. The knife buried itself in the muscle of his right thigh. He couldn't scream out his pain, for the wind had been knocked from him. Rolling over onto his back, he pulled the knife from his leg. His light-blue cords darkened in an ever-growing circle. The blood quickly soaked the whole leg of his pants. As he began to recover his breath, some movement in the doorway of the house caught his attention.

Standing in the doorway was the evil creature. Slowly the screen door opened and the dark bulbous eyes bore into Mike's. Adrenaline pumped through Mike, fighting against the fear already there. He struggled to his feet, the knife still firmly in his hand, as the creature stepped out onto the front landing.

The incubus looked up and down the street. The neighborhood was deserted in the quiet hush of the snowy evening. Again the creature locked his gaze upon the boy, and now he began to case out his illusion. It took a moment for the illusion to filter through the boy's fear and pain, but in the end he could not resist.

Mike looked toward the door where Paula stood naked to the waist. His pain faded. All he could feel was his desire for Paula—so beautiful, he thought, as he gazed at her image. She smiled warmly at him and he moved one step toward her.

Shiny white fragments exploded in her hair like a snow flurry, dancing about her head. Her smile faded abruptly as the hideous creature collapsed to the sidewalk in her place.

Stan stood over the beast, a determined look on his face and the remains of Mrs. Kawaguchi's table lamp in his hand. For a moment the pain in his own head was so severe that he was sure he was going to faint. He did not; instead, he looked up and turned to face Mike, the pain in his head already lessening. Stan knew they didn't have long before the creature would rise up again.

"Run, Mike, run," he said, his voice fading away like the vapor trail of his breath.

Mike turned, just in time to see the incubus raise its head. Mike ran, the pain throbbing upward through his entire body. He ran as fast as his gimpy leg would carry him, each step a struggle against blacking out. He had run a short distance down the street when, behind him, he heard a metallic clang, and he glanced over his shoulder to see what it was. All he saw was the screen door banging against the side of the house; neither the evil creature nor Stan was in sight.

* * *

Stan had kicked the beast out into the snow-covered yard, then quickly locked the screen door behind himself and shut the heavy wooden door. He ran for the kitchen. Once there, he heard the screen door being ripped open and flung against the side of the house.

Stan grabbed a knife from the cutlery strewn around the kitchen and then rummaged frantically through the cupboards, knocking cans of soup and vegetables onto the floor with a sweep of his hand. Finally he found a canister of Morton's salt and tore open the top. He heard the front door creak, then crash loudly; quickly, he poured a circle of salt around himself and sat down inside it.

As he heard the evil growl and the clickety-click of talons on the linoleum, Stan crossed himself with the pentacle of protection and recited the protection spell. He held the tip of the knife blade against his chest, pointing at his heart—determined to plunge it in, despite his fear, if the creature broke through the spell.

Keeping his head down and his eyes open only a crack, he continued reciting the protection spell as the inhuman feet stepped into his field of vision. He pushed the point of the knife into his chest, and the pain reinforced his determination as he continued speaking the words of the incantation.

The beastly feet inched closer and closer, until they touched the circle of salt. Then they stopped. Stan felt strands of his hair moving from the creature's breath. The foul odor from the incubus, devoid of illusion, made Stan want to vomit.

Stan braced himself, ready to die by his own hand rather than submit to more filth, humiliation, and pain from the creature. The creature did not move closer, but he now spoke to Stan in a raspy singsong voice that sounded as if it came from the depth of Stan's worst nightmares.

". . . pretty pretty Stan . . ."

Stan's eyes were squeezed shut, so he did not see the great ugly feet walk away, but he listened to the clickety-click of talons until he heard the scraping sound the screen door made as Bargolas pushed it aside as he ran out into the night. Stan knew, as long as he lived, he would never forget the sound of those talons against the linoleum. He sat there, the chill from the outside washing over him. He did not want to move.

Here, in the circle of salt, he was safe. He pulled the knife away from his chest, blood darkening a spot on his shirt. He wondered if the creature *had* broken through the circle, would he really have been able to kill himself? He shivered as the cold made him more uncomfortable.

Guilt and dread washed over Stan. Here he remained, safe in his spot, while Mike ran in terror. Why had Mike been limping? Obviously, he was hurt. Even without an injury, he couldn't overcome the superhuman strength of the creature— at least, not without Stan's help.

Gripping the hilt of the knife, he cut into the circle and pushed some of the salt to the side. He stood up and stepped cautiously from the circle. A noise from the other room propelled his heart into his throat. Stan held the knife in front of himself and took another step, then another. He rounded the corner and peeked fearfully into the living room. Newspapers fluttered in the cold breeze. Stan relaxed a bit and approached the front door, standing open and battered.

Night had fallen hard during the preceding hour, but the snow brightened the atmosphere outside; Stan almost believed this was a sign of hope. He tried to think where Mike would have run to. It seemed strange that he hadn't taken his truck. But how could he take the truck—he didn't have the keys! Stan ran back into the bedroom and grabbed Mike's coat, picking his own up on the way out. He found the keys in Mike's coat pocket. Jangling them, Stan slipped his own coat on and rushed out to the Ranchero.

He hurriedly got in, brushed the glass off the seat, and started the truck. It purred to life; Mike always took good care of his truck. Stan shifted it into gear and slowly let the clutch out. It dawned on him now where Mike would have gone—Bill's house. It was only a few minutes away. Stan flashed back to only two days ago when he had crouched outside Bill's window—casting a spell to make Bill sick—all just to prove to Mike that there was something to his studies of the occult. And now they were both in the middle of a nightmare . . . Stan turned right at the next corner and headed for Bill's, recklessly sliding to and fro on the slick road.

Soon he turned down Larch Street and felt gratified to see Mike up ahead—pain from his wound and the freezing cold had taken its toll. Mike was leaning against an old battered yellow Ford. He had covered over four blocks on his wounded leg but he could go no farther. Bill's house was still at least two blocks away, but that didn't matter now—Stan had beaten the monster to his intended prey. He honked the horn several times and slowed his pace, preparing to stop.

Mike turned his head toward the sound, looking confused; then he seemed relieved. He waited for Stan beside the old Ford. Great gasps of steam issued from his mouth. Ice and snow covered his pants and shirt where he had fallen during his escape; his hands and face were crimson.

All at once, from behind the small house, the creature leapt out and bounded toward Mike. He was as white as the snow, but the grotesque expression on his face was plainly visible. He hit the street between Stan, in the truck, and Mike. Mike screamed and began to hobble-run once again toward Bill's house. The creature recognized Stan in the truck and paused. Stan lowered his eyes to evade the illusions and drove straight for the creature.

Bargolas stood in the middle of the icy road as the truck raced toward him. Focusing all of his will, he cast out his illusion, thinking it irresistible. But the little red truck only increased its speed. Stan felt the impact—pain all over his body—and heard the headlights shatter. He felt still more pain as the vile creature bent from the impact, then flew upward and hit the roof of the truck, careened off and landed in a heap to the side. The Ranchero stalled and rolled to a halt. Stan himself lay crumpled inside the cab.

Mike rested against a parked car, shock and hypothermia threatening to settle in. He saw movement inside the truck: Stan was painfully sitting up in the driver's seat. Mike started toward the truck but stopped. The beast, too, was moving again. Mike tried to scream, but his voice was only a raspy whisper.

The stillness was broken by the cranking of the truck's engine. Oily blue smoke erupted from the tailpipe. Stan began to drive toward Mike, unaware that the creature was already running for the truck.

The beast put its fist through the passenger window. Stan's reflexes jerked the steering wheel, and the truck hit the curb with great force, again killing the engine. The creature's head popped into the cab, and the foul stench of its breath filled the cold air as Stan bent his head down to keep from meeting the creature's gaze.

The next second he was gone. Stan looked up through the window the creature had smashed and saw him running full speed toward Mike as Mike just watched, his mouth agape. Stan started the truck again and backed up, cranking the wheel hard as the tires slid. By the time he had straightened the wheel and begun to move forward again, the incubus had scooped up Mike and had thrown him onto his back like a sack of potatoes. The beast took off running and turned the corner before Stan reached the end of the block. Rounding the corner, Stan could see Mike flopping helplessly against the back of the creature as it headed out across the snow-covered fields toward the abandoned farmhouse.

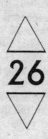

26

Othello, 1951

A new moon, a sliver of luminescence, shone through the windows of the bedroom gable. Lydia stared unblinkingly at the crescent and listened to Seth's heavy rhythmic breathing. Drawing a deep breath of her own, she clenched her eyes tight and tried to will away her body's craving. The bed creaked loudly as she turned over to face Seth.

His disheveled hair stuck to the pillow. Even in the dim moonlight, Lydia could see the stubble of his beard. His lips seemed dry and lifeless, but his chest rose and fell. Her hand trembled as she traced the outline of his lips. They twitched, but otherwise he remained still. Desperation fueled her boldness, a boldness reminiscent of the days long ago in Denver, before she met Seth. She slipped her hand under the covers, inched her fingers toward his chest; she felt the heat of his body even before she touched his wiry chest hairs. He remained still.

Fighting frustration for the sake of her need, Lydia ran her hand slowly down his chest to his belly, rounded now—not taut and flat like it had been when they first met—and she felt a wave of pride in her cooking. She touched the indentation of his navel and noted how the hair around it thickened, then continued downward.

Her hand poked under the elastic band and slid beneath the

smooth fabric of his jockey shorts. She could feel his flesh in
her hand, so hot it almost burnt her. Then the heat stirred
into movement as blood rushed to the call of her kneading
fingers. Bolder now, she reached forward with her other hand
and brushed against her husband's chest. She slowly drew
her lips nearer his, smelling his sweet-sour breath—

"Wha . . . what is . . . YOU HARLOT!" he croaked into
her mouth, pushing her away roughly. Sitting up, he leaned
over her and spoke in the voice with which he commanded
his congregation. "Don't you EVER do that again!" Through
her fear, she saw his eyes in the dim light, glaring at her.

Seth dropped to the bed, rolled onto his side facing away
from Lydia, and pretended to go back to sleep.

Lydia lay still for over two hours, aching with need and
seething with anger and embarrassment. She had already made
up her mind about what she was going to do, but first she
had to make sure Seth was asleep. From the sound of his
breathing, she knew that he too had lain awake for a long
time. Finally, his breath deepened and she could feel the
tenseness of his body melt into sleep.

She waited another half-hour before she slowly pulled the
covers back and threw her legs over the side of the bed. She
glanced at the clock. It was 2:45 A.M. when she crept out of
the bedroom. She didn't even bother to put on her slippers
before walking down the stairs. In the living room, she
stopped and reconsidered, but she hesitated only for a moment before she walked soundlessly across the kitchen floor
and opened the basement door.

The door squeaked slightly, and she stared into the abyss
before her. The darkness was so complete that her eyes created a ghostly display of fireworks for her. She gazed upon
the shadows of red explosions and gossamer white Roman
candles. She took the first step into the basement.

She didn't bother to turn on the lights, or even carry a
candle with her. She knew very well that she was going into
a realm of illusion, where everything would be provided for
her pleasure—even the light. Before she reached the bottom
of the stairs, she shuddered, trying to imagine what Bargolas
must really look like, but her need canceled out her repulsion
and she continued her decent into darkness.

At last her foot lighted upon the dirt floor. She saw no

light, no Bargolas, nothing. She waited a few minutes, wishing for the hot touch of her lover, knowing that his passionate embrace, bordering on violence, would consume her and grant her the grace of release. But there was only darkness, nothing more. Not a sound . . . not a glimmer of light, not a touch. She stifled a groan of agony as she returned to the stairs and began the long climb back to her bedroom.

She was halfway up the stairs when she saw the dark silhouette waiting at the top. "Seth!" she gasped. Taking a deep breath, she prepared herself for an explanation. He surprised her by taking a step down the stairs toward her. She stopped and waited. He made no sound, and as he drew nearer she caught the familiar smell of ripe olives . . . Bargolas!

She took a step back and almost lost her balance. Turning her head to look around, she noticed that the basement had taken on an eerie glow and was getting brighter by the minute. Then Bargolas swept her up into his arms and carried her down a gleaming white marble staircase.

Bearing her lightly across the blue-green and white marble floor, Bargolas gazed longingly into her eyes. She went limp in his arms as he nuzzled the warm fullness of her breast. She gasped with the sharpness of pleasure; her head lolled back and her hair flowed down across his arm, almost reaching the floor. His footsteps rang against the marble, then became muffled as he crossed onto a thick carpet of pure silk. She heard a splashing and turned her head toward an enormous steaming bath of indigo water.

Bargolas set her down lightly upon her feet and stepped back to admire her. "You are so beautiful," he muttered in his mellow tone.

She felt herself blush and tilted her head downward in mock embarrassment. It was then that she noticed that she, too, had changed. She was both fearful and pleased. She was no longer the demure preacher's wife who wore print dresses and pulled her mousy hair back—pinned stiffly down against the nape of her neck. Now her hair was the color of gold, with highlights that were almost pure white; the flickering of the torches picked up the color and reflected it. A fine, almost transparent silk of the palest lavender was draped across her shoulders, cascading downward and pooling at her feet.

Bargolas stepped toward her and unfastened the gold clasp

at her neck, letting the ethereal robe fall to the floor. It vanished, melting into the carpet. Lydia was exhilarated, thrilled; never before had she been allowed to see herself as part of the illusion.

Yes, of course, it made sense. The longer she allowed Bargolas to influence her, the stronger the illusions became! For a moment she thought about it. She could remember all the other times, the wonderful pleasures. Each time, after returning to her "real" world, she would feel revolted with what she had done, would swear to herself that she would repent. But after only a day or two the desires would return, growing into a need that she couldn't deny. Each time she surrendered to her need, she would find the illusion richer and more complex. It seemed that after each surrender, Bargolas would learn more about her hidden desires, and one by one he would make them come true. Now the illusions were so strong that—

Bargolas laughed and Lydia fell . . . down into the deep well of illusion. She turned her head to see Bargolas walking slowly backward into the bathwater. His teeth gleamed like pearls.

"Come to me, Lydia, my love."

She stepped forward, feeling the weight of her hair as it swung from the motion; the golden strands brushed against her knees. She waded into the steaming water. Bargolas was now up to his chest in the bath, his arms floating upon the surface. A moment later, her hair spread upon the surface like an exotic flower; she pushed herself toward her lover.

He submerged. The oil torches set in the wall blazed brightly, reflecting the ripples from his sudden movement. She could not see where he had gone; then she felt him, soft as a feather, lightly touching her thighs. He emerged in front of her, and her golden hair now formed a web that held them together, intertwining with his own dark locks and covering his arms and chest. She leaned forward and kissed him. He devoured her in an embrace so tight she thought she had stopped breathing. She felt his manhood stiffen against her belly; she flushed hotly in anticipation.

He lifted her in his arms and carried her to the side of the bath, where he laid her upon warm tiles that glistened with

ever-changing patterns and colors. He crouched over her to
lick the water from her face and breasts. She arched her back
and he continued downward until he reached the tender flesh
between her legs. She moaned, gently opening her legs wider.
A moment later he stopped and placed his hands beside her
shoulders. She could feel the hot, erect flesh poised at the
entrance to her desire, teasing, not entering.

Her nails dug into his flesh, the water from the bath
dripping from the dark ringlets of his hair onto her face.
She ground her pelvis against his, thrusting, but he still
waited. She grew desperate as he covered her breasts with
his warm breath and an occasional flick of his tongue. Her
face burnt with the flame of desire, her body convulsed
with its need.

She tilted her head back so far she thought it would surely
snap . . . her eyes turned backward . . . then finally, he entered her. She screamed. It was pain—more pain than she had
ever felt before—but it was merged with desire . . . because
that was all there was. She screamed again as Bargolas' breath
quickened and his thrusts became even more powerful,
deeper, more painful. Suddenly he gripped her shoulders hard,
and the pain from his grip merged with the pain deep inside
her abdomen. She shook violently in a wave of heat that
burned a path to her release.

"Lydia . . . Lydia! Are you down there?"

Somewhere deep in her consciousness she heard the question but ignored it. She couldn't be bothered. There was no
more pain, no more desire—nothing except blissful emptiness.

Suddenly she became cold, and she knew that Bargolas no
longer covered her body with his—and then there was an
explosion of light. She was momentarily blinded, but heard
heavy footsteps descending toward her.

"Lydia, what . . . ?"

She blinked, shielding her eyes with her hand, and looked
up at Seth as he stood about two-thirds of the way down the
stairs. He wore his black bathrobe, and his hair stood up
comically from his head. A look of disgust was plain upon
his face. Her eye caught movement beyond Seth's feet, in
the space behind the unfinished stairs, and when she focused
her eyes there, what she saw made her shudder with fear and

revulsion. She couldn't see behind the stairs clearly, but she saw enough of the monstrous face and sooty black skin to make her nauseated. Seth approached as far as the bottom step.

"Look at you!" he screamed. "You are disgusting!"

She swallowed hard and did as he demanded: she looked at herself, lying naked upon the dirt floor of the basement. Her hair, matted by sweat and soil, hung across her forehead. Drying blotches of foul-smelling slime covered her skin. When she moved her legs to try to stand up, she felt the heavy stickiness and the soreness of her genitals. Looking down, she was assaulted by the ugliness of her body. She was ashamed of how she looked, and mortified by the realization of how low she had sunk to satisfy herself. Sticky fluid dripped down the inside of her thighs and mingled with the dirt on her legs. Tears from her eyes created streams of mud running down her face.

"Are you so shameless?" began Seth in his preaching voice. "Is this what was trying to move me to make love this evening? Is this what my wife has become—a whore to herself, without self-control, without dignity? God in heaven! Lydia, you make me sick!"

"Yessss," she hissed. "This IS what I have become. Because I married a man, but haven't *had* a man for a husband. THIS is what I have become, but it is what you have made me—you, with your pious bullshit. You, with your guilt. We fucked before we were married, and just as you always suspected, you were not the first. We fucked before we were married and you blamed me. Sure, I seduced you—but you were more than willing. I saw you watching me, wanting me."

"Shut your filthy blasphemous mouth!"

"I will not! I am nothing to you. You use me only for decoration: a preacher must have a wife. You don't love me, you *can't* love me, because you can't love yourself—and you sure as hell can't love your God. You, YOU are the one who's repulsive. You are a mockery of everything you pretend to stand for—and it is YOU that make *me* sick."

"Silence, you blasphemous whore! Beware the wrath of God!"

For a moment there was indeed silence. Both quivered from the emotions that wracked their bodies.

At length, Lydia spoke, her voice calm and level. "I'm pregnant," she said, hoping at last to crush the final pretense of their marriage.

"Whore! Adulteress!" he spat, barely able to stand as the enormity of her confession took its toll on him. His age lines seemed suddenly etched to a much deeper level, and he now wore a face of unforgiving hate. "Who?" he demanded, his voice high and out of control.

Lydia stood, silently looking through him.

He tried again: "Who?"

"Him!" she screamed, pointing under the stairs. "I conjured him from hell." She began to laugh insanely, shaking her head back and forth; the loose dirt formed a halo around her.

Seth frowned at her, only now realizing that she was mad. He stepped from the last step and grabbed her by the shoulders. She struggled and continued her insane laughter. He slapped her. The laughing stopped abruptly, and she looked directly into his eyes. She smiled at him and spoke in a little girl's voice. "You don't believe me, do you?"

Lydia glanced back through the stairs where she saw Bargolas crouched in the darkness. Seth slowly turned his head, trying to follow her eyes. He saw nothing at the top of the stairs. He turned back to Lydia, almost feeling compassion. She was seeing something that was not there; undoubtedly she was not pregnant, either. He almost felt sorry for her—almost, but not quite.

"Go upstairs and clean yourself," he commanded.

She looked back into his eyes, smiling. "You still don't believe me?" She paused, smiling more broadly. "Bargolas! Bargolas, show yourself!"

Seth shook his head in a gesture of pity—but stopped when he heard a scraping sound from behind. He couldn't let himself believe there was someone here. Then he felt something brush against him, and he whirled around just in time to see someone—no, some*thing*—run up the stairs—something naked and male, but not human.

Lydia began to laugh again when she saw the expression on her husband's face. In the space of a few seconds she had seen him go from confident and self-righteous to confused and terrified.

Cautiously he stepped back, staring into her eyes in disbelief. Suddenly he could see nothing. He could not move. Lydia's insane laughter echoed in his mind as he fell to the dirt floor and lost consciousness.

27

Othello, 1970

Darkness. Limbo. Smothering, freezing darkness, clawing away at the raw edges of flesh on his face, carving an icy vision of death across his soul. Everything touching him—everything that *was* him, his arms, his legs, his face, his blood—seemed, in that darkness, in the basement of that house, to become ice.

He didn't see, nor did he hear; but then again, perhaps he couldn't—perhaps he was already dead. His mind smiled to itself. Surely death could be no worse than this frigid darkness. He willed movement, but there was none. But wait: perhaps *that* was movement. Is *that* how it feels? I can't remember . . . yes, I think that *is* how it feels . . . but perhaps not . . .

A tickle. Ants. Red fire ants, hot with activity. Warmed by the movement: ants deep inside him. Ants in his lungs, shards of glass, grinding-frozen-flesh-imploring-prodding-demanding . . . tickle . . . tickle . . . tickle. A great thundering cough erupted in his lungs, and the horrible icy pain made him forget to wonder if he was alive; now he only wished he were dead. To end the pain to end the horror please God to sink at least back into the great gray soup of oblivion to wait for the final—

Another cough. Another . . .

Something wet and foul slipped from between his lips and drooled down upon his arm—or was it his knee? He felt a small river run down his arm. It was cold. It came from deep inside him, and it was *cold*! Ah, movement—but wait; it was not him. It must be . . .

From the edge of darkness, an incalculable distance, farther than the forever of cold surrounding him, a soft scraping drew near. An unwelcome rational thought bled forth from his mind: My fuckin' cough woke it up!

Fear drove the last rational thought from his mind, and he sank back into the cloying fuzz of unconsciousness.

The coughing echoed through the freezing basement and stirred the incubus from his slumber. He thought of food, blood, warmth. Hungrily, he pulled himself upright. Holding onto his ridged arousal with one hand, he reached up to the bare wooden beams of the ceiling and stretched the sleepiness from his muscles. As he flexed, he listened to the uneven breathing of the boy; this excited him even more. He cast out his illusion, a familiar one, the one of the girl, Paula, but it simply drifted off into the darkness. The boy was dying; the beast could smell it. Letting go of the ceiling beam, he slithered over to the unconscious boy.

"Wake up, pretty Mike . . . pretty pretty Mike . . . wake up for me."

There was no movement. The evil creature's nostrils flared with fury. Once again he caught the scent of blood. In the darkness, the incubus craned his head over the boy, sniffing out the smell of blood, and he found it. A gash, covered with frozen dried blood on Mike's leg. Bargolas pushed the boy with one hand, but he didn't move. Gently he traced the outline of the wound with his talon, but still the boy did not move. Abruptly, Evil stuck his long claw into the wound until it met the hard resistance of bone. The boy screamed to life. The sound of pain and fear whetted the creature's appetite; he pulled his claw out and put it to his cracked cold lips— sucking it.

Stan was bundled up, but the icy wind from the two broken windows tore at his clothing and penetrated what little warmth was left in his body. Nonetheless he increased his speed, pushing the little truck as fast as it would go down the highway and toward the house.

Despite a nagging helplessness, he also felt stubbornly determined, and his determination had given him some presence of mind. He had returned to his home before heading for the creature's lair; he quietly walked inside, trying not to wake up his family in the early morning hours. He rummaged around in the locked trunk in his bedroom until he found what he needed. Putting the objects into a paper bag, he started to sneak out as quietly as he had come in; but his parents had been waiting up and he ran into his father, emerging from the bedroom, his jockeys drooping under his belly. Stan's mother followed.

They began by demanding an explanation for his coming in so late, then they saw the look on his face, a look they had never seen before. Both parents raged with their concern and anger. They shouted about the deaths and wild animals, they screamed at him for being unreasonable and sick. They felt apprehension, and fear, but in the end all they could do was just stand there, grainy fatigue in their eyes, watching their son walk out the door. When he was gone, they glared angrily at one another, each blaming the other for not stopping him.

Stan hopped into the damaged Ranchero, turned the engine over, and drove away. He doubted that he could destroy the creature, but he knew that he had to save Mike. He felt the heavy weight of responsibility clawing into his shoulders and neck. It was his fault—he had unleashed the creature. It was true, he had no love for his classmates, they had never treated him with very much kindness. But did they deserve death—a death that ripped them to pieces? No, they didn't . . . What would his own life be worth after all of this was over? Probably not much, even if he lived. Stan stopped thinking about it as he drove through the icy streets, heading for the highway and the old house.

Bargolas was confused. He wanted this man-child, but he preferred him alive and vibrant with lust; however, he was unable to cast an illusion to arouse the boy. In the past, when faced with this situation, he had simply killed. Death was at once soothing and exciting. The blood nourished and stimulated him. He should kill the boy; he could bask in the moist warmth of his youth and satiate himself. But something kept him from his pleasure. It was the other boy—Stan, the one who had awakened him from the deep sleep of abandonment. Because of Stan, somehow . . .

Bargolas removed his finger from his mouth. The fresh blood and cries of pain drove him to the brink of losing control. The boy whimpered softly below him, calling to him, demanding the lust and release that he knew Bargolas could give him. He groaned louder and turned onto his back.

Bargolas could no longer contain himself. Dropping to his knees, he put his mouth to the bleeding wound in Mike's thigh and sucked the warm blood up into his mouth. The fresh taste gnawed away at his desire, excited him. While plunging his tongue deep into the wound, he felt his loins fill out; his own bloodlust pounded inside his head like some ancient drum . . . demanding . . . killing . . . eating.

The pain jolted Mike sharply, clearing his mind briefly from the fuzziness hypothermia had induced. He could not see the terror, but he felt it with every nerve. His body bucked against the agony. His arms unfolded and his fists clenched, and he began to pound upon the bulk above him. The blows struck solidly but seemed to have no effect. Mike jerked the wounded leg downward, flat upon the dirt floor, then brought it back up with all the strength he had left. He felt his knee connect with something solid; he heard a grunt, and the weight of the dark creature was gone.

The knee cracked against the creature's mouth and nose. He jumped to his feet and a black rage, sharp as knives, sliced through to his brain. The pitch-black basement was filled with his piercing shriek.

The screams echoing in the darkness became ugly fat worms, slithering their way toward Mike. The terror reached out to him; he couldn't run—he could only wait. Soon the slithering worms covered him and bored into his sanity as if it were an overripe piece of fruit. His body shook in spasms. Death, he felt, was surely preferable to this.

Bargolas felt the boy's convulsions. Abruptly, there was silence, and the incubus crept over to Mike. He listened to the terror in his breathing and relished the suffering.

"Mike . . . pretty pretty Mike, let me in, please let me in, and everything will be . . . pretty pretty . . ."

Trying once again, Bargolas cast out his illusion; once again, he found Mike's mind shattered into millions of disjointed pieces and unable to retain the illusion. Undaunted, he placed his hand upon Mike's knees to prevent being kicked again, and leaned over the boy. With his short arms he caught at Mike's arms, drawn close to his chest for protection. Bargolas lowered his weight onto the struggling boy. He squeezed and felt breath rushing out of Mike, warm and full upon his own face. But again, Bargolas could not bring himself to suck the life away . . . not yet anyway.

28

Othello, 1951

For two days, Seth slept. Lydia saw to the preparations for Sunday and invited a substitute minister to preach to the congregation. Still, with all that had happened, Lydia was concerned about Seth.

Although it was too late to undo it, she was feeling remorse for the incident that had occurred almost three nights earlier. She felt ashamed whenever she came near Seth, and her overwhelming guilt was pushing her to continue on in that sham of a marriage.

Carrying a tray with toast, coffee, and two eggs fried sunny-side up, she climbed the stairs to the bedroom. The aroma of the food made her aware of her own hunger, but her duty was to take care of her husband first.

Seth was still asleep. Lydia set the tray on the night table and sat down carefully on the bed beside Seth. He didn't stir. Softly she traced her finger down the unshaven side of his cheek. He twitched, and his eyes fluttered open. A flicker of recognition registered on his face, then his eyes lost their focus and he stared off blankly.

Lydia took the plate again and began cutting the eggs up. Soon the plate was swimming with the warm yellow yolks. She scooped up a forkful and moved it toward Seth, but he wouldn't open his mouth. She held the eggs there a moment, the yolks dripping onto his chin, hoping that the smell of warm food would bring him out of his shock, but he just continued to stare off into space.

Not allowing herself to become frustrated, she picked up the tray and walked back downstairs. She sat at the kitchen table and began to eat the breakfast herself, wondering if and when Seth was going to come out of this state. She couldn't allow herself to look too far into the future, because if she did, she knew she wouldn't be able to see any normalcy in their lives.

Without warning, her mind turned toward Bargolas. Even with the shame and uncertainty she felt, she could not rid herself of the need, the desire to be possessed by him—to escape into the beautiful, intricate illusions he wove. She hadn't seen Bargolas for the past two days, ever since he had bolted up the basement stairs. She feared that she might never see his beautiful face again. She admitted to herself that this would be the best thing for all involved, for she knew that as long as Bargolas existed, she could never return to her own life—with or without Seth—but still she longed for her lover.

Othello, 1970

Gertie Johnston wrapped the dirty yellow scarf around her hair to protect it from the incessantly blowing dust. She pulled on an old smock—also not really for warmth, but to keep the dust off her clothes.

She closed the back door sharply behind her and quickly crossed the hundred yards between her house and the barn. She wondered where Walter had been all morning. Although Walter seldom checked in with her during the day, she was used to seeing him puttering around the farm as he completed his chores. He better not have snuck off to Charlie Ryan's to play cards, she thought to herself. There was always so much to be done around the farm and never enough hours in the day. Oh, well.

Gertie was almost two hours late in getting around to milking old Bessie; that ol' cow was going to be cranky as all get out. Sometimes Gertie just didn't know where the time got off to, but it sure as the dickens got away from her. She shook her head in the blowing dust, tasting the grit in her mouth. She headed for the small door set in the large sliding doors of the barn; once there, she opened the latch and stepped over the high lip of the sill.

Immediately she knew something was wrong; it was far too quiet. She had expected old Bessie to be bawling her head off, teats full and aching with too much milk. But she didn't hear a thing. She stopped at the threshold, set the pail on the straw-covered floor, and quietly closed the door behind her. The quiet was eerie, and there was something else—an odd smell she couldn't place in her memory.

The barn contained one milk cow and two horses. There was a chicken coop built onto the side of the barn, where they kept between ten and fifteen laying hens—depending on whether or not they had chicken for dinner that week. There wasn't a sound except for her own breath. She walked over to the entrance to the extension they had built with their own hands and entered the coop.

White feathers were strewn everywhere. Clumps of feathers were matted together with dried blood; some were still attached to a scrap of chicken. The picture grew worse when she realized that their entire flock had been ripped to shreds. Her first thought was wolf: she had seen the handiwork of wolves in Montana. But there weren't any wolves in the Columbia Basin.

Her heart sank as she looked about at the destruction. Horrified, she noticed that some of the chicken parts had been flung against the walls and had stuck there, the blood gluing these scraps of flesh to the wall. The room reeked with death; the drying blood almost overpowered her. That was it, she thought—blood. That was what she had smelled when she walked into the barn.

Gertie left the chicken coop and returned to the main part of the barn, fear dogging her every step. She wished Walter were here with her, but she was determined to get to the bottom of this senseless destruction. She heard something— was it behind her or above her? She looked up into the hayloft but saw nothing. A pitchfork hung upon a nail in the wall;

suddenly feeling vulnerable, Gertie lifted the tool from its place.

She held the pitchfork out in front of her like a demon housewife, gripping it tightly, and cautiously made her way back to the stalls where Bessie and the two horses were kept. Her spirits fell when she looked toward the stalls and did not see the shoulders or heads of the animals. The rich odor of blood and manure told her what she didn't want to know. Approaching, she spied one of Bessie's hoofs sticking out from the side of the stall. Gertie felt sick; the remainder of the cow's leg was nowhere to be seen.

Gertie didn't know if she could stand to see old Bessie and the horses torn to pieces, but she was a strong farm woman who had endured much hardship, and she would cope with this as well. She took a step forward, craning her head to see into the stall.

What was left of Bessie was strewn all over the stall. The hay was dark with blood and matted together in muddy clumps. Like the chickens, poor Bessie had been torn apart, and there wasn't enough of her left to make a whole cow again.

Gertie felt sick. Her impulse was to run and find Walter—to get out of there—to call the police. But she was a staunch woman, and she intended to see the rest, no matter how grisly. She took another step sideways, lifting the tines of the fork higher. She swallowed hard and resolved not to vomit, expecting a scene in the horses' stalls similar to that with Bessie and the chickens.

But she didn't expect to find Walter. She didn't see much of him, except his head—which had been cleanly severed from his body and still wore a grimace of pain and terror. She didn't notice that his pants were wadded up in the corner and that there was a pile of bones half-buried in the bloody hay. Gertie stared at the head of the man who had been her loving husband for twenty-two years, not even aware that she was screaming.

Her screams woke the incubus from his gluttony-induced slumber. Half-buried in the hay, and half-hidden by the remains of the horse, the creature raised its gore-covered head and looked sleepily at Gertie.

It took a moment before this newest horror registered in

Gertie's brain. She tried to react, to scream—but she was already screaming. She watched in terror as the beast pulled itself to a half-standing position and smiled a wide, blood-stained, toothy grin.

Gertie shoved the pitchfork forward. Her aim was off and the fork veered sideways, the outermost tine piercing the creature's longer right arm and coming out its other side. Gertie dropped the fork, and its weight dragged his arm down to the ground. The beast wailed in fury and reached his other hands down to release his arm from the fork.

Gertie turned on her heels and ran screaming for the house. Out in the dusty wind, her head scarf took flight across the barnyard. Halfway to the house, Gertie glanced back over her shoulder; she saw the barn door swing open, and the evil thing stepped out into the sunlight.

Bargolas' black glassy eyes squinted in the bright daylight. His two shorter arms held the injured one up on his distended belly, full from a whole night of gorging himself. He slowly brought his eyes to focus upon the woman running for her life, then began to gallop after her. After a couple of steps, however, he slowed to a walk; he was too full to run.

Gertie yanked the screen door open. Inside the house, she bolted the door and ran for the bedroom to get Walter's shotgun. Shuddering, she returned to the kitchen with the gun. She checked to see if it was loaded, then snapped it together again, looking back at the door. It was secure. She stumbled over to the wall phone and picked up the telephone receiver. She dialed "0" and waited for the operator.

"Operator."

"Gwenn, it's Gertie Johnston." Her voice shook. "For God's sake, get the sheriff out here right away!"

"Gertie, honey, are you all right?"

"Gwenn! Just get the sheriff!"

"Okay, okay."

Suddenly there was a sound at the door. She wasn't sure if it was the wind or if it was— There it was again. She started to step toward the door but felt dizzy. The floor beyond the barrel of the shotgun seemed to swim up at her. For a moment she thought she was going to faint. In the back of her mind, she heard a scraping just outside the door—then something else, perhaps a crash. Still looking down at the floor wavering in front of her, she saw her dress billow up in the wind now blowing in through the broken door.

Looking up, she was surprised to see Walter. He was standing there with the biggest grin she had ever seen on his face. It didn't occur to her that it was unusual for him to come in from the outside without any clothes on. He just continued to smile his toothy smile as he began to walk slowly toward her. She blushed as she glanced down at his private parts; they were swelling up in arousal, and as proud as could be.

She giggled as he covered her mouth with his in a wet kiss. Pretending to resist, she pulled her head away—and his teeth tore open her throat. Blood spurted in hot streams, covering the incubus and spattering the kitchen floor. The beast took a swipe with his talons, and Gertie's head landed with a wet plop on the floor in a puddle of blood, rolled away, and came to a stop almost facedown.

The incubus held the body upright; leaning over into the network of veins and arteries that the woman's head had been connected to, he lapped up the gushing blood and giggled with his eyes closed.

Othello, 1951

Just as Lydia approached the sink, an intense pain stabbed through her right forearm and she dropped the breakfast dishes, smashing them into a thousand pieces on the kitchen floor. Biting her lip in agony, she searched her arm for any sign of a wound but found none. She gripped her arm with her left hand; the pain continued until it brought her to her knees. She screamed.

Seth lay like a great gray lump in their bed. He didn't allow himself the luxury of thinking; it was as if his brain resisted a rational approach to the situation, as if some inner sense told Seth that thinking about it would only bring madness. Better the state of suspension in which he now rested. He gazed across the room toward the dappled morning light blotting out the patterns on the wallpaper. It wasn't that he couldn't hear or respond to Lydia—no, he was repulsed by her. He had married a harlot and a—

The scream drifted up the stairs into the bedroom as if it were simply a proper part of the morning. Such a normal sound, it took Seth a moment to realize its passing. His eyes shifted to the hallway outside the bedroom. Slowly he swung his legs out of bed and planted his feet on the floor. He stood up unsteadily, naked except for his stained jockey shorts which hung askew on his hips. He walked to the stairs, weaving slightly and wondering what delightful circumstance could have befallen Lydia to cause her to scream so. Perhaps it was God's punishment, swift and mighty.

In the meantime, most of Lydia's pain had subsided and she had begun to pick up the shards of crockery. She bent down now to pick up the pieces of the shattered juice glass. Her hand slipped, plunging her finger against the sharp edge of one piece, and it sliced her finger swiftly and cleanly to the bone. Droplets of blood stained the floor even before she could feel the sting and pull her hand back.

"Shit, what a morning," she swore softly under her breath as she inspected her bleeding finger.

She glanced up to see Seth staring down at her; his eyes appeared to be glazed over as if he were in a trance. As the blood ran swiftly down Lydia's finger, through her palm, and down the edge of her wrist to drip slowly onto the white linoleum floor, a smile spread gradually across Seth's face, his dry lips cracking.

Lydia frowned at him and stood up to wash the blood off in the sink and apply a Band-Aid. She dried her hands and searched through the cupboard, feeling self-conscious because she knew Seth was watching her every movement. Then she heard a sort of hissing from his direction. Turning her head quickly, she saw that he was laughing, but with his teeth clenched shut. He quivered as he spoke.

"That's the beginning of God's punishment. Whore . . . WITCH!" He tried to scream, but his voice cracked under the strain. He turned and skulked away.

A chill passed through Lydia's body as she tried to stretch the white strip over the gash on her finger. But her finger was wet and the Band-Aid would not stay in place, so she just wrapped a napkin around it until the bleeding stopped. Con-

cerned about Seth, she now followed him back upstairs to the
bedroom.

Before she reached the top of the stairs, she heard whispering. For a moment she thought Bargolas had returned, and
the two of them—no, that was crazy. More quietly now, she
finished climbing the stairs. Peering into the bedroom, she
saw Seth kneeling on the floor beside the bed, praying like a
child does before he goes to bed. He whispered conspiratorially to his God while his head bobbed and his eyes rolled.
Suddenly, as if he had heard Lydia, he shifted his eyes and
looked briefly at her, then rolled his eyes back into his head
and returned to his prayers. Lydia turned and walked back
down the stairs.

She returned to the kitchen and picked up the broom and
dustpan from the corner beside the back door. She carefully
swept up the glass fragments and dumped them into the trash.
Finally, as she wiped a damp cloth over the surface to pick
up the remaining slivers of glass, she heard the front door
slam and, a few seconds later, the car starting. She stood,
wondering . . . and an uneasy feeling grew in her. Just where
was Seth going—and was he ever coming back . . . ?

Othello, 1970

Sheriff Gordon rested his head in his hands. He could smell
the vomit on his breath as he looked out the patrol car's window into the whirling dust. It was the worst thing he had ever
seen. He recalled the time Dennis Miller had got caught under the harrow bed, and that one time when the state cops
had requested his help on a bad accident. That accident had
given him nightmares for weeks—those poor kids. But as bad
as those scenes were, they were nothing compared to the
condition of Gertie and Walter. This was something different.
The brutal killings of the '50s gnawed at his memory.

Gertie's head, with her salt-and-pepper curls, swam before
his eyes. A smile crept across her face just like it did when
she was serving her famous apple and peach pie, a smile that
said "I know you're gonna like this!" Abruptly, the face was

hacked by contortions, the gleam in her eyes faded to be replaced by dark ugly mystery—the shattered remains of one eye plastered to her cheek with blood and retinal fluid, forming a squash of pink—no more cookies, no more pies, no laughter, only the obvious pain of an unimaginable death.

The sheriff gripped the steering wheel tightly as he tried to squint his eyes dry. The wonderful smell of her baking pies and Walter's silly hunting stories haunted him, all of a piece with the bright kitchen, the lacquered table and chairs—and now, the rank odor of drying blood. He sniffed, hawked, and rolled down the window to spit. The sharp metallic smell of blood seemed to eat away at the inside of his nose. The blood was everywhere. There were footprints of blood tracking across the once well-scrubbed floor, forming circular patterns that suggested a dance of delight. Horrible, horrible, the sheriff thought.

Tooth marks were all over Gertie's body. In most places it appeared that random bites had been taken out of her flesh. It was impossible for Sheriff Gordon to tell if the cannibalism had taken place before or after the violation—the rape—that left her torso ripped apart, her guts sagging through the rents of muscle and flesh. Ten feet away her skull had been crushed, and most of her gray matter emptied . . . and across the floor, the bloody footprints of a dance of delight.

Sheriff Gordon had stumbled back to the patrol car to radio in for an ambulance, but he decided to wait until his nerves settled before calling. He wasn't even sure he'd be able to put two sentences together. So he had just waited in his car, allowing these thoughts to chase each other through his mind.

He happened now to glance up and saw some movement in his rearview mirror. There he saw the reflection of a horrible face, ash-white and covered with flecks of drying blood. In that instant Sheriff Gordon knew why he hadn't been able to get the smell of blood out of his nose, and in that instant the creature wrapped its filthy talons around his face.

He reached up with his own strong hands and grabbed onto the creature's wrists. He was amazed, briefly, at the size and strength of those wrists. "Briefly" was all the time Gordon had, for in the next instant the incubus's shorter arms closed upon his neck and slowly squeezed off his air.

Bargolas enjoyed the act of killing; the more horrifying it

was to the victim, the more gratifying it was to him. With delight, he positioned a talon over each of the struggling lawman's eyes. The sheriff kicked his feet desperately; his left foot lodged firmly under the brake pedal as he kicked out wildly with his right foot. He knocked the two-way radio from its hook and began to scream as the talons pressed lightly upon his eyelids. He gagged and started to lose consciousness from lack of air; Bargolas eased his grip on the man's throat.

The monster paused, drinking in the entire experience. The man's fear oozed in putrid globs, attaching themselves to the soul of the creature; the incubus felt invigorated. Gradually now he increased the pressure of his talons on Gordon's eyelids. The sheriff scrunched his eyes shut tightly; the creature, chuckling, gripped the folds of skin between his fingers and pinched, first with his right claw, then with his left.

Slowly, carefully, Bargolas pulled Gordon's eyelids apart and extended his own head over the top of the sheriff's balding hairline to look directly at him. Gordon tried to scream louder, forced now to gaze into the hideous face.

With the folds of the man's eyelids still firmly clenched, the incubus jerked his hands away violently. For a long, satisfying moment, there was nothing but silence as he popped the two bloody flaps of skin into his mouth. He smiled in delight as the sheriff began a high-pitched keening. Letting go of the creature's wrists he covered his bloody eyes with his hands.

The evil creature giggled. "Good . . . good taste good . . ."

Twenty minutes ago, Bargolas had been too bloated from the old woman to care much about anything except sleep, but now the taste of new flesh rekindled his bloodlust. He reached over the seat and grabbed both of the sheriff's wrists. Holding the man's hands away from his eyes, Evil leaned down and began to lick away the blood from the lidless eyes. The sheriff continued his endless, pitiful screams, which now took on the gravelly texture of hoarseness.

Abruptly, he let go of the sheriff's hands, but before they could fly back and form a protective covering for his damaged eyes, Bargolas brought his own hands back and positioned his talons, once again, over the bloody eyes. With a quick flick of the chipped talon on his right index finger, he popped

the right eye like an egg yolk. A renewed frenzy of struggle
and screaming gripped Gordon as the incubus leaned over the
man to suck out the delicious liquid.

Othello, 1951

Lydia had been staring at the exquisite beauty of Bargolas
for several minutes. She hadn't seen him come into the room,
but once he was there, she'd known it. As usual, he stood
before her naked, save for the glittering bloodred beads
draped across his shoulders and chest and covering his sex.
He simply stood there and watched her watch him. He could
feel her arousal but wanted to increase it to an unforgettable
level before even touching her.

She rose to her feet unsteadily, her arms outstretched. But
Bargolas stepped back and said, "Wait. You must wait."

"I—I can't." She took another step toward him, her quivering arms still calling to him.

"No." He stepped back again.

She ran to him, seizing upon his bejeweled body with her
demanding lips. Sparkling beads of red now covered her neck
and face as she licked at the mysterious warm dark crevices
of his body.

Ecstasy lifted her high into the air and then brought her
down firmly into the incubus's possessive embrace. Lost in
the endless warp and weave of her desire, she felt the warm
sweet breath of her lover against the back of her neck. If there
was illusion, it was wasted, for Lydia saw nothing and heard
nothing—she only thrashed about in a web of lust, like a
trapped insect. She felt him enter her, and almost immediately, her passion culminated in her release.

29

Othello, 1970

Freezing air reached deep into Mike's lungs and pulled forth a rasping cough, and that in turn brought movement to his almost frozen body. He tried to open his eyes, but they seemed to be glued shut. Wrinkling his brow and nose, he reached up with one knuckle and dug into his eye—at the tears of his fear and desperation that had matted his eyes together. Mike repeated the procedure for the other eye, roughly brushing the sticky matter away, and forced his eyes open. He saw nothing; the blackness remained.

Not knowing what else to try, he decided to sit up. The pain wracked his body; his leg throbbed, and he felt like his guts had been rearranged. Bringing his hand around, he discovered that his pants had been torn to shreds. Suddenly the memory of what had happened slapped him sharply in the face, and he almost cried out in despair and anger. Instead, he slid back down on the cold dirt floor, closed his eyes again, and gave up.

From high up the wall inside the attic gable, the incubus peered through a crack at the little red Ranchero driving up the road to the house. He smiled and clicked his teeth together, relishing the thought of what was to come. Now he

felt content. His boy, Stan, had arrived, and they would take
care of each other.

"Mine, mine, mine . . ." chanted the creature softy to
himself as he slid down the bare wood of the attic wall and
waited impatiently, huddled on the floor, excited by the
knowledge that his new protector was here at long last, and
that he was safe once again to roam the realm of humanity.

While the beast slept, the presence of the house—the good
force that the witch Maria had discerned—began to reassert
itself; the timbers creaked while the force surged through the
beams and floorboards, seeking its way to the boy lying,
nearly dead, in darkness. There was very little time. The
house had to use what strength it had left quickly if the evil
was to be destroyed.

Stan stood outside the truck, half-frozen from the frigid
draft that had blown through the broken windows during the
drive from town. He looked toward the house, feeling everything, feeling both the good and the evil—but he didn't really
know what it was that he felt. He worried that Mike might
be dead, though his sensibility told him he might not be. The
evil creature wanted him, Stan, for some special reason, and
he believed that his own life was not in danger. Still, he
needed to call on every ounce of his courage to proceed. He
leaned into the truck now through one broken window and
pulled out the bag of objects he'd brought along.

The still air here seemed almost warm compared to the
bitter cold en route. Stan took his first few crunchy steps
toward the house and stopped. He turned and looked at the
little red truck—a symbol of safety and escape, and a re-
minder of Mike; then he exhaled a long sigh that hung in the
cold air for a moment before disappearing. He didn't hesitate
after that moment, he walked up the stairs to the porch and
around the corner into the house.

Bargolas listened intently as he heard the steps upon the
porch. He stirred sexually when he realized what they meant:
it was time. Smiling to himself with his crooked, stained teeth,
he dug his talons into the wooden beams and pulled himself
upright. Stooped and apelike, he walked to the access hole

leading into the little room, where his bloody handprints from Maria's death were visible, and her clothing lay, together with a couple of large bones, near the stained mattress in the corner. Slowly he eased himself through the hole and dropped lightly to the floor. He heard the boy's feet crunching against the broken window glass downstairs. Yes, it was time.

Inexplicably, heat radiated up from the dirt floor. Without really thinking, Mike drew himself closer to the source of the heat, until he lay directly over it. Quietly, he absorbed the energy. His hand began to tremble and seemed to take on a life all its own; his fingers began to scrape lightly at the frozen earth near his chest. Mike became aware now that some outside force was controlling the movement of his hand. At first he thought this had some connection to the horrible creature, but every time he thought about the evil thing, the calming warmth would surge through his body. No, this was something different. A spark of hope was ignited; Mike blew on it gently, biding his time until the spark might flare into a fire to fuel this desperate, renewed attempt at survival.

Mike's hand now clawed at the frozen ground, and despite the pain in his fingers, he dug now with increasing determination. He imagined his hand bleeding into the dirt, creating mud, and it became easier to dig toward whatever lay buried there.

A handful of dirt hit his face, and he shook his head. He suppressed a sneeze, fearing that the noise would bring Bargolas back . . .

Bargolas!—The name echoed in Mike's mind there in the indivisible darkness. He knew that the name Bargolas did not come from him, just as the determination to dig into the earth or the warmth that had brought him back to life could not be originating in his own person. But where was it coming from? From Stan? Impossible. The name was lost in darkness, forgotten.

The ceiling above him creaked, and he feared that the creature was returning. Footsteps sounded lightly, moving toward the door. Fear slapped him into action. The one hand that seemed to have a life of its own was joined by his other. He began to dig furiously. In his mind, or perhaps in his soul, he knew that he must find the Peridot and Carnelian. It was only the power of these stones that—

Stones! Now he knew what he was looking for—a red stone and a green one. He raised himself to his knees. The pain in his thigh was tremendous, but he gained his balance and clawed at the earth with all his strength. The footsteps above drew closer to the door.

30

Othello, 1951

Lydia held her hands over her ears. The incessant pounding had been going on for over six hours, and now it seemed as if Seth's hammering was inside her head. Each blow of his hammer hit a different nerve, although they were all linked together in a bond of pain. She didn't know what he was doing—and she didn't care; she only wished he'd stop.

When he had returned, she was asleep in the dirt of the basement once again. This time, Seth didn't bother to come looking for her. No, he went straight to work. When she finally found the strength to drag her body, naked and filthy, up the basement steps, and then up the main stairs to the bathroom, she paused to look at Seth. He was doing something to the door of her sewing room, but she hadn't the strength even to be curious.

He glared coldly at her, knowing what she had been up to. She felt no shame this time—only a great weariness that penetrated to her bones, a fatigue that reached into her soul, or what was left of it.

She continued past him in the hallway, on her way to the bathroom. He stared with hatred at her nakedness; he smelled the odor of sex on her. Her feet left sticky gray footprints on the floor. For an instant, Stan was tempted to take the hammer and bring it down on the top of her skull. But he restrained himself. God had already spoken to him; He had commanded Seth, and Seth would do his duty.

Seth returned to his work with an increased fury. He nailed the reinforced door frame in the place of the old one. When it was secure, he grasped it with both hands, pulling from side to side to make sure it held; then he walked into the little room. He picked up armfuls of her sewing things and heaved them outside in a noisy clatter of falling hoops, tin boxes, paper bags, and knitting needles. He pushed her Singer out. Within minutes, the room was bare. Seth walked back into the hall, roughly kicked aside a pile of unfinished skirts, picked up the old door, and threw it into the room.

Fury fueled his muscles as he pulled the special door up and set it on the hinges of the frame. After driving the pins into the hinges, he quietly closed the door and stood back, admiring his work. Set into the door at the level of Seth's eyes was a small, custom-made window. The glass was extra hard and reinforced with wire.

Seth smiled to himself and set about the final task of his project. From a paper bag he pulled out a heavy-duty hasp and padlock. He quickly drove the screws into the wall so that the door could be locked only from the outside. It swung inwardly, ensuring that the lock could not be forced from the wall by pushing on the door from the inside.

Still enraged, Seth stormed into the bedroom and dragged the mattress off the bed. He pulled the mattress awkwardly across the floor, out into the hallway, through the new doorway and into the otherwise empty little room. He skulked back into the bedroom to retrieve a pillow and some blankets, and then he noticed the large, darkly-bound book lying on the floor. He guessed it must have been between the mattress and the box springs. He picked up the old book and read the title. *The Maleficuarm.*

He opened it and read for a few minutes, his knuckles growing white and his pulse quickening. Then, unable to read further, he screamed, "Lydia! Lydia, you will burn in hell! With God's help, I will see to it!"

He dashed into the bathroom, where he found Lydia lying exhausted in a hot bath. She lay there, trying in vain to block out her husband's mad ravings. Seth screamed and threw the book at her, the corner striking her nose. A wild-animal

scream erupted from her throat. Wet and soapy, she slithered
slowly from the tub, blood trickling down the side of her
face. Suddenly she lunged at Seth.

She caught him off guard, and her momentum knocked him
against the sink. He crashed against the mirror, shattering it,
and a sliver of glass lodged itself into his head. He regained
his footing and rushed at Lydia, the shard of glass still firmly
embedded in his scalp. He grabbed at her with both hands
but was unable to gain a hold on her wet and soapy body.
She slipped away and brought her hand up sharply across his
face. Seth slapped her back, knocking her to the floor.

He stepped over to the bathtub and fished the book from
the sudsy water. He raised it over his head and threw it as
hard as he could at Lydia. She was almost on her feet when
the heavy book struck her on the leg. She yowled in pain and
fell back to the floor. Seth retrieved the book and bashed her
about the head and shoulders with it. Within seconds, she lay
at his feet, sinking into unconsciousness.

Seth, his chest puffed up with righteousness, grabbed a
handful of Lydia's hair and dragged her through the hallway
and into the special room with the lock. He tossed her carelessly upon the mattress and slammed the door.

Vaguely, Lydia heard the lock click shut.

Standing high on the wind-blown edge of a rocky gully,
the creature looked out across the desert at the dust devils as
they swirled their dirt of grays and reds upward into a steel-
blue sky. Skeletons of old tumbleweeds twisted in the dirt,
leaping and singing with the wind. Behind him, on the horizon, the sun had begun to sink, coloring the sky overhead
with gentle streaks of pink and purple. The fleshy pinks reminded him of Lydia.

The salty taste of Lydia was still upon his tongue, her musk
still in his breath. His lust was momentarily softened by the
memory of her sweet passion and its release. He looked back
behind himself toward the sunset and muttered over and over,
"Lydia, sweet pretty Lydia . . ."

All at once he felt a blunt blow across his face; he cupped
the hands of his shorter arms to his nose, waiting for the
blood, but there was none. Anger filled his brain, and he
turned back toward the house several miles away across the

desert. He started his run with a leap across the gully of
jagged rocks, but in midair he felt a sharp pain in his leg,
and he landed awkwardly on the lip of the small gully. His
legs slipped over the side. His feet scrambling, he knocked a
stone loose from the dirt wall, and it tumbled the thirty feet
to the bottom of the small ravine. Then one of his sharp talons
gained hold on a rock, and he pulled himself up toward the
edge. Before he could haul his midsection to the top, more
blows rained down upon his head and shoulders. His grip
loosened and he slipped over the edge, bounced against the
rocky side of the gully, and landed in a heap thirty feet below.

Seth peeked smugly at Lydia through the small window in
the door. She hadn't moved since he had thrown her into the
room an hour earlier. The mattress was still wet with the
water that had dripped from her naked body.

Smiling to himself, Seth muttered, "Amen . . ."

He continued to stare at his wife, and her nakedness sud-
denly stirred something within him he hadn't felt for a while.
For a minute he allowed the feeling to soften his anger, but
when the stiffening in his groin began, he regained control.
"Whore!" he shouted. "Your nakedness tempts me, witch.
It is the work of Satan!"

Tramping loudly back into the bedroom, he looked around
for some clothing to cover Lydia. He grabbed her robe and
started to return to the little room, but, thinking again, stuffed
the robe into her chest of drawers and pushed the chest out of
the bedroom, grunting, to the door of the locked room. Checking carefully to make sure Lydia was still unconscious, he unlocked the door and pushed the chest of drawers in, beside the
mattress. Still Lydia did not move. Stooping over her, Seth
watched for the rise and fall of her chest, steeling himself against
the temptation of her flesh. Satisfied that she was breathing nor-
mally, he turned, strode out the door, and again secured the
padlock behind himself.

Half an hour later, Seth knelt beside the coffee table in the
living room, ignoring the clamor upstairs. Holding the large,
leather-bound Bible his father had given him back in Georgia,
Seth prayed for Lydia's soul—though he yearned for her punishment. As the sounds of her hollering and pounding contin-

ued, he thought about what he, as God's anointed servant, should do. He considered beating and starvation, but neither option seemed satisfactory.

He stood now, rubbing the soreness out of his knees, and walked into the kitchen. Idly, he looked through the cupboards for something to eat. He found some crackers and bananas and poured himself a glass of milk.

When he had finished them, he became aware all of a sudden that Lydia had grown quiet. That didn't seem right; she should express her suffering. Troubled, Seth left the kitchen and headed for the stairs to check on her.

There was a crash overhead. "Wha—? What was that?" he mumbled to himself.

Seth dashed up the steps and, seconds later, stood peering into the room. He didn't see Lydia. He fumbled with the padlock before it clicked, then he flung the door open. His mouth widened when he saw that the gable window had been shattered and Lydia was gone. Enraged, he ran down the stairs and outside. He circled the house, craning his neck to spot Lydia on the roof.

"God will strike you down, witch!" he screamed. But she was nowhere to be seen.

Seth continued circling the house, puzzled. He stepped toward the edge of the back lawn to get a better angle of view toward the roof, and heard a faint crash from somewhere within. He dashed back around the side of the house and tripped hard over a root jutting up from the soil around the base of the old oak tree. Suppressing a curse, he got to his feet again and hurried up the porch and in through the front door, then clambered madly back up the stairs.

He had left the door to the little room open. Passing through it now, Seth saw that the access panel in the ceiling stood open and the chest of drawers lay toppled on its back. He had been tricked! A wounded scream lifted off the top of his lungs and filled the entire house. He turned and vaulted down the stairs to look for his wife.

It took Bargolas only a few minutes to climb the sheer wall of rock and reach the top. No sooner had his foot touched the flat surface than he was running at full speed back toward the house. His talons clicked loudly against the rocks, keeping time with the musical howling of the wind.

Anger rose from his stomach and burned his mouth. Sweet Lydia was in danger. Now, as he ran, he heard a scream of death in his head; still he ran, even knowing that he was too late.

Seth ran shrieking into the kitchen, knocking furniture aside. He looked at Lydia, and his anger filled the kitchen. She held a ten-inch butcher knife.

Seth bared his teeth at her like a cougar and advanced. She too stepped forward, her hand a blur. The knife blade sliced through Seth's flesh. Blood spattered the white cupboards and floor as he landed in a heap. Lydia stepped closer, again raising the knife over her head to plunge it mightily into Seth.

Othello, 1970

He crawled on all fours, groping his way around on the dirt floor. He clutched the stones in his hand, certain that they were his salvation. The darkness was an ocean, and he had the impression of trying to swim in it—but the undertow of his own confusion and fear threatened to suck him under. Drawing in a deep breath of frigid air, he tasted his own sour breath. Something brushed, feather-light, against his cheek. He touched it with his hand, stirring up the recent horrible memories, and he screamed.

Mike threw himself to the dirt; his leg sent lightning bolts of pain into his mind. He screamed again, and immediately cursed himself for revealing his position in the dark. He rolled away as quietly as he could. Loose dirt covered his face, and his ear came to rest on something very cold. He sat up quickly and sucked in his breath, trying not to vomit.

Suddenly, as he watched, the outline of his hand became visible. He hadn't even known, before this moment, if his eyes had been open—the darkness had been so complete. Mike stared down at the strange stones, still clutched in his fist. A soft, silvery luminescence bathed his hand, and he began now to pick out details in the dirt floor, where he thought he saw shadows growing longer and longer. Tilting his head up, Mike gazed full into a towering figure, cloaked and hooded; one gnarled hand poked forward, resting atop the ornately carved handle of a cane. The silvery light slipped through the man's burled fingers like moonbeams.

As Mike watched, the figure moved closer. Mike vaguely noticed the details of the basement fading again in the darkness. Mainly, however, his attention was centered upon this figure that seemed to float in the darkness, coming closer and closer to him.

A moment later, the hem of the stranger's dark robe was almost touching Mike's hand. A great coldness, unloving, flowed out from under the robe, washing over Mike's hand and face. It was not like the clean cold of a winter chill, but rather like the cold of hatred.

I will give you your life . . . if you give me the stones.

The wheezing voice was flat and very old. The cruelty of the pitch was absolute, leaving no room for mercy. This specter held Mike's life under his illuminated hand.

Mike was, by now, in no condition to reason this situation through. His grip loosened, and he felt the stones tumbling inside his fist. Then heat began again to course through his hand, and he remembered that it was this warmth, the warmth from these stones, that had returned him to life.

"No!" Mike wasn't sure whether he shouted his answer out loud, or whether it sounded only within his head.

You dare to refuse me? the robed figure said sternly.

"NO! I won't give them . . ." Mike's voice trailed off into the darkness, becoming a strand of light streaming, it appeared, into the handle of the cane. Mike screamed again and looked around in the eerie glow for the stairs—but he couldn't find them. The wall shimmered with undecided form. The place was not the same as it had been before, and again Mike screamed, turning away from the quicksilver glow and into the darkness.

Stan's heart pounded violently when he heard the muted scream. It was Mike! Still alive! Stan ran through the living room and into the old dining room. After all these years, there was still one of the dining room chairs left it lay in the corner, broken, its rotting wooden pieces scattered.

Suddenly, he heard footsteps running toward the dining room—running toward him. He whirled around, ready to face the creature, but there was nothing there. He waited, glanced around, decided he had imagined the sound, and took another step toward the basement where his desire to help Mike was drawing him—but turned once more when he heard the running footsteps again and a crazed voice screaming, "Whore! Bitch! You will burn in hell!"

Stan held his breath as the words echoed around him. He heard footsteps above him, and a clickety-click that struck dread deep into his heart. Behind him there was a *crash*. He spun around in time to see the chair hit the wall.

"Witch! Whore! Bitch! I will KILL you!"

Stan was hurled to one side against the wall. He watched in shock as a maniacal man picked up the chair and flung it into the corner. Then he heard the curse again.

"Whore! Bitch! You will burn in hell!"

Seth ran into the kitchen. Stan stood up and stepped softly across the carpet; he leaned across the polished dining room table to peer into the kitchen, where he saw the man step backward, lose his balance, and fall, a sunlit spout of blood spraying through the air all the way into the dining room. Several drops spattered the table; one large drop landed on Stan's arm.

Unable to take his eyes from this spectacle, Stan stared at the fallen man, who was holding his hands over his face. When the man pulled his hands away, Stan saw that the knife had sliced cleanly through his nose. A flap of cartilage and flesh hung by a single piece of skin against his cheek. A woman stepped into view, holding a long, bloodstained knife over her shoulder. In a blur of motion, she brought the knife down and plunged it into the belly of the man as he lay helpless on the floor. The woman lost her balance and fell on top of him.

The man screamed and gurgled, and the dying voice made Stan's guts churn. The metallic smell of blood was all around him. The shiny white floor of the kitchen was stained with red, and the stain flowed outward from the man's body. As the woman rolled off the man and began sobbing, Stan listened to her; between her cries she spoke what sounded like a name—spoke it over and over—but he couldn't make it out.

The incubus stared at Stan. He saw the paper bag gripped tightly in Stan's hand and wondered about it. The boy had his back to him and didn't appear concerned about his own danger. Bargolas took a noisy step toward the boy, glass crunching beneath his horny foot, but the boy still did not turn. The creature then cast out the great fat worms of illusion, trying to ensnare Stan; they were wasted, and the worms drifted off aimlessly, dissipating into the air like wisps of smoke. Suddenly, Bargolas heard his name called. The voice was melodic, familiar. It was Lydia.

Lydia rolled over onto the floor, sobbing. Her cries shook the walls of the house, and it seemed as if the house groaned in accompaniment.

Then Seth moved.

Blood slid out from between his lips—a soup of bile, blood, and spit that joined the liquid gushing from his nose in a confluence that ran down his chin in foamy bubbles. Both hands came up together and wrapped around the handle of the knife. With an angry jerk Seth pulled the knife free, releasing yet another river of blood which pooled rapidly under his waist.

Lydia sobbed, but the name on her lips was not that of her dead husband; it was the unholy name of the incubus. The name wheezed from her lungs, across the many years of death, fouling the ears of the present.

Bargolas stood transfixed, looking past Stan into the kitchen, still angry about those events of nineteen years past, events which had happened because he had arrived too late. Lydia called and called to him—but Lydia was dead, pretty pretty Lydia is dead . . . Bargolas stared on in agony, and his talons dug into the rough flooring.

Lydia rocked with sobs, oblivious of everything but her own deluded world. Seth pulled himself upright and slowly turned toward Lydia. Then he rotated his head back and looked directly at Stan. One of his eyes swam in blood that now dribbled downward, adding to the ocean of scarlet in which he was drowning. Still tightly gripping the knife, he shifted his weight and rolled forward onto his knees. His shirt, plastered wetly to his back with blood, began dripping as he stood up.

Lydia heard the wet slurpy sounds nearby and bolted upright. She stared now into eyes that could never have been her husband's. She didn't even try to move as he brought the knife down, swiftly slicing her right cheek and exposing her teeth.

Bargolas stood in the dining room, towering over Stan, looking over his shoulder; the scene before him filled him with fury, and yet he found it exciting. The bodies, the house, all shimmered, but they faded into blowing dust and the flat range as he ran, vaulting over sagebrush, to save his beloved Lydia. Suddenly, as he was leaping over a half-buried boulder, he felt white-hot pain across his cheek and fell, tumbling over and over, to the desert ground. He pulled himself upright and continued racing back to the house. Then he felt the knife plunge deep into his loins. An angry, gurgling scream— "Whore!"—echoed in his mind, as he fell again to the dusty ground, entangling himself in sagebrush.

Screaming "Whore!" over and over, Seth pulled the knife from the soft folds of Lydia's flesh and, wrapping both hands around the hilt, plunged it again deeply into his wife's body. His strength almost gone, he attempted to pull the knife out of her and stab her once again. But his strength was now gone and he crumpled to the floor.

Suddenly, the back door leading into the kitchen burst open, and Bargolas rushed forward. Seth turned his head at the sound and tried to scream, but the horrible sound roaring forth from the hellish creature numbed him to his very soul. Seth could do no more than stare in abject horror when this bearer of death knelt over him swinging a deadly claw. The knife fell to the floor as the talons caught Seth across the face, leaving nothing but bone and ragged tissue.

Stan stood paralyzed on the brink of insanity. He watched as the faceless man lying on the floor twitched, his head, legs, arms, and chest jerking. He had no mouth to scream, and only a liquid growl gurgled from his throat.

The beast crouched atop Seth's writhing body and licked

at the shredded face, pulling flesh off bit by bit with his teeth. He savored the taste but gazed longingly at the lifeless body of Lydia. Hatred now, not pleasure, drove him again to the attack, and he slowly, cruelly sank his jagged teeth into Seth's throat, ever so gradually ripping it open. The last of the man's blood pumped warmly from the arteries and washed over the evil face.

Bargolas, alone again, shrieked his anguish, and the house recorded the horror of his deeds—and the deeds of Seth, and, yes, those of Lydia—in its walls, floors, and foundation.

Covered in blood, the creature stood and stepped over to his dead lover. With one hand, he turned her over and looked into her dead face. He leaned down and kissed her on the remains of her lips, red and pink foam clinging to his own as he pulled his mouth away. He stood and glanced about himself.

Now he stared directly into Stan's eyes and began to stumble toward him. Stan remained in such a state of panic that he could do nothing except watch the creature approach. An instant later, the incubus was upon him. Stan saw the blood dripping from his great hulk, smelled the putrid odor. And then, the horrible creature walked right past him.

Stan stood very still. He expected to be attacked from behind at any moment. But nothing happened. Slowly, carefully, he turned his head. The creature now stood only a couple of feet from him, staring past him into the kitchen. Stan, too, looked back into the kitchen. Now he saw nothing except for the dirty, worn linoleum and the vandalized cabinets. In the distance—below him?—he heard the desperate screams of Mike.

Quickly now, he turned back to the creature. The beast still hadn't moved, but suddenly his eyelids closed in gauzy layers and reopened. Stan bolted for the kitchen—the only direction of escape left to him.

His first thought was to run out the back door and try to get away with the truck. As he reached the back door, however, he became conscious of the paper bag still in his hand. Then he heard another scream—that of the incubus—but as the beast's hellish roar died, Stan heard the weaker cry of Mike, now clearly coming from the basement.

Stan turned from the back door toward the basement. He reached for the knob and flung the door open, just as the creature poked its head around the corner and grinned at him. Stan glanced into the darkness below and reached his foot downward, but there was no wooden step to catch his weight; he fell through the space where the basement had been, through the same door that Mike's terror had opened. He fell headlong into the suffocating blackness.

32

Mike heard the voices, soft as heartbeats, and limped in the shadows toward them. A moment later he stood beneath the sounds—thumping, cries, and running steps. He turned his face upward toward the distant noise and saw what appeared to be crevices in a stone ceiling.

"Lydia, you whore!"

A pause.

"Whore! Witch!" The shout drifted through the stone again, as Mike felt a furrow of fear dig itself into his brow. Suddenly something wet dripped from the dark stone onto his face. Several more drops rained upon his shoulder, and more upon his face. He wiped his hand across his cheek and looked at the dark smudges. Unable to tell clearly what it was, he walked over to one of the sparsely scattered torches stuck into the cracks of stone.

The torch didn't make sense to him, but nothing during the past week had made sense to him.

"Goddamned Stan," he whispered to himself in the flickering light of the torch. He wondered where the torch had come from and looked at the blackish streak across his hand. Now, however, he saw that it wasn't black—it was red. Blood! He didn't know if he could retain his sanity in a place where blood dripped from rocks; in fact, he wondered if he had it still.

"Torches," he muttered, looking at the burning globs atop the sticks of wood. "Someone will come . . ." Bathed in the flickering firelight, he felt naked and exposed. He had stared into the flame too long, and now he could see nothing beyond it except darkness.

He pushed himself from the wall, feeling the pain stab through his leg, and found himself again submerged in shadows. Minutes passed before his eyes adjusted to the darkness and he could see the jagged outlines of the stone walls curving into corridors. The corridor in front of him forked into two paths; one was very dark, the other dimly illuminated. His instincts told him to take the one that was darker, but he could not make his legs obey.

"What the fuck is this place?" he hissed to himself. The sound of his own voice told him he was alive and awake; he must accept what he saw before him. He squeezed the two stones in his sweaty hand.

What if I go back the way I came? he thought. Maybe I can find my way back upstairs. He wondered if he was in some cave beneath the house, maybe where the monster lived. He shook his head and felt a sudden wave of dizziness. He thought of Stan and the circle of salt. Salt, he thought, if only he had a box of salt, he could make a circle with it, crawl inside, and wait this nightmare out.

He turned around and began to limp back the way he had come, but the memory of the cloaked figure now reentered his mind and stopped him. Confused, he turned again to face the fork in the corridor. He took a step toward the better-lit path but halted once more when he heard a crashing behind him and then—what was that?—a moan? a growl?

Cocking his head toward the sound, he heard a shuffling in the darkness and decided it was time to get the hell out. He ran for the darker corridor, looking for a place to hide as nightmarish images pummeled his brain—the incubus, its teeth, and waving arms, the cloaked figure with his menacing demands. He heard their footsteps, their breathing, and he ran.

Stan landed hard on the dirt floor. He pulled his face from the dust and wiped the grime from his mouth and cheek. He wondered where the stairs had disappeared to, but knew he didn't have time to stop and think about it. He had to help his friend.

The darkness was deep but not total. Off to the right, Stan saw a corridor, a cave of rough stone walls illuminated by a flickering yellow light. He caught his breath, fearful now that he'd lost his paper bag, but he saw it then in the shadows a few feet away. Quietly, he crawled on hands and knees toward the bag and, just as his outstretched hand grasped it, warm liquid dripped from above onto his face. Some of it ran into his mouth, and he recognized its taste: blood—the blood of the murder he had witnessed only minutes ago.

Through the darkness before him he saw a speck of light. From the shadows behind him came a high-pitched, nasal voice.

". . . pretty pretty Stan . . . now, now you are here . . . home."

Without another thought, Stan was on his feet and running in the direction of the light. A moment later he passed a torch stuck in the wall, and he knew that he was no longer in the normal world; he knew he was in the world he and Mike had been in when they had tried to rid themselves of the creature in Lea's bedroom, he was now in the world of the horrible creature.

As he ran, he heard a faint scratching sound and then a thud behind him. Once again, but farther away, he heard the voice call out to him.

"Where did my pretty Stan go . . . where are you?"

Stan continued to run. He didn't think; he couldn't think. Escape. All that was on his mind now was to escape.

Again he heard the voice, this time closer. "Pretty pretty Stan . . ."

He felt shame and humiliation as he ran. He passed from shadowed stretches into stretches lit by torches, and back into shadows. Every time he approached a lighted area he expected to see some horror, and each time he passed through, he welcomed the darkness on the other side.

The steps behind him grew closer and closer. Suddenly he stopped, realizing escape was hopeless. He stood in the shadows, waiting for the beast to overtake him. The steps grew closer, the creature's labored breaths echoed off the stone walls. Stan turned to face the darkness. In a moment it would all be over: hell was not far away.

A hand seized his shoulder and pulled him into the deepest shadows. Stan stumbled backward. The hand covered his mouth, and another jerked him into a tight crevice. His captor, squeezed up against him, whispered, "Shut up, asshole."

Seconds later, footsteps sounded in the corridor, passing them. Neither had the courage to peek out and look, but they both knew who it was. It was evil—and, for at least one of them, it was death. Several minutes passed.

Then Stan spoke. "He'll be back in a minute, I'm sure of it."

Silently, Mike flattened himself against the stone, trying to fit himself into a niche where the sharp rocks did not jab him in the back. Neither of them spoke now. They closed their eyes.

More time elapsed—minutes, an eternity. Then they heard a scream of fury and hate, at first distantly but then echoing off the stones surrounding them until their ears were numbed by the volume. In the last desperate moment, unable any longer to endure the sound, both boys were ready to step from behind the protective stone and end their lives.

Then it passed. The sound drifted off into the darkness.

Mike spoke. "He'll try the other corridor or go back."

"Back where?" Stan thought for a moment. "The house? The real world? I don't think we can get back there from . . . We may not even be . . ."

"How are we gonna get out of here?"

Stan stood still and looked solemnly into the darkness of the crevice, trying to see his friend's face. "We have to kill the creature first."

The silent darkness seemed to agree with him.

For a minute, Mike didn't speak. He knew Stan was right; they had to try. If they didn't, he'd always be looking over his shoulder for the creature. There was no other way.

"Well," Mike said, "if we're gonna kill it, I guess we'd better find it." His voice sounded weak, even in that narrow crevice. "Maybe these will help," he said, extending the Peridot and Carnelian in his hand.

Stan frowned in the gloom and reached his hand out. He held the stones in his hand and felt a sudden surge of heat that spread gradually through his body.

"Heat!" he whispered.

"Yeah, I know. I think it was those rocks that kept me alive in the basement, in the freezing . . ." Mike's voice trailed off as he remembered what he had been through, though it seemed a distant memory—almost as distant a memory as home. He wondered if he had in fact had any life other than this; had he perhaps died ages ago, after some unspeakable sin, and was this his hell? "Shit!" he exclaimed, his voice resonating from the stone walls. "Too much smoke . . . this nightmare is *real*."

Stan wondered if Mike was starting to slip back into the soupiness of shock again. But no, he thought, Mike was just on the edge of reason. Like me.

"We'll make it, we'll get out of here." Stan's voice was flat and determined. He squeezed his hand tightly around the stones. Closing his eyes made him feel dizzy, but he clenched them shut tightly and took several deep breaths. Colors exploded in his mind, and the force knocked him from his feet.

Mike knelt beside him, frightened that Stan had died and left him alone again in this hellhole. But Stan moved, opened his eyes, and sat up.

"Hold onto the stones, Mike," he said. "We gotta hurry. The creature—the incubus—is coming back."

Mike watched Stan reach into his bag, pull out a container, and pour out a circle of salt, larger than the one he had made in Lea's room. Mike could feel sweat dripping down his rib cage as he recalled the terrifying blackness that ceremony had cast them into; then he realized that the darkness surrounding them now was the very same.

"We're in that same place where—"

"I know," Stan said gently.

From the paper bag Stan removed candles and his *Athame*. He had never before made the circle of salt this big, almost ten feet in diameter, and he hoped the larger size would make it more effective. Inside the circle he poured out a small pentagram, dug a hole in the middle of it, and planted six candles—four white ones and two violet ones. These would allow him to call upon all the purest energies, or so he hoped.

He laid the *Athame* in front of the pentagram and then took from the bag a piece of paper rolled into a scroll. He set the scroll down beside the candles and unrolled it.

Pointing to the break in the circle, Stan motioned for Mike to enter. When they were both inside, Stan closed the entrance and poured out a smaller circle; he then instructed Mike to sit within this smaller circle. Mike obeyed as Stan walked to four different positions in the larger circle, one by one, at each position pouring out a small pentagram and a number: nine twice, two once, and fourteen once. Each time, after pouring out the number, he crossed himself with the pentacle of protection and recited the protection spell.

That done, he asked Mike for the stones. These he dropped beside the candles before removing the final object from the bag. It too was a candle, a short, fat candle, black as the shadows that threatened to swallow them up. Stan took a book of matches from his pocket and lit the wicks of the four white candles. Immediately a wail, soft as the wind, began to blow through the corridor of stone. Now Stan lit the violet candles, and by the time the flame touched the second one, the wail had grown into a bone-piercing scream.

The corridor ahead of them began to glow a deep red. Wind howled through their hair. Their hair whipped about their eyes, their clothes flattened against their bodies from the force of the wind—but the candles barely flickered. Getting to his feet, Stan fought to stand up. Thrusting his arms into the howling darkness, he began to chant his incantation.

INDWELLING SUN OF MYSELF
MY FIRE! WITHIN THOU EIGHTFOLD STAR
INITIATOR! INITIATOR! SANGRAAL!
BREATH OF MY SOUL, LUST OF MINE
FIGURES OF WHITE BURNING WITH MY FIRE
THOU DOST REMEMBER, THOU ART ANGELS
ONE OF THE EYE, THE SECOND THE LUST
OF THE GOAT, THE THIRD MICHAEL,
AND THE LAST, GABRIEL

HO FOR THE SANGRAAL!
HO FOR THE BURNING CUP OF BABYLON

HO FOR THE ANGELS BURNING BRIGHTLY
BEFORE ME BURNING, PROTECTING ME!

Mike watched in amazement as the six candles in the front
of the circle burned brighter and brighter. The plasma of the
flames grew higher and higher, merging, until the flames had
reached a greater length than the host candles. Stan's hair
whipped about his face in the wind, stinging his eyes and
forehead. The red glow grew more evil, and the same deep
drumming they had heard in Lea's room, like heavy footsteps, drew near.

> ABRASAX, SABRIAM
> THOU ART THE GREATER
> OF THE LOWER,
> OF THE LUST OF THE GOAT
> ABRASAX, SABRIAM
> THOU BURN BRIGHT
> THOU ART THE TWO VIOLET
> BURNING BEFORE ME
> NUITH! HADITH!
> RA-HOOR-KHUIT!
> HAIL, GREAT WILD BEAST!

Suddenly the fury of the wild beast was there, standing
before them, undefined but unmistakable in its power. Its
screams toppled Stan. Falling, he reached out to Mike and
caught his hand. Stan's weight pulled Mike from his sitting
position and dragged him across the small circle as Stan himself tumbled across the rim of the large circle. There was a
flash of fire as his legs slipped over the edge into the void,
and he screamed from the searing pain. Momentarily sus-
pending his disbelief and amazement that the circle was surrounded by an abyss, he held fast to Mike and tried to pull
himself back up onto the bright platform defined by the circle
of protective salt.

Mike, prone, was pulled toward the edge. Finally, he spread
his legs wide for balance, planted his chin firmly on the solid
edge of the circle of salt, and grabbed Stan's arm with both of
his hands while Stan's other hand clutched the circle of salt.

As Mike pulled Stan back up inch by inch, he looked into

the abyss below. Faintly luminous, seemingly deformed human shapes floated in the darkness, drifting toward Stan until one of them finally attached itself to Stan's leg. Stan's cry of pain echoed over the howling wind, and he suddenly found the strength to clamber back up into the circle, using Mike's body as a ladder. As Stan's leg trailed across his shoulder, Mike could feel blood dripping from it onto the side of his own face. The wound itself gave off a fiery heat.

Wiping the blood from his face, Mike turned and saw Stan limp back to his altar of candles. From the knee down, his leg had lost its covering of pants and looked like raw hamburger, oozing blood and clear fluid. Mike bent his head in a silent prayer, not knowing if he could take any more. Then he heard Stan's words ring out into the abyss:

> THOU DOST DEVOUR ME!
> BUT I AM NAUGHT!
> I WILL THEE
> I AM HE, THE BORNLESS SPIRIT
> I AM HE, THE BEGETTER
> THE MANIFESTER
> UNTO THE FLAME!
> THE HEART GIRT WITHIN THE SPIRIT
> UBEROUS, THAT IS MY NAME!
>
> I WILL THE SABAF
> I DEMAND THEE
> DIATHARAA
> SHOW ME IMMORTAL
> MANIFESTER UNTO THE LIGHT
> BEGETTER OF THOSE WHO HATE!
> SUCH ARE THE WORDS
> SHOW THYSELF!

Silence. Stillness. The howling wind, with its angry red and black screams of anger, had died. Quiet. Before them stood the ancient cloaked figure carrying his cane, the scepter of power. The handle sent out streams of light that pulsated through the old one's gnarled fingers.

What do you want? came the whispers, from deep within the folds of the hood.

"I . . . I want the creature's . . . name."

No. I will not give you his name.

"I will destroy him."

Mike was surprised at the power and conviction in Stan's voice.

"But first you *will* tell me his name."

NO! The reply was deafening.

Stan paused. Looking down at the candles, he knew he had no chance of destroying the creature without its name. Then his answer sparkled up from the dirt near the candles. It was the Carnelian and Peridot. Reaching down to pick up the stones, he heard the cloaked figure scream his rage. Stan held the stones up in the palm of his hand.

"TELL ME!"

The old one drifted nearer, and the darkness within his hood came toward them, grew wider and wider, opened into the mouth of hell, and vomited forth a terrible vision of the past: the incubus plowing his organ of lust through the guts of a mutilated figure tied with rope to the walls of darkness; the incubus licking the blood that oozed together with his own semen from the fleshy rents . . . *BARGOLAS* . . . a nun lying with a monk, their bodies moving urgently . . . *BARGOLAS* . . . a holy man engaged in the unholy rape of a boy amid the pain and cries of redemption, crystalline smiles of uncorrupted lust spinning around and around, calling "Mother . . . Mother," a rosary flung to the feet of the incubus, two stones rolling from the shattered icon—one red, one green—carried by the creature back to the edge of darkness . . . *BARGOLAS! BARGOLAS* . . . white, pure, nightfallen snow, spattered with blood, Stan running, Peterson torn to shreds, more blood spattering the cold, clear purity . . . *BARGOLAS* . . . *BARGOLAS* . . . *BARGOLAS!*

Both boys lay on their bellies in the dirt. The enormity of evil crushing their will, corrupting . . . disintegrating their souls, killing them. Their fingers dug furrows in the darkness, searching for something to grab onto, something like a shred of sanity. But they found none. Suddenly, close to death, Mike's arm launched out and fell upon the injured raw leg of Stan. The pain crept up slowly, registering incrementally in Stan's brain until he remembered . . .

Stan turned his head forward and looked at the burning

candles. Their light, the light of the angels, had shone unin-
terruptedly through the incessant parade of violence. He
pulled himself upright, ignored his pain, fought against the
tide of illusion. He grasped the black candle, holding it high
into the raging storm, and screamed:

"I NAME THIS *BARGOLAS!*"

Then he lit the candle from the fire of angels.

Once again there was silence. The boys now knew their
enemy—and feared him even more. They looked around
themselves and felt the oppressive darkness closing in. These
corridors, they now understood, were the original home of
the incubus.

Stan held the black candle high over the circle and commanded:

"BARGOLAS, come to me!"

A distant roar of anger and pain tore vainly at the stone
walls around them. The flat racing footsteps, the clickety-
click, grew closer and closer by the second. Stan and Mike
stared into the blackness. Just then, Bargolas burst into sight
and, before the boys could think, sprang at them in a fero-
cious leap.

They saw the beast flying through the air toward them, and,
in a final act of friendship, Mike grasped Stan by the wrist.
Both of them screamed and shut their eyes tightly.

Seconds elapsed. They didn't dare to look, and the seconds
seemed like hours. But the pain they anticipated didn't come.

Hesitantly, they looked up. Stan still held the burning black
candle. The incubus lay on his back outside the circle, twitching and groaning.

Mike whispered, "Can you feel his pain?"

Stan shook his head. He knew that the circle protected
him—protected them both.

Slowly, the creature turned over onto its side and rolled up
onto its feet. It took a step toward the circle, and Mike said,
"Paula! It's Paula, and she's hurt."

Stan slapped Mike as hard as he could. Mike put his hand
up to his cheek.

"What the fu—!"

"Don't look at it! Don't look into its eyes."

The beast inched up to the edge of the circle of salt and
stopped there. Stan realized that now was the time; it must

be now. He held the black candle over the burning bright light of the angels. As it began to melt, Bargolas began to howl like an animal on fire. Stan continued to hold the candle, the icon of evil, over the white light, and the wax dripping from it was consumed by the fire of the angels.

Bargolas was burning. His head, arms, and shoulders blazed, and he felt the unbearable heat of the flame that had destroyed his mother. Thoughts of his mother were singed into his mind, merging with the fire on his body and burning into the timbers of the house. The house creaked and moaned, content to allow the cleansing of the evil.

"Look!" cried Mike over the creature's screams. "There are the basement stairs—let's go!"

"Wait!" Stan yelled. "Open the circle. When it's open, run to the Ranchero as fast as you can, and wait for me there. But don't stop running until you're out of the house."

Mike nodded and opened a space in the back of the circle near the steps. As soon as he did so, he felt the icy chill of winter. He looked back at Stan for a moment and saw that he had collapsed in agony, twitching from the heat of the flames, apparently no longer protected from the creature's pain now that the circle was broken. Stan watched in frustrated agony as the only hope, the black candle, sputtered in the dirt.

Mike glanced up to see the rafters burning brightly; he reached out for the black candle and, holding it over the flame of the white and violet candles, listened to the roar of the creature, roars that were echoed in the pitiful cries of Stan. Mike didn't know what to do. Already the flames had spread upward; he could see through the ceiling at one point into the kitchen.

Then he saw, lying on the dirt floor, the *Athame*. He grasped the blade and dug a hole in the dirt beside the candles. He stuck the knife's handle in the hole, tilting the blade over the white flame, and packed the earth firmly around the handle. He then tried to impale the black candle from its bottom end onto the tip of the blade. It slipped off, and the blade sliced into his palm. Hardly feeling the cut, he tried now to impale the other end of the candle—the burning end, hot and soft. The flame continued to burn and the whole candle dripped into the flame of the angels. Both Stan and

the incubus shrieked deafeningly, their pain increasingly
pushing them closer to death.

Mike grabbed Stan by the shoulders and pulled him from
the circle as a beam fell in from above, crashing onto the
floor near them in a burning mass. Mike dragged Stan to the
foot of the stairs, but there his strength failed him, the terror,
pain, and loss of blood had made him too weak. Another
piece of the ceiling collapsed into the fiery basement. The
blindingly bright flames seemed to tear at Mike's eyes. Still
another blazing chunk fell, this time directly onto the incubus. Stan screamed even more loudly than before and reached
up toward Mike.

Mike looked down at Stan as he reached up with one hand
for his friend. Mike looked back toward the top of the stairs.
Flames were beginning to lap around the side of the door.
Tears welled up in his eyes, blurring the whole scene into a
smear of light. He knelt down beside his friend knowing that
Stan was dying, knowing that he was paying for bringing the
creature into the world again. But still he could not turn his
back on him. Wheezing from the effort Mike reached around
Stan's shoulder and tried to haul him to his feet. But there
was no more strength left for heroism and he fell onto the
suffering teenager. Looking square into Stan's face only a
couple of inches away from his own, he watched Stan's eyes
flicker open. The eyes were glazed over with tears and pain
and a frown creased his brow. Then suddenly a smile broke
through the agony of imminent death and words filled the
silence of Mike's weary heart.

"Go . . . save yourself. You cannot die for me . . . go . . ."

Mike watched as his friend sank back into the horrible
aloneness of his agony. Reluctantly, he released the grip on
his friend. Suddenly part of the wall above the stairs collapsed in flames. One of the pieces of burning timber landed
on Stan's hand. Stan did not even move as his flesh sputtered
and turned black. Mike stood and pushed it away with his
toe as he turned toward the stairs. He barely had the strength
to limp up the steps. At the top, he put his arm over his face
to shield it against the flames. He could smell his hair burning
as he burst through the back door and out into the purity of
the crystalline night.

* * *

More than half an hour passed before the fire truck arrived. Mike sat on the hood of his Ranchero and watched the flames leaping high into the night. He thought of Stan, thought of their friendship, rough and uneven, and he felt cheated. He didn't know if he would miss that friendship or feel happy that he was now safe. His tears froze into snowflakes as they hit the Ranchero's fender.